ONCE AND FUTURE ANTIQUITIES IN SCIENCE FICTION AND FANTASY

Bloomsbury Studies in Classical Reception

Bloomsbury Studies in Classical Reception presents scholarly monographs offering new and innovative research and debate to students and scholars in the reception of Classical Studies. Each volume will explore the appropriation, reconceptualization and recontextualization of various aspects of the Graeco-Roman world and its culture, looking at the impact of the ancient world on modernity. Research will also cover reception within antiquity, the theory and practice of translation, and reception theory.

Also available in the series:

ANCIENT MAGIC AND THE SUPERNATURAL IN THE MODERN VISUAL AND PERFORMING ARTS
edited by Filippo Carlà and Irene Berti

ANCIENT GREEK MYTH IN WORLD FICTION SINCE 1989
edited by Justine McConnell and Edith Hall

CLASSICS IN EXTREMIS
by Edmund Richardson

FRANKENSTEIN AND ITS CLASSICS
edited by Jesse Weiner, Benjamin Eldon Stevens and Brett M. Rogers

GREEK AND ROMAN CLASSICS IN THE BRITISH STRUGGLE FOR SOCIAL REFORM
edited by Henry Stead and Edith Hall

HOMER'S ILIAD AND THE TROJAN WAR: DIALOGUES ON TRADITION
Jan Haywood and Naoíse Mac Sweeney

IMAGINING XERXES
Emma Bridges

JULIUS CAESAR'S SELF-CREATED IMAGE AND ITS DRAMATIC AFTERLIFE
Miryana Dimitrova

OVID'S MYTH OF PYGMALION ON SCREEN
Paula James

THE CODEX FORI MUSSOLINI
Han Lamers and Bettina Reitz-Joosse

THE GENTLE, JEALOUS GOD
Simon Perris

VICTORIAN CLASSICAL BURLESQUES
Laura Monrós-Gaspar

VICTORIAN EPIC BURLESQUES
Rachel Bryant Davies

ONCE AND FUTURE ANTIQUITIES IN SCIENCE FICTION AND FANTASY

Edited by Brett M. Rogers and Benjamin Eldon Stevens

BLOOMSBURY ACADEMIC
LONDON • NEW YORK • OXFORD • NEW DELHI • SYDNEY

BLOOMSBURY ACADEMIC
Bloomsbury Publishing Plc
50 Bedford Square, London, WC1B 3DP, UK
1385 Broadway, New York, NY 10018, USA

BLOOMSBURY, BLOOMSBURY ACADEMIC and the Diana logo are trademarks of
Bloomsbury Publishing Plc

First published in Great Britain 2019

A catalogue record for this book is available from the British Library.

Library of Congress Cataloging-in-Publication Data
Names: Rogers, Brett M., editor. | Stevens, Benjamin Eldon, editor.
Title: Once and future antiquities in science fiction and fantasy / edited by
Brett M. Rogers and Benjamin Eldon Stevens.
Other titles: Bloomsbury studies in classical reception.
Description: London : Bloomsbury Academic, 2019. | Series: Bloomsbury
studies in classical reception.
Identifiers: LCCN 2018040890| ISBN 9781350074880 (pbk.) | ISBN 9781350068940 (hardback)
Subjects: LCSH: Science fiction—Classical influences. | Classical literature—Influence.
Classification: LCC PN3433.6 .O53 2019 | DDC 809.3/8762—dc23 LC record
available at https://lccn.loc.gov/2018040890

ISBN: HB: 978-1-3500-6894-0
       PB: 978-1-3500-7488-0
       ePDF: 978-1-3500-6895-7
       eBook: 978-1-3500-6896-4

Series: Bloomsbury Studies in Classical Reception

Typeset by RefineCatch Limited, Bungay, Suffolk

To find out more about our authors and books visit www.bloomsbury.com
and sign up for our newsletters.

CONTENTS

Contents

ILLUSTRATIONS

Figures

Illustrations

Tables

CONTRIBUTORS

Frances Foster is Senior Teaching Associate in Classics Education at the Faculty of Education, University of Cambridge. In addition to her research on Servius, she has published on classical reception in children's and YA fantasy. She has particular interests in the presentation of ancient hero culture for young audiences and in the recurrence of the themes surrounding the land and shades of the dead.

Tony Keen teaches Classical Studies for the University of Notre Dame London Global Gateway, and the University of Reading. He is an Honorary Research Affiliate at the Open University. Since 2002 his research has focused on Classical Reception in popular culture, especially science fiction and fantasy. He has written widely for academic publications, and also for sf and comics magazines.

Claire Kenward is Archivist Researcher at the University of Oxford's Archive of Performances of Greek and Roman Drama. Her publications include 'The Reception of Greek Drama in Early Modern England' in *A Handbook to the Reception of Greek Drama* (Wiley, 2016) and "Sights to make an Alexander? Reading Homer on the early modern stage" (*CRJ Special Issue*, 2017). She is currently co-editing the forthcoming *Epic Performances, from the Middle Ages into the Twenty-first Century* (OUP).

Ortwin Knorr is Associate Professor of Classics at Willamette University and Director of its Center for Ancient Studies and Archaeology (CASA). He is the author of *Verborgene Kunst: Argumentationsstruktur und Buchaufbau in den Satiren des Horaz* (Olms, 2004) and several articles on Greek and Roman comedy, Latin poetry, and late-antique anti-heretical literature.

Suzanne Lye is Assistant Professor in the Department of Classics at the University of North Carolina at Chapel Hill. She has published on ancient epic, magic and religion, representations of gender and ethnicity, ancient and modern pedagogy, and classical reception.

C. W. Marshall is Professor of Greek at the University of British Columbia in Vancouver, Canada.

Alexander McAuley is Lecturer in Hellenistic History in the School of History, Archaeology, and Religion at Cardiff University. Beyond classical receptions in popular culture, his research focuses on the ancient dynamics of 'globalism' in the society and culture of the Hellenistic world on the Greek mainland. He also works on the dynastic ideology and practices of the Seleucids and Ptolemies, with particular interest in the role of royal women.

Contributors

Stephen B. Moses earned his BA in Classical Studies at the University of Puget Sound. Since graduating he has taught juggling in Haiti and currently works with youths and teens in Berkeley, CA.

Jennifer Ranck is an independent scholar who holds a BA in Religious Studies from the University of Rochester and a BA in Latin and Greek from Hunter College – City University of New York. Her academic interests include ancient Greek tragedy and performance, early Christianity, and classical reception in television and film.

Brett M. Rogers is Associate Professor of Classics at the University of Puget Sound. He has co-edited three volumes: with Benjamin Eldon Stevens, *Classical Traditions in Science Fiction* (Oxford University Press, 2015) and *Classical Traditions in Modern Fantasy* (Oxford University Press, 2017); and, with Stevens and Jesse Weiner, *Frankenstein and Its Classics* (Bloomsbury Academic, 2018). He is the author of numerous articles on classical literature and its receptions in popular media (comics, sci-fi, and fantasy).

Benjamin Eldon Stevens is Visiting Assistant Professor at Trinity University. He is the author of *Silence in Catullus* (University of Wisconsin Press, 2013) and co-editor, with Brett M. Rogers, of *Classical Traditions in Science Fiction* (Oxford University Press, 2015) and *Classical Traditions in Modern Fantasy* (Oxford University Press, 2017). He has also edited, with Rogers and Jesse Weiner, *Frankenstein and Its Classics* (Bloomsbury Academic, 2018). Beyond classical receptions, he has published on underworlds and afterlives, the senses in literature, and ancient linguistics, and has translated Spanish poetry and French literary prose.

Vincent Tomasso is Assistant Professor in the department of Classics at Trinity College in Hartford, CT. He researches and teaches about ancient Greek epic poetry and popular culture's reception of classical antiquity. In the latter category, he wrote about science fiction's interaction with ancient Greece in the television series *Battlestar Galactica* for the volume *Classical Traditions in Science Fiction* (Oxford University Press, 2015), edited by the same individuals responsible for this fine volume.

Catherynne M. Valente is the *New York Times* and *USA Today* bestselling author of over thirty works of science fiction and fantasy, including the Fairyland novels, *Space Opera*, *Deathless*, *Radiance*, and *The Refrigerator Monologues*. She has won the Tiptree, Andre Norton, Lambda, Hugo, Sturgeon, and Grand Prix d'Imaginaire awards, and been a finalist for many others. She lives with her partner on a small island off the coast of Maine.

Jesse Weiner is Assistant Professor of Classics at Hamilton College. He has co-edited, with Rogers and Stevens, *Frankenstein and Its Classics* (Bloomsbury Academic, 2018). He is the author of numerous articles on classical literature and its modern receptions.

Laura Zientek is Visiting Assistant Professor of Classics and Humanities at Reed College. She has published articles on Latin epic poetry, particularly Lucan's *Bellum Civile*, and landscape studies. Her research focuses on the intersection of representation and experience with interests in natural philosophy, ecocriticism, and literary and artistic treatments of natural and built environments.

PREFACE

If science fiction and fantasy take us to other worlds – alien planets, schools of magic, ghostly underworlds – then perhaps we might say the same for the study of Greek and Roman antiquity. This volume explores that intriguing similarity in how science fiction, modern fantasy, and classical antiquity all involve *displacements* from the world around us. Although each is distinct – science fiction is routinely linked to speculation about the future, fantasy regularly imagines different underlying rules for the universe, and classical antiquity consists of cultures and contexts both familiar and strange in their own ways – all three areas represent meaningful differences from any given present time and place. As such, science fiction, fantasy, and the classics have in common the effect of inviting us to reconsider (by speculating, by imagining, by contextualizing) our own world anew.

In this vein, *Once and Future Antiquities in Science Fiction and Fantasy* seeks to explore some ways in which the modern genres of science fiction and fantasy make use of the ancient world in order to bring about such sensations of displacement. Indeed, the general field – of 'classical receptions in science fiction and fantasy' – has been a subject of burgeoning interest, leading to an increasing number of courses, conferences and publications. Building on earlier publications, our own prior collections – *Classical Traditions in Science Fiction* (2015), *Classical Traditions in Modern Fantasy* (2017), and *Frankenstein and Its Classics: The Modern Prometheus from Antiquity to Science Fiction* (2018) – have sought to help put the field on a firmer foundation, to propose possible theoretical frameworks, and to identify and treat more systematically some of the great many topics in need of attention.

Once and Future Antiquities continues in that vein by presenting what we believe is the first collection of essays in the field with a shared *thematic* focus – namely, 'displacement'. Our hope is that this volume highlights many ways in which reception scholars are thinking about science fiction, fantasy, and classics as modes that 'displace'. We also intend the volume to help 'displace' the field itself, offering a diverse array of texts and approaches so that we might reorient ourselves as the field continues to develop in diverse and striking directions. We are, as ever, humbled and honoured to be able to publish so much interesting work by so many scholars, representing a range of research specialties, institutional affiliations and experience in the field, and personal backgrounds. All fourteen essays (as well as the Introduction) are published here for the first time. The volume represents developments that started in a conference on *The Once and Future Antiquity: Classical Traditions in Science Fiction and Fantasy*, held 27–28 March 2015 at the University of Puget Sound, in Tacoma, Washington (USA). This conference was co-organized by us alongside Dr Laura Zientek (Reed College), whose incredible efforts spanned from conference planning to her own contribution to this volume. To Dr Zientek we owe greatest thanks.

Preface

Over the several years from that conference to the appearance of this volume, many people have played important roles. Above all, we wish to thank the contributors for sharing their work and for allowing us to publish it here. Special thanks go to the team at Bloomsbury, including Alice Wright, Senior Commissioning Editor for Classical Studies and Archaeology; Emma Payne, Editorial Assistant for the same; and Terry Woodley, cover design. We are also grateful to the University of Puget Sound for a Faculty Research Grant in support of this volume and the Katharine Gould Chism Fund for the Humanities and the Arts for supporting the conference that preceded this volume.

Rogers would like to thank the students in his courses on classical receptions, especially those in the spring 2015 course, who helped pull together *The Once and Future Antiquity* conference. He also wishes to thank several colleagues at the University of Puget Sound – Kane Anderson, Bill Barry, Amy Fisher, Aislinn Melchior, Claudia Moser, Eric Orlin, Jess K. Smith, and especially Laura Zientek – who offered terrific support for the conference. Most special thanks are due to Jennifer, who patiently and pregnantly endured the conference and subsequent editing process, and to Elinor, who was polite enough to wait a few more weeks before springing into the world. And, of course, myriad thanks to Ben, who, Atlas-like in his own right, always shares the burden so everyone can enjoy golden apples.

Stevens would like to thank the students in his courses on afterlives of antiquity (fall 2017) and antiquity and diversity in contemporary literature (spring 2018) at Trinity University, the former for their haunting readings of Oyeyemi's *White is for Witching*, the latter for their warm embrace of difficult material. Trinity's Department of Classical Studies remained a productive setting for finishing the work, and a research student – erstwhile *katabant* and estival Mellon fellow Maggie Lupo (Trinity '21) – was a thoughtful interlocutor as the volume neared completion. There can be no end of thanks, now four volumes in (... and counting?), to Brett, without whom academic life would have been very different.

INTRODUCTION
DISPLACING ANTIQUITIES IN SCIENCE FICTION AND FANTASY
Brett M. Rogers and Benjamin Eldon Stevens

Since at least the middle of the twentieth century, science fiction and fantasy (SF&F) have been crucial and popular modes for representing and thinking about life in the modern world. Both science-fictional speculations about the future and fantastic imaginings of alternative worlds – to oversimplify each complex genre – have provided vivid fictional settings for thought experiments about the world at hand. So successful have SF&F been in that capacity that, in the early twenty-first century, these narrative modes are everywhere, taking various forms in literature and the visual arts, perhaps most obviously exerting a strong hold on film and television. One need only note, for example, that of the fifty highest-grossing films worldwide to date, fully forty-five – 90 percent! – are SF&F.[1] Thus SF&F would seem to form a core or mainstream component of how the modern world reflects on itself, at least in popular culture.

It is therefore fascinating to observe how these significant modern genres are deeply rooted in the past. Beyond commonly cited precursors – including medieval romance and early modern collections of fairy tales – SF&F draw on the myth, philosophy, literature, history, and arts of the ancient Greek and Roman worlds.[2] In other words, two of the most important and popular *modern* modes, by transmitting and transmuting *ancient* Greek and Roman materials, are rich sites for 'classical receptions'.[3] Thus recent scholarly work has sought to articulate and describe the sorts of connections or genealogies that may extend, for example, from Plutarch's *Lives* and Juvenal's *Satires* (both early second century CE) through William Shakespeare's *Coriolanus* (c. 1605–1608), Pierre Corneille's *Cinna* (1643), and Edward Gibbon's *The History of the Decline and Fall of the Roman Empire* (1776–1789) to Isaac Asimov's *Foundation* series, the *Star Trek: The Original Series* episode "Bread and Circuses" (dir. Senensky, 1968), George Lucas's *Star Wars* Episodes I–VI (1997–2005), and Suzanne Collins's *The Hunger Games* trilogy (2008–2010).[4]

The present volume, *Once and Future Antiquities: Displacing Classics in Science Fiction and Fantasy* (*OFA*), seeks to make a new kind of contribution to this field by centering on a single, complex theme: 'displacement'. We derive the notion of 'displacement' from David Sandner, who, in a brief yet sweeping account of fantastic literature, describes the 'fantastic' thus: "The fundamental characteristic of the fantastic is displacement; the fantastic signifier does not point, even superficially, to any clear signified and so causes the reader to experience a lack, a disruption, inviting (if not provoking) an interpretation."[5] Sandner's particular term 'displacement' points usefully to multiple aspects of the process of reading or viewing SF&F – pointing not only to the experience of disruption

1

and the invitation to interpretation (as Sandner argues), but also to the many senses of distance and difference (spatial, temporal, linguistic, cultural, racial/ethnic, etc.) the reader or viewer may feel from their own empirical environment or the contemporary world.[6] We co-editors have argued elsewhere that an epistemologically similar form of 'estrangement' is to be found in studying the ancient past: just as science fiction may posit potential futures, and fantasy may imagine entirely different realities, so too does classical antiquity require our figurative transportation from the known world of the present.[7] That epistemological similarity means that all three areas are productively considered 'knowledge fictions' – and so may be productively compared with each other at a deeper level than formal comparison alone.

A principal aim of the volume is thus to explore what appears to be a central, even essential, feature shared by modern SF&F and ancient classics alike – once again, 'displacement'. This kind of comparative study stands to shed light not only on the modern materials but, just as significantly, on the ancient materials as well. To that perhaps-surprising end, *OFA*'s fourteen essays explore a wide range of interconnections amongst ancient and modern materials, stories, media, and genres. Together the essays serve as an invitation for readers to consider how the 'displacements' required by ancient classics may help to deepen their appreciation of – and indeed, authors', filmmakers', and other artists' construction of – modern SF&F. Finally, we hope that these essays may serve to 'displace' what (up until this point) has constituted the parameters for studies of reception in SF&F by de-centering some of our collective thinking about space, time, points of origin, and genre.

To these ends, we were delighted to see such displacements occur at the conference where many of the chapters were first presented (*The Once and Future Antiquity*, University of Puget Sound, March 2015), and we hope that readers will find that experience replicated in their own consideration of the chapters here. We believe that one of the most significant upshots of the comparative study of ancient classics and modern SF&F is to help constitute precisely the diverse community of readers for whom such comparison is 'natural' – that is, readers for whom the 'displacements' of science fiction, fantasy, and antiquity could serve as an invitation to a kind of intellectual and cultural homecoming. Our hope, then, is that the collected chapters will vividly exemplify the richness and excitement of this burgeoning field in ways that will invite readers to continue – and to correct! – the work thus far. We hope that this will help to invite further research in this exciting area, to foster interest in the ancient world and the classics more generally, and – with the great diversity of approaches and purposes in mind – to inspire additional 'creative' works of the type studied by the contributors.

Outline of volume

The chapters are organized into thematic groups. The chapters in the first section, 'Displacing Points of Origin', consider different ways in which contemporary SF&F

have been configured relative to – and therefore develop images of – certain eras of classical scholarship or other areas of passionate interest in antiquity.

Building on this Introduction's brief consideration of theoretical principles, Tony Keen offers a more detailed survey of methods in "More 'T' Vicar? Revisiting Models and Methodologies for Classical Receptions in Science Fiction". Keen revisits in particular his own foundational blog post (2006) – a 'point of origin' in its own right – to discuss some ways in which theoretical frameworks and practical approaches to the field have developed over the past twelve years. Especially of interest is the prospect of increased and deepened communication and collaboration between scholars of classical receptions or Classics generally and scholars situated more squarely in SF&F studies.

In "*Saxa loquuntur?* Archaeological Fantasies in Wilhelm Jensen's *Gradiva*", Jesse Weiner discusses how Jensen's 1902 historical novel – about an archaeologist with an immoderate love of ancient materials – is framed by psychoanalytical approaches *in* the field and *to* the field. Noting that Jensen's novel lies behind Sigmund Freud's influential *Delusion and Dream*, Weiner argues that *Gradiva* offers not an 'accurate' depiction of classical archaeology, but a dreamlike vision of how encounters with antiquity are made to speak to personal desire.

Turning from 'high' literature with institutional endorsement to 'low' media and genres at the centre of modern popular culture, in "Time Travel and Self-Reflexivity in Receptions of Homer's *Iliad*", Claire Kenward examines how the story of the Trojan War appears in a series of episodes in the beloved television series *Doctor Who* and in a contemporaneous comics series centred on Norse myth, Marvel's *Thor*. Emphasizing that, in each disparate storyline, characters experience antiquity directly via time travel, Kenward argues that such central tropes make science fiction something of a natural fit for classical reception, which in its own right practises a kind of 'time travel'. In this way, classical receptions in popular culture serve to draw attention to the epistemological status of fields like Classics.

As a final example and further development of that idea, in "Monuments and Tradition in Jack McDevitt's *The Engines of God*", Laura Zientek resumes Weiner's interest in archaeology, in this case in a form that is not fantastic but science-fictional . . . at least at first. Discussing McDevitt's references to the history of classical archaeology and related fields, Zientek argues that McDevitt's scholarly characters encounter 'antiquities' in ways that render even the science-fictional a matter of fact, contiguous with human experience in the present. From this perspective, the more science-fictional or fantastic the depiction, paradoxically the closer popular culture might come to representing actual scholarly experience of antiquity, a 'displacement' of perspective on academic disciplines that imagine themselves as *simply* factual or true.

Turning from such interests in theoretical and historical groundings of scholarly disciplines – from Foucauldian archaeologies – the chapters in the second section, 'Displaced in Space', consider a range of materials in which 'displacement' is literal, i.e., spatial. In these concrete examples, the epistemological or otherwise figurative displacements of SF&F and classics are mapped onto physical spaces with special effect, including the Arctic, the Underworld, and various locations called 'home'.

In "Lyra's Odyssey in Philip Pullman's *His Dark Materials*", Ortwin Knorr adds to readings of Pullman's trilogy as a take on Milton's *Paradise Lost* by considering its relationship to an antecedent epic, Homer's *Odyssey*. Noting similarities between main characters Lyra and Odysseus, as well as parallels in episodes and themes, Knorr argues that *The Golden Compass*, *The Amber Spyglass*, and *The Subtle Knife* all together offer a complex recasting of an odyssean journey, through which Pullman's Lyra emerges as a leader more competent than ancient Odysseus.

In "Displacing *Nostos* and the Ancient Greek Hero in Hayao Miyazaki's *Spirited Away*", Suzanne Lye discusses how Miyazaki's beloved film syncretises an assortment of myths, including those from ancient Greece and Rome. Lye argues that narrative and thematic parallels between *Spirited Away* and Greek epic stories of homecomings (*nostoi*) and Underworld journeys (*katabaseis*) work to displace the viewer's understanding of 'homecoming' so as to offer a richer, if untraditional, notion of what it means to reach home.

A similar authorial use of classical reception is to be found in "'The Nearest Technically Impossible Thing': Classical Receptions in Helen Oyeyemi", in which Benjamin Eldon Stevens examines how each of Oyeyemi's five novels to date sets classical myths alongside stories from other cultures, above all Oyeyemi's ancestral Yoruba (Nigerian) traditions. In context of her seemingly contradictory impulses *both* to converse mainly with 'dead' authors *and* to 'correct' older stories, Stevens argues that, for Oyeyemi, the displacement intrinsic to classical receptions makes them a powerful means of expressing the 'fantastic' nature or 'technical impossibility' of modern life.

Moving away from space or place as such, the chapters in the third section consider SF&F materials whose stories or characters are 'Displaced in Time'. These chapters challenge the notion that ancient narratives and figures move in simple, diachronic, or unidirectional ways. From the perspective of these modern stories, ancient narratives, too, are subject to unforeseen and often unpredictable temporal movements and recursions, such that past, present, and future remain in complex dialogues.

In "Dynamic Tensions: The Figure(s) of Atlas in *The Rocky Horror Picture Show*", Stephen B. Moses and Brett M. Rogers seek to add a missing link – or missing hunk? – to characterizations of the beloved cult classic *The Rocky Horror Picture Show* in ancient classical terms. Although scholars have described the film loosely as 'saturnalian' or 'Dionysiac', Moses and Rogers focus on the film's rather more overt – and strangely overlooked – engagement with traditions about the mythic Titan Atlas. Building on Atlas's appropriation by the well-marketed bodybuilder Charles Atlas, Moses and Rogers argue that the film's multiple figurations of Atlas contribute to its complex presentations and critiques of modern queer masculinities.

In "Drinking Blood and Talking Ghosts in Diana Wynne Jones's *The Time of the Ghost*", Frances Foster examines the formative role played in the novel by an ancient episode of encounter with the dead – namely, Odysseus's *nekuia* in *Odyssey* book 11. Considering explicit references as well as implicit structural parallels, Foster shows that the ghostly experience of Jones's characters – their encounter with a nearly deceased sister – expressly recalls the general structure and particular details of Odysseus's own emotional meeting with the dead. Foster thus argues that Jones's novel exemplifies the potential for sophisticated classical receptions in young adult fantasy.

Switching from page back to screen, in "Finding Cassandra in Science Fiction: The Seer of *Agamemnon* and the Time-Travelling Protector of *Continuum*", Jennifer Ranck explores parallels between the SF television series *Continuum* and certain tropes in classical tragedy, especially the figure of the *mantis* or 'seer' Cassandra in Aeschylus's *Oresteia*. Ranck details parallels between that ancient seer and the series' time-travelling main character. Ultimately, Ranck argues that such classical receptions, in context of storylines recalling police procedurals and conspiracy theories, offer an image of modern female 'heroism' that is implicitly both a response and a corrective to long traditions.

The final section of scholarship, 'Displacing Genre', returns, in a sense, to the theoretical considerations of the Introduction and first chapter by examining receptions that are not limited to 'mainstream' literary or televisual SF&F but appear in related genres like historical fiction and in a variety of media, in these cases especially role-playing games (RPGs) and tabletop games.

In "Classical Reception and the Half-Elf Cleric", C. W. Marshall examines the Monster Manuals of the foundational RPG *Dungeons & Dragons*. Applying a philological or textual-critical approach to the manuals, Marshall tracks which classical 'monsters' have appeared in which editions and with what descriptions or forms. In context of the RPG's penchant for syncretism – its love of bringing together monsters from many different cultural traditions – Marshall argues that *D&D*'s relatively stable set of classical monsters have formed an important source of information about Greco-Roman myths for generations of players and readers.

In "The Gods Problem in Gene Wolfe's *Soldier of the Mist*", Vincent Tomasso identifies a similar function fulfilled by, in this case, historical fiction. Focusing on how Wolfe's novel complicates an ancient distinction between 'mythologizing' and 'rationalizing' modes of explanation, Tomasso argues that the story's mixture of the two – the divine apparently exists but is not present, and the novel frames itself as a historical discovery in our real world – represents a complication to any simple modern understanding of ancient myth – and indeed, of thought about the gods in the modern world.

In "The Divine Emperor in Virgil's *Aeneid* and the *Warhammer 40K* Universe", Alexander McAuley combines the preceding chapter's interests in games and historical fiction to consider how Games Workshop's *Warhammer 40K* universe of tabletop games and novels imagine a fictional future history that strongly recalls ancient literary representations of imperial Rome. Drawing on documentary evidence including interviews with *Warhammer* creators and authors, McAuley focuses in particular on deliberate similarities between *Warhammer*'s figure of the divine emperor and portrayals of Rome's first emperor, Augustus Caesar, especially in Virgil's epic poem, the *Aeneid*.

The volume ends with a special epilogue, 'Finding a Place in Displacement'. In "Just Your Average Tuesday-Morning Minotaur", beloved speculative-fiction author

Catherynne M. Valente offers a uniquely personal contribution, discussing how her own longstanding love of ancient classics, especially Greek language and myth, played a formative role in her development as an author. Valente's essay, like Sandner's understanding of 'displacement', not only disrupts the scholarly voice of this volume, but also invites readers to reconsider their own possible roles in how we, collectively, may (dis)place our own narratives about the relationship between SF&F and classical antiquity.

Notes

1. Box Office Mojo: http://www.boxofficemojo.com/alltime/world/. Accessed 8 May 2018.
2. On 'medievalism' and the history of modern fantasy, see usefully Gessert 2017 and Folch 2017. This is not to claim that Greco-Roman or even, more broadly, Mediterranean antiquity uniquely contributes as a source for SF&F.
3. On classical receptions, see, e.g., Butler 2016, Jenkins 2015, Hardwick and Stray 2008, Martindale and Thomas 2006, Hardwick 2003.
4. For collections of scholarship on SF&F and classics, see esp. Weiner, Stevens, and Rogers 2018 on *Frankenstein* and related works (including Plutarch); Rogers and Stevens 2017 on fantasy; Rogers and Stevens 2015 on SF (including *Star Trek* and *The Hunger Games*); and Bost-Fiévet and Provini 2014 on SF&F (likewise including *The Hunger Games*). Brown 2008 also offers a survey of SF and classics. On *Star Wars* and classics, see Winkler 2001 and Keen 2012a, b.
5. Sandner (2004: 9).
6. Cf. Mathews 1997, who argues that disciplines focusing on distance and difference – archaeology, anthropology, and philology – are important for SF&F because they explore and recover the past that is "at the heart of the fantasy impulse", such that "time travel is an archetypal impulse … [and] [a]ntiquity – history – is one gateway to infinity" (26). On archaeology in SF&F, see Weiner and Zientek (this volume); on time travel, see Kenward (this volume).
7. Rogers and Stevens (2017: 7–14), (2015: 11–19), and (2012: 131), after Suvin 1979, usefully analysed by Freedman 2000; cf. Csicsery-Ronay 2011.

PART I
DISPLACING POINTS OF ORIGIN

CHAPTER 1
MORE 'T' VICAR? REVISITING MODELS AND METHODOLOGIES FOR CLASSICAL RECEPTIONS IN SCIENCE FICTION
Tony Keen

The study of classical reception in science fiction (SF) has only been a coherent subject for about twenty years.[1] There was some early work in the 1970s by Fredericks.[2] But the first scholarly panel of which I am aware took place at the 1999 UK Classical Association conference in Liverpool.[3] It was about this time that classical reception was starting to emerge as a distinct part of the scholarly landscape. Martindale's *Redeeming the Text* was published in 1993; in 2003, reception was considered seriously enough to get a volume in the *Greece and Rome New Surveys in the Classics* series.[4] At the same time, important studies on reception in popular culture, in particular in cinema, were being produced.[5]

In the twenty-first century there has been an increasing interest in the interaction of classics and SF and fantasy (SF&F). This has exploded in the six years between 2012 and 2018. Conferences have taken place in France (*L'Antiquité gréco-latine aux sources de l'imaginaire contemporain: Fantastique, Fantasy & S-F*, Rouen and Paris, 7–9 June 2012), the UK (*Swords, Sorcery, Sandals and Space*, Liverpool, 29 June–1 July 2013), the USA (*The Once and Future Antiquity*, Tacoma, WA, 27–28 March 2015), Germany (*Antikenrezeption in der Science-Fiction-Literatur*, Cologne, 9 May 2015), and Sweden (*Reception Histories of the Future: A Conference on Byzantinisms, Speculative Fiction, and the Literary Heritage of Medieval Empire*, Uppsala, 4–6 August 2017).[6] There has also been a series of panels and roundtables at the Society for Classical Studies Annual Meeting. Two non-conference volumes of papers have also appeared.[7] Other surveys of the field have appeared, by Brown, Bourke, Nisbet, Rogers and Stevens, and Gloyn.[8]

As both an SF fan and a Classicist since childhood, I began working in this area in 2002. In 2006 I posted a long, and in the event surprisingly significant, article on my weblog *Memorabilia Antonina*: "The 'T' stands for Tiberius: Models and Methodologies of Classical Reception in Science Fiction".[9] This was a revised and expanded version of a paper I had presented at that year's UK Classical Association conference in Newcastle-upon-Tyne. The paper was originally based on a structure I had developed in 2000 for a paper on classical reception in the television shows *Doctor Who* and *Star Trek*; this had been intended in the first instance for an SF convention.[10]

In this chapter I revisit the ideas and models advanced in 2006, in light of the following decade's work. How far do the models proposed still stand up? What should a theoretical approach in 2018 look like? How can these models and theories be applied? What directions should future research follow? I first assess the post and its legacy, and how it has become embedded in scholarly study of the subject area. I then address what I now believe to be methodological challenges facing scholars working in this field.

Revisiting the original post

There was a degree of frivolity in how I wrote the original post. The terms were chosen with at least half an eye on a cheap laugh, but there remained a serious intent beneath it. Originally, I had only the central four categories, *appropriation*, *interaction*, *borrowing*, and *stealing*; I added the others (*retellings*, *allusion*, and *ghosting*) as I developed the ideas (for a summary of the meanings of these terms, see Fig. 1.1). I put the paper out quickly on my blog in the spirit of sharing discussion, and to put down a marker that this was a field I was interested in. I then proceeded to completely ignore this model in almost everything I have written since – it certainly does not appear in my own later methodological pieces.[11] Nevertheless, without my realizing it, the post became widely cited, largely because no one else had even attempted to theorize in this area.[12]

As noted above, in the intervening period there have been a number of surveys of the field, with greater or lesser degrees of theorizing.[13] What I learn most from these pieces is that the field is vast and can accommodate a number of different approaches, whether that be Brown's genre-based study or Nisbet's engagement with the idea that popular perceptions of antiquity are extremely difficult for scholars to get moved on in the light of new academic thinking. I have also contributed some generalist pieces.[14]

Coming back to my own schema twelve years later, how do I feel it stands up? It is evidently the product of someone who had read very little in the way of literary or reception theory. There is reference to Martindale, but this was written before I had read *Redeeming the Text*; Hardwick's *Reception Studies* is only mentioned in a note.[15] I would not write in quite such naïve terms now.[16] I would certainly address more the ideas of Martindale (see below) and Hardwick, noting that the reception vocabulary she devises almost all relates to active and serious engagement with an ancient source.[17] There is little room in her vocabulary for my *allusion* or *ghosting*.

There are weaknesses in my schema. My theoretical proposals display a disinterest in fantasy that I have since abandoned. I attempted to differentiate the appearance of gods in modern-day settings in fantasy series from that of gods in an SF setting. I now see this as tendentious. My schema does not really deal well with alternative history, despite my attempt to crowbar it into *interaction*. Meanwhile, Paula James has separately come up with the concept of 'cultural companions', where there is no suggestion that the creators of a modern text have deliberately used antiquity or ancient texts, but nevertheless illuminating parallels can be drawn.[18] I think that I now prefer that concept to my *ghosting*, but they might not actually be the same thing: 'cultural companions' comes from a comparative literature perspective, whereas *ghosting* is perhaps more historicist.

By and large, though, I think the model stands up – but with the very large *caveat* that the boundaries between the categories are much less clearly delineated than I may have implied. Is *2001: A Space Odyssey* merely something that alludes to Homer in its title, or a reworking of the epic?[19] Is *Battlestar Galactica* (either version) a cultural companion of Virgil's *Aeneid*, or a straight steal?[20] How can we decide? And, of course, a single text can, and often does, fall under several different categories of my schema – see *Galactica* again.

Theoretical engagements

Since the publication of the piece, there have been two major theoretical engagements with it. The first is an alternative schema devised by Marshall, who proposes dividing receptions into five categories: *cosmetic reference, indirect reference, envisioning, revisioning* and *engagement*.[21]

Rogers has produced a chart that summarizes the schemas and shows the relationship between the two.[22] This oversimplifies, and the actual network of links is far more complicated; for instance, the Romulan empire, which Marshall sees as a *cosmetic reference*, which Rogers links with my *allusion*, I would place in the category of *borrowing*. But the fundamental difference is in what the two schemas are trying to assess. Marshall is looking specifically at expectations of audiences and what knowledge they need to fully appreciate a reception. Mine focuses upon the level of use of the ancient world/texts, which Marshall rightly points out "blurs authorial intent and the narrative being presented".[23] Nevertheless, I think both schemas are useful, especially if mine is modified in the light of Marshall's comments.

The other engagement is by Rogers, who develops the concept of *ghosting*.[24] Rogers notes that I do not provide any testable criteria by which an example of *ghosting* may be identified. He proposes the use of the semiotic concept of "syntagms", "ordered combination[s] of signifiers forming a meaningful whole".[25] This seems to me to be a valuable modification of my original schema.

Methodological challenges

In light of such theoretical engagements, and given other work – including my own – over the years since the original post, certain methodological challenges arise. Here I identify five, all of which, I think, affect other fields of reception to one degree or another.

Challenge #1: Science fiction is big. Really big.[26]

The field is vast. There really is nothing we can do about this. No study can be comprehensive – though the database Rogers and Stevens are compiling will certainly be extremely useful in this respect.[27] But it will never cover everything, and it will never be completed.

Challenge #2: The lure of positivism

As I alluded to in the original post when mentioning *2001*, it is too easy, once one parallel has been found, to search for more, and to force the receiving text into something it is

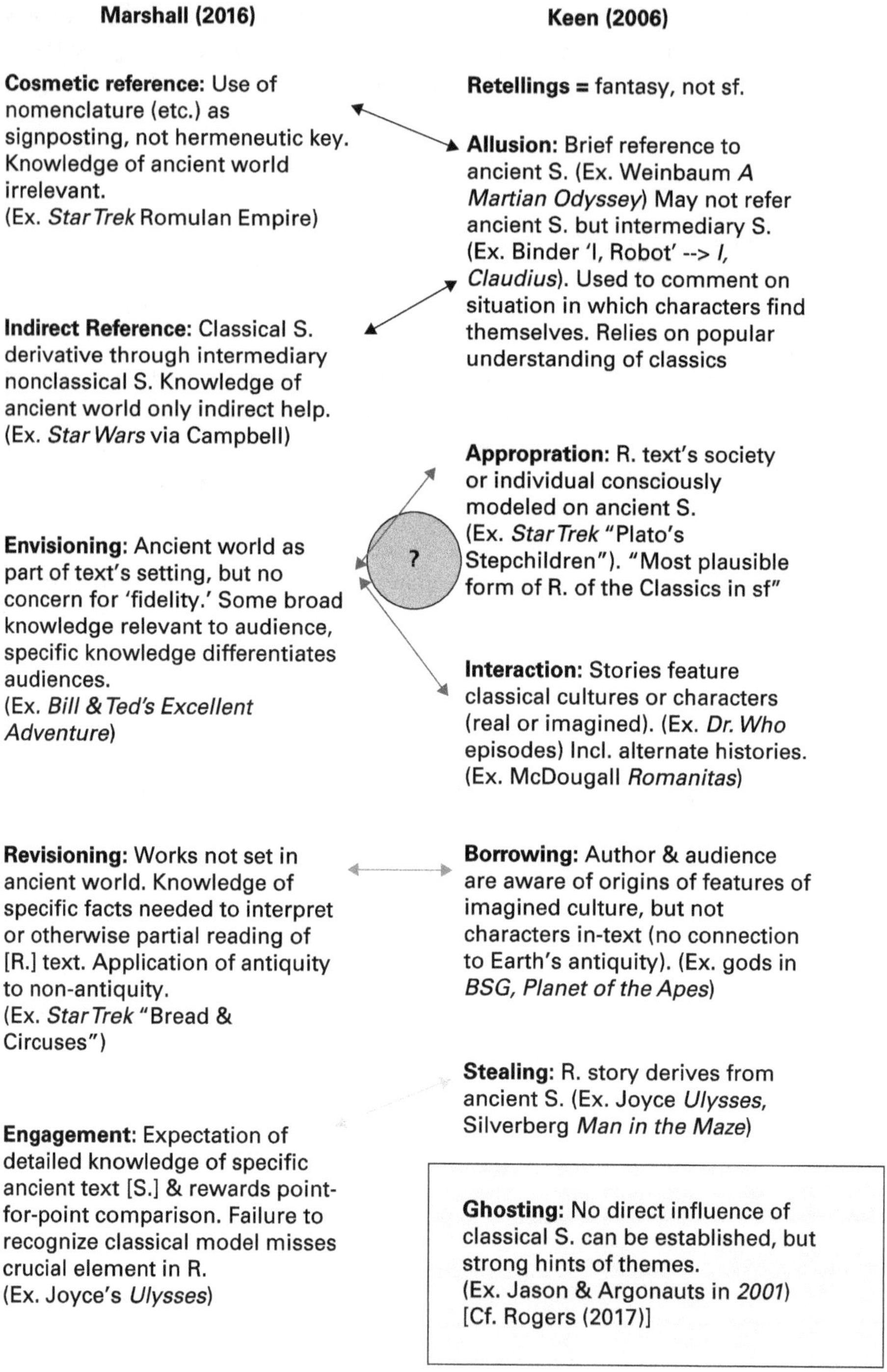

Marshall (2016)   **Keen (2006)**

Cosmetic reference: Use of nomenclature (etc.) as signposting, not hermeneutic key. Knowledge of ancient world irrelevant.
(Ex. *Star Trek* Romulan Empire)

Retellings = fantasy, not sf.

Allusion: Brief reference to ancient S. (Ex. Weinbaum *A Martian Odyssey*) May not refer ancient S. but intermediary S. (Ex. Binder 'I, Robot' --> *I, Claudius*). Used to comment on situation in which characters find themselves. Relies on popular understanding of classics

Indirect Reference: Classical S. derivative through intermediary nonclassical S. Knowledge of ancient world only indirect help.
(Ex. *Star Wars* via Campbell)

Appropration: R. text's society or individual consciously modeled on ancient S. (Ex. *Star Trek* "Plato's Stepchildren"). "Most plausible form of R. of the Classics in sf"

Envisioning: Ancient world as part of text's setting, but no concern for 'fidelity.' Some broad knowledge relevant to audience, specific knowledge differentiates audiences.
(Ex. *Bill & Ted's Excellent Adventure*)

?

Interaction: Stories feature classical cultures or characters (real or imagined). (Ex. *Dr. Who* episodes) Incl. alternate histories. (Ex. McDougall *Romanitas*)

Revisioning: Works not set in ancient world. Knowledge of specific facts needed to interpret or otherwise partial reading of [R.] text. Application of antiquity to non-antiquity.
(Ex. *Star Trek* "Bread & Circuses")

Borrowing: Author & audience are aware of origins of features of imagined culture, but not characters in-text (no connection to Earth's antiquity). (Ex. gods in *BSG, Planet of the Apes*)

Stealing: R. story derives from ancient S. (Ex. Joyce *Ulysses*, Silverberg *Man in the Maze*)

Engagement: Expectation of detailed knowledge of specific ancient text [S.] & rewards point-for-point comparison. Failure to recognize classical model misses crucial element in R.
(Ex. Joyce's *Ulysses*)

Ghosting: No direct influence of classical S. can be established, but strong hints of themes.
(Ex. Jason & Argonauts in *2001*)
[Cf. Rogers (2017)]

Fig. 1.1 The relationship of the schemas of Marshall and Keen. Chart by Brett M. Rogers (June 2017).

Note: R. = Reception; S. = Source.

not. This is a particular concern in respect to cultural companions, as formulated by James. People have seen parallels between Virgil and the reimagined *Battlestar Galactica*, and sought to develop them further, by locating a Dido figure – and I simply do not think there is one to be found.[28] In the case of *2001*, David Bowman might be an Odysseus figure – but only if Odysseus is reduced to such a degree that he loses everything that makes him Odysseus and not a generic sea captain. If scholarship is doing the equivalent of saying "well, you can see the parallel if you look at it this way" whilst squinting and holding a hand over one eye, then the parallel may be illusory.[29]

Related to this is the danger of seeing classical reception as the most important element of a text's makeup. Undoubtedly this is true in some cases. But in others the creators are drawing on a wide range of different sources and periods, to create a unique palimpsest, and we must remember not to over-privilege classical reception because it is the reception in which we ourselves are interested.[30]

Challenge #3: Theory, what theory?

As reception scholars, we are often terrible at theorizing our case studies. I am as guilty of this as anyone. We are too prone to the historicist studies of which Martindale complains, studies that assume that issues in reception can be known and explained.[31]

Of course, there is a problem here for scholars of reception and SF. One of the prime reception theorists of the past twenty years is Martindale, and he is often hostile to popular culture, even when he claims not to be.[32] I have engaged with this in my *Foundation* editorial.[33] The most effective demolition of Martindale I have seen is in an unpublished discussion post by Claire Greenhalgh.[34] She shows how Martindale uses reception theory in the service of canon creation, and prefers the more broadly based approach to reception of Simon Goldhill.[35] Goldhill's case is that Martindale focuses upon the individual in the chain of receptions, e.g., Martindale reading Dante reading Homer. This, Goldhill suggests, neglects broader contexts for receptions.

Whether one sides with Martindale or Goldhill, the point remains that we do not theorize our work enough, and we should. As Neville Morley writes, "most of the radical theoretical agenda that first inspired the movement has been quietly abandoned".[36]

Three recent developments will change how reception studies are done. The first is the resurgence of the concept of the classical tradition, once thought to have been largely displaced by reception.[37] A large reference work was published in 2010 entitled *The Classical Tradition*, though the approach is quite positivist, aiming to ensure 'correct' understanding of development of the tradition.[38] Rather more sophisticated is the work of Silk, Gildenhard, and Barrow, who make a strong case that, while reception and the classical tradition overlap, they are not the same thing, and that reception has not displaced the classical tradition.[39]

Secondly, there is the challenge of Butler's 'Deep Classics'. Butler argues for a perspective that sits between the classical tradition and reception, one which he sees as stratigraphic, digging through the layers of reception and looking at them from a sideways perspective.[40] Butler's work is a new perspective, which has not yet fully worked its way into theoretical approaches, though its influence is showing more and more.

Finally, there is Willis's excellent book, *Reception*.[41] Willis addresses the fact that Classics, always a very text-based discipline, deals in text-to-text receptions, in contrast with, for instance, reception in film studies, which is much more concerned with audience responses.[42] Willis explores all the different approaches to reception studies, and it is to be hoped that exposure to this will result in new approaches to classical reception.

Challenge #4: Voici la fantastique!

Bost-Fiévet's and Provini's volume, the Cologne conference, and the French popular-culture-focused Antiquipop project all mean that we in Classics and SF studies must stop pretending that non-anglophone scholarship does not exist.[43] This is actually a problem that is endemic to reception; I know of no other field of classical studies in which writing in German, French, and Italian is so completely ignored.[44] In SF&F reception in particular, there has not yet been much scholarship in any language, so we are perhaps not as guilty of this form of Anglocentrism. But we must ensure that we do not make the mistake already made in other fields. If we allow that to happen, we will miss out on important scholarship, such as Wenskus's study of reception in *Star Trek*.[45]

Challenge #5: Becoming SF scholars

In my *Foundation* editorial I wrote "the best scholars in Classical Reception are those who are already credible both as Classicists and scholars in the receiving field".[46] I now think that is exclusionary (and a bit pompous), and in my revision amended that to "the best scholars in Classical Reception will be those who are able to become credible both as Classicists and scholars in the receiving field".[47] It is possible to be credible as both – but the work has to be done. In our field, that means being up to date with critical thinking within SF. And that means, and I cannot emphasize this enough, going beyond Darko Suvin.[48] The problem is that to concentrate upon Suvin is potentially reductive in two ways: firstly, it restricts the theoretical approaches to which one is exposed; secondly, Suvin's definition of what constitutes SF is itself reductive. The danger is that some of the richness of the field, the very thing that makes it attractive, may be lost.

Suvin's 1979 book *Metamorphoses of Science Fiction* is an important work, and the concepts of the 'novum' and 'cognitive estrangement' are important critical tools in SF.[49] But Suvin has not solved the problem of the definition of SF. As Kincaid says, Suvin's definition is a prescriptive one, and one that is enmeshed in SF as essentially about grand narratives of science. SF can be that, but it does not have to be.[50] Suvin's definition can exclude much that is generally thought of as SF, particularly in film and television. This is not an issue to Suvin – he would quite happily exclude the likes of *Star Wars*.[51] But if a definition of a genre excludes what most people think of as being part of that genre – indeed, even typical of it – then I think there is something wrong with the definition.[52] Knight's definition, that SF is what we mean when we point to something and call it SF, recognizes that a definition of SF must include texts generally considered as SF. As I said in my contribution to *Classical Traditions in Science Fiction*, this is the only definition of SF that makes any sense and can stand up to robust interrogation (whilst at the same time being a massive cop-out).[53]

So Suvin should no longer be the end point of engagement with SF theory, or even the starting point. I want to see more works on SF and classics that take as their starting point the James and Mendlesohn *Cambridge Companion*, or Kincaid's *What It Is We Do When We Read Science Fiction*, or Csicsery-Ronay's inspiring *Seven Beauties of Science Fiction*.[54] This does not necessarily mean that one has to become a 'fan', to touch on an issue Gloyn raises in a 2015 post on her blog.[55] But, as Martindale rightly says, work on the reception of classics in a particular genre must be credible to scholars of that genre, as well as to Classicists.[56] Again, the REF summary highlights this failure to engage as a general weakness in some papers in reception.[57]

So, classical reception scholars need to read SF criticism, and publish in SF venues. Taking courses in science fiction is also advisable. In the UK the Science Fiction Foundation runs Masterclass in Science Fiction Criticism, a three-day course in the summer that has been a boon to many scholars in the field over the past decade.[58]

Those then, are the challenges I think we face in studying classics and SF.

Notes

1. I am grateful to Brett M. Rogers, Benjamin Eldon Stevens, and Laura Zientek for allowing me to speak at the conference, to Rogers and Stevens for their patience over the final text, and to everyone I've discussed this subject with since 1999.

2. Fredericks 1975, 1976 (reprinted as Fredericks 1978), 1977, and 1980.

3. One of the papers from the 1999 CA conference was eventually published as Morley 2000, and one as D'Angour 2001. The third, Shone 1999, I believe remains unpublished.

4. Martindale 1993; Hardwick 2003.

5. E.g., Wyke 1997a.

6. The French conference is published as Bost-Fiévet and Provini 2014. A selection of papers from the Liverpool conference were published in *Foundation* 118 (2014). *The Once and Future Antiquity* is published in this volume. For the German conference, see Kleu 2015. There may be others I have missed, and a comprehensive list of scholarly writings on the topic is beyond the scope of this chapter. Links between SF&F and the medieval period are explored in Paz and Kears 2016.

7. Rogers and Stevens 2015 and 2017.

8. Brown 2008; Bourke 2011; Nisbet 2011; Rogers and Stevens 2012; and Gloyn 2015b.

9. Keen 2006a. The title of the present chapter is a punning reference to the original blogpost and a stereotypical remark often found in dramas and comedies set in English country villages. The original post may be found at http://tonykeen.blogspot.com/2006/04/t-stands-for-tiberius-models-and.html and an annotated version at http://tonykeen.blogspot.com/2018/07/t-for-tiberius-revisited.html.

10. The first half of this eventually appeared as a book chapter (Keen 2010), while the second was posted to my blog in 2007 (Keen 2007a).

11. Keen 2014a (revised as 2015b), 2016a, and 2017. It is not even mentioned in the chapter that grew out of the paper for which I originally developed the schema (Keen 2010). I have, however, used it in Keen 2018.

12. E.g., Saylor (n.d.); Rogers and Stevens (2012: 142–143); Provini and Bost-Fiévet (2014: 32); Rogers and Stevens (2015: viii); Gloyn 2015b; Marshall (2016: 20, 23); Quinn 2016; and Rogers (2017: 216–217).

13. Brown 2008; Bourke 2011; Nisbet 2011; Rogers and Stevens 2012; Provini and Bost-Fiévet 2014; Rogers and Stevens 2015a; Gloyn 2015b; Rogers and Stevens 2017a. Kovacs 2011 is also relevant.

14. Keen 2011, 2014a (revised as 2015b), and 2017.

15. Martindale 1993; Hardwick 2003.

16. However, I retain the view that it is best to be theory-aware rather than theory-driven. For my initial thoughts on theory (theory being a never-ending process), see Keen 2009 and 2016b. For my understanding of theory, Culler 1997 and Rice and Waugh 2001 [1992] have been key.

17. Hardwick (2003: 9–10).

18. James (2009: 239).

19. There is an inclination in various treatments towards the latter, though I think wrongly: e.g., Gilbert (2006: 32). For an extreme example of this, see Wheat 2000. On deeper Homeric themes in *2001*, see Keen 2006b, Rogers (2015: 217–222), and Keen 2018.

20. Kubrick 1968; Larson 1978; Moore 2003–2009. On *Galactica*, see Potter and Marshall 2008, Tomasso 2015a, and Wenskus (2017: 455–456).

21. Marshall (2016: 19–23).

22. I am grateful to Brett Rogers for permission to include this in the present chapter.

23. Marshall (2016: 20–24).

24. Rogers (2017: 216–218).

25. Ibid., 217, citing the *Oxford English Dictionary*.

26. Paraphrasing Adams (1985: 39): "Space . . . is big. Really big."

27. The database is located at http://tinyurl.com/ctsfmfdatabase.

28. For *Battlestar Galactica* (Moore 2003–2009) as a re-imagining of the *Aeneid*, see Nokes 2006, Higgins 2009, and Pache 2010. The more academic study of Tomasso (2015a: 253) spends little time on this aspect of *BSG*.

29. See Rogers and Stevens 2012 and 2015a.

30. Hodkinson and Lovatt (2018: 17, 35n38), citing Lowe (forthcoming: 13).

31. Martindale (2006: 9) and (2013: 170–171). This is hinted at in the subject summaries from the most recent Research Excellence Framework (REF) in the UK, which identifies work on reception as often "of mixed quality"; REF (2015: 60). I am grateful to Joanna Paul for bringing this to my attention. On issues with the REF, see Sayer 2014.

32. Most notoriously in Martindale in Martindale and Thomas (2006: 11); cf. Martindale (2013: 176).

33. Keen (2014a: 5–6).

34. Greenhalgh 2015.

35. Goldhill 2010.

36. Morley 2014. There are good introductions to reception in the *Oxford Classical Dictionary*, but these should be merely the start of methodological work; Michelakis 2012, Lowe 2012, and Martindale and Hardwick 2012.

37. For the relationship between reception and tradition, see Budelmann and Haubold 2008.

38. Grafton, Most, and Settis 2010a; for the approach, see ibid., x.

39. Silk, Gildenhard, and Barrow (2014: 4–5).

40. See Butler 2016a; the concept is worked through in specific instances by the various contributions to Butler 2016. See also Morley 2014.

41. Willis 2017.

42. Ibid., 35. For film studies, see King 1998 and Maltby (2003 [1995]: 549–553). Perhaps the only scholar in classical reception taking this approach is Potter (e.g., 2009).

43. Bost-Fiévet and Provini 2014, Kleu 2015, and https://antiquipop.hypotheses.org/ (accessed 29 April 2018).

44. A glance over the bibliography to Hardwick and Stray 2008 shows that there are non-anglophone works present, but often not more than one or two per page in a bibliography that runs to fifty-one pages (482–532).

45. Wenskus 2011; an English summary of some of her ideas can be found in Wenskus 2017.

46. Keen (2014a: 6).

47. Keen (2015b: 2).

48. For an approach heavily dependent on Suvin, see Rogers and Stevens (2015a: 11–19).

49. Suvin 2016 reprints Suvin 1979 with new introductions by Suvin and Gerry Canavan. See also Suvin 2014.

50. Kincaid (2008: 13).

51. Not explicitly stated by Suvin, but that this is a consequence of Suvin's thinking is made clear by Freedman (2000: 19); see also Csicsery-Ronay (2003: 119).

52. In this I concur with Freedman (2000: 19).

53. Knight (1996: 11) and Keen (2015a: 109–110). Compare Folch (2017: 163–164), who argues for using Wittgenstein's "family resemblances" when defining fantasy.

54. James and Mendlesohn 2003, Kincaid (2008: 3–11), and Csicsery-Ronay 2011. For further recommended reading for classical reception scholars working in SF, see Keen 2012b.

55. Gloyn 2015a, further developed in Gloyn 2015b. The similarities between classical scholarship and fandoms, and the need for scholars working in cult areas to acknowledge and engage with their own fannishness is variously discussed in Kovacs (2011: 6–7), Nisbet (2011: 1–2), Rogers and Stevens (2015: viii), and Keen 2015c.

56. Martindale (2006: 9).

57. REF (2015: 60).

58. For the Masterclass, see https://www.sf-foundation.org/masterclass (accessed 29 April 2018).

CHAPTER 2
SAXA LOQUUNTUR? ARCHAEOLOGICAL FANTASIES IN WILHELM JENSEN'S *GRADIVA*
Jesse Weiner

Introduction

Pompeii and Herculaneum are dramatic loci for exploration of the fantastic. Since their rediscoveries, the ruins of Pompeii and Herculaneum have captured the imaginations of classicists and popular audiences alike. The twin cities preserved by ash in the midst of their daily motions conjure sublime, grandiose visions of apocalyptic destruction, while nearly unprecedented levels of preservation offer some of the best material evidence for reconstructing the everyday lives of ancient Romans. Bread still baking in the ovens, pets chained to their posts, and walls decorated with graffiti and erotic frescoes all contribute to a richer picture of daily life in classical antiquity while tantalizingly suggesting the possibility of revivifying the past. In the words of Genevieve Liveley, "Pompeii has long been a site of delusion and dream, illusion and fantasy, inspiring in generations of visitors the desire to travel back in time so that they might see the "City of the Dead" and its citizens brought back to life."[1] These delusions and fantasies have, at times, taken erotic turns. In particular, as Daniel Orrells observes, "the archaeological excavation of Pompeii [has also] provided a site for modern men to voice their fantasies about ancient women".[2]

This essay examines such tensions – between scientific archaeology and erotic fantasy – in a dreamlike psychological novella inspired by and set among the ruins of Pompeii, Wilhelm Jensen's 1903 *Gradiva: A Pompeian Fantasy* (*Gradiva: Ein pompejanisches Phantasiestück*). The novella's protagonist, a classical archaeologist named Norbert Hanold, wanders the excavated city in a hallucinatory haze, obsessed with a woman from an ancient bas-relief, whom he names Gradiva, "the girl who is splendid in walking" (*die Vorschreitende*; 9).[3] Norbert struggles to separate imagination from reality and to distinguish figures from the Roman past from his own acquaintances. *Gradiva* thus posits a nexus between scientific archaeology and erotic fantasy.

After providing initial context for the novella and its reception – *Gradiva* is little-known today and less read by audiences outside of the academy – I argue that *Gradiva* sets scientific archaeology in binary opposition to fantasy, only to collapse the distinction. While much recent scholarship has focused on Sigmund Freud's reading of *Gradiva*, I focus on Jensen's novella itself to suggest that Norbert's science inherently contains something of the fantastic and, despite his pretensions, the archaeologist cannot help but interpret the classical past through his own aesthetic preferences and prejudices. Archaeology and fantasy each wrestle with and rely upon displacement, and *Gradiva* illuminates not only classical influence on fantasy but also fantasy's influence on Classics. I suggest that *Gradiva* celebrates a role for the fantastic in antiquarian scholarship. Therefore, I conclude by asking, speculatively but hopefully, whether there might be something gained by embracing a rightful place for the fantastic in the scholarly practices of classical archaeology and philology. Such a reading thus aligns with the perspective offered by Edmund Richardson (2013: 75):

> In the space between the nineteenth century and the classical past, imagination richly flourished. Often that past was not long lost – it was close enough to touch, and could be conjured into life again. The space between it and the present could fall away; that was a promise which bordered upon an enchantment. For many, the ancient world was their world; it belonged to them and they belonged to it. History was a narrative to make one's own – where past and present danced, but suspiciously, together.

Gradiva calls attention to the estranging gulfs – temporal, cultural, material – between classical antiquity and the classicist, and offers fantasy as a path for exploring these voids. I argue that the fantastic is an essential component of Norbert's 'science', and that *Gradiva* celebrates a place for the fantastic in Classics. Only when Norbert abandons his pretense of positivism can the past come back to life. Finally, I offer that this inclusion of the fantastic within its vision of classical scholarship opens Jensen's novella to a feminist reading.

Gradiva and its readers: the archaeologist, the psychoanalyst, and the witch

To summarize the novella in brief: Norbert Hanold, an independently wealthy German archaeologist, becomes obsessed with a woman depicted mid-step in an ancient bas-relief. The relief itself is not fictional: Jensen borrows the Gradiva sculpture from a neo-Attic Roman relief depicting the Agraulides.[4]

Norbert names the figure Gradiva and he vividly dreams that he bears witness to the woman's death in Pompeii during the Vesuvius eruption of 79 CE (*Gradiva* 16–19). During the dream, Gradiva's presence in Pompeii "seemed natural" to Norbert, "as she was, of course, a Pompeiian girl . . ." (17). According to the novella's narrator, Norbert's dream of Gradiva's death in Pompeii is characterized by "excitement over the danger to her life" (21). After all, says Freud, "this was the wish, [the fantasy] comprehensible to every archaeologist, to have been an eyewitness of that catastrophe".[5]

Norbert then travels to Pompeii, where he believes he sees and interacts with Gradiva herself amongst the ruins.[6] The reader is held in suspense while Norbert wrestles with the mystery. Is he mad? Does he really meet Gradiva's ghost? Is Gradiva a material, revivified woman? *Gradiva*'s narrative thus relies on what Rosemary Jackson calls "fantasy's central thematic issue: an uncertainty as to the nature of the 'real', a problematization of categories of 'realism' and 'truth,' of the 'seen' and 'known'".[7]

Fig. 2.1 Bas-relief known as "Gradiva". Hadrianic period, second century CE. Museo Chiramonti. Photo Credit: Alinari/Art Resource, NY. © 2018 Artists Rights Society (ARS), New York/ADAGP, Paris.

Eventually, the living Gradiva is revealed to be Norbert's childhood friend, Zoë Bertgang, whom Norbert failed to recognize in his obsession with the classical past. Zoë's name, Greek for 'life', playfully represents a dead past brought back to life. Once she reveals herself, Norbert asks Zoë to marry him, and the novella ends with the couple's engagement. Because *Gradiva*'s fantastic elements take place in our world (rather than in a secondary world) and are, ultimately, anchored to reality, the novella is best classified as 'low fantasy' (as opposed to 'high fantasy') and 'delusional fantasy'.[8] *Gradiva* suggests that studying antiquity is itself a kind of fantastic activity, which depends upon the metaphysically impossible for any truly unmediated encounter with the past.

Beyond *Gradiva*'s Pompeian setting and classicist protagonist, another classical connection is to the story of Pygmalion. As a misogynistic bachelor who fixates upon and fetishizes a white sculpture of a woman that subsequently comes to life, Norbert is easily read as a Pygmalion figure.[9] Pygmalion's sexual repression (he shuns contact with women, though he ultimately desires them) and deviance (he falls in love with a sculpture), present in Ovid's version of the story (*Metamorphoses* 10.243–97), are recognizable in Norbert. Classical sources aside from Ovid depict Pygmalion falling in love with a statue of another's creation, and Norbert does the same with the figure in the ancient bas-relief.[10] The surrealist painter André Masson connected Jensen's novella with

Fig. 2.2 Masson, André. "Gradiva" (1939). Musée National d'Art Moderne. © CNAC/MNAM/ Dist. RNM-Grand Palais/Art Resource, NY. © 2018 Artists Rights Society (ARS), New York/ADAGP, Paris.

the classical myth, since Masson's *Gradiva* (1939) (Fig. 2.2) derives from his less successful *Pygmalion* (1938).[11]

As Masson's use of Gradiva as a surreal subject suggests, Jensen's *Gradiva* was immediately influential, for its fantastic and psychological elements alike. Freud seized upon Gradiva in his 1907 treatise *Delusion and Dream in Wilhelm Jensen's Gradiva* (*Wahn und die träume in W. Jensens Gradiva*) to propose archaeology as a metaphor for psychoanalysis. Beyond Masson, surrealists including André Breton, Paul Éluard, and Salvador Dalí drew upon Gradiva in their paintings and writings. Dalí used Gradiva as a nickname for his wife, Gala. Gradiva also appears in the mime-plays of Jean Cocteau and, more recently, in the music of Maxence Cyrin.[12]

Even before Carl Jung mailed him a copy of Jensen's novella in 1906, Freud had written of archaeology as a metaphor for psychoanalysis. Just as the archaeologist uses scientific tools to revivify the past by decoding its secrets, so the psychoanalyst does with human memory and the subconscious. Freud's 1896 essay "The Aetiology of Hysteria" "describe[s] how the archaeological expeditions of psychoanalysis might be able to distinguish ancient fact from fiction".[13] Freud imagines the archaeologist as an "explorer [*forcher*] arriv[ing] in a little-known region where his interest is aroused by an expanse of ruins. . . . If his work is crowned with success, the discoveries are self-explanatory". The ruins reveal a symbolic language, which "yield[s] undreamed-of information about the events of the remote past, to commemorate which the monuments were built. *Saxa loquuntur!*"[14] The stones speak!

As Orrells observes, Freud's *saxa loquuntur* metaphor alludes to Lucan's *Bellum Civile* (*BC*) 6.618, in which the witch Erichtho declares, "*Rhodopaeaque saxa loquentur*" ("the rocks of Rhodope will speak").[15] Erichtho revives a corpse for the purpose of disseminating knowledge. Thus, both the archaeologist and the witch turn to the dead past in the hope that material remains will reveal secrets with a clear, unambiguous voice: "so that the mouth of a cadaver might speak with a clear voice" (*ut . . . cadaveris ora / plena voce sonent*; *BC* 6.621–622). Freud's *saxa loquuntur* finds clear resonance in Norbert, who surrounds himself with "objects from the distant past" because "for his feelings marble and bronze were not dead, but rather the only really vital thing". Norbert immerses himself in Greek and Roman antiquity "with no need of any other intercourse", suggesting that he, too, fancies that the stones speak back to him in some unmediated fashion (*Gradiva* 25).

In addition to the connection with Freud, I think we might rightly situate Norbert's scholarly approach and pretentions within its nineteenth- and early-twentieth-century contexts. August Boeckh, for example, contends that philology and historical enquiry are "productive" activities that, properly exercised, reanimate the past: "The productive capacity is the principal thing in philology. . . . To relearn what has been known, to present it in a pure state, to remove the falsifications of time, to make an apparent into a real whole, these are not superfluous activities; they are necessary to the very life of knowledge."[16] For Boeckh, as for Freud, antiquarian scholarship requires exploration of the subconscious, since "the interpreter must bring to clear awareness what the author has unconsciously created, and in so doing many things will be opened to him, many windows will be unlocked which have been closed to the author himself".[17] The activities of archaeology and textual exegesis, then, share much with psychoanalysis, which brings us back to *Gradiva*.

In light of this preexisting interest in connecting archaeology and psychoanalysis, it comes as little surprise that Freud should show interest in *Gradiva*. *Delusion and Dream* represents Freud's first foray into literary analysis and his first attempt to perform psychoanalysis on fictional dreams. Today Freud's text is materially inseparable from Jensen's: the two come joined in the same volume in which Freud's presence engulfs Jensen's *Gradiva* – Freud's portrait dominates the cover, while *Delusion and Dream* looms behind the novella; thus recent scholarship on *Gradiva* has tended to focus on Freud's reception in *Delusion and Dream*.

Orrells ventures that "no literary critic would dare claim that they had read *Gradiva* without already having read Freud's essay".[18] While the spectre of Freud does indeed loom over Jensen's text – literally, on the book's cover – I here aim to shift attention back from Freud's text onto Jensen's novella, its depiction of Classics as a discipline, and Norbert's archaeological fantasy of the dead reanimated and stone brought to waking, walking life. My own focus moves away from the manifestly fantastic episodes of the novella to explore Norbert's "science" (*Wissenschaft*; *Gradiva* 9) as an exercise in reader response. I look at Jensen's archaeology not as a metaphor for psychoanalysis, but on its own terms, as a depiction of and commentary on scholarly classical inquiry.

If, for Freud and Jensen's protagonist, the fantasy is that stones might speak (*saxa loquuntur*), Norbert's behaviour in *Gradiva*, his discursive strategies and hallucinations, suggest the very opposite – namely, that we classicists inscribe our own aesthetics, desires, and fantasies onto antiquity. Today, this idea is hardly radical. In the wake of Roland Barthes and Stanley Fish, developments in the sociology of science, and the rise of classical reception studies, readers of the classics are increasingly predisposed to recognize and even to celebrate the subjectivity of scholars, researchers, and readers.[19] Jensen wrote his "Pompeian fantasy", however, at a place and time when pretentions of scientific objectivity dominated the discipline of Classics. *Gradiva* collapses the boundaries between science and fantasy. While Norbert seeks unmediated connection with the past, his very science negates this possibility. His Pompeii is at best a fantasy, at worst a delusion reminiscent of trends in Classics and Art History that sought to whitewash the classical past.

Archaeological fantasies

I aim to show that Norbert's science is inherently fantastic and that Jensen's novella celebrates the fantastic in Classics. Only when Norbert abandons his pretense of positivistic *Wissenschaft* can the past come back to life. In the final analysis, I offer that despite the misogyny, racism, and classism of Norbert's science, Jensen's novella ultimately offers itself to a feminist reading.

From the outset, Jensen nominally presents archaeology as a precise science. Almost immediately, the novella's narrator names archaeology Norbert's "science" (*Wissenschaft*; *Gradiva* 9). Norbert's "science" governed by "critical judgment" compels him to conduct "mathematically formulated" experiments to interpret the female figure in the bas-relief (13). Jensen repetitively names archaeology a science on numerous other occasions throughout *Gradiva*.[20] As scientist, Norbert is frustrated by the possibility that the artist's rendering in the bas-relief may not correspond to reality (16). Despite this protestation, Norbert's science is ultimately fetishistic, as Andreas Mayer argues, since "his interest for an object is never purely scientific but also aesthetically and erotically tinged".[21]

Norbert is a product of nineteenth-century European classicism, which voiced the potential to access and reconstruct antiquity with scientific precision. For instance, as Orrells observes of approaches to classical epigraphy, William Wordsworth's 1810 *Essays Upon Epitaphs* suggests that inscriptions are permanent with a meaning "legible for a universal posterity", while Freud's "*saxa loquuntur!*" insists that epigraphs offer "readers a direct and unmediated view into the originating contexts behind those words".[22] August Boeckh held that the philologist might objectively establish "what is meant in a work".[23]

Perhaps ironically, this *Wissenschaft* contains within it elements of the fantastic. For example, Boeckh argues for a spiritual component to scholarship: "A deeper penetration into the mind and spirit of the author must be effected. No man will be a good interpreter who does not see it as his chief business to immerse himself in the authors and from them to draw the drafts of their very being."[24] Recalling Boeckh's philological methods and theory, Norbert's science is defined by a combination of meticulous academic rigor and the possibility of almost metaphysical communion with antiquity. This fusion of science with fantasy is established very early in the novella, as "his desire for knowledge transported him into a scientific passion in which he surrendered himself" (14). When Norbert wakes from dreaming that he bears witness to Gradiva's death in Vesuvius's destruction of Pompeii, "he did not succeed, even by the use of critical thought, in breaking from the idea" that his dream represented reality (19–20).

When Lucan's Erichtho raises the dead and claims the stones will speak (*saxa loquentur*), the corpse is charged not with revealing the historical past but with prophecy of present and future events. Likewise, even before Norbert slips entirely into delusion and dream, his "science" reveals as much or more about himself than it does about the classical past and his knowledge of it. As Victoria C. Gardner Coates observes, "Norbert does not fixate on the classical original [of the bas-relief] but rather on his modern copy, which is a very different object".[25] This not only provides an important early clue to the living Gradiva/Zoë's modernity but also is indicative of modernity's influence on Norbert's *Wissenschaft*.

So let's meet Norbert. Norbert is a post-PhD German scholar, who, even before he "brilliantly passed examination in philology", had felt compelled since childhood to emulate his father as a "university professor and antiquarian" (*Gradiva* 23–24). Norbert is independently wealthy (23) and he continuously expresses disdain for the less educated and those of lower socio-economic class. For instance, Norbert thinks of the people around him in sub-human, animalistic terms (generally as birds or, worse, flies). When Norbert is "compelled" to observe them on his train to Italy, he finds that "although ... they were all German country people, his racial identity with them awoke in him no feeling of pride" (29). To escape these other travellers, Norbert moves into a third-class coach hoping "to find there an interesting and scientifically useful company of Italian folk types", but instead finding "nothing but the usual dirt, Monopol cigars which smelled horribly, little warped fellows beating about with arms and legs, and members of the female sex, in contrast to whom his coupled countrywomen seemed to his memory almost like Olympian goddesses" (35). Norbert's own classist and racist aesthetics ultimately inform his interpretation of the Gradiva figure as well as his fantasies about her. The repressed Norbert believes he has no standard according to which he might compare modern beauty with "the sublime beauty of antiquity" (30). Nevertheless, Norbert constantly inscribes his modern aesthetics onto antiquity.

Norbert, who previously "had never given his feminine contemporaries the least consideration" (14), tries to interpret Gradiva's gait through empirical observation of modern women. Norbert thus seeks "enlightenment" on the classical past through "observation from" his own, contemporary "life" (ibid.). One of his very first observations about the Gradiva sculpture is that "obviously she did not belong to a lower class but was the daughter of a nobleman" (10). This hopeful deduction may well originate from

Norbert's prejudices, but it also stems at least in part from his contemporary aesthetics. The Gradiva figure wears a long skirt, which falls down to the ankles. The narrator, who focalizes through Norbert, reflects that in his Germany, "almost no one but housemaids wore short skirts" (14–15). While Norbert may not consciously connect Gradiva's dress with this observation, the narrator's pairing nevertheless suggests that Norbert's assessment of Gradiva's class is a product of his own discursive community.[26]

Even before he dreams Gradiva's death in the Vesuvius eruption of 79, Norbert whimsically decides she lived in Pompeii (11): "On his Italian journey, he had spent several weeks in Pompeii studying the ruins; and in Germany, the idea had suddenly come to him one day that the girl depicted by the relief was walking there, somewhere, on the peculiar stepping stones which have been excavated." This, of course, is emblematic of Pompeii's grip on the modern imagination. However, Norbert simultaneously deduces Gradiva is of Greek, not Italian ancestry (12–13):

> The cut of her features seemed to him, more and more, not Roman or Latin, but Greek, so that her Hellenic ancestry became for him a certainty. The ancient settlement of all southern Italy by Greeks offered sufficient ground for that, and more ideas pleasantly associated with the settlers developed. Then the young "domina" had perhaps spoken Greek in her parental home, and had grown up fostered by Greek culture. Upon closer consideration he found this also confirmed by the expression of the face, for quite decidedly wisdom and a delicate spirituality lay hidden beneath her modesty.

Here, Norbert seems again conditioned by his *fin-du-siècle* German identity; an inheritor of the art historian Johann Winckelmann's cultural patrimony, Norbert privileges Greek over Roman culture as an ideal. During the nineteenth century, German archaeology, which was increasingly viewed as a science, came to be dominated by philhellenism. As Eric Downing argues, this German interest in Greece was "at least in part in keeping with the self-conscious rise in German nationalism, which led to a self-distancing from the Roman, Italian, and French world and a more exclusive investment in ancient Greece alone as the original model for German *Bildung* and identity".[27]

Like Winckelmann, Norbert conflates "ethical nobility with formal simplicity", and his assessment of Gradiva's "delicate spirituality" and modest appearance recalls Winckelmann's assessment of the Greek ideal as "a noble simplicity and a calm grandeur" (*eine edle Einfalt und eine stille Grösse*).[28] Norbert's discursive position thus leads to a rather perfunctory judgement that the figure on the bas-relief represents an actual Pompeian woman of high social status and Greek descent. Likewise, Norbert's "understanding" of the sculpture deduces that Gradiva's physical features show she died with stoic repose (*Gradiva* 20).

His science and his racial biases also lead Norbert to project absolute whiteness onto both the sculpture and its referent, the woman of his fantasies.[29] As he travels south to Pompeii, Norbert eavesdrops and focuses intensely on one particular conversation between lovers, which shows his own erotic obsession with whiteness (38):

"I fear the sun there would be too hot for your delicate complexion and I could never forgive myself that."

"What if you should suddenly have a negress (*eine Negerin*) for a wife?"

"No, my imagination fortunately does not reach that far, but a freckle on your little nose would make me unhappy."

Norbert is obsessed with whiteness as an ideal. When Norbert first dreams of Gradiva on Pompeii's day of destruction, he visualizes that "her face became paler as if it were changing to white marble" (*wie wenn es sich zu weißen Marmor umwandle*; 18). Whiteness as an ideal is put forward even more strongly when Norbert first fantasizes Gradiva coming to life in Pompeii. Norbert notes the figure coming to life in vivid color that diverges from the "uniform colorlessness" of stone and "cold marble white". Nevertheless, the lifelike colour of Gradiva's clothing and hair remains "in bold contrast to her alabaster countenance" (57).

Norbert's fetishization of whiteness informs not only his erotic fantasies but also his archaeological science: a product of his time, Norbert seems to acknowledge ancient polychromy only to ignore it. Norbert imagines "lively colors, gaily painted wall surfaces, pillars with red and yellow capitals" (11) in Pompeii, yet he simultaneously visualizes classical sculpture *in situ* as "gleaming, white" (12). The archaeologist projects whiteness as an ideal back onto antiquity. This echoes the then-prevailing belief that the gaudy painting of Greek and Roman statuary must have been later, apocryphal additions, which led to such actions as the stripping of authentic paint from the Elgin Marbles.[30] Norbert's assessment also prefigures contemporary pushback against those who bring ancient polychromy to the public eye by some who would (ab)use Greece and Rome to perpetuate anachronistic and racially charged conceptions of 'Europe'.[31]

A place for fantasy?

Norbert thus fills in holes in the archaeological record, albeit subconsciously, with his own preferences and desires. But does this necessarily make him a bad archaeologist or a bad antiquarian? Richard Armstrong has earlier reflected on archaeology's lacunae as they relate to our fascination with the ruins of antiquity: "The ancient archive fascinates and entices not just because of its moments of presence, like the charming insistence of Gradiva's gait caught forever in stone, but because of its absences, its fragmentation and temporal *dis*-location, its quality of being otherwise and other-where."[32] Armstrong's observations point not only towards displacement but also towards estrangement, which, at least in certain formulations, lies at the very heart of fantasy and the fantastic.[33] *Gradiva* invites us to meditate on archaeology and philology themselves as fantasy (at least in part) and to view our most scientific attempts to reconstruct antiquity from ruins as inherently imaginative and creative. This activity is rendered fantastic not by imagination and creativity alone but, ultimately, by metaphysical impossibility. This is not to negate the validity of archaeology's scientific methods and claims to historical knowledge but rather to complicate the positivism of *Wissenschaft* and to highlight the active role of the archaeologist as 'reader' of material culture. Can exploration of the classical past help but be informed by our own desires and biases? Should it?

So far I have been rather harsh on Norbert Hanold, whom the past century has made an easy target. In the wake of the Second World War and the Civil Rights Movement, poor Norbert's world view has not aged particularly well, nor has his scholarship. His scholarly and social beliefs are, at best, dated relics of a bygone and deeply flawed past. Anecdotally, the vast majority of my students whom I have subjected to reading *Gradiva* and *Arria Marcella* find both Jensen's Norbert and Gautier's Octavien unsympathetic, even unreadable, protagonists. To a contemporary audience reading with the benefits afforded by a century's worth of hindsight, *Gradiva* serves as a reminder that scientific inquiry tends to reify social, cultural, and political orders and hierarchies of the present. In the specific case of Norbert Hanold, the activity of scientific archaeology is "designed to fabricate and secure his privileged, socially important, but always tenuously grounded German identity".[34] Nevertheless, Jensen's novella suggests that embracing a role for the fantastic has much to offer classical studies. As Downing argues, "Jensen's text seems to suggest a different relation between science and *Phantasie*, one that insists on their inseparability."[35]

The gap between Norbert's expectations for *Wissenschaft* and its execution points towards feminist movements in classical studies, which highlight the impossibility of unmediated encounters with the past and tend to view claims to scientific humanistic inquiry with some amount of scepticism. This mirrors broader epistemological trends that privilege the role of social construction in scientific knowledge.[36] Alison Wylie summarizes the tension between social relativists and scientific positivists within contemporary archaeology:

(with hindsight) ... some of the best, most empirically sophisticated archaeological practice has reproduced nationalist, racist, classist, and, according to the most recent analyses, sexist and androcentric understandings of the cultural past. Some archaeologists conclude on this basis that however influential the rhetoric of objectivity may be among practitioners, the practice and products of archaeology must inevitably reflect the situated interests of its makers. A great many others regard such claims with suspicion, if not outright hostility. They maintain the conviction – a central and defining tenet of North American archaeology since its founding as a profession early in this century – that archaeology is, first and foremost, a science and that, therefore, the social and political contexts of inquiry are properly external to the process of inquiry and to its product.[37]

In her introduction to *Feminism and Classics*, Barbara McManus argues that "one strong feature of the disciplinary self-image of classics is provided by positivism". Like Norbert:

Many classicists see themselves as participating in an empirical, unmediated encounter with the textual and material remains of ancient Greece and Rome. Using precise intellectual tools to evaluate and assess this evidence, philologists attempt to establish definitive texts; historians, to establish the "facts" of the past as it actually was; archaeologists to establish definitive catalogues and analyses of the material record as it exists today.[38]

As one of six proposed tenets for feminist classical inquiry, McManus calls for a turn away from postitivism to include, amongst other things, "conjecture".[39]

Shelby Brown is even more forceful in articulating a place for fantasy in Classics.[40] Brown distances feminist archaeology from New Archaeology (or Processual Archaeology), and she argues that positivist archaeology is itself biased and subjective. Brown's critique of Lewis Binford, a leading proponent of New Archaeology, implicitly recalls the postivist pretentions of German philological methods and theory of the nineteenth century:

> From the feminist perspective, Binford's scientific approach can also be viewed as biased and subjective for many reasons, including its establishment of the arcaheologist as the empowered possessor of a special insight, and its assumption that objective facts can be obtained from approaches still invented today largely by the same people who were inventing them in the nineteeth century, namely upper-middle class, European and Anglo-Saxon males, often legitimizing the ideals of the modern technocratic West, and operating as colonialist interpreters of their subjects of study.

For Brown, "the admitted subjectivity of the researcher is perhaps the most significant and defining issue" in feminist archaeology. Alternative narratives import new ways of seeing the past into the discipline, enlivening antiquity while still permitting "the validation of facts and the consideration of alternatives".[41] This is, of course, not to say that scientific objectivity or poitivism need be an all-or-nothing affair, but a feminist archaeology will give attention to and allow some space for the subjectivity of the researcher and alternative modes of reconstructing the past.[42] Fantastic, ficitional narratives, "while not meant to stand alone", can "accompany more conventional sources" to enrich our reproduction of the classical archive.[43] It is perhaps no surprise, then, that the figure of Gradiva has become a feminist trope.[44]

On the surface, *Gradiva* pits the science of Classics in oppositional tension with fantasy. For instance, the narrator presents Norbert's "lively imagination" as "a corrective of a thoroughly unscientific sort", opposed to *Wissenschaft* (26). As Norbert slips deeper into delusion, Jensen depicts this transition explicitly in binary terms of departure from science. When Norbert arrives at Pompeii, he loses the aesthetic capacity for empirical observation, realizing that he has become "aimless, senseless, blind, and deaf. . . . For his traveling companion, science, had, most decidedly, much of an old Trappist about her, did not open her mouth when she was spoken to, and it seemed to him that he was almost forgetting in what language he has communed with her" (44). Science becomes an increasingly silent partner, and, in order for the stones to speak (*saxa loquuntur*), Norbert must first forget the scientific language: "What it [science] taught was a lifeless, archaeological view and what came from its mouth was a dead, philological language" (55). Norbert's dream of Pompeii's destruction is more descriptive and vivid than his waking scientific observations, and "that sixth sense was awakened in him" (53). As he slips deeper into delusion, Norbert, who "possessed a certain skill in deciphering" difficult graffiti and epigraphy, temporarily forgets how to read Latin (54–55):

> Not only had all his science left him, but it left him without the least desire to regain it; he remembered it as from a great distance, and he felt that it had been an old, dried up, boresome aunt, dullest and most superfluous creature in the world. What she uttered with puckered lips and sapient mien, and presented as wisdom, was all vain, empty pompousness, and merely gnawed at the dry rind of the fruit of knowledge without revealing anything of its content, the germ of life, or bringing anything to the point of inner, intelligent, enjoyment.

What science offers as a path to knowledge, fantasy complements as an avenue towards utility and enjoyment. It is at this moment that "the dead awoke, and Pompeii began to live again" (56). Whereas *Wissenschaft* – scientific archaeology – had previously been Norbert's language to commune with the dead, the reanimation of the classical past is now marked by loss of this "dead" language.

Before losing his grip on reality, Norbert "woeful[ly]" reflects that the Gradiva bas-relief is, "in a way, a tombstone" (20). Norbert as scientist is forced to confront the sublime inaccessibly of the classical past. In a sense, he experiences what Sean Gurd might call "text-critical melancholy". Norbert's pursuit of Gradiva, the referent of a modern copy of an ancient sculpture, is characterized by "melancholic reflection on history as separation and loss".[45] But despite Norbert's initial frustration and sorrow, Jensen's novella is ultimately celebratory – it is only when the archaeologist abandons his scientific pretentions that the past begins to come alive. If the fantastic is, in part, defined by estrangement and metaphysical impossibility, Gradiva's unknowability suggests fantasy as a path for exploring the voids of history and, with them, the psyche of the researcher. Fantasy achieves what science alone could not; it revivifies the classical past such that *saxa loquuntur!* The stones speak, not with their own voices but with ours.

Notes

1. Liveley (2011: 105).
2. Orrells (2011a: 185). Gardner Coates (2012: 70): "Imagining who these ancient Pompeians might have been and weaving elaborate fantasies around them became increasingly popular. While some of these creations were male ... most were female – imaginary women of the past conjured to satisfy contemporary desires."
3. Throughout, I use Downey's translation, republished in Jensen and Freud (2003), for quotations from *Gradiva* and Sigmund Freud's *Delusion and Dream*. Where particularly useful or necessary, I reference Jensen's German text. In Latin, *Gradiva* is a feminine adjective derived from the verb '*gradior*' ('to walk' or 'to advance').

4. The relief is pictured and discussed in Hauser (1903: 79–107).

5. Jensen and Freud (2003: 286).

6. This plotline is very much evocative of Théophile Gautier's "Arria Marcella: Souvenir de Pompéi" (1852), a short story also about an upper-class male tourist to Pompeii, who, in a dreamlike encounter with the past, experiences a revivified Pompeii and falls in love in Vesuvius's shadow. *Gradiva* thereby participates not only in the early time-travel genre but also in the tradition of early Pompeii fantasies. See Liveley (2011: 107). The name of Augustus, a minor character whom Norbert observes in *Gradiva*, may well signal an intertext with Gautier's story via his protagonist, named Octavien.

7. Jackson (2003: 48–49).

8. On delusion and the definitions of 'low fantasy', see Clute and Grant (1997: 264, 597; authors David Langford and Brian Stableford, respectively). Freud himself comments on *Gradiva* in similar terms, which conjure a binary between science and fantasy: "Jensen . . . has, of course found no occasion, as yet, to explain to us whether he wishes to leave us in our world, decried as dull and ruled by the laws of science, or to conduct us into another fantastic one." See Jensen and Freud (2003: 160) and Downing (2006: 118–119).

9. See, e.g., Hite 2011; Lothane 2010; Knight (2004: 94n15); Bergstein (2003: 299); Rand and Torok (1997: 58).

10. On non-Ovidian versions of Pygmalion, see Salzman-Mitchell (2008: 291–293), citing the lost version of Philostephanus, paraphrased by the Christian authors Clement of Alexandria (*Protrepticus* 4.57.3) and Arnobius (*Adversus Nationes* 6.22).

11. Chadwick (1970: 415).

12. Ibid. Cyrin's album, *The Fantasist* (2012), features a piano solo entitled "Gradiva". On *Gradiva*'s legacy, see Gardner Coates 2012.

13. Orrells (2011a: 186).

14. Freud (1953–1974: iii.193). This passage is quoted and discussed in Orrells (2011a: 187–192) and Orrells (2014: 330–332).

15. Orrells (2011a: 193).

16. Boeckh (1968 [1877]: 13).

17. Ibid., 56.

18. Orrells (2010: 166).

19. In classical scholarship, see especially Hallett and Van Nortwick 1997.

20. On archaeology as science, see especially Jensen and Freud (2003: 25–26).

21. Mayer (2012: 562).

22. See Orrells (2014: 330–331); Wordsworth (1974: ii.59–60).

23. Boeckh (1968: 85).

24. Ibid., 88–89.

25. Gardner Coates (2012: 71).

26. Interestingly, as Mary Bergstein (2003: 289–290) observes, Freud's 1876 letters from Trieste "presaged that [experience] of Norbert Hanold . . . in an eerie, almost uncanny, manner", since "the unmarried Freud, occupied as he was by looking at life through a microscope, was haunted on his day off by human fertility in the romantic guise of an ethnic other".

27. Downing (2006: 95). Downing (87–103) offers a good overview of the intersections between 'scientific' archaeology and the production of cultural and political identity in nineteenth- and early-twentieth-century Germany; cf. Hartman (2008: 508).

28. Potts (2000: 1). Winckelmann coined his famous phrase in his 1755 essay, *Gedanken über die Nachahmung der griechischen Werke in der Malerei und Bildhauerkunst* (translated and republished as Winckelmann 1985). The bibliography on Winckelmann's privileging of Greek aesthetics and culture as the German national ideal is massive; see, e.g., Nisbet (1985: 6–8), Porter (2006: 8–13), Valdez 2014, Fox (2015: 75).

29. For an extended discussion of whiteness in *Gradiva*, see Downing (2006: 135–46).

30. Lamenting the trouble her beauty has caused, Euripides' Helen wishes that it could be rubbed away like paint from a statue: "My life and deeds are a wonder, partly because of Hera and partly because of my beauty. If only I could be rubbed off like a statue and again assume a baser appearance instead of beauty" (τέρας γὰρ ὁ βίος καὶ τὰ πράγματ᾽ ἐστί μου, / τὰ μὲν δι᾽ Ἥραν, τὰ δὲ τὸ κάλλος αἴτιον. / εἴθ᾽ ἐξαλειφθεῖσ᾽ ὡς ἄγαλμ᾽ αὖθις πάλιν / αἴσχιον εἶδος ἔλαβον ἀντὶ τοῦ καλοῦ; *Helen* 260–264). Thus, to strip a statue of its paint and therefore of its colour was to disfigure it.

31. See for example *Artforum* 2017, which details death threats received by Sarah Bond after publishing an article on ancient polychromy (Bond 2017).

32. Armstrong (2005: 19), quoted and discussed in Liveley (2011: 111).

33. Sandner (2004: 9).

34. Downing (2006: 136).

35. Ibid., 119.

36. See, e.g., Pinch and Bijker 2012 with bibliography.

37. Wylie (1997: 80). Thomas (2000: 1): "The New Archaeology can be identified as a unitary project, because its practitioners believed that there was a single truth about the past that could be accessed as long as one had the right approach, and did the right kind of science."

38. McManus (1997: 4).

39. Ibid., 19.

40. Brown draws upon Tringham (1991), especially "Fantasy > Fact".

41. Preceding quotations from Brown (1993: 250–254), whose critique is focused on Binford 1989. Cf. Tringham (1991: 124).

42. Brown (1993: 254); Wylie (1997: 98–99). On the potential for feminist archaeology to challenge positivist epistemologies, see also Conkey and Gero 1991, Wylie 1991, and the essays in Wright 1996.

43. Brown (1993: 254).

44. Blum (2008: 43–90).

45. Gurd (2004: 97).

CHAPTER 3
TIME TRAVEL AND SELF-REFLEXIVITY IN RECEPTIONS OF HOMER'S *ILIAD*
Claire Kenward

"This is not Troy. This is not even the world. This is the journey through the beyond." These lines are spoken by Katarina, handmaid to the Trojan prophetess Cassandra, as she flees the destruction of Troy, only to find herself inside the incongruous interior of a 1960s British police-box.[1] The iconic time machine hurtles the Trojan from twelfth-century BCE Earth to arrive, in *Doctor Who*'s next episode, at the farthest edge of the Milky Way in 4000 CE. Katarina's notion of a "journey through the beyond" encapsulates the concerns of this chapter. Collapsing distinctions between time and space, Katarina renders Troy a "not Troy" – where 'Troy' can stand for the classical past or the classic text. This "not Troy" is paradoxically created in the fictional world shared by modern receptions, which both resurrect and annihilate, as they overwrite, an ancient original. There is also a meta-dramatic irony to Katarina's pronouncement, as her grief for a lost past is expressed inside a time machine.

Such irony proves key in the science-fiction (SF) receptions explored in this chapter. Indeed, one of the hallmarks of SF is that its speculations function as displaced commentaries on their own historical moment.[2] That SF narratives address at least two disparate time frames makes them analogous to acts of classical reception; that they do so ironically makes the genre suited to such meta-reception. Thus Sarah Annes Brown surmises that "SF's preoccupation with various kinds of time disruption, whether literal time-travel or an alertness to the cyclical, gives a special edge to its engagement with the classics".[3] This chapter explores that "special edge" by literalizing Brown's metaphor and analysing the spatial and temporal dimensions of that edge or "interface".[4]

To that end, I examine the surface on which the collision between ancient – specifically, the Trojan war in Homer's *Iliad* (*Il.*) and *Odyssey* (*Od.*) as well as Virgil's *Aeneid* (*Aen.*) – and modern occurs in two media that provide dominant vehicles for SF: television and comics.[5] Focusing on *Doctor Who*'s "Myth Makers" story (BBC 1965) and the *Thor Annual #8: Thunder Over Troy* (Marvel 1979), I investigate how iconic SF tropes, particularly space/time travel, combine with each medium to provide alternative perspectives from which to explore Homer's epic. I argue that these two examples offer complex and vibrant meta-receptions that challenge our relationship with Homer's text and the history of its reception. Both demonstrate that the playful and irreverent should not be dismissed as frivolous or irrelevant.[6]

"Watch the scanners": *Doctor Who* and the televised Trojan War

> The time and space voyagers in the good ship *Tardis* come down to Mother Earth for their latest adventure – but to a world as remote from our own as any distant planet. [. . .] Once, some thousands of years ago, it witnessed the most famous clash of arms ever sung by a poet: the Trojan War.
>
> *Radio Times* p. 6 (14 October 1965)

Doctor Who's "Myth Makers" story begins as the Doctor and two human companions, Vicki and Steven, arrive during Achilles' and Hector's final battle (*Iliad* book 22) and ends, four episodes later, as they flee Troy's destruction after helping Odysseus build the Trojan Horse (*Odyssey* book 8; *Aeneid* book 2). The episodes, directed by Michael Leeston-Smith and written by Donald Cotton, who had previously adapted Greek myth for radio, were broadcast weekly from 16 October to 6 November 1965, in the series' third season.[7] All four are lost, although the audio survives with eight photographic stills and around sixty amateur clips recorded from television.[8]

The *Radio Times*' reference to the poet singing "of arms" echoes the *Iliad*'s opening line and its reformulation in both the *Odyssey* and the *Aeneid*: "sing the rage of Peleus' son Achilles" (*Il.* 1.1); "Sing to me of the man" (*Od.* 1.1); "I sing of arms and of the man" (*Aen.* 1.1).[9] Thus, while promising historical veracity enabled by the time machine, *Radio Times* primes readers to approach "Myth Makers" with Troy's epic origins in mind. A tension is posited between the depiction of 'real' historical events played out in the ostensible present and the audience's awareness of literary versions paradoxically lying in the war's future whilst acting as the drama's ancient antecedent. This tension is exploited throughout Cotton's script, which sees characters ironically reference Homer, Virgil, Shakespeare, and Poe, and by Leeston-Smith's direction, which encourages actors to display a knowing theatricality.

Although evoked by *Radio Times*, the *Iliad*'s extradiegetic narrator, Homer, is absent from *Doctor Who*. The drama limits itself to the intradiegetic level, in line with television 'realism', experienced and vocalized solely by characters within the fiction. Cotton's screenplay suggests that the fourth wall is not broken and the camera acts as an impartial witness – predominantly static, not aligned with any one character's point of view.[10] In this way, television realism helps to underscore an orthodox SF engagement with the legendary past: the time-travel trope enables the Doctor, his companions, and the audience to experience Troy 'as it really was'. However, all film is shaped by the extradiegetic 'voice' of the director/editor determining shots, angles, pacing, juxtapositions, and more. "Myth Makers" not only points to the Trojan war's literary incarnations but also subverts the illusory objectivity of the television screen. The TARDIS is a neat analogy for television, that other technological box ('the Box') that could transport the 1960s spectator to infinite possible worlds: past, present, or future, factual and fictional.[11]

"Myth Makers" also emphasizes the role of the screen in mediating the Trojan past by making the TARDIS's scanner a focal point in establishing the action. Episode One opens with an establishing exterior shot: "*a dry plain near the coast of what would now be north-western Turkey. The walls of a great city stand in the distance. Two warriors are engaged in a sword battle*" (1.1). The ensuing dialogue names "Trojan", "Achilles" and "Patroclus [who] died like a dog, whimpering after his master" (1.1), allowing the audience to place the scene and, if they know their Homer, to date the action to the final year of the war. From this exterior shot we cut to the TARDIS interior, where the Doctor, Steven, and Vicki are watching the control room's scanner – watching, as the BBC's twentieth-century human audience have just done, the same fight on a similar monitor. The television screen is thus an interface between ancient and modern.

Unlike the audience, the Doctor and his companions cannot hear the dialogue, and the Doctor exits to ask where/when they have materialized. The subsequent six scenes move swiftly back and forth between exterior and interior, between the ancient past of the Trojan plain and the fantastical future of the control room. The Doctor's interactions with Homeric characters – Hector, Achilles, Odysseus and his soldiers – are intercut with an equal number of shorter scenes (1.4, 1.6, 1.8) in which Vicki and Steven watch the footage on their scanner and attempt to interpret what they see (1.8):

> STEVEN: Well, the Doctor said they were Greeks. We're probably in Greece.
> VICKI: Oh, but that would be wonderful, wouldn't it? We might meet the heroes.
> STEVEN: Those men who carried off the Doctor wouldn't be heroes.

For Steven and Vicki, both from Earth's distant future, expectations of ancient Greece are based on memory of "the Heroes" that they ascribe to "Homer" (2.7, 3.3) and "a story I heard a long time ago" (2.9). Because the silent footage fails to match their expectations, Vicki and Steven misread events. Mirroring the BBC's audience, the focus on Vicki and Steven as spectators exposes the process by which everything is read against an individual's "horizon of expectations", built on knowledge of prior texts and generic conventions to help audiences interpret action and fill gaps.[12] Regardless of the technological advances that brought them to Troy, the TARDIS/television still requires an interpretative, imaginative leap; the interface between ancient and modern is tied to a subjective memory of the Homeric text and its receptions. The loss of the original episodes adds another level to this metatheatrical process, as a modern viewer can only listen to Vicki and Steven watching their silent scanner and imagine the scene based on their knowledge of extant contemporary episodes of *Doctor Who* and/or the fragmentary stills and clips from this story.

For each scene that Vicki and Steven spectate, the audience joins the Doctor for 'unmediated' access to the ancient past. This dramatic irony, in which the audience watches Vicki and Steven misled by memories of Homer, affirms the 'reality' of Cotton's war. In refusing to evoke classical associations, the drama asserts fidelity to a historical truth antedating poetic embellishment. Ironically, however, Cotton draws his Trojan war from Homer's *Iliad* and *Odyssey*, as well as their receptions in Virgil's *Aeneid* and Shakespeare's (and Chaucer's) *Troilus and Cressida*.[13] The impossibility of isolating Cotton's multiple sources becomes a metatheatrical feature of the episodes. This multiplicity is signified in the title, with "Myth Makers" encompassing the Doctor and his companions, the Greeks and Trojans they meet, and the multiple sources that embed the Trojan War myth in the collective cultural imaginary.

The audience's familiarity with the myth engenders a sense of Fate: dramatic tension is generated from *how* – not if – the episodes will fulfil plot points of the well-known story. Unusually for *Doctor Who*, the audience's assumed knowledge allows them to share in the main characters' superior insight. The most significant example of this centres on the Trojan Horse. The audience's anticipation of the Horse is toyed with from the opening scene in which Achilles calls Hector a "Barbarian horse-worshipper" and a "stable keeper" (1.1), to the characterization of the Trojans as horse-mad, worshipping the "Great Horse of Asia" (2.3, 3.6, 3.15, 3.16). Episode Two opens with the TARDIS dragged into Troy in a foreshadowing re-enactment of the horse being brought into the city (4.1–3). Paris presents the TARDIS as an "offering to the gods of Troy" (2.3), but Cassandra recounts her dream: "out on the plain the Greeks left a gift and […] we brought it into Troy. Then at night, from out of its belly, soldiers came and fell upon us as we slept" (ibid.). Dramatic irony renders the moment a bathetic parody of the classical scene: the audience knows that the TARDIS *is* capable of concealing an army, but the oblivious Paris mocks Cassandra, asking, "just how many soldiers do you think you can get inside that?" (ibid.), just as Vicki emerges with a "disarming" smile (ibid.). While the audience is privy to metatheatrical nods that Trojans will "do anything for a horse" (2.9), the Doctor, imprisoned in the Greek camp, disavows the horse's feasibility (2.7):

STEVEN: Why not the Wooden Horse?
DOCTOR: Oh! My dear boy, I couldn't possibly suggest that. The whole story is obviously absurd. Probably invented by Homer as some good dramatic device.

Although Cotton plays with the parallels between the horse and the deceptive TARDIS (2.3), for the Doctor the horse is Homer's invention. This creates a pleasing paradox for the viewer: the Doctor only suggests the horse to Odysseus (at 3.4) because he knows of it from Homer's *Odyssey*, which will only be written because the Doctor suggests the horse.

A similar temporal paradox surrounds Vicki, a twenty-fifth-century Earth teenager, who, renamed Cressida by Priam, falls in love with Troilus and remains behind when the TARDIS dematerializes. Cressida is a medieval addition to the classical tradition; the revelation here that she is a displaced future-human inserted into the 'original' historic war offers the knowing viewer another intertextual joke.[14] The medieval romances to which Cressida belongs – drawn from spurious eye-witness accounts of first-century Dictys and (no later than) sixth-century Dares – created an alternative tradition of reception that dominated the Northern-European conception of the Trojan war long after the Renaissance 'rediscovery' of the Greco-Roman classics.[15] Shakespeare's dramatization of this so-called 'anti-Homeric' tradition, *Troilus and Cressida* (c. 1602), is referenced when Cotton's Troilus, jealous of Vicki/Cressida's friendship with Diomede (Steven in disguise), recites the Shakespearean line: "Has Cressida played me false?"

(4.12).[16] Although "Myth Makers" is imbued with the cynical or bathetic dramatization of Homeric material offered by Shakespeare, Cotton's spurious camera-eye-witness account insists on a happy ending for Cressida/Vicki, who escapes with Troilus to help Aeneas found Rome (4.19).

Once the episode disavows the medieval tradition of punishing Cressida as a lesson for false women, *Doctor Who's* false Cressida/Vicki segues back into the classical tradition. Vicki, remembering the *Aeneid*, reassures Troilus: "We can start again. With your cousin's help . . . we can build another Troy" (4.19). That Vicki's future will be to live Virgil's *Aeneid* adds retrospective significance to the fact that the Doctor first meets Vicki stranded on the planet Dido, after her transport ship crash-landed en route from Earth to 'Astra', where she was destined to help establish an outpost for the human empire ("The Rescue" 1965).[17] The Doctor then takes Vicki from Dido to ancient Rome, where she witnesses Nero burning the city: "Isn't it strange . . . to think that people will read about that in books for thousands and thousands of years" ("The Romans: Inferno" 1965).[18] Again, Vicki equates classical events with the continuing reception of literary sources. Vicki may be the medieval Cressida, but she defies her medieval origins to guide Aeneas and will, presumably, be stranded (again) at Dido's Carthage while en route to found the new Empire at Rome – a city she has already witnessed burn. All this renders her an anomaly in time: a temporal glitch caught in replays of the *Aeneid* anachronistically shot through with alternative texts and traditions. Oscillating backwards and forwards through time frames, Vicki lives a history of reception: replaying, revising, and overwritten by texts she read in her past that help guide her understanding of the present.

Helping to establish the conventions of what would become an orthodox SF 'interaction' with the classical past, "Myth Makers" sets out to rationalize classical elements considered alien or irrational within our cultural understanding of the world.[19] The gods are exposed as "propaganda" (1.9), and supernatural elements are misinterpretations ascribed by ancient characters to phenomena beyond their scientific knowledge: for naïve Achilles, the Doctor's sudden appearance, "*by a curious quirk of timing*" (1.3), with a thunderclap makes him a manifestation of Zeus, and his "supernatural knowledge" (1.10) lends credence to Achilles' conclusion. At the story's denouement, Trojan Katarina enters the TARDIS and declares that she has died and awoken in "limbo", making the Doctor a "great god" (4.20). The Doctor's power over time *does* render him omnipotent; a box beyond the laws of physics, which traverses time and space, *is* a form of limbo; and Katarina's death is merely postponed (she will be the first companion to die a few episodes later).

Cotton's screenplay employs bathos to undercut suggestions of Homeric heroism or epic grandeur. Achilles' Homeric epithet, "swift runner", for example, becomes sarcastic insult (hurled by Hector and Odysseus) to mock his tendency to run away: "Out of breath so soon, my light-foot princeling?" (1.1). The reason for the war is neither honour nor Helen (who is never seen) but Agamemnon's ambition "to take over Asia Minor [and] trade routes through the Bosphorus" (1.9).[20] Agamemnon's greed is complemented by corporeal gluttony: the viewer meets him "*eating like a pig*" (ibid.). His brother, Menelaus, is a cowardly drunk: "*he drinks from a pitcher of wine* [and] *replies in a slurred voice*" (ibid.). Displaced from the *Odyssey*, Cyclops is a mute man with an eye patch who, ironically, acts as Odysseus's chief spy. On the Trojan side, Priam is a sentimental old fool, Cassandra is cruel and vindictive, revelling in doom-laden prophecies, while a lecherous Paris has "gone somewhat to seed".

As these *précis* indicate, *Doctor Who*'s Homeric characters are stripped of complexity, drawn in broad strokes loosely evocative of sins: Agamemnon personifies greed; Menelaus, sloth; Odysseus, wrath and pride; Paris, lust; and Achilles, envy. This subtext is, for the dominant Christian culture of 1960s Britain, a shorthand for universal human failings: mythic heroes are merely fallible humans. To be drawn in such broad strokes, however, pushes the characters into caricature, reinforced by the Doctor's opening reference to the "Grecian *costumes*" (1.2; emphasis added). Realism is undercut as the Greeks and Trojans veer into self-conscious vaudeville. Francis De Wolff's Agamemnon, for example, wears the same costume that De Wolff had worn as Agrippa in *Carry On Cleo* (an outlandish 1964 parody of the 1963 film *Cleopatra*). That the actor carries his 'classical' costume from a (parodic) cinematic Rome to small-screen Greece/Troy adds a metatheatrical twist. Sharing the same performance heritage as the *Carry On* films, the well-known revue-artist Max Adrian plays Priam, while Broadway musical star Barrie Ingham plays a compulsively punning Paris.

Television realism and the rationalization of myth are thus counterbalanced by a performance style indebted to the traditions of the self-consciously frivolous English music-hall.[21] This adds a veneer of theatricality to the ancient characters, especially in comparison with the series' permanent cast (Vicki, Steven, the Doctor), seeming to endorse a view of populist SF and/or television receptions as mere banalities. Yet this underestimates the effect of metatheatricality on the spectator, which reduces the distance felt between viewer and character. A character who acknowledges their own fictionality, and by extension the existence of the audience, ironically intensifies the viewer's empathy. Bathetic subversion of epic only increases the audience's emotional attachment, heightening the pathos of the story's conclusion.[22] This sympathetic response derives from and again confirms this televised war's 'reality' against its 'later' literary embellishments.

"Meanwhile, on another dimensional plane at the self-same time": Marvel's *Thor Annual* #8: *Thunder Over Troy*

From *Doctor Who*'s 1965 black-and-white, all-too-human affair, we jump to the four-colour, god-filled, multiple dimensions of Marvel's 1979 *Thor Annual* #8: *Thunder Over Troy* (*Thunder*).[23] The comic shares the framework of the SF interaction that "Myth Makers" helps to establish: 'alien' interlopers – Thor and Loki – displaced in time and space find themselves at Troy in the war's final year and become responsible for Homeric detail. However, in contrast to the ironic, impudent "Myth Makers", *Thunder* is unswerving in its self-proclaimed fidelity to Homer's *Iliad*. Motivated by writer Roy Thomas's life-long appreciation, the comic is an homage to his "favourite work of literature" (47).

In an appendix entitled "A Few Ounces of Troy" (47), Thomas explains how his desire to write a "comicbook adaptation of THE ILIAD" was thwarted when Marvel produced a version without him.[24] Consequently, Thomas fixed on *Thor* as a means to allow him to engage with Homer: "I decided that even putting a northern diety [sic] like Thor into the story of the Trojan War wouldn't do any more violence to Homer than had already been done." As the suggestion of "violence" evidences, Thomas reveals an anxiety over his desire to "do" the *Iliad*. From the self-deprecating "A Few Ounces", to the insistence that "what [Homer] said about [...] Achilles and Agamemnon and Hector [is] sacrosanct", and that "research help [was needed] on bringing Thor into the Trojan War without changing the details of the story", Thomas defends himself against accusations of "taking liberties" as he displaces and condenses epic into comic.

Thomas reveals that his desire to rewrite the *Iliad* is entwined with a journey through receptions, starting in childhood with a *Classics Illustrated* comics adaptation of the *Iliad* and A. J. Church's "young-people's illustrated abridgement", before progressing to "Samuel Butler's prose translation".[25] During college, Thomas studied Pope's translation ("I forced myself to finish, but it was hard sledding – and for a chaser I went back to and read Butler's version again"); then he states that, during the 1960s and 1970s, he "pored lovingly" over the "translations of Richmond Lattimore and Robert Fitzgerald". Every *Classics Illustrated* concludes with the invocation: "NOW THAT YOU HAVE READ THE CLASSICS *Illustrated* EDITION, DON'T MISS THE ADDED ENJOYMENT OF READING THE ORIGINAL, OBTAINABLE AT YOUR SCHOOL OR PUBLIC LIBRARY"; as Thomas itemizes his progress, he not only asserts his credentials but also locates the value of *Thunder* as the 1979 equivalent to *Classics Illustrated*. Posited as a gateway edition for children, Thomas exposes and plays on the cultural acceptance regarding the worth of comics: *Thunder* should be judged kindly as a first step on a journey to Homer rather than as a 'violent' hack job scarring Homer (an accusation levelled, implicitly, at the prior Marvel attempt).

A shared visual language renders *Thunder* as much an aesthetic homage to *Classics Illustrated* as a paean to Homer: the depiction of gods invisible to humans via broken outlines; a bleaching of all colour except a light cyan shading (Figs 3.1 and 3.2), and the arrangement of each comic's final splash-page. In *Classics Illustrated*, epic's narratorial voice is assumed by captions drawn as scrolls unfurling across the panels, while obscure terms are glossed in plainer rectangular captions linked by asterisks (e.g., "Apollo*" is glossed as: "*God of manly beauty"). In *Thunder*, Thomas inserts himself into the comic as scholarly mediator, with a similar set of authoritative signed captions in which "Roy" or "R.T" explains, e.g., that Aphrodite is the Greek version of Venus (8.4).[26]

As "R.T's" asides imply, the comic rarely assumes its reader's classical knowledge. Although sending Thor to Troy may have been a means for Thomas to visit the landscape of the *Iliad*, it also provides the means for guiding young readers into unfamiliar classical terrain. The comic begins in Asgard with Thor and Loki battling their adversaries, the Storm-Giants (*Thunder* 1–3). Thor remembers a nearby "crevice" through which he fell "unbidden", finding himself in "ancient time-defying Olympus" (3.3).[27] Loki discovers this "yawning fissure" and Thor, fearing "what vile mischief Loki might cause" in "eternal

Figs 3.1 and 3.2 *Thunder Over Troy* offers an homage to *Classics Illustrated*'s *Iliad* through its shared visual language: the depiction of gods via broken outlines and a light cyan shading. Fig. 3.1 from *Classics Illustrated No.77: Homer's* Iliad (12.6). Fig. 3.2 from *Thor Annual #8: Thunder Over Troy* (16.5–6). Roy Thomas (w.), John Buscema (a.), and Tony DeZuñiga (i.). Copyright: Marvel Comics.

Olympus" (6.1), follows Loki inside, through a mist that wipes his memory, and emerges, alone, in a forest.

As the action moves to Troy, the narrator's voice, already familiar in *Thor* comics, subsumes epic's narratorial voice. The narrator is omnipresent, referencing events in Thor's past and future, but not objective. Comments are at turns judgemental, ("for those who cause war are not always its bravest warriors"; *Thunder* 31.2), speculative ("It's the gods will, it's said … but who heard them speak their will?"; 23.1), and conspiratorial ("thus do instincts rule us all … aye, even those among us who may be divine"; 7.2). The result is a narrator who, unlike *Classics Illustrated*'s literary Homeric scrolls, prompts a moralistic engagement with the story.

The amnesiac Thor stands for the unknowing reader, providing impetus for Aeneas, who finds Thor in the forest, to explain the war's origins (*Thunder* 8–11).[28] The comic traverses temporal boundaries by complementing Aeneas's "strange tale" (8.4) with a flashback, demarcated by thicker, sketchier panel outlines: the character's memory is less clear-cut and more obtrusive than the narrator's. Aeneas commandeers the narrator's captions, but quotation marks remind us that this is Aeneas's voice, while the panels themselves fall silent. A change in page layout further marks the flashback; the change – from the predominant three-tiered, 2-2-2 panel formation used for present-action to a 2-1-2 (9) and then 1-1-1 (10) composition – slows the pace. Aeneas offers a measured reflection on accumulated events, encapsulated as silent tableau rather than action-sequences.[29] In evoking his role from Virgil's *Aeneid* (books 2–3), Aeneas's narration subtly aligns the reader's sympathies with the Trojan's cause.

In contrast to "Myth Makers", intertextual irony is almost entirely absent in *Thunder*. The aesthetic of *Classics Illustrated* is implicit here, as reference to any receptions is always unacknowledged. For example, despite the fact that all characters – Greek, Trojan, the gods Thor and Loki – and even the narrator speak in a pseudo-Elizabethan idiom, Marlowe's famous line is only obliquely alluded to, awkwardly reformulated by Aeneas: "Ships a thousand strong, launched by one unforgettable face" (*Thunder* 9.4). Despite the lexicon of "thee", "thou", "thy", "methinks" and "in sooth", a frequently inverted syntax, and a preponderance of compound adjectives, it still jars when Thor refers to "the fair-domain of Graeco-Roman Gods" (6.2). "Graeco-Roman" belongs outside of the action, to the narrator's or R.T's extradiegetic commentary; it is the vocabulary of those looking back on classical antiquity from afar, not of those living within it. However, unlike *Doctor Who*'s technology-enabled trip to a point in human history, Thor's mythological Asgard is linked with *mythic* Olympus, said to "co-exist with the Earthly Olympus, and yet on another dimensional plane at the selfsame time" (18.3). In this "ancient time-defying Olympus" (3.3), an "eon-lost land" (45.5) of "age-forgotten days" (1), temporal laws do not apply – the gods are simultaneously Greek *and* Roman.

For the comic-book page, constructed entirely of juxtaposed panels, the depiction of simultaneous dimensions, "far distant as a star, yet near as a heart-beat" (*Thunder* 22.2), is effortless. The gutter dividing and linking panels can be as geographically wide as the illustrations depict or as temporally diverse as the narrator states: "next instant" (7.4), "soon …" (11.5), "meanwhile" (26.1), "moments later" (34.5), "days later" (43.1). The narrator thus provides movement through time, occasionally reinforcing the illustrations' movement through space: "on the plain below" (18.2), "nearby" (30.2), "upon the field of battle" (43.2). Juxtaposed panels operate like the screen in *Doctor Who*, allowing for the co-existence of multiple time frames. Here, however, the split is between gods and mortals, and neither comes from a time in which Homer's *Iliad* is considered the authority on the events occurring on the Trojan plain. Instead, Homer's authority lies 'beyond' the comic with its contemporary creators and, potentially, its readers looking on from their own dimension. Unlike *Doctor Who*, the fantasy realm of comic-book heroes provides closer fidelity to the *Iliad* by allowing the gods to be depicted as gods.[30]

Inclusion of the gods allows Thomas himself, and Thor, to encroach on Homer's "sacrosanct" text (*Thunder* 47): "After all Homer was a man [and] even if Homer was able to see [. . .] he could only have guessed what Zeus said to Hera" (ibid.). Accordingly, Thor's interventions into Homer's plot consist entirely of actions that Homer 'mistakenly' ascribed to Greek gods rather than the displaced Norse god: Thor pushes aside Pandarus's arrow so that it doesn't kill Menelaus (22; cf. *Il.* 4.147–159); Thor lifts the wounded Aeneas from the battlefield (27; cf. *Il.* 20.366–400); and the warring gods are revealed to be just Zeus and Thor (35–44; cf. *Il.* 20). The thunder over Troy, which in *Doctor Who* is a meteorological event and "quirk of timing" (1.3), is here a battle so loud that the narrator declares, "in truth it seems to those below that all the deities of Olympus take part in this clash of Titans – and so shall Blind Homer, whoever he may be, record" (38.1). With the exception of Thomas's appendix, this is the comic's only reference to Homer and one of its few instances of ironic intertextuality. Homer is implicitly located as one of "those below" the battle, a yet-to-be poet whose identity remains unknown – even to the omnipresent narrator. The reference to Homer paradoxically asserts the comic's divergence from and fidelity to the *Iliad*: the narrator's truth lies beyond human perception, but this eyewitness Homer will still "record" the events "in truth" (ibid.).

The battle between Thor and Zeus rages behind a rainstorm, shrouded in a relative time dimension: minutes pass for Thor but months pass for the humans beneath. This allows for a succinct scene-to-scene montage of episodes to advance, as they condense, the epic (*Thunder* 42–43): Patroclus fights in Achilles' armour; Hector kills Patroclus; Achilles kills Hector; Paris kills Achilles; Philoctetes kills Paris. The reader thus 'witnesses' snapshots from the mortal timeframe of Homer's *Iliad*, yet experiences them fleetingly because they are tied to Thor's experience of time. The unavoidable abridging of epic is, then, presented not as a result of limitations of the comic form, but rather a feature of a sophisticated collision of timeframes. Whereas the viewer of *Doctor Who* is party to rational demystifications, *Thor*'s reader is godlike: Homer's epic proceeds far below, and the reader's skimming of highlights is posited as the divine experience of mortal time.

The 'epic' battle is concluded rather perfunctorily when Thor, remembering his identity, proclaims himself son of Odin and Zeus recalls an inviolable pact between Olympus and Asgard. Thor returns to Troy, wishes Aeneas goodbye, and comes across

Loki as he searches for the crevice back to Asgard. Although absent (and forgotten by Thor) for the entirety of the comic, Loki has been conspiring with the Greeks to end the war through subterfuge: "a man after mine own heart, by the name Odysseus / We call that which we did jointly create / the wooden horse!" (*Thunder* 46.1–2). There is no implication that knowledge of classical epic inspired the interloper to suggest the horse; rather two "vile" minds "have made certain" (46.1) that Troy's fate will be infamous. The final page reveals Loki's meddling, concluding both the comic and the war with a two-thirds splash (Fig. 3.3). Chaotic violence is evoked by distortions to the perspective. Strong right-to-left diagonals are created by the edges of buildings, off of which men are thrown and women swoon; these clashing diagonals lead the eye to the page's centre and the mass of tiny figures being engulfed by flames, which, cutting across the opposite left-to-right diagonals, lap upwards across the page where they intersect with the elongated neck of the giant horse as it tilts from page-centre to top-left. The competing tilts seem to bend sightlines around the horse, so that the reader is at once looking down on the slaughter yet up at the ominous horse.

Simultaneously allied with, but above, the Trojans, the reader occupies the position of Thor who, from the panel above, looks down on "yonder nightmare" (46.1). The narrator's voice disappears with the arrival of Loki, and this final panel, with its wide-angled survey of Troy's destruction, acts similar to a camera tracking away from the action, signalling Thor's, Loki's, and the readers' withdrawal from the story. Loki's dramatically spiked-caption naming "the wooden horse" links the page's two panels and presents the scene of destruction, but extradiegetic voices have the last word, drawing the reader out of the story. A three-volume 1885 reference work, *Bulfinch's Mythology*, is "paraphrased" in three single-edged boxes to elucidate the wooden horse. Below Bulfinch, a double-edged box signed "Roy Thomas" trails the promised content of next year's annual: "the untold saga of Aeneas and of the true founding of Rome" (46.2); and, finally, the word "fin" appears, cinematically, bottom-right in a heavy Blackletter font, inside an unfurling scroll (echoing "The End" in *Classics Illustrated*).[31]

The inclusion of Bulfinch interrupts the comic's immediacy, returning the American reader, at least, to a familiar textual landscape.[32] With the withdrawal of the narrator – or the submergence of that voice under Bulfinch – the comic's action becomes, as Thor ironically 'prophesises', "a story to be echoed down through untold ages" (*Thunder* 45.6). While Thomas may be focused on Homer's telling, the comic introduces an array of voices. In contrast to both the monophonic epic and *Doctor Who*, *Thor* is not only multi-vocalic but also ties these voices to disparate timeframes and perspectives: the intradiegetic characters (whose voices are not subsumed by that of the narrator as in epic); the extradiegetic narrator (who urges the reader to question the material); the metadiegetic "R.T" (who annotates the narrator); the Latinist (who is responsible for a voluminous nineteenth-century reference work that popularized Greek myth); and the 'voice' of the illustrators (who shape the composition of the pages and the perspective of each panel). To these can be added additional external voices as the story is intercut with advertisements, predominantly exhorting the reader to a more heroic, imagined existence: sports trading cards with the reader's name and photo, so as to be "just like the

Fig. 3.3 Loki and the Trojan horse. From *Thor Annual #8: Thunder Over Troy* (46). Roy Thomas (w.), John Buscema (a.), and Tony DeZuñiga (i.). Copyright: Marvel Comics.

pros except you're the star!" (33); "stage your own battle of the Shogun warriors" (29); "re-live again the famous battles of the American revolution" (32); "be a master of self-defense" with Kung Fu (48); or "shape a new you" with "Wate-on" (40). The focus on heroism and fantasy, the collection of American norms of masculinity (sports-stars, soldiers, warriors), and the juxtapositions of timeframes (an improved future you, travelling back to historic battles) replicate the comic's main narrative. Although they disrupt the main narrative's flow – typically as two-page spreads located after minor cliff-hangers to increase dramatic tension – they echo and exacerbate *Thunder*'s competing voices, moving the reader in and out of various timeframes as the comic circles around the receptions through which Thomas locates Homer's *Iliad*.

Travelling through time: classical reception as science fiction

In his conclusion to *Antiquity Now*, Thomas Jenkins asks readers to imagine that it is the year 4015, that "Martians" have landed on Earth, and that the only surviving "record of Earthling history between the Bronze Age and the Fall of Rome is this book: *Antiquity Now*".[33] Jenkins's deployment of this trope is designed to bring the current state of classical reception into sharper focus by inserting temporal distance and cultural displacement. Yet Jenkins's descriptive embellishments – "planetfall on a barren post-apocalyptic Earth", "the Parthenon [...] sadly evaporated in the 7th World War" and "warp-drive technology" – go beyond perfunctory support for his "thought experiment" to build an imagined future indebted to SF tropes.[34] Carol Symes similarly employs the vocabulary of SF, asserting that, "[i]n the early modern period [...] the new model of humanist education valued an elusive ideal of authenticity; [humanists] dreamed that the close imitation of Classical styles could be a vehicle of escape, a literary time-machine".[35] Less explicit or extensive than Jenkins's speculative world-building, the casual insertion of a "time-machine" into a discussion on early modern Europe nevertheless attests to the metaphor's potency.

As quintessential tropes and idioms of SF become incorporated within mainstream reception studies, it is clear that the genre offers a common conceptual vocabulary well suited to discussing issues of time and history that lie at the heart of both Classics and classical reception. A central concern of classical reception is awareness of the temporal gulf separating a reader from not only an ancient Greek or Roman text and its original context, but also each historical moment of that text's subsequent receptions – and the impact of those receptions on our interpretation of the original. Anxiety over how to read ancient texts and their multiple historic (re)interpretations, without misreading or "contaminat[ing]" them from our "'situatedness' in the present", drives the methodological approaches of Cultural Materialism, New Historicism, and Presentism.[36] It prompts Jenkins's reflection on the subjective "narrative of Greece and Rome" that Martian and Earthling philologists might construct from fragmentary evidence.[37] It motivates Charles Martindale's call for classical reception to adopt a "dialogic model", in which the post-classical reception enters into a "significant dialogue with antiquity" in order to provide "mutual illumination", and it fuels Terence Hawkes's presentist belief that a dialogue with the past is always an act of ventriloquism enacted by the present.[38]

SF engagements with ancient classics, as both *Doctor Who* and *Thor* demonstrate, can offer speculative wish-fulfilment for those seeking to commune directly with the classical past. Quintessential tropes of the genre – resurrection or reanimation, space-time travel, the experience of time as uncannily cyclical or syncretic – offer means by which to reach the past. Yet, as my opening quotation from *Doctor Who* asserts, this journey cannot but recall the multiple co-existing fictional worlds of numerous receptions. In other words, SF seems suited to engaging with ancient classics partly because of how classical reception can be understood as depending on 'science-fictional' tropes and practices. Thus if it has increasingly been clear that SF and fantasy are sites for classical reception, in this chapter I have tried to show how those genres may also be studied for extended and explicitly self-aware engagement with issues at the heart of Classics and reception studies. Nor are examples limited to *Doctor Who* and *Thor*, or for that matter to television and comics, but range widely across modern SF and fantasy.[39]

Indeed, similar fantastical receptions of Homer's Troy go far back beyond *Doctor Who* or even SF as such to the early modern period. In 1609, in the midst of his thirteen-year project that would culminate in the first full English translation of the *Iliad* (1611), George Chapman resurrected the ghost of Homer in the poetic-dialogue *Euthymiae Raptus: or The Teares of Peace*. Chapman envisions a messianic Homer, a "sacred bosome [...] so full of fire, / That t'was transparent; and made him expire / His breath in flames" (A3v).[40] Although this is essentially a dream poem, Chapman defies that genre's convention by declaring that the ghost of Homer did not "vanish with this slight vision", but rather "brought me / Home to my Cabine" to help work on his translation (F2r). Intimately tied with the moment in which the text of the *Iliad* first became accessible in English, Chapman's dialogue effectively casts Homer as an omniscient time-traveller: "past, and future things, he sawe; / And was to both, and present times, their lawe" (A3v). While various classical texts, notably Lucian's *True Story* and Aristophanes' *Birds*, have been used to argue that a strain of fantasy, and even proto-science fiction, is detectable in ancient classics, I argue that engagement with classics, including the often 'invisible' act of translation, has always involved an engagement with fantasy.[41] A leap of imaginative speculative fantasy is the (often unacknowledged) analogue in all contact with the classical past.

Notes

1. *Doctor Who*'s "Myth Makers", Episode 4, Scene 20 (hereafter 4.20).

2. Suvin 1973 and 1979 for SF as a "literature of estrangement".

3. Brown (2008: 416).

4. Cf. Paul (2007: 311) on film.

5. Kovacs and Marshall 2011 and 2016; for TV, Rogers and Stevens (2015: chs. 9, 11, and 14).

6. Cf. Martindale (2013: 177).

7. See Cotton's *Echo and Narcissus* (1959), *The Golden Fleece* (1962), and *The Tragedy of Phaethon* (1965) for the BBC Third Programme. The episodes are: One: "Temple of Secrets" (16 October 1965); Two: "Small Prophet, Quick Return" (23 October 1965); Three: "Death of a Spy" (30 October 1965); Four: "Horse of Destruction" (6 November 1965).

8. See Keen 2010.

9. Translations used throughout: *Il.*, Fagles 1996; *Od.*, Fagles 1990; *Aen.*, West 2003 [1990].

10. The camera is not tied to the perspective of the Doctor and his companions. The static nature of the camera work may be assumed to be based on the limitations of the heavy mounted cameras of the time. It is also rare for *Doctor Who* to break the fourth-wall convention.

11. An initial feasibility study stressed that "television science fiction drama must be written *not* by SF writers, but by TV dramatists" (Bull and Frick [1962: 3]) because "SF is not itself a wildly popular branch of fiction" (2).

12. For 'horizon of expectations', see Jauss 1970.

13. See Keen (2010: 104).

14. For the medieval Cressida, see the romance epics of Benoît de Sainte-Maure (*c.* 1160), Guido delle Colonne (1287), and Chaucer (*c.* 1385), and their reformulation by John Lydgate (*c.* 1420), Raoul Lefèvre (*c.* 1465), and William Caxton (1473).

15. For the romances, see Frazer Jr. 1966; for the resultant reception of 'Troy', see Kenward 2016.

16. In "Myth Makers", it is not only Troilus who fears Vicki/Cressida's infidelity but also Cassandra ("show me a sign that she is false"; 2.8). Cotton claims Diomedes died from his wounds, but by wearing Diomedes' clothes and sneaking into Troy, Steven gestures to not only *Iliad* book 10 (Diomedes and Odysseus spying on the Trojans), but also a resurrection – a wry nod that allows for his differing fates in post-Homeric versions, where he is either granted immortality (as in Pindar) or appears in Hell (as in Dante's *Inferno*).

17. The name 'Astra' adds a further allusion to Virgil: Apollo's reference to a journey to the stars, *sic itur ad astra* (*Aen.* 9.641).

18. Although not referenced in the *Doctor Who* episodes, Nero's burning of Rome is often figured as replaying Troy's destruction, e.g., in accounts of Nero singing about the destruction of Troy as Rome burns (Tacitus *Annals* 16.39; Cassius Dio 8.17–18).

19. See Keen 2006a on this 'interaction' as peculiar to SF, whose *locus classicus* is *Doctor Who*.

20. Keen 2006a discusses Helen's exclusion as a feature of SF. I read Helen's absence as another intertextual joke by Cotton about competition between his multiple sources.

21. Episode Two's title, "Small Prophet, Quick Return", shares Paris's punning impulse; Episode Four was originally titled "Is there a Doctor in the Horse", but was renamed "Horse of Destruction" in light of the story's violent climax.

22. See also the modern reviews of the "Myth Makers" audio CDs: "The shift into tragedy half way through Episode Four is a little uncomfortable"; "it's slightly reminiscent of 'Blackadder' ... Rather moving and tragic at the end as well" (BBC 2014).

23. Roy Thomas (w.), John Buscema (a.), Tony DeZuñiga (i.), and George Roussos (c.), *Thor Annual #8: Thunder Over Troy* (Marvel, November 1979).

24. Thomas does not identify this prior comic, but it is safe to assume that he is referring to *Marvel Classics Comics #26: The Iliad* by Elliot S. Maggin (w.) and Yong Montaño (a.) (Marvel, January 1977). Thomas got to realize his ambition with the 'Marvel Illustrated Imprint' editions of *The Iliad* (December 2007–July 2008), *The Odyssey* (September 2008–April 2009), and *The Trojan War* (May–September 2009), all adapted by Roy Thomas (w.). See Marshall (2016: 8–11).

25. Homer (w.), Alex A. Blum (a.), *Classics Illustrated #77: The Iliad* (Classics Illustrated, November 1950).

26. All citations for comics use the following format: *Title* Issue Number: Page(s).Panel(s). Thus (*Thunder* 8.2, 4) means *Thunder* page 8, panels 2 and 4.

27. As a caption by "Roy" tells us, Thor refers here to "Annual #1 1965" (1). It is somewhat ironic that in 1979 Thor is used to guide the reader into the classical world, given that Thor was introduced as a major Marvel character in 1940 because Stan Lee, Jack Kirby, and Larry Lieber felt "that audiences were overly familiar with Greek and Roman divinities"; Dethloff (2011: 112).

28. The conceit is somewhat unnecessary, as the comic itself later concedes, after Thor regains his memory, "that city's history be unknown to us of Asgard" (45.6).

29. Aeneas's flashback also recalls *Classics Illustrated*'s two-page 'preface' in which seven scene-to-scene panels jump vast swathes of time to depict the marriage of Helen, her abduction, and the start of a war that has now entered its tenth year. I follow here the terminology of McCloud 1993.

30. On gods and SF, see Keen 2006a.

31. This final panel echoes that of *Classics Illustrated*, which also ends with a two-thirds splash page in which an unidentified Trojan woman (Cassandra?) watches the Horse being pulled into the city as the narrator informs the reader that "the Greeks, emerging from the horse, finally took the city in the tenth year of the siege".

32. As Richard (2009: 33) notes, *Bulfinch's Mythology* is "one of the most popular books ever published in the United States and the standard work on classical mythology for nearly a century".

33. Jenkins (2015: 221).

34. Ibid.

35. Symes (2016: 100).

36. Grady and Hawkes (2007: 3).

37. Jenkins (2015: 221).

38. Martindale (2013: 177), Hawkes 2002.

39. A pertinent example is Dan Simmons's *Ilium* (2003) and *Olympos* (2005), centered on a future re-creation of Homer's *Iliad* by nanotechnologically enhanced post-humans observed through the eyes of a time-displaced professor of Classics. In a central conceit, the consciousnesses of literary geniuses (esp. Shakespeare and Proust alongside Homer) are "like naked singularities [that] can bend space-time … and collapse probability waves into discrete alternatives" (*Ilium* 373). Receptions thus endow 'originals' with enough energy to burst into existence in parallel dimensions. See Brown 2008, Laimé 2014, and Grobéty 2015.

40. This light-emitting Homer recalls an iconographic tradition dating back to late-fourth-century Christianity; see Hanfmann (1980: 78). For classical texts, characters, and authors figured throughout the early modern period as ghosts or corpses, see Kenward 2016.

41. For the invisibility of the translator, see Venuti 1995 and 2008. For the debate surrounding nascent SF in the classics, particularly Lucian's *True History*, see, e.g., Fredericks 1976, Suvin 1979, Brown 2008, and Keen 2015a.

CHAPTER 4
MONUMENTS AND TRADITION IN JACK MCDEVITT'S *THE ENGINES OF GOD*
Laura Zientek

When experimental science fiction (SF) offers commentary on society, it does so in a way that allows and even impels self-reflection and self-judgement through the portrayal of alternative, hypothetical, and speculative worlds.[1] Albert Wendland, in *Science, Myth, and the Fictional Creation of Alien Worlds*, uses the analogy of a pane of glass – reflective or transparent – to illustrate how SF focalizes observations about culture.[2] Using a mirror as an artifact to view reality recalls the fantastic voyages of Lucian's *True Histories* (*VH*), in which Endymion, king of the Moon, shows the narrator a mirror that can be used to view all aspects of the Earth (26).[3] Lucian's narrator can observe his own culture from an alternative world and thereby achieves a perspective otherwise unachievable. This offers a useful parallel to modern SF, which provides a simulated external perspective on culture, as if viewing the Earth from the Moon. To be sure, some modern SF has moved from fiction to fact, for example, in the wake of NASA's Apollo missions. Nevertheless, many modern SF works continue to displace the viewer into the rest of the solar system, to more distant astronomical locations, or forward into the future, thus returning this otherworldly perspective to us.[4] This move also grants the same ability to reflect on our culture – and the traditions that are foundational to it – through the 'mirror' of reception.[5]

Distance from the classical tradition makes moments of sameness stand out more clearly in Jack McDevitt's 1994 novel, *The Engines of God* (hereafter *Engines*), a text that features twenty-third-century Earth and fictional planets beyond the solar system.[6] When evidence of extraterrestrial life and culture is discovered, it is ancient, and this antiquity prompts allusions to the classical past within the novel itself, inviting a reading that incorporates a comparison to the cultures of Greece and Rome. In *Engines*, the first discovery of any creation beyond Earth is also the closest to Earth: an ice sculpture on Iapetus, one of Saturn's moons. The statue, surrounded by footprints matching the shape of its feet, is thought to be a self-portrait of its creator. This sculpture is the impetus for interstellar explorers to seek out and ultimately discover seventeen huge structures, called 'Monuments'; a handful of planets with ruins of advanced extraterrestrial civilizations; and even an extant, moderately advanced civilization (in McDevitt's *Odyssey* 161).[7] The Monuments introduce the central mysteries in *Engines*: the identity of their Makers, the purpose of their construction, and their proximity to the ruins of alien civilizations. The ancient ruins also evoke the classical world, but most of McDevitt's interaction with the classical tradition occurs in his representation of research and scholarship. In *Engines*, archaeologists, cryptologists, and philologists enjoy a new "golden age" of discovery (15).

In an exo-archaeological mystery that spans millennia and an entire arm of our galaxy, McDevitt engages with the classical tradition in a way that supersedes reception of an individual text or image. McDevitt mirrors the development of the tradition itself – its collection of texts, images, textual transmission problems, researchers, research methods, and celebrities both notorious and celebrated – in a vast new context. This displaced perspective on the materials and practices of the classical tradition is augmented by modern mythology with pop-philosophical theories about the nature of the universe and its inhabitants. Alongside references to Troy as explored by nineteenth-century archaeologist Heinrich Schliemann, *Engines* presents the Monument-Makers as a play on 'ancient astronauts', technologically advanced beings that can be interpreted as divine by the less-advanced civilizations that they meet.[8]

Engines has two major narrative impulses: first, a race to preserve as much evidence as possible from an exo-archaeological site before the planet involved undergoes terraforming; second, an attempt to decipher an inscription on a nearby Monument, which can be used to find the Monument-Makers. McDevitt's application of classical elements shapes the structure of the novel but, because *Engines* is not in dialogue with a *single* text or image, a broader approach is more useful in analysing his multifaceted incorporation of archaeology, philology, and myth from the classical world.[9] More importantly, by identifying connections between McDevitt's SF premise and the classical tradition, we have a platform from which to observe the tradition itself. In other words, we can revisit from another perspective how material, linguistic, and narrative evidence from the Greco-Roman world is inextricably intertwined, how that evidence is interpreted and develops into a tradition of knowledge and scholarship, and even how we may extrapolate its continued presence and development in the future.

In this chapter, I examine how the development, content, and scholarly personae of the classical tradition play a role in *Engines*, and explore how these can contribute to both our reading of the novel and our perspectives on the classical tradition. Material, linguistic, and narrative aspects of the tradition are treated individually: first archaeology; then language and philology; and finally mythology, which includes Greco-Roman myth, McDevitt's fictional ancient mythological system, and the modern ancient astronaut myth. Within *Engines*'s narrative, we find the reception of ancient mythologies and the deconstruction of modern mythologies. The displacement of familiar patterns into these fictional settings ultimately reflects the enduring character of the classical tradition and of its study, also enduring, into – and beyond – our modern time.

Exo-archaeology and the monuments

J. J. Winckelmann and Heinrich Schliemann are associated with the study of classical culture in eighteenth- and nineteenth-century Germany. It is no coincidence that these two names also make their way into *Engines*. As the protagonist, Priscilla Hutchins

(Hutch) travels between archaeological sites; she pilots a ship called the *Johann Winckelmann*. The historical Winckelmann is famous for his study of Greek art and is considered a founding figure in the study of archaeological artifacts as art history.[10] Winckelmann saw the value in classical literary sources, relying on authors such as Pausanias for inspiration on his approach to art and its meaning.[11] He held a particular, fanatical enthusiasm for the Homeric poems, reportedly reading from the *Odyssey* in lieu of the Gospels during church services.[12] But what makes his name most fitting for Hutch's ship is Winckelmann's approach to evaluating extant art objects for their meaning and aesthetic value without necessarily relying on ancient descriptions. The *Winck* is intended for the evacuation of the archaeologists and as many artifacts as possible from a soon-to-be destroyed dig site. Essentially, all extant artifacts from this particular site will be those preserved on board the *Winckelmann*. The ship itself thus becomes an incarnation of Winckelmann's literary opus, *Geschichte der Kunst des Altertums*, in which the author sought to "construct a textual monument" of surviving art from the Greek and Roman worlds.[13]

Like Winckelmann in the field of art history, Schliemann has a similar foundational role in modern field archaeology, though his reputation and findings have always been the source of academic debate, due in part to his determination to use the Homeric poems to find and identify ancient sites.[14] Since the 1970s in particular, significant re-examination of his findings has taken place on the basis of the pursuit of methodological and scholarly accuracy.[15] It seems that some consensus may be reached in the consideration of Schliemann as an important early figure in classical field archaeology who, despite his propensity to exaggerate and lie in his writing and his lack of precise tools for recording excavations, nevertheless paved the way for future study and contributed greatly to modern knowledge of ancient sites such as Troy and Mycenae.[16]

In *Engines*, however, Schliemann's historical notoriety persists. When the team of archaeologists at one exo-archaeological site (Quraqua) must evacuate, they lament their dedication to stratigraphy and detailed recordkeeping. The character Richard Wald, a well-known and well-regarded archaeologist, reflects, "It turns out we were too cautious. Should have plowed right in. Like Schliemann" (52). The novel picks up on the popular villainizing of Schliemann's methodology, but retrospective study of these methods shows something different. The historical excavations were not so careless as this: between 1871 and 1873, Schliemann's hired photographer, Panagos Zaphyropoulos, took more than 100,000 photographs to document the progress of the excavation at Hisarlik and the artifacts discovered there, a practice emulated in *Engines* by the excavators of Quraqua in the days leading up to their departure.[17] *Engines*'s reception of Schliemann and his work prompts a renewed examination of the man himself. To understand the full importance of Schliemann's historical influence for *Engines*, however, we must consider the scope of exo-archaeological study in the novel.

In a report about his 1873 excavations at Troy, Schliemann described the site and its significance as "a new world for archaeology".[18] McDevitt makes this metaphorical statement literal, as archaeology in *Engines* encompasses the Monuments as well as several advanced civilizations (15). The ice statue on Iapetus, Saturn's moon, was the first find and the catalyst for subsequent exploration and discovery. By the beginning of *Engines*, several other Monuments are known (3):

a cloudy pyramid orbiting a rocky world off blue-white Sirius, a black cluster of crystal spheres and cones mounted in a snowfield near the south pole of lifeless Armis V, a transparent wedge orbiting Arcturus.... Most spectacular among the relics was an object that resembled a circular pavilion complete with columns and steps cut from the side of a mountain on a misshapen asteroid in the Procyon system.

The civilizations include one extant example, Inakademeri, and two extinct examples known only through archaeological study, Pinnacle and Quraqua; one more, the home of the Monument-Makers, is discovered in the course of the novel. *Engines* focuses on the study of the ruins on Quraqua (and of the nearby Monument on the planet's moon), the artifacts and epigraphic evidence, and the cultural information that can be gleaned from both.

The central site on Quraqua is the Temple of the Winds, a complex built over several historical eras (and many millennia) that reflects periods of technological development and stagnation, containing both epigraphic evidence that allows the decipherment of its language and artifacts that bear images from local myth. The researchers there rely on the stratigraphy of the site to establish historical eras, something Schliemann himself did at Hisarlik, and by the time of their evacuation, they are occupied with one of the lowest and oldest parts of the Temple.[19]

The Temple of the Winds is the most thoroughly explored location on Quraqua and is matched in significance by Oz, a massive facsimile of a city on Quraqua's moon. Only by comparison with findings on Quraqua do Wald, Hutch, and the other researchers come to see Oz as one of the Monuments. Numismatic evidence links Oz to Quraquat culture, and while the Quraquat had never travelled to their moon, artifacts at the Temple site were the best hope for understanding the Monument (*Engines* 13). Compared with other Monuments, Oz was massive, the image of a city without the function, its geometry eerily disrupted by ruined sections (53–54).[20] McDevitt sets Oz in dialogue with classical sources when, upon seeing Oz, Hutch recalls "old textbook representations of Troy" (53). Implicit here is Schliemann's role in uncovering the ruins at Hisarlik and identifying them with Troy and, beyond that, the adoption of this knowledge into popular understandings of ancient Near Eastern and classical history. That Hutch thinks of Troy when confronted by mysterious Monumental ruined walls speaks to the pervasiveness of this knowledge but also elides Schliemann's role in obtaining it. The Oz–Troy dialogue, however, does encompass both the fictional exo-archaeologists and Schliemann's historical persona. In fact, by using myth to direct their search for the Monument-Makers and in their ultimate interpretation of the ruins of the Monument-Makers' civilization, Hutch and the others become futuristic images of Schliemann.

Later, after leaving Quraqua behind, Hutch and crew arrive at Beta Pacifica, the home of the Monument-Makers. At this point, the *Winckelmann* takes on so much damage that they must abandon the ship; Winckelmann's influence is no longer applicable.[21] The characters are less concerned with the preservation of artifacts, but instead are driven by a Schliemann-style quest of discovery. In order to best understand the role of myth in these new exo-archaeological pursuits, it is necessary to consider how archaeologists from one planet (educated in the field methodology and archaeological history of civilizations such as ancient Greece) can understand the myths of an alien culture. The answer requires a detour into the representation of philological and linguistic study in the novel.

The decipherment of Linear C

When McDevitt uses the term 'philology', he alludes to the varied forms of language study that can exist in the kind of archaeological context described in the novel: the discovery of symbols and text, the identification of characters, the decipherment of language itself, epigraphic study, translation of texts, and interpretation of the content of those texts. The central character in *Engines*'s portrayal of philology is 'exophilologist' Maggie Tufu, who assists with and directs excavation, identifies a syllabary, deciphers the language, and translates what fragments of text the team collects (*Engines* 140). The texts she works with come from the ruins on Quraqua, primarily at the Temple of the Winds, and from Oz. If we revisit the analogy of SF as a mirror, in McDevitt's refiguration of philology the glass is cracked and the reflection is accordingly disrupted; it is manifold rather than unified. The practice of philology that we can identify from our own tradition appears in pieces: cryptology in the mode of Michael Ventris, poetic interpretation in the style of scholars like C. M. Bowra, and glimpses of how the Rosetta stone impacted Egyptology.

The scale of Maggie's linguistic achievements is truly clear upon examining the parallels between the discovery and decipherment of one Quraquat language, dubbed 'Casumel Linear C' in *Engines*, and that of Linear B in the nineteenth and twentieth centuries. Inscriptions in Linear B were initially identified in Knossos on Crete, but inscriptions from mainland Greece were later included in the classification. The process of identification and decipherment was long and complex, from the first excavation of undeciphered inscriptions on tablets, seals, and other objects on Crete, through attempts to record and categorize hieroglyphic signs on these objects, to the distinction between a variety of scripts and contexts in the Minoan and Mycenaean worlds, to the ongoing work of philologists and linguists to decipher Linear B itself.[22] Alice Kober, who worked on identifying potential noun paradigms for Linear B under the assumption that it was an inflected language, noted the difficulty of deciphering an unknown language written in an unknown script and stated that, even with bilingual comparanda, such work was essentially impossible. Only by having knowledge of the language could the unknown script be deciphered.[23] This complication stalled the decipherment of Linear B, and only when Ventris came to suspect a connection between the Greek language of the ancient historical period and the language conveyed by Linear B, and later when his research partner John Chadwick assisted and then continued Ventris's work, did the decipherment proceed in a conclusive way.[24] Over half a century elapsed from the first discovery of unknown symbols by Evans in the 1890s to the decipherment by Ventris, Chadwick, and others in the 1950s.

By calling the alien script in his novel 'Linear C', McDevitt places it in line with the real languages of Linear A and B, implying both a similarity in significance and a lack of any comparable archaeological mystery on Earth in the intervening centuries. His narrative of its discovery and decipherment is much more streamlined than its historical model, however, and thus appears relatively uncomplicated. Unknown scripts are associated with the Monuments from the very beginning, appearing as inscriptions on or near them, but it is only in the course of the excavation of the Temple site on Quraqua that the Casumel script is shown to undergo the more thorough process of identification and eventual translation (*Engines* 4). McDevitt writes about the textual tradition of Quraqua in terms of its languages: a more recent language that is already deciphered and translatable, and the language spoken by the more ancient Quraquat who wrote in Linear C (another reflection, perhaps, of the temporal range of the Greek language). A people called the "Scriveners" (due to their prolific and detailed record-keeping practices) preserved literature from earlier periods in the more recent text and language of their own period (115–116). In her translations of this literature, Maggie converts Quraquat dates to correspond to our timeline: the Scriveners flourished between about 1400–1000 BCE, making them conveniently contemporaneous with the use of Linear B by Mycenaean Greeks in the Mediterranean. The people who used Casumel Linear C, however, were much further removed than the Mycenaeans were from the classical Greeks or even from the time period of the novel itself, dating from the ninth millennium BCE (64). In *Engines*, Maggie's initial work results in translated poetry and mythography likely dating from the time of the Scriveners, while her later focus is on Linear C.[25]

The ongoing decipherment of Linear C is what determines the direction of excavation in the final days at the Temple, as the search for a multi-lingual inscription (a Rosetta Stone) becomes desperate. Hutch learns that the Lower Temple was built over a military post controlled by the Linear C language speakers, and that this location, therefore, suggests the possibility of examples of the script more significant than the scattered fragments and inscriptions that the team had thus far recovered (*Engines* 89). The collected knowledge and information about Linear C is a clear parallel to the pre-decipherment work on Linear B. Like Linear B's small, extant corpus of textual fragments, Linear C is known from about 500 samples of text, often inscribed on tablets, mostly made up of small groups of signs, gathered from a handful of excavation sites and given meaning by the context of their discovery.[26] Maggie's work had progressed to the reconstruction of a syllabary and identification of some vocabulary items (140–141). However, where the key to deciphering Linear B was understanding that its language was a form of Greek, Maggie's breakthrough comes thanks to the discovery of a printing press with moveable type set into its chases (141, 174). The decipherment of the mysterious Linear C inscription on Oz happens quickly, as the information gleaned from the printing press and a new set of tablets discovered near the Lower Temple allow Maggie to work out the meaning in less than five months (194).[27]

The printing press is a striking artifact for its level of technological advancement. Though the text it printed was Casumel Linear C, the comparatively primitive technology of the Mycenaean Greeks makes the Quraquat printing press seem all the more alien. The correspondences between our classical tradition and the fictional ancient Quraquat tradition make this fictional technological achievement emphasize the distance between the Mycenaean users of Linear B and study of them in the modern world. We may even observe a kind of wish fulfilment of Mycenaean studies, in light of the Phaistos Disk, an artifact discovered in the early twentieth century on Crete. Found in a Minoan palace and covered with an undeciphered script that has as yet foiled attempts at translation, the Phaistos Disk is said to display a primitive "typeface" or an "anticipation" of printing, pre-dating printing technology with moveable type in Europe by more than 2,000 years.[28] The Quraquat printing press takes this technology to its logical, yet fantastic, end.

McDevitt's description of Maggie's philology engages with the efforts of archaeologists, philologists, and linguists who worked to identify and discover the languages of the Minoans and Mycenaeans. Moreover, it does so in a way that makes the fantastic real, at least within the realm of this fictional future. While we may never know the meaning or purpose of the Phaistos Disk, McDevitt's characters *do* find their typographic 'Rosetta Stone' and can solve the mystery of the Oz inscription (*Engines* 64). Maggie completes work reminiscent of that done by Kober, Ventris, and Chadwick, but does so independently, in such a brief time, and with such surety and completeness, that this emphasizes not so much her ability as an exophilologist as much as her impossibility as a philologist at all. Like the archaeological site, the fragments of Casumel Linear C, and the larger mythological narratives woven through the story, Maggie herself takes on a sense of futuristic improbability, becoming a sort of mythological heroine-scholar.

'Hercules' versus the Monument-Makers

McDevitt's creation of a fictional (and alien) mythic tradition that appropriates ancient Greco-Roman mythical patterns makes the narrative a reflection of myth's place in our own tradition; the addition of the 'ancient astronaut' concept introduces a modern mythos as well. With this tripartite mythological system, reception of the classical tradition is a primary concern, as the intersection of mythologies here – Greco-Roman, Quraquat, 'ancient astronauts' – helps dictate the portrayal of both archaeology and philology.

The Temple site on Quraqua yields bas-reliefs, tablets, and other art objects depicting an ancient Quraquat hero, Malinar, comparable to, and contextualized by the characters as, a culture-hero along the lines of Hercules (*Engines* 202).[29] As with Hercules, heroic stories about Malinar include his childhood and often involve the taming or defeat of mythical monsters.[30] To Hercules' hydra, Geryon, and Nemean lion, we can compare Malinar's 'horgon'. The archaeological context of these discoveries, moreover, also places Hercules and Malinar in parallel positions. Art from the classical Greek world, such as the series of metopes from the Temple of Zeus at Olympia showing Hercules' Twelve

Labours, depicts Hercules as hero, something mirrored in the artifacts at the fictional Temple site on Quraqua.[31] Through knowledge of the Hercules tradition, the full significance of this mythic/heroic parallel emerges. Not limited to the interconnected sources and media of this fictional archaeological site, the parallel reveals how an understanding of mythology creates expectations about mythic systems in general. With the 'Hercules' heroic figure borrowed from the past – or rather, from *our* past – and located instead in the fictional ancient tradition of the Quraquat, characters and readers can anticipate other aspects of the Greek heroic tradition: the oral component of myth; epic, epinician, or tragic contexts; and the adoption of an early myth by later cultures. Much of this process of mythical development is omitted in *Engines*, however, and what the Herculean Malinar really reveals about the original Hercules mythos is the tradition's richness and pervasiveness. We know Greek and Roman mythical stories were varied, conflicting, and alternately local or global; the fictional mythic tradition of the Quraquat is, by comparison, monolithic and even monumental.

McDevitt's focus is not on the creation of an ancient tradition on Quraqua to rival that of the Greeks and Romans; the western mythological tradition is a reference point, a touchstone for readers to be able to grasp the implied antiquity and cultural significance of figures like Malinar (*Engines* 202–206). Rather, through his use of ancient myth, both Greco-Roman and Quraquat, McDevitt makes the third type of mythical tradition – the modern 'ancient astronauts' myth – into something 'real' within the scope of his narrative. The ancient astronauts theory posits that visits from technologically advanced extraterrestrials in Earth's distant past led to the creation of culture, the building of monumental artifacts (e.g., the Pyramids at Giza, the Nazca lines in Peru) and the understanding of these visitors as 'divine beings' due to the technological gap between them and the ancient humans who witnessed them.[32] One of the earliest and most significant purveyors of this theory, Erich von Däniken, has been accused by archaeologists of working with muddled evidence, as he claims artifacts from around the globe – despite their spatial and chronological distance from each other – as evidence for his theory.[33] McDevitt effectively 'revs up' the engines on Däniken's *Chariots of the Gods*: the Monuments in *Engines* avoid the cultural confines of Earth's ancient cultures and, therefore, fulfil Däniken's desire for evidence on a grand scale. Like the ancient astronauts of myth, the Monument-Makers travelled widely, used advanced technology to create their Monuments and, to the Quraquat at least, were seen as comparable to divine figures. Early in the novel, a bas-relief depicting one of the Monument-Makers as an iconographical Death figure spurs interest in a connection between the Quraquat and the builders of the Monuments; this interest is sharpened due to the fact that the Monument on Quraqua's moon dated to the same period as the bas-relief (20, 54). A poem and an inscription locate the Monument-Makers within the ancient astronaut narrative and highlight the distinction between Däniken's and McDevitt's ancient astronauts. Unlike the alien 'gods' of Däniken's theory, the Monument-Makers did not *create* culture. Instead, they used it (as Quraquat myth) to communicate and to give directions back to their home. The inscription and its translation are also the driving force of the latter half of *Engines*: a search for Beta Pacifica, the Monument-Makers' world. Here, McDevitt's approach to archaeology, philology, and myth comes full circle, as Hutch, Maggie, and the others use ancient text and material evidence to pursue the reality behind a myth. They become futuristic avatars of Schliemann for the reason he was admired by ancient astronaut theorists like Däniken and mocked by contemporary Classicists.[34]

Both of the texts that lead Hutch and her companions to the Monument-Makers are ancient. The poem comes from a book of devotionals found near the Temple and describes the streets of a major religious centre as its people wait for some destructive cosmological event (*Engines* 115–116). There is an awareness of some advanced alien force ('the engines of God' of the novel's title) set in a religious context – a narrative perfectly in line with Däniken's theories. The inscription is key to both the ongoing plot of the novel and to the interpretation of the ancient astronauts myth. Though unknown to the people of Quraqua, it is discovered by the archaeologists from Earth on a tower in Oz. It was written in the same language and using the same syllabary, Casumel Linear C, as the most ancient tablets and texts in the lowest level of the Temple, a discovery that is essentially the equivalent of finding a Mycenaean Greek inscription written in Linear B on a clearly constructed (i.e., not naturally occurring) object on Mars. Moreover, the inscription communicates by adopting the concepts of ancient myth: it bids the reader "farewell and good fortune. Seek us by the light of the horgon's eye" (194). Beyond recalling the interactive nature of ancient Greek and Roman inscriptions, which also made requests/commands of their readers, the Oz inscription can use the horgon as a directional reference because, like Greco-Roman mythic figures including Hercules and Hydra, it became part of the local constellations.[35]

Conclusion

In McDevitt's novel, the ancient astronaut myth becomes something true, at least for the tradition built by the people of Quraqua. The subsequent portion of von Däniken's theory – that these ancient astronauts must then be perceived as gods – does not follow in *Engines*, especially for Hutch and her companions. Through the discoveries made at the Temple site and interpretation made possible by Maggie's translation work, Hutch and the others become reflections of Schliemann. In this way they also break the mould borrowed from von Däniken because, like Schliemann, they deconstruct the monumental nature of the artifacts' creators. Schliemann both revered and eventually de-mythologized the literary monuments of the Greek past, the Homeric poems. As James Porter writes about the effects of Schliemann's work, "the past was a foreign country indeed. Homer had become its alienated witness, and in his alienation he stood closer to 'us'".[36]

This displacement is mirrored again in *Engines*'s conclusion. The Monument-Makers' homeworld reveals information about the decline of these ancient astronauts. Advanced technology *preceded* a space station where the level of visible technology had been surpassed on Earth in the twentieth century (*Engines* 303). All the artifacts on board are familiar and quotidian enough to seem unremarkable and, despite their antiquity, almost recent (310). For Hutch, the revelation is disappointing. The deconstruction of the god-motif in the modern myth is clear in her journal entry: "The Monument-Makers seem to have vanished, to be replaced by pathetic creatures who build primitive space stations and kill themselves when things go wrong. Where are the beings who built the Great Monuments? They are not here" (311). This absence had been predicted by Maggie Tufu before their arrival at Beta Pacifica: "the Monument-Makers are gone. Just as the Classical Greeks are gone. I mean, no one seems to be running around making Monuments anymore" (229). In Maggie's words, the distance from the Monument-Makers, like the distance from ancient Greece, is temporal. To Hutch, the grandeur of the species is lost in their ruins.

In a way, this debunking of the ancient astronaut myth distinguishes Hutch from Schliemann: though both followed a myth with success, Hutch's disappointment is a sharp contrast to Schliemann's continued enthusiasm.[37] Where Schliemann kept the myths and added faces, Hutch and her crew deconstruct the myth, concluding that "there were no aliens. They all turn out to be pretty human" (*Engines* 414). In identifying with the Monument-Makers, Hutch's perspective shows how the only remaining displacement of familiar patterns to unknown settings is from the classical tradition onto *Engine*'s narrative of exo-archaeology, philology, and mythology. Since such displacement is effectively rationalizing, the modern myth is no longer fantastic. For readers, the perspective afforded by knowledge of the classical world and its academic reception since the eighteenth century remains as a way to observe both the underlying structure of the novel and how it allows, encourages, and even impels reflection on the development of Classics and its knowledge base as we know it today. In *Engines*, McDevitt invigorates, then re-examines, the desire to re-enact the past that was so prevalent in the early practice of classical archaeology, especially for Schliemann. The combination of the ancient astronaut myth and the fantastic archaeological quest are, by necessity, grand and often monolithic, both in *Engines* as well as in other modern franchises, such as *Stargate* (1994), *Indiana Jones and the Kingdom of the Crystal Skull* (2008), and *Prometheus* (2012). In familiar narrative patterns that reflect both the ancient world and its examination by scholars, *Engines* shifts the focus from the stories themselves to our ways of telling, understanding, and, ultimately, relating them back to ourselves.

Notes

1. Wendland (1985: 23–27); cf. Hardwick (2003: 109).

2. Wendland (1985: 6–7); cf. Roberts (2006: 14).

3. On Lucian's SF, see Georgiadou and Larmour 1998, Swanson 1976. For ancient SF, see Roberts (2006: 38–42). For qualifications on *VH* as SF or fantastic literature, see Rogers and Stevens (2015: 6).

4. Roberts (2006: 26) uses the film *Apollo 13* (1996) as an illustration of space flight as a concept that moved from the future to the 'real' and finally to the past.

5. See Martindale (2007: 298) on the "two-way process" of reception.

6. Hardwick (2003: 8–9) calls this 'critical distance', which allows the reader of ancient texts to move beyond their own cultural 'horizon of expectation'. Cf. Suvin (1979: 3–15) on 'cognitive estrangement'.

7. *Odyssey* (2006) follows *Engines* in the *Academy Series*.

8. On the 'ancient astronaut' mythos, see sources below, n. 32.

9. Hardwick (2003: 12) describes how reception itself is multifaceted, in that it includes "the balance between borrowed, traditional, and new perspectives in individual works of art and literature, in philosophy and historical writing, and in broader cultural movements".

10. See Marchand (1996: 7–16), Orrells (2011b: 173), Schindler (1992: 135), and Wohlleben (1990: 198).

11. See Marchand (1996: 10), Pretzler (2010: 199, 209).

12. Wohlleben (1990: 198–199) quotes Winckelmann as saying "I prayed in Homeric similes."

13. Orrells (2011b: 172–173).

14. See de Jong (2005: 2–3), Maurer (2009: 305–306), Schindler (1992: 140), and Wohlleben (1990: 210). As to his reputation, Schliemann is in turns "a rascal" in Calder (1981: 247) and "notorious" as the excavator of Troy to Wohlleben (1990: 198), as a businessman to Giesecke (2003: 38n10), and as a liar to Arentzen (2001: 189); Marchand (1996: 117) calls him a "maverick philhellene".

15. Easton (1998: 335) summarizes the mixed impressions of Schliemann in modern studies, from "a half crazy human being who has no idea whatsoever of the meaning of his excavations" to "the father of scientific archaeology" who was "without a doubt a scholar". Easton also cites the dozen articles going back and forth on Schliemann's reputation and findings between himself and Traill between 1981 and 1994 (see Bibliography).

16. See Arentzen (2001: 189), Easton (1998: 335–336).

17. See Maurer (2009: 309–310). Due to picture quality, only 270 of these photographs were published in Schliemann's 1874 atlas (*Atlas trojanischer Alterthümer: Photographische Abbildungen zu dem Berichte über die Ausgrabungen in Troja von Dr. Heinrich Schliemann*). See Marchand (1996: 106–107) for Schliemann's pioneering role in the use of photography in archaeology.

18. Marchand (1996: 122–123).

19. Easton (1998: 340) calls stratigraphy "one of [Schliemann's] strong points".

20. Oz's size: the walls of the city are arranged in a perfect square and in a ratio 2000:1 in length and height (8.32 km per side, 41.63 m tall); urban appearance: "an utterly sublime mystery. It really is no more than a rock sculpture in an airless place"; ruins: "Long sections had fallen away, and there were places where the wall appeared to have been hammered in to the ground. Rubble lay along its base."

21. Maurer (2009: 315) notes that Schliemann was "never enthusiastic about Winckelmann".

22. Excavation and discovery was begun by Sir Arthur Evans and later became the object of study for many other archaeologists and philologists. Kober (1948: 82) describes the state of knowledge about the "Minoan scripts" before the decipherment of Linear B, citing six separate but related scripts: a pictographic script, the script found on the Phaistos Disk, Linear A, Linear B, the mainland scripts, and the Cypro-Minoan scripts.

23. Kober (1948: 102) uses the decipherment of Egyptian hieroglyphic script as an example: "The Rosetta Stone was found in 1799. Champollion began his intensive work in 1814, but it was not till 1824 … that he was able to publish convincing proof that he had found the clue to the decipherment of Egyptian." Chadwick (1959: 26) offers a similar perspective: a bilingual inscription could offer immense help to the process.

24. Chadwick 1959.

25. The exact time period is not clear in the novel, but context and the characterization of the Scriveners make them likely candidates.

26. See Chadwick (1959: 15–16).

27. Evacuation of the team on Quraqua begins in June 2202; Maggie Tufu sends her translation of the inscription in a message on 19 October 2202.

28. Whittaker (2005: 31) describes the "stamped typeface" and the "enigmatic" nature of the Disk. Chadwick (1959: 19) describes the Disk and its proto-printing "use of standard forms". For further discussion of the Disk, see Duhoux 2000, Ephron 1962, Mackay 1965, Pomerance 1976, Schwartz 1959a, b, c, and Timm 2004.

29. On Hercules as culture hero, see Papadimitropoulos (2008: 131). On the concept of the culture hero in Greek myth, see Delcourt and Rankin 1965 and Thomas (1989: 205, 280n129). For 'ancient astronauts' as culture heroes, see Grünschloß (2007: 14).

30. On Hercules, see Bowra (1952a: 95). Cf. Pindar, *Nemean* 1.37–47 for one of our earliest references to the infant Hercules strangling the snakes sent by Hera to kill him; see Gantz (1993: 377) and Stafford (2012: 52–53).

31. Stafford (2012: 23–30).

32. On the 'ancient astronaut' theory, see Andersson 2012, Grünschloß (2007: 14), Hiscock (2012: 164–165), Rathje (1978: 4–5), and Richter (2012: 223). For a more direct treatment, see the works of Erich von Däniken, in particular his 1968 treatise, *Erinnerungen an die Zukunft* (title translated as *Chariots of the Gods*); a literal translation of the title, *Memories of the Future*, corresponds to the kind of fictional retrospective future we see in *Engines*. On the meaning of von Däniken's title, see Cohn 2015.

33. Richter (2012: 234) calls this *interpretatio technologica*.

34. Grünschloß (2007: 7); Calder 1980 recounts an anecdote about Wilamowitz dressing up as Mrs Schliemann at a party and reciting faux-Homeric verses about the discovery of 'Priam's Treasure'.

35. On Hercules as constellation, see Dionysius of Halicarnassus *Antiquitates Romanae* 1.41.

36. Porter (2002: 71).

37. Calder (1981: 247) cites an anecdote about Schliemann deforming his son Agamemnon's face to make it more 'classical' in appearance.

PART II
DISPLACED IN SPACE

CHAPTER 5
'LYRA'S ODYSSEY' IN PHILIP PULLMAN'S
HIS DARK MATERIALS TRILOGY
Ortwin Knorr

Philip Pullman's bestselling fantasy trilogy, *His Dark Materials* (*HDM*), published between 1995 and 2000, is a remarkable example of creative adaptation and an intertextual tour de force.[1] Pullman conceived it as a "*Paradise Lost* for teenagers in three volumes".[2] Yet his work engages a plethora of other intertexts apart from Milton's epic, including one whose importance is still widely underappreciated – namely, Homer's *Odyssey* (*Od.*). So far, the few scholars who have considered the *Odyssey* in the context of Pullman's trilogy have focused almost exclusively on the third book, *The Amber Spyglass* (*AS*), with its obvious allusions to earlier Underworld journeys, including Odysseus's encounter with the dead (*Od.* book 11).[3] Readers have overlooked, however, that Homer's entire epic plays a central role in Pullman's work. The reason for this omission may be that the British writer has turned Homer's adult male hero, the cunning king of Ithaca, into a pre-pubescent girl, clever little Lyra, who is only eleven years old at the outset of the trilogy (*The Golden Compass* [*GC*] 238). In addition, Pullman replaces Odysseus's mythical but still recognizably Mediterranean environment with a fantastic multiverse of many parallel worlds. Moreover, his Lyra is not simply a female copy of Homer's Odysseus displaced into a new genre, the modern fantasy novel. The Homeric echoes in Pullman's text emphasize Lyra's specific nature as a heroine for whom her home and family remain a shifting and elusive goal. Whereas Odysseus famously manages to regain his former home, his family, and his royal status, Lyra's 'Odyssey' ends in the permanent yet inevitable displacement of growing up. In this chapter, I focus first on the connections between Odysseus's and Lyra's characters. Then I analyse the trilogy's references to the Telemachy, the coming-of-age story of Odysseus's son, Telemachus. Third, I discuss the themes of homecoming and displacement in the trilogy. Throughout, I address what effect Pullman's displacement of the Homeric plot and characters has on our appreciation of *His Dark Materials*.

'Lyra's Odyssey'

The entire *HDM* trilogy shows so many echoes of Homer's *Odyssey* that it deserves the subtitle 'Lyra's Odyssey'. The initial clue of Pullman's interest in the Homeric epic appears on the very first page of the trilogy, where Pullman introduces the figure of Pantalaimon, Lyra's dæmon (*GC* 3).[4] In Lyra's world, a universe parallel to ours, humans are always accompanied by their personal dæmon.[5] Not unlike Pinocchio's 'Official Conscience'

Jiminy Cricket in the 1940 Disney movie *Pinocchio*, these dæmons constantly converse and argue with their humans.[6] They are so closely linked to their humans that a human's death automatically results in that of her dæmon (e.g., *GC* 104). In other words, Pullman's dæmons are the external manifestation of a human's soul or conscience in animal shape. The character of a human's dæmon and the type of animal on which it settles after puberty reflect that human's innermost nature (167).[7] Accordingly, Lyra's dæmon reveals what kind of person Lyra is.

In Lyra's case, the same is also true of her dæmon's name, Pantalaimon. Derived from ancient Greek, the name also subtly links Lyra to Homer's Odysseus. The first part of the name, the prefix παν- (*pan-*), means 'all'. The second part, ταλαι- (*talai-*), seems to be derived from τάλας, τάλαινα, τάλαν (*talas, talaina, talan,* 'suffering, enduring').[8] The third part, -μων (-*mōn*), is a common Greek adjective suffix. In short, the name Pantalaimon signifies something like 'all-suffering, all-enduring'.[9] Accordingly, the name of Lyra's dæmon closely resembles the nearly synonymous adjective or epithet that Homer frequently (and exclusively) uses in connection with Odysseus, namely πολύτλας (*polytlas*) or "much-suffering" (e.g., Homer *Iliad* [*Il.*] 8.97; *Od.* 5.171 and *passim*). As Lyra's dæmon and constant companion, Pantalaimon functions like the physical incarnation of a Homeric epithet.

That said, the name Pantalaimon also signals the extent to which Lyra differs from Odysseus. Replacing the prefix *poly* with *pan* seems only a subtle shift from 'much' to 'all'. Yet it declares that Pullman's Lyra is not just a simple copy of Homer's Odysseus. On the contrary, her dæmon's name foreshadows that the adventures of Pullman's child protagonist are going to surpass those of the ancient Greek hero. In particular, Pantalaimon's name prepares the reader for Lyra's visit to the World of the Dead. There, Lyra and Pantalaimon do not just suffer much, they 'suffer all', that is, the worst that can happen to a human and her dæmon in Lyra's world: they have to endure the painful rupture of the invisible physical bond that ties them together (*AS* 283–286). Lyra voluntarily submits to a harrowing near-death experience whereas Homer's Odysseus emerges physically unaffected from his encounter with the dead.

Readers who pick up on the significance of Pantalaimon's name will soon notice a number of other points of contacts between *HDM* and the *Odyssey*. One is that little Lyra turns out to be a veteran warrior, just like Odysseus. The children of Lyra's Oxford are constantly "engaged in deadly warfare" (*GC* 35) against each other. For example, the kids from Lyra's Jordan College battle children associated with other colleges, or all the college kids band together to fight the townies. In these battles, Lyra frequently assumes leadership roles. In one instance, she negotiates a temporary truce between college kids and townies so that they can jointly attack the children of the socially inferior brickburners (ibid.). Another time, she commands a raid on the boat of a Gyptian family (36). Lyra's wars only involve children, but, in her way, she is a seasoned commander of troops.

As a commander, however, Lyra also differs from Odysseus, as anyone aware of *HDM*'s Odyssean intertext is bound to notice. Lyra does not struggle with the same kind of leadership problems Odysseus does. Odysseus's men repeatedly disobey him. After raiding the Cicones, for example, they refuse to leave town and instead want to celebrate their victory (*Od.* 9.44) – a decision for which seventy-two men pay with their lives, six from each of Odysseus's twelve ships (9.60; cf. 159). Later, when Odysseus's ship is within sight of Ithaca, his men, jealous that the keeper of the winds, Aeolus, gave only Odysseus a present, open the bag of winds and unleash a storm that drives them far away from home (10.34–49). Finally, Odysseus's men disregard his warnings and eat the cattle of the sun god Helios, a sacrilege that costs all of them their lives (12.260–419). Lyra's friends, in contrast, not only obey her; once, when kids from another college have captured her, they sneak into enemy territory to rescue her (*GC* 35). On occasion, Lyra even inspires enemies to follow her lead. For example, when Billy Costa, a little Gyptian, disappears, presumably abducted by the Gobblers, Lyra organizes a search for the missing child that involves both her Jordan college friends and their "enemies", the Gyptian kids (57). In short, Lyra seems to be a more inspiring leader than the hero from Ithaca.

In addition to being leaders, Lyra and Odysseus also share the experience of fantastic adventures in far-flung lands. Odysseus's most famous adventure is his near-fatal encounter with the Cyclops, Polyphemus (*Od.* 9.177–535). At first, as Odysseus and his crew enter the Cyclops's cave, they are unaware what kind of creature resides there. After seeing the immense size of everything inside, however, the men start to worry and want to leave as soon as they have raided the Cyclops's stores. Odysseus, though, becomes curious and insists on staying "in order to see him and find out if he'd give me gifts" (ὄφρ᾽ αὐτόν τε ἴδοιμι καὶ εἴ μοι ξείνια δοίη; 229). Odysseus's ill-advised curiosity and greed cost six of his men their lives, even if his ingenuity then allows him to escape the Cyclops's clutches with the rest of his party. Worse still, once he deems himself safely out of the Cyclops's reach, Odysseus feels the urge to taunt the monster and tell him his true name (502–505). Odysseus's boastfulness then enables the Cyclops to call on his father Poseidon for help and curse Odysseus and his companions (526–535). Overall, this episode shows Odysseus's leadership skills in a rather ambiguous light.

In comparison, Pullman's Lyra acquits herself far better against the Gobblers. These Gobblers are the trilogy's equivalent of Homer's man-eating Cyclops because they acquired their name from being, as Gyptian kids explain to Lyra, "cannaboles" who eat kids: "They gobble 'em up" (*GC* 56).[10] A few weeks later, after the Gobblers have kidnapped Lyra's best friend, Lyra is staying in the apartment of a brilliant female explorer, Mrs Coulter, whose expedition to the Arctic Lyra hopes to join in order to find and free Roger. There Lyra not only learns by chance that the Gobblers are an organization of the Church, the General Oblation Board, but also that Mrs Coulter is herself intimately involved with them (89). Unlike Odysseus, Lyra then immediately runs away. Her wise decision to flee at this point rather than stick around enables Lyra to liberate not only her friend Roger from his imprisonment but numerous other children as well.

The people who help Lyra on her flight from Mrs Coulter and her Gobbler associates, the Gyptians, invite comparisons with Homer's Phaeacians. These Gyptians are a nomadic, seafaring community of East Anglia and travel on canal boats across Lyra's England. Some Gyptians come to Lyra's rescue just as two men with nets are trying to capture her (*GC* 97–103). Unlike Homer's Phaeacians, Pullman's Gyptians do not possess magic boats, but in many other ways they recall Homer's master sailors. Most importantly, Homer's

Phaeacians offer Odysseus temporary rest from Poseidon's persecution, and they convey him back to Ithaca unharmed (*Odyssey* books 6–13). Pullman's Lord Faa, the king of the Gyptians, similarly provides Lyra with temporary sanctuary from the clutches of the Church and Mrs Coulter. The Gyptians cannot bring Lyra back home, however, because Oxford is no longer safe for her. Instead, they take Lyra along with them on their dangerous journey to the far North, where they hope to free their children from the Gobblers.

Lyra's and the Gyptians' destination in the North, Bolvangar, is another place with Homeric echoes. A remote, fortified research station whose name means "the fields of evil" (*GC* 187), Bolvangar is Pullman's version of the Cyclops's cave. Here the Gobblers subject the children they have kidnapped to human experiments that ultimately kill them. Read against the Homeric intertext, this episode reveals that Lyra surpasses Odysseus here as well because she manages to sneak both into and out of Bolvangar. Odysseus famously tricks the Cyclops by assuming a false name, 'No One' (Οὖτις: *Od.* 9.366). Lyra also assumes a false identity, that of slow and dim-witted Lizzy Brooks, the daughter of a fur trader (*GC* 237), but she uses it to infiltrate the station, not as part of an escape plan. When Lyra finally makes her getaway, she rescues not just her friend, Roger, but also all the other children that the Gobblers have imprisoned (302). Odysseus, by contrast, manages to save only half of the men that had entered the cave with him.

Other differences from Homer similarly show off Lyra to her advantage. In Homer, Odysseus makes the Cyclops sleepy by giving him strong wine. He then blinds the sleeping Cyclops by ramming a fire-hardened, burning-hot wooden stake into the giant's single eye (*Od.* 9.375–394). Lyra does not drug her captors. Instead, she blinds them first metaphorically, then literally. In the first instance, she also works with fire: she sets a diversionary fire in the kitchen that distracts (that is, metaphorically blinds) the Gobbler personnel (*GC* 287). Later, she blinds her enemies in a literal, if temporary way, when the kids try to run away and heavily armed Tartar guards block their escape. "[The Tartars] were all in padded mail, and they had no eyes – or at least you couldn't see any eyes behind the snow slits of their helmets" (269). Lyra realizes that the helmet slits offer the soldiers only limited vision. She succeeds in blocking her opponent's sight completely by throwing a snowball right at his eye slit. All the other children join in, and "in a few moments the Tartars were stumbling about, spitting and cursing and trying to brush the packed snow out of the narrow gap in front of their eyes" (290). Lyra's quick thinking and ingenuity match that of Odysseus, but the scene also comically inverts its Homeric intertext. Rather than with hot fire, Pullman's Lyra blinds her visually challenged captors with the opposite of fire, an icy snowball.

Another major adventure that Lyra shares with Odysseus is her journey to the World of the Dead. This episode recalls not just Odysseus's encounter with the dead in *Odyssey* book 11, but conflates and reworks several other famous literary Underworld trips as well, in particular those in Vergil's *Aeneid* 6 and Dante's *Inferno*. Since other scholars have already discussed Pullman's reworking of older traditions here in some detail, I will keep my discussion of this episode brief.[11]

Pullman alerts his readers to the Odyssean subtext of Lyra's visit to the Underworld almost from the start. The leader of the Harpies who tries to stop Lyra from entering the

World of the Dead is called "No-Name" (*AS* 260). This is a striking, if displaced, allusion to the pseudonym "No One" that Odysseus uses in the Cyclops's cave (*Od.* 9.366).

More important is that Lyra does not make the dead come to her, like Odysseus, but enters the Underworld herself. While Odysseus succeeds in conjuring up the ghosts of the dead with the blood of animals he sacrifices, Lyra sacrifices herself. In order to see her friend Roger and apologize to him for unwittingly delivering him to his death, she voluntarily submits to a kind of half-death that is similar to the painful intercisions to which the Gobblers had subjected the children at Bolvangar (*AS* 281–287).

For both Lyra and Odysseus, the Underworld episodes represent important turning points. Odysseus meets the ghosts of Agamemnon and Tiresias and learns from them the only way to survive the impending encounter with Penelope's suitors: he cannot confront them openly like a hero, but must assume a disguise, tell lies, and bide his time. Lyra's experience in the Underworld, by contrast, inverts the Homeric parallel. Lyra is a practised liar, and she tries to talk her way into the Underworld by telling the Harpies a vastly inflated story of her adventures, just as she has done numerous times before in front of other audiences.[12] Odysseus is a similarly skilled liar; once he tries to fool even Athena, his patron goddess, with one of his 'Lying Tales'. Yet in contrast to Athena, who reacts to Odysseus's lies with amusement and admiration (*Od.* 13.291–292), the leader of the Harpies responds to Lyra's fabrications by attacking the girl with her claws and screaming, "Liar! Liar! Liar!" (*AS* 292): "And it sounded as if her voice were coming from everywhere, and the words echoed back from the great wall in the fog, muffled and changed, so that she seemed to be screaming Lyra's name, so that *Lyra* and *liar* were one and the same thing."

Up to this point in the trilogy, lying has already been an essential part of Lyra's identity. Lyra lies often, and she is good at it. In London, for example, she frightens off a potential child molester by telling him that she's waiting for her dad, a professional murderer (*GC* 100).[13] In the fen town of the Gyptians, she impresses an audience of children with her trumped-up version of the attempted poisoning of Lord Asriel (*GC* 130–131). Later in Bolvangar, after Mrs Coulter recognizes her at the last minute and saves her from the intercision machine, Lyra conceals the fact that she ran away from Mrs Coulter's apartment in London by inventing a story about having been abducted by Gobblers (281). So Lyra is a practised liar. Moreover, she enjoys the challenge of lying convincingly. While she is trying to fool her mother in Bolvangar, Lyra muses (ibid.):

> [N]ow that she was doing something difficult and familiar and never quite predictable, namely lying, she felt a sort of mastery again, the same sense of complexity and control that the alethiometer gave her. She had to be careful not to say anything obviously impossible; she had to be vague in some places and invent plausible details in others; she had to be an artist, in short.

Lyra considers her lying an art form. Not surprisingly, she is rather proud of it. Later, she even boasts in front of Will that she is "the best liar there ever was" (*SK* 103).

In Pullman's World of the Dead, however, Lyra learns a lesson about lying that is diametrically opposed to what Odysseus takes away from his own sojourn among the dead. Purely by accident, she discovers that she needs to stop lying and tell the truth. After forcing her way into the Underworld past the Harpies, Lyra encounters the ghosts of many dead children who have almost forgotten what is was like to be alive. They beg her to tell them about the world of the living. Moved by pity, Lyra tries to describe the world above to her deceased age-mates as truthfully as she can. Her truthful account captures the essence of being alive as a child so powerfully that even the Harpies are "spellbound" (AS 315). As a result, the Harpies agree to a truce. In the future, they will give a chance to escape the World of the Dead to all the dead who agree to give them a truthful and nourishing account of their life. They will then guide the ghosts to the place in the Underworld where Will with his magic knife has cut an opening into the world of the living. In this way, the dead can dissolve back into the universe and again become part of all living things (AS 318). In sum, Lyra learns that the truth can be even more powerful than her masterful tall tales; it can set one free, even from death.[14]

Although several of Lyra's adventures recall Odysseus's travels, Pullman has also made sure that Lyra does not follow the waystations of Odysseus's journey too closely. Consequently, several of the most famous challenges from the Odyssey, like the Sirens or Scylla and Charybdis, do not appear in HDM. Lyra also encounters people and creatures that are very different from any in the Odyssey, such as the foul-smelling cliff-ghasts, armoured polar bears (panserbjørne), flying witches, and cruel Tartars. Moreover, Lyra travels much farther than Odysseus. Odysseus reaches many half-magic, uncharted lands after a gigantic storm drives him away from the Peloponnese. These strange places, however, resemble his own world closely enough that later generations tried to track his journey around the Mediterranean, equating, for example, the island of the Cyclopes with Sicily and the land of the Phaeacians with Corcyra.[15] Lyra, in contrast, crosses into completely different worlds that exist outside her own world. One of these worlds, the world of Cittàgazze, the City of the Magpies, does resemble the Mediterranean, but it is ravaged by frightening, soul-sucking Specters. Another world is inhabited by creatures unlike anything Odysseus encounters, the Mulefa. They are gentle, cow-like beings with horns and trunks, and they move around on giant wheel-shaped seed-pods. Lyra's world is part of a multiverse of innumerable worlds that exist side by side, much larger than that of Odysseus.

In addition to their travels, Lyra and Odysseus also have in common being pursued by a vengeful adversary with religious associations. Odysseus's pursuer is the sea god Poseidon. Because Odysseus blinded Poseidon's son, the Cyclops, the sea god hounds him until he finally manages to leave the god's realm. Pullman replaces Homer's divine nemesis with a human religious institution. The Magisterium of the Calvinist Church, the source of all power in Lyra's world, pursues her and her friend Will. The Church tries to prevent Lyra from fulfilling her mission as the 'Second Eve' by sending an assassin priest after her. Lyra, however, is fated to reenact the 'Fall of Man' together with Will and thus to save the world (AS 67–68, 464). Poseidon's wrath concerns only him and Odysseus. Lyra's struggle against the Church, however, has implications that reach far beyond the girl's own fate.

As a result, the showdowns that conclude both Homer's *Odyssey* and Pullman's trilogy are very different in scale and effect. Odysseus almost singlehandedly overcomes an incredibly superior force of 108 suitors, and he is rewarded by regaining control of his own home. The showdown in Pullman's work features gigantic armies on both sides and, in the end, Lyra and her allies wrest control of the multiverse from the evil angel Metatron and kill both him and "the Authority" (aka God) in whose name he had been fighting (*AS* 403–410). Even more important is that Lyra and Will have their first and only sexual encounter in the battle's aftermath. Somehow, their tryst reverts the flow of cosmic Dust so that it again falls to earth and nourishes all living beings (470). In effect, Odysseus restores only his own family and fortune, whereas Lyra and Will save the entire multiverse.

Echoes of the Telemachy

Given how clearly Pullman's trilogy reworks the *Odyssey*, it cannot surprise that he has also created a character whose experiences recall those of Odysseus's son Telemachus. In fact, *HDM* contains two such characters. One of them is Lyra, the other is her friend Will. Both, however, differ from Homer's Telemachus in significant ways.

In the *Odyssey*, Telemachus goes on a quest to visit Odysseus's old comrades, Nestor, and Menelaus, to find out if his father is still alive. From both, he hears stories about his father's past heroic exploits (*Odyssey* books 3 and 4). Menelaus also informs Telemachus of a prophesy he received during his travels that Odysseus is trapped on the island of Calypso and has no means of getting home (4.555–560). Yet instead of trying to find this island and free his father, Telemachus then simply returns home.

Unlike Telemachus, Lyra at once decides she wants to rescue her uncle, Lord Asriel, when she learns that the Church keeps him imprisoned in the North, guarded by ferocious armoured bears (*GC* 95, 109, 119). Along the way, she learns from the king of the Gyptians, Lord Faa, that Lord Asriel is not just her uncle, but actually her father (121). Just like Telemachus, who gets to know his father better through the stories he hears from King Nestor, King Menelaus, and Queen Helen, Lyra learns from Lord Faa about her father's bravery and daring. She hears how Lord Asriel saved her live when she was a baby (122–124) and how he has repeatedly stood up for the Gyptians, defended their rights, and risked his own life to save those of Gyptian children (135). All this serves to reinforce Lyra's resolve to rescue her father and to bring him her alethiometer, a rare scientific instrument that once belonged to him (302–303).

The reunion of Lyra and her father, however, turns out very differently from that of Telemachus and Odysseus. Telemachus sees Odysseus after Athena has just given him a magic makeover. The older man looks so impressive that Telemachus becomes afraid of him, thinking he is facing a god (*Od.* 16.181–185). Odysseus needs to reassure him that he is indeed his father who has finally returned before they hug each other and cry (186–219).

Pullman has reversed this situation in ways that are bound to disturb anyone aware of the Odyssean references. In *HDM*, it is the father who inexplicably reacts with shock when he suddenly faces his child. Lord Asriel staggers back from Lyra in horror and cries "Get out! ... Turn around, get out, go! *I did not send for you!*" (GC 364, italics in the original). He only calms down when he sees that Lyra has not come alone but brought her friend Roger along. The reason for Asriel's mysterious reaction only becomes clear the next day. It turns out that he needs to kill a child as part of a scientific experiment that would create a temporary bridge between two parallel worlds and, for a moment, he thought he had to kill his own daughter (380). While Telemachus encounters a lost father who looks even more impressive than he could ever have imagined him, Lyra's father turns out to be a mad scientist who betrays his daughter in the worst way possible, by killing her best friend for the sake of one of his experiments.

The second character in which Pullman has reworked Homer's Telemachus figure is Lyra's friend and companion, Will Parry. Will is a twelve-year-old boy not from Lyra's world but from a world like ours. He evokes Telemachus because he also grows up as a half-orphan whose soldier father has been missing since he was a baby. John Parry, an ex-Royal Marine turned professional explorer, disappeared on an expedition to the north of Alaska in the year of Will's birth (SK 9–10; 81). Will's mother, a latter-day Penelope, has never remarried and refuses to believe that her long-missing husband is dead. The entire situation sounds as if it came straight out of Homer, except that it has been adapted to our own time.

The way Pullman has modernized many of the details of Telemachus's story in the *Odyssey* is very clever. Will cannot plausibly treat his mother the same way Telemachus does when he first asserts his new role as man of the house by telling his mother to go to her room and take care of spinning and weaving (*Od.* 1.356–359). So Pullman has her suffer from mental illness in order to explain why Will, despite his young age, is taking care of his mother and running their common household (SK 8–9). Pullman also replaces the abusive suitors that harass Penelope with secret service agents who grill Will's mother about her husband's whereabouts and are searching for the letters that Will's father sent from his final expedition (11–12). Penelope's loom has been exchanged for an old treadle sewing machine that plays an unexpectedly crucial role: one of its compartments is the place where Will's mother hid her husband's old letters (6).

Compared with Telemachus, Will appears far more mature and independent. He has had to cope with his mother's increasing paranoia since he was only seven years old (8). Not much later, Will learned to take care both of himself and of his confused mother. Fearing that the authorities could take her away from him, he shops, cooks, and does other household chores (10–11). Whereas Telemachus only ineffectually tries to assert himself and drive his mother's suitors out of his house (*Od.* 1.372–375), the much younger Will twice manages to throw secret service agents out of their house when they try to interrogate his mother (SK 11–12). The men persist, however, and surreptitiously search the house while Will and his mother are out. Again, Will takes charge even though he is no more than twelve years old at that point (71). He finds a safe place for his mother to stay, then returns to their house and discovers the letters that the men have been looking for (12, 111–114). Trying to escape unnoticed by the agents, who have again broken into his house, Will accidentally kills one of them (7). In one of the last books of the *Odyssey*, Telemachus also kills a man, but only while fighting at his father's side, during the final battle against the suitors (22.284). Will is forced to grow up and act like an adult much faster than Telemachus is.

Will's quest for his father also looks very different from Telemachus's hunt for news of Odysseus. Like Lyra, Will is interested in more than news; he wants to rescue his father (*SK* 10). Before he can do that, however, Will needs to locate him by tracking down all information about his father. Telemachus tries to do the same by travelling around the Peloponnese and talking to his father's old war buddies. Will instead goes to the public library where he finds old newspaper articles about his father's expedition (80–81), and he reads the three letters that his father wrote to his mother before he disappeared (111–114). Again, Pullman has skilfully modernized Will's research efforts.

When Will finally tracks down his father, this reunion also turns out very differently from Telemachus's first encounter with Odysseus in *Odyssey* book 16. Both teenagers encounter a worn-out old man (*Od.* 16.181–182; *SK* 321). Whereas Odysseus's beggar costume is only a disguise, however, John Parry's shaman dress reflects his actual status in Tartar society (*SK* 214). Moreover, Parry is dying because he has spent too many years in a world different from his own (*SK* 215; cf. *AS* 363, 485). Worst of all, though, the minute that Parry and Will finally recognize each other, a jealous witch shoots the old man dead (*SK* 321). Whereas Telemachus gets to enjoy a future with his dad, Will has to be content with taking up his father's shaman mantel and complete on his own the task his father gave him (324).

Homecoming and displacement

Two of the most pervasive and interrelated themes in both *Odyssey* and *HDM* are home and family. Will, for example, "longs for his father as a lost child yearns for home" (*SK* 307). At the same time, however, Pullman and Homer treat them differently. Whereas the *Odyssey* is a story about homecoming, Pullman's trilogy is a story about displacement.

In the *Odyssey*, Odysseus has only one mission: to come home to his family and resume his throne. That mission is threatened in various ways. On one hand, there are dangerous monsters and people like Scylla and Charybdis, the Sirens, the Cyclops, and the Laestrygonians, that threaten Odysseus's life and kill many of his men. In the end, they consume the entire flotilla of twelve ships with which he had set out from Troy (9.159). On the other hand, Odysseus repeatedly has to resist the lure of women who offer him substitute homes, such as the witch Circe, the nymph Calypso, and the Phaeacian princess Nausicaa. And once he escapes these temptations, he has to battle his way back to being the husband of Penelope and the undisputed ruler of Ithaca.

Lyra, in contrast, has no family to speak of almost from birth. She is the product of an adulterous love affair between two extremely ambitious and self-centred scientists, Lord Asriel and Mrs Coulter, and neither of her parents is interested in raising the child. By court order, Lyra is placed with the Sisters of Obedience in Watling (*GC* 123).[16] Even there, she cannot stay. Lord Asriel, opposed to anything smacking of religion, abducts the baby and entrusts its upbringing to the scholars of Jordan College instead (121). Lyra is too young to be aware of her displacement, but she is basically a lost child.

That said, for around ten years, Jordan College becomes Lyra's home (69). The Master of the college and the resident Scholars love her as if she were their own child (127). Staff members like Bernie Johansen, the pastry cook, and Mrs Lonsdale, the housekeeper, look after her (64, 125). Mrs Lonsdale, however, is often gruff and impatient with Lyra. Once, ordered to give the girl a bath and make her presentable, Mrs Lonsdale scrubs Lyra's knees so hard that they turn "bright pink and sore" (64). Moreover, the Scholars do not really know what to do with the little girl in their charge. Some try to teach her, but soon abandon this project when Lyra resists their efforts (82). As a result, Lyra grows up like a little wild "barbarian" (34). In the end, Jordan College is a substitute home that cannot fully replace a real family.

Lyra experiences what it is like to live in a family for the first time when she lives with her mother, Mrs Coulter, in London. Lyra herself, however, is unaware of Mrs Coulter's true relationship to her. She was told that her parents had died in a zeppelin accident (88). At first, Lyra enjoys that Mrs Coulter likes to spoil her. Soon, however, she feels trapped in Mrs Coulter's apartment. Then homesickness turns to horror when Lyra learns that Mrs Coulter is the mastermind behind the Gobblers that have kidnapped her friend Roger. Instead of family, she has found a fiend.

After that, Lyra finds refuge with the Gyptians, but it can only be temporary. Lyra adjusts quickly to her new environment, starts speaking like a Gyptian, and begins "to think of herself as gyptian" (112). Unlike Odysseus, who resists the temptation of staying with the Phaeacians, Lyra, who does not have a real home to return to, almost succumbs to the lure of the substitute home that the Gyptians seem to hold out to her. Yet Ma Costa, her former Gyptian nurse, sets Lyra straight (ibid.):

> "You en't gyptian, Lyra. You might pass for gyptian with practice, but there is more to us than gyptian language. There's deeps in us and strong currents. We're water people all through, and you en't, you are a fire person. What you are most like is marsh fire, that's the place you have in the gyptian scheme; you got witch oil in your soul. Deceptive, that's what you are, child".

Even among the Gyptians, who mean well with her, Lyra remains a displaced child.

When Lyra finally reaches her father, however, she feels even more lost. At first, though, it seems to her as if she has finally come home. Everything about the stately house on Svalbard where Lord Asriel spends his exile reminds Lyra of Jordan College, the "coal fire blazing in a stone grate; warm naphtha light glowing on carpets, leather chairs, polished wood" (364). The illusion of home is so strong it brings "a choking gasp to her throat" (ibid.). Her father, however, reacts not with joy, but with horror to her unexpected presence (ibid.), and he is not even interested in the alethiometer that Lyra has brought him at great sacrifice (365). Disappointed and hurt, Lyra scolds her father (368):

"You en't human, Lord Asriel. You en't my *father*. My *father* wouldn't treat me like that. Fathers are supposed to love their daughters, en't they? You don't love me, and I don't love you, and that's a fact. I love Farder Coram, and I love Iorek Byrnison; I love an armored bear more than I love my father. And I bet Iorek Byrnison loves me more'n you do."

During her journeys, Lyra does indeed meet a number of men who are better fathers than her actual birth father. One of them is the aeronaut Lee Scoresby, who promises the witches that he will try to be a better parent to Lyra than her real parents (*SK* 52). At the end of the second book, Lee even sacrifices his life for Lyra's sake, explaining, "I love that little child like a daughter. If I'd had a child of my own, I couldn't love her more" (299). Singlehandedly, he holds off a platoon of Church soldiers pursuing Will's father, John Parry, because Parry assures him that his sacrifice will ultimately help Lyra (299). What Lee cannot provide Lyra is a home because Lee, a displaced Texan, himself lives far from home.

Lyra's second ersatz-father is the *panserbjørn* Iorek Byrnison. He cannot offer Lyra a home either since he too lives in exile. In fact, it is Lyra who restores Iorek to his home and throne. Using her mastery of lying, she manages a near-impossible feat and tricks the usurper of the bear throne, King Iofur Raknison, into agreeing to a duel with Iorek that Raknison loses. In gratitude, Iorek bestows a new name on the girl, "Lyra Silvertongue", baptizing her, as it were, like a father (*GC* 348). After that, Lyra could live with him in Svalbard but she realizes that she is not a bear and so "wouldn't really fit in there" (*AS* 514).

Will, who is only slightly older than herself, seems to offer Lyra the opportunity to found her own family and home. She and Will first become friends, then lovers. Together, they harrow hell (*AS* 417–418) and replay the Fall of Man (465–466). In the end, though, they have to separate. Humans cannot live in any other world than their own without getting sick after some time (*AS* 363, 485). So Will and Lyra have to say goodbye and live separate lives (488). Instead of establishing a life and home with Will, Lyra needs to return to her own world where she imagines herself living a bit like Penelope except that she has no hope of ever seeing Will again (517).

At the trilogy's end, Lyra returns to Oxford and Jordan College, but now she experiences the displacement of growing up. She tells the Master and Dame Hannah, the head of a women's college: "I came back to Jordan because this used to be my home, and I didn't have anywhere else to go. [...] But really, I don't know what to do anymore. I'm lost, really, now" (514). Lyra has gotten too old to return to her old, unrestrained life at Jordan College. It is time for her to think about her education and her future. Lured by the idea that she could regain by hard work and study her former ability to read the alethiometer, Lyra agrees to join St Sophia, Dame Hannah's college. St Sophia might not become her home, Dame Hannah suggests, but it could become her school (515).

Conclusion

Pullman's fantasy trilogy, *His Dark Materials*, is even more complex and multi-layered than scholars have realized so far. The trilogy not only reworks Milton's *Paradise Lost*, it also responds to Homer's *Odyssey*. In particular, Pullman's protagonists, Lyra and Will, invite us to read them in contrast to Homeric figures such as Odysseus and Telemachus. Compared with their Homeric counterparts, Pullman's characters emerge as even better leaders, more independent, and more mature. Moreover, readers who set Pullman's text against the Homeric epic will notice that Homer's *Odyssey* is a story about a homecoming, whereas Pullman's trilogy focuses on Lyra's inability to find a true home and family and on the displacement of growing up.

Notes

1. For surveys on Pullman's intertextuality, see Lenz (2001: 123–126) and Squires (2006: 115–137). On his use of Milton, William Blake, and Heinrich von Kleist, see Pullman's acknowledgements at the end of *The Amber Spyglass* (*AS* 520) and the essays by Shohet, Scott, and Matthews in Lenz and Scott 2005. On his use of C. S. Lewis and Tolkien, see Hatlen 2005, Smith 2005, and Kölzer 2008.

2. Parsons and Nicholson (1999: 126); cf. Pullman's statement in Eccleshare (1996: 15). The title of the trilogy, *His Dark Materials*, quotes from *Paradise Lost* 2.916.

3. On the resemblance between Lyra's journey to the World of the Dead and the Underworld episodes in Homer, Vergil, and Dante, see Jacobs 2000, Lenz (2001: 133), and Holderness (2007: 279); Syson 2017 focuses only on Vergil. *En passant*, Michael Chabon has also compared Lyra's flights of fancy in the Underworld with Odysseus's 'Lying Tales' (2005: 13).

4. Quotations come from the title and page numbers of the first American edition. In the United Kingdom, *GC* is known by its original title, *Northern Lights*.

5. Pronounced like the English word 'demon'; cf. Pullman's note before the table of contents in *GC*. On the link between this pronunciation and the demons in the poetry of Blake, see Matthews (2005: 129–130).

6. In *Pinocchio*, a fairy appoints Jiminy Cricket as Pinocchio's conscience, and at the end he is awarded with a golden 'Official Conscience' badge. A nameless talking cricket with a similar, but much shorter role, already appears in the 1883 book that inspired the Disney movie, Carlo Collodi's *The Adventures of Pinocchio*. Robert Butler has noticed a talking insect sidekick in Pullman's illustrated children's novel, *Spring-Heeled Jack* (1991), where "a mournful moth flutters around as the villain's conscience", and argues that it prefigures the author's later concept of dæmons (Butler 2007). The *daimonion* of Socrates in Plato's *Apology*, which is often named as a possible inspiration for Pullman – see, e.g., Bruner and Ware (2007: 16) – differs in that it has no body but is a mere voice in Socrates' head (*Apology* 31c7–d2). Moreover, it speaks to the philosopher only when it needs to warn him against making a morally bad decision.

7. Every dæmon "communicates to the reader an immediate impression of a character's essence"; Lenz (2001: 139). For recent, comprehensive discussions of dæmons, see Frost (2008: 263–272) and Kölzer (2008: 285–289).

8. Solhaug (2008: 322) instead wants to link Pantalaimon's name to the Greek god Pan and to Panteleimon (i.e., Παντελεήμων), the Greek name of St Pantaleon, meaning 'all-compassionate'.

Tucker (2007: 141) similarly translates the name as 'all-merciful'; neither of them explains how the stem *eleē-* could turn into *alai*.

9. It should not concern us too much that the name Pantalaimon does not occur in real ancient Greek. According to Liddell and Scott (LSJ), the standard Greek–English dictionary, only two synonymous adjectives exist, *pantalas* and *pantlēmōn*, which LSJ translates 'all-wretched', although 'all-suffering' would be equally appropriate. Pullman takes similar liberties with names derived from Latin or Italian; e.g., Lord Asriel's snow leopard dæmon is called Stelmaria (*GC* 11), not *stella maris*, 'Star of the Sea'. Similarly, the City of the Magpies would have to be Città di Gazze in Italian, not Cittàgazze (*The Subtle Knife* [*SK*] 59).

10. I am grateful to my daughter, Isabelle Knorr, for pointing out the link between the gobbling Gobblers and the cannibalism of the Cyclops . . . but not the Laestrygonians?

11. For the medieval Christian background ("the Harrowing of Hell") of *AS*'s Underworld episode, see Lenz (2001: 126) and Holderness 2007. Others have claimed a link to the Greek myth of Orpheus and Eurydice (e.g., Smith [2005: 144] and Squires [2006: 129]), but the resemblances seem less significant. Several reviewers have briefly commented on the connections between Pullman's Underworld and those of Homer, Vergil, and/or Dante, e.g., Jacobs 2000, Lenz (2001: 126, 133), and Simpson (2007: 129–130). For a more detailed discussion, see Syson 2017.

12. For example, Lyra amazes the Gyptian children by telling them half-fictitious "tales of her mighty father, so unjustly made captive" (*GC* 130–131).

13. In contrast, at *Od.* 13.250–286 Odysseus pretends himself to be a murderer in exile to keep a young cowherd (Athena in disguise) from trying to steal his treasures. Ironically, Lyra's lie is truer than she herself knows because her father, Lord Asriel, did, in fact, once kill a man (*GC* 121–124), as my daughter, Isabelle Knorr, has pointed out to me.

14. On Pullman's engagement with Aeschylus's *Oresteia* in this scene, see Pullman's own comments in Mustich 2007; the scene is also discussed in, e.g., Squires (2006: 91–92), Tucker (2007: 109), Syson (2017: 244–247).

15. The ancient geographer Eratosthenes famously mocked these attempts by quipping, "one will find where Odysseus wandered when one finds the cobbler who sewed up the bag of winds" (φησὶ τότ' ἂν εὑρεῖν τινα ποῦ Ὀδυσσεὺς πεπλάνηται, ὅταν εὕρῃ τὸν σκυτέα τὸν συρράψαντα τὸν τῶν ἀνέμων ἀσκόν; Strabo *Geography* 1.2.15).

16. This placement is the starting point for *The Book of Dust*, the prequel to *HDM*.

CHAPTER 6

DISPLACING *NOSTOS* AND THE ANCIENT GREEK HERO IN HAYAO MIYAZAKI'S *SPIRITED AWAY*

Suzanne Lye

Spirited Away's opening scene depicts a farewell card addressed to a girl named Chihiro, which is nestled in a bouquet of pink flowers and held by a despondent girl in the back seat of a moving car. The girl's posture identifies her as the recipient of these gifts and communicates her resistance to her current state and to her powerlessness in the face of her parents' decision to relocate the family. The farewell card is a reminder that, while her body is in one place, her thoughts and desires are somewhere else, focused on a home the audience never sees. Chihiro is introduced as a passive character, the victim of more powerful forces (first, her parents; later, the supernatural) that control her identity and location. As she makes the transition between her old home and a new one, Chihiro and her parents inadvertently stumble into a third place – the spirit world. By introducing the audience to three locations in rapid succession, *Spirited Away* (SA) frames itself as a narrative of displacement. As details emerge about the depth of Chihiro's displacement, *SA* links dislocations in space to displacements of Greek myths into a Japanese story about the spirit world.

Scholars have long made connections between Japanese film and mythic traditions rooted in ancient Greece and Rome.[1] Classical influences on *SA* have received little attention, but *SA* engages directly and persistently with the myths of two major Greek heroes – Odysseus and Orpheus. Director Hayao Miyazaki uses Greek myths to create displacements that motivate the events of *SA* and give a broader context to his characters. In the following, I show how *SA* incorporates Greek myths and discuss Miyazaki's historical engagement with Greek myths, particularly from Homer's *Odyssey* (*Od.*). Next, I focus on how the story patterns from Greek myths lead to displacements that challenge characters' identities. I conclude by considering how Miyazaki reconfigures the myths of Odysseus and Orpheus to fit Chihiro and his own idea of the hero.[2]

Off the path and into Greek myth

Within sight of their new house, Chihiro's father Akio takes a shortcut on a smaller road, which ends at what looks like an abandoned theme park but is actually a bathhouse for the gods. Akio finds food among the empty stalls and encourages his family to eat with him. A rebellious Chihiro rejects this offer and wanders around the stalls. As the sun sets,

Fig. 6.1 Chihiro's parents turn into pigs, like Odysseus's men in the Circe episode (*Odyssey* book 10). From *Spirited Away* (dir. Miyazaki, 2001). Studio Ghibli.

ghostly images emerge around her. Frightened, she runs back to her parents only to find that they have been turned into pigs (Fig. 6.1). Lost and afraid, she tries to run away but encounters a deep body of water blocking the path to the family's car.

The transformation of Chihiro's parents into pigs is the first indication of the film's connection to Greek myth. The motif borrows directly from the famous Circe episode in Homer's *Odyssey*, where Odysseus's companions turn into pigs after eating her enchanted feast. Miyazaki thus frames *SA* within the context of Greek myth and analogizes Chihiro's character to Odysseus. Her story ends, however, not with a return to a beloved home but with acceptance that her original home cannot be recaptured and that her displacement is permanent. Through references to the *Odyssey*, Miyazaki plays with the ancient narrative motif of *nostos* ('homecoming'). With this Greek concept as an underpinning, he constructs Chihiro's journey as a 'displaced homecoming'. By denying Chihiro a full homecoming, Miyazaki challenges the *Odyssey*'s ideas that *nostos* restores order and marks the success of a hero. Instead, the filmmaker suggests that one's 'sense of place' can reside within the individual, divorced from ties to a physical location.

Miyazaki's connection to Greek myth

Miyazaki and his production company Studio Ghibli have a history of using ancient Greek myths and folklore as source materials for his films. *Nausicaä of the Valley of the Wind* (*Nausicaä*) is the most obvious example, as Miyazaki has said in interviews that he combined a Japanese folktale called *The Princess Who Loved Insects* with the personality of Homer's Phaeacian princess Nausicaä.[3] In the introduction to the manga series

Nausicaä, whose initial publication predates the movie, Miyazaki describes his first encounter with Greek myths and the *Odyssey*:

> Nausicaä was a Phaecian [*sic*] princess in *The Odyssey*. I have been fascinated by her ever since I first read about her in Bernard Evslin's Japanese translation of a small dictionary of Greek mythology. Later, when I actually read *The Odyssey*, I was disappointed not to find the same splendor there as I had found in Evslin's book. So, as far as I am concerned, Nausicaä is still the girl Evslin described at length in his paperback. I can tell that he was particularly fond of Nausicaä as he devoted three pages to her in his small dictionary, but gave only one page to both Zeus and Achilles.[4]

Miyazaki is thus familiar with the famous episodes of Odysseus's journey and tries to find synergies between Greek and Japanese myths. Additionally, he approves of Evslin's creative licence in expanding the personality of the young princess and in eliciting a more emotional response from his audience than the Homeric original.

Miyazaki's familiarity with the ancient world can also be traced through popular media and manga's tradition of importing elements from ancient Greek myth.[5] *SA*'s continuous dialogue with the *Odyssey*, however, indicates Miyazaki intends a deeper and more direct conversation with the ancient Greek tradition than in *Nausicaä*. *SA* refigures multiple myths to create Chihiro's story via 'revisioning' and 'engagement'.[6] Of course, the film is comprehensible and enjoyable to a general audience, but reading *SA* alongside ancient Greek heroic myths sharpens Miyazaki's messages about the dangers and challenges of modern society.

Miyazaki's debt to Greek myth is explicit in some cases but also relies on the recognition of mythic tropes by his audience. In *SA*, Miyazaki follows a cinematic tradition of inserting specific references and story patterns from Greek myths into unexpected, modern settings.[7] While some references are overt, others tap into the web of myths "that have become integrated into our wider cultural discourse after percolating through the ages into story-patterns and archetypes".[8] Miyazaki cannot escape the influence of the classical sources as he engages with cinematic forebears and peers, but he goes further by invoking certain heroic stories from Greek myth that involve supernatural encounters. In *SA*, a coming-of-age story centring around a young, sheltered Japanese girl is compared primarily to the circuitous homecoming of a battle-hardened, aging Greek warrior. *SA* is a tribute to both the Greek mythic tradition and to Miyazaki's early cinematic and storytelling forebears even as it promotes a message particular to the transient and sometimes dislocated existences of people in the modern world.[9]

Miyazaki's films have a reputation for creating outlandish characters and imaginative engagements between humans and non-humans. What differentiates *SA* from his other popular animated films is *SA*'s emphasis on the strangeness of his heroine's situation and her existential dislocation via motifs involving Odysseus and heroic *katabasis* (descent into the Underworld). These motifs include: a journey to the spirit world, taboos about food, separation between the worlds of mortals and immortals, discussions with supernatural guides and gatekeepers, the importance of memory and forgetfulness, and the treatment of the spirit world as an extension of the real world, albeit a foreign one, whose practices and laws parallel those of the protagonist's home.

The major mythic sources for *SA* can thus be traced not only to the Japanese *Kojiki* but also to Homer's *Odyssey* (books 11 and 24), the *Homeric Hymn to Demeter*, and the myth of Orpheus as told in Ovid (*Metamorphoses* book 10) and Virgil (*Georgics* book 4).[10] Smaller details similar to those appearing in Aristophanes' *Frogs* also echo Miyazaki's construction of *SA*'s spirit realm, including the idea of spirits having bodily needs and the importance of remembering and following instructions so as not to get stuck forever in an undesirable place through inadvertent forgetfulness.

Displacement in *Spirited Away*

In *SA*, 'displacement' occurs when a character is moved from his or her native place to a new, unfamiliar space. Moving and leaving one's native city for a new home is not unusual in the modern world, and Chihiro's parents refer to it as a big day for the family. Chihiro, who has no decision-making power in the family, struggles, however, to come to terms with her displacement from a beloved home, possibly the only one she has known. Her feelings of being in the wrong place, physically, expand and ripple outward as the film progresses, causing a chain reaction of displacements that affects other characters and ultimately changes the power structure of the spirit realm. These events reflect back on her so that by the end of the film, she finds strength in a re-claimed human identity. Through contact with Chihiro, almost all the characters in the film 'lose their place' at some point, forgetting what initially defined them. These displacements occur physically, psychologically, or socially.

To accomplish this variety of displacements, Miyazaki uses cross-cultural displacement to connect ancient supernatural beliefs with modern problem solving. On a meta-narrative level, Miyazaki's references to Greek myths point the audience's attention to alternative narratives that encourage comparisons between values portrayed in ancient Greek myth and modern Japan. Displacement in *SA*, therefore, operates on two levels – for the characters and the audience – and refers to two phenomena: 1) moments when a character feels 'out of sorts' because they find themselves in a new location or role and 2) moments when a story pattern from Greek myth appears in the film. The first of these is easily recognized because the character either complains or acts surprised by where they are or an unexpected thing they encounter. In the latter case, the audience members who recognize the borrowed myth must situate its occurrence in the film against their knowledge of the original Greek myth.

Reading the *Odyssey* in *Spirited Away*

While *SA*'s story is set in Japan and its spirits operate within a Japanese mythic framework, Miyazaki populates his spirit world and narrative with details from supernatural encounters in Greek myths. While he displaces Japanese myths and characters in favour of those from the *Odyssey*, he also allows the modern Japanese setting to displace the expectations of the borrowed Greek myths. The replacement of Odysseus with a young girl and the lack of a true *nostos* displace the expectations of homecoming and heroic glory that analogizing *SA* to the *Odyssey* implies. As the film closes, the audience knows that she still has to face her original displacement of moving to a new home. It is only through negotiating the *Odyssey*'s idea of homecoming with the more fluid concept of 'home' in Chihiro's modern Japanese world that she and the audience can return from the spirit-world digression.

Odysseus's encounter with Circe provides the basic frame narrative for Chihiro's journey. *SA*, like the *Odyssey*, uses a sorceress's spell to generate encounters with the supernatural. Miyazaki extends this initial link into a larger engagement with a particular group of Greek myths related to Underworld encounters. In both the *Odyssey* and *SA*, the hero must make a journey to the spirit world as a result of interactions with a sorceress. Chihiro's journey to the spirit world thus engages with the story pattern of *Odyssey*'s *Nekuia* (book 11), the famous Underworld episode in which Odysseus interacts with ghosts and learns about the rules of the afterlife. Motifs from the *Nekuia* further expand the film's access to other Greek myths involving encounters with the spirit world, particularly the story of Orpheus. With each of these micro-displacements of Greek myth into *SA*, Miyazaki produces a different kind of *nostos*, which displaces his Homeric model and favours a new, more personalized definition of 'homecoming'.

The main plot of Chihiro's journey closely follows Odysseus's visit to Circe's island. After the Ogino family unwittingly enters the lair of the sorceress Yubaba, Chihiro's parents Akio and Yuuko are turned into pigs upon eating forbidden food. Chihiro finds herself trapped by a body of water that was not there when she and her parents entered the seemingly abandoned buildings. With no other recourse, she turns back and has a moment of despair as her body starts to fade. She is found by a mysterious young boy called Haku. He designates himself her protector throughout the film, originally warning Chihiro to leave with her parents but then helping her survive in the magical realm by giving her enchanted food that prevents her body from disappearing completely. With him and other supernatural companions as her guides, Chihiro embarks on her mission to rescue her parents and return to the human world. Along the way, she takes on other tasks, such as rescuing Haku and finding a home for the outcast spirit Kaonashi. During her spirit-world adventure, Chihiro's desire to return to her original 'home' is displaced in favour of a more general conceptualization of home as 'the human realm'.

In the *Odyssey*, Odysseus sends his crew to scout out signs of habitation on Aeaea, where they find the house of the goddess Circe (10.210–211), a dwelling incongruent with its wooded surroundings. Even stranger are the friendly wild animals, such as lions and wolves, that greet the men (212). Despite their fear and the hints that they are entering a supernatural realm, Odysseus's companions press on, lured by Circe's voice and promised feast. Those who enter are welcomed by the hospitality of the goddess and enjoy delicious food. They do not realize, however, that their food is enchanted and that Circe has mixed a potion to make them forget their homeland (236). Afterwards, she transforms them with her wand so that they have the "heads, voice, bristles, and form of swines", then places them in a pen, throwing them slops (233–243). The men retain their human mental faculties and mourn their displacement into animal bodies. The audience now infers that the friendly wild animals had similarly been transformed from previous travellers who had encountered the sorceress.

While Odysseus's men follow their ears, Chihiro's father follows his nose, lured by the scent of food, until he finds a stall laden with a feast. The pull of his senses overwhelms reason, such that he and his wife do not notice warning signs that the food is enchanted and their presence unwelcome. After gorging themselves, they are shown surrounded by the detritus of food and dishes, like pigs wallowing in slops, until they are chased away and later put into pigpens. Thus, Odysseus's men and Chihiro's parents fall into the same trap. The incongruity of their new animal bodies in their original human clothes emphasizes their dehumanization and underscores their displacement from the human sphere into the spirit world. Unlike Odysseus's men, however, Akio and Yuuko do not recollect their previous humanity. Only Chihiro remembers their true identities, and Haku warns that she must retain this knowledge in order to rescue them.

Once Homer's *Odyssey* enters the mindscape of *SA*, other details close the gap between the two narratives and invite viewers to split their attention between the narrative at hand and the Greek myths they refigure. The sorceress Yubaba's bathhouse, like Circe's island, is surrounded by water and approachable primarily by boat.[11] Both Yubaba and Circe pervert the expectations of hospitality by using food to change visitors' physical appearances against their will. Like Odysseus, Chihiro escapes a sorceress's magic and must use her wits along with the help of supernatural guides to rescue companions. More importantly, however, Chihiro, like Odysseus, has to remember who she is and where she comes from.

Other details strengthen connections between *SA* and the *Odyssey*. Chihiro's reluctance to accept the feast laid before her mirrors that of Odysseus's companion Eurylochus, the only man who escapes Circe's initial magical attack (*Od.* 10.231–232). Both resist the enticing feast but are powerless to prevent others from eating it. Later, Chihiro's introduction to Yubaba imitates Odysseus's approach to Circe in the *Odyssey*. Before entering Circe's house, Odysseus is given magical, protective food by the god Hermes who appears "in the likeness of a youth" (277–279). In *SA*, the youthful deity Haku plays Hermes' role by giving Chihiro special food that allows her to survive in the spirit realm. Like Hermes, Haku instructs his protégé how to defeat a malicious sorceress's schemes. In the *Odyssey*, Odysseus pulls out his sword to threaten Circe until she yields; Chihiro must endure both the initial indifference of the spider-like boiler-room manager Kamaji and the malevolent intimidation of the sorceress Yubaba to demand a job in the bathhouse so she can gain her parents' freedom.

In both the *Odyssey* and *SA*, identity is treated as a highly valued currency in the supernatural world. To stay in a sorceress's realm, both Odysseus and Chihiro must temporarily displace their identities. Odysseus becomes Circe's consort, giving up thoughts of homecoming for a year until reminded by his men (*Od.* 10.469–474). Chihiro also forgets her identity and her purpose until Haku returns her original clothes, including the farewell card with her name. *SA* makes clear that Chihiro has experienced a more explicit displacement from her identity than even Odysseus does in the *Odyssey*, and the audience discovers the fundamental impact of her contract with Yubaba. To get her job in the bathhouse, Chihiro had to relinquish her name, and thus her identity, to Yubaba, who renamed her "Sen". In the bathhouse, she fully becomes Sen, living out the life of the lowest-ranked "new girl", until she is jolted out of this alternative identity by the tokens from her previous life as Chihiro. Miyazaki cleverly changes Chihiro's name to "Sen" by showing how her signature on a contract with Yubaba transforms from one name to another. In Japanese, Chihiro's name literally means "one thousand fathoms" (荻野千尋), but when parts of her name are removed, the change produces the unique kanji "Sen" (千) meaning simply "one thousand". The character "Sen" is an intrinsic part of the name Chihiro, but only a part of her full identity. By displacing names through her magic, Yubaba displaces the memories of her victims so that they cannot escape.[12] Like Odysseus's men, whose porcine appearance belies their internal human consciousness, Chihiro's concept of self becomes disrupted with the dismemberment of her name.

Although she looks like the same girl, Chihiro's human identity becomes displaced from her consciousness the longer she is in the spirit realm. For much of the film, she *is* Sen, a clumsy employee who does not fit in with her surroundings or co-workers because of her youth, origins, and kindness. Only Haku knows her original name and complete story, and he warns Chihiro not to misplace her clothes or forget her human identity. Indeed, the threat of forgetting looms over her and the other characters. As a cautionary tale, Haku reveals that he himself is subjugated to Yubaba because his memories have been displaced, and he cannot remember his original name or identity. He must walk a fine line between his role as Yubaba's apprentice and his friendship with Chihiro, which the audience later discovers antedates his employment at the bathhouse.

Haku's conflict of identities leads to the only moment of true despair for Chihiro. After Chihiro signs her contract, Haku leads her into the main hall of the bathhouse to introduce her to the other employees, who complain about her being a human. While there, he treats her with a cruelty that makes her ask her co-worker friend Rin if there are two Hakus. The other servants defer to him with a combination of respect and fear, calling him "Master Haku", and Rin warns Chihiro, "He's Yubaba's henchman, stay away from him." In this moment, Chihiro's utter displacement from everything she knows and everyone she loves becomes visible. Haku later repairs his relationship with Chihiro privately when he shows her where her parents are being kept and comforts her with energizing food, but he cannot stop her gut-wrenching sobs. Thus Miyazaki reveals how troubling each displacement is – and how common.

Complicated characters

After remembering her name and sobbing cathartically, Chihiro moves forward with renewed purpose, leveraging her ability to exist with two identities (Chihiro and Sen) and adapting successfully to other characters and new situations, in a way reminiscent of Odysseus and his characteristic epithets *polumētis* ('many-wiled') and *polutropos* ('crafty', 'complicated'). As Sen, Chihiro adapts to the rhythms of the bathhouse and is subject to harassment by her co-workers, who shun her for being a human and deride her for being incompetent. She can barely keep up with the other workers and moves clumsily through her tasks, from cleaning the floors (she stumbles) to filling the soaking tubs (she falls in). The foreman and Yubaba assign her undesirable jobs, as happens when she is told to care for the "stink spirit", whose smell is so strong that it rots food and sickens the other spirits, who flee or turn away. Chihiro eventually discovers that the stink spirit is sick when he directs her to grab onto a "thorn" in his side. As she and others pull it out, a wave of discarded junk comes along with it, including bits of metal fencing, a barrel, and a broken bicycle. Her compassion and bravery reveal that the stink god is actually a revered river god, whose identity had been displaced. In the place of his initial form as a plodding, muddy, long-suffering stink god, he emerges as the glowing, buoyant, laughter-filled river god that he had been before his river was polluted by human activity. From this scene, we see that when Chihiro became Sen, a self-centred, whiny young girl transformed into a hardworking, compassionate, and reliable worker. Each character who enters the bathhouse discovers and expresses new aspects to their identities: Chihiro and her companions tap into multiple aspects of their identities to survive, just as Odysseus does.

Another nod to Odysseus's fluidity of identities is the character Kaonashi, who changes identities to suit his immediate environment. Kaonashi's name literally means "No-face", suggesting he has no recognizable identity, yet he later transforms into many different identities based on his surroundings. Odysseus similarly chooses to change into temporary identities and denies having any identity when calling himself 'Nobody' (*Outis*) at the Cyclops's cave (*Od.* 9.365–366).

A drifter lingering at the edges of society, Kaonashi is in an almost permanent state of displacement when he appears in the film, having no distinct core identity. When he enters the bathhouse at Chihiro's invitation, he adapts to the new environment by changing his appearance and identity to reflect the characteristics of those around him so that he embodies the workers' greed, pettiness, and sense of entitlement. Chihiro, recognizing that the bathhouse is unhealthy for Kaonashi's well-being, lures him away from the others and makes him disgorge the workers he has eaten by tricking him into eating the magical medicine she received from the river spirit. This sequence parallels the story of the overthrow of Cronus by his son Zeus in Hesiod's *Theogony*. In the Greek myth, Cronus, king of the Titans, consumes his children whole. His wife Rhea then tricks him by substituting a rock in place of their last child Zeus, whom she secrets away. Zeus eventually returns and makes his father vomit up all the offspring he had consumed (493–497). These siblings become Zeus's allies in overthrowing their father and the Titans. Similarly, Chihiro manages to make the rescued bathhouse workers her allies by the end of the film: they cheer for her when she rescues her parents and foils Yubaba's plan to trick her.

Kaonashi is an extreme example of a 'many-wiled' individual, a 'nobody' who can be 'anybody', displacing identities to fit new situations by absorbing information and substance from those around him. Only after turning away from borrowed identities does Kaonashi find his own, as a friend and companion to Chihiro and permanent helper to the sorceress Zeniba, Yubaba's estranged sister. Kaonashi represents the extreme version of the 'displacement' that the other characters in the movie experience. He has no distinct face, no home, no voice, and, at times, no body. Before Chihiro intervenes, he lives on the margins of spirit society, and other spirits fear or despise him for lacking a distinct identity. Particular music marks his presence, even when he is invisible, signifying to viewers through sound what has been displaced from sight. Finding a home with Zeniba and companions who value him removes him from the permanent state of displacement that was his fate as a "no-face" spirit.

Greek Underworld myths in *Spirited Away*

While echoes of the Circe episode recall Homer's *Odyssey*, SA is still at its core a story about an encounter with the supernatural spirit world and the heroic actions of its protagonist Chihiro as she transitions between stages of life. The *Odyssey* remains a narrative counterpoint to SA in this regard. Odysseus's encounter with Circe leads to his most challenging trial (*Od.* 10.496, 566–567): the hero and his crew must seek out the ghost of the seer Tiresias. During this encounter, Odysseus gains information to contextualize his travels, reaffirms his goal of returning home, and then returns to Circe's island before embarking on his actual journey home. Chihiro's journey throughout SA, particularly her quest to save Haku, reiterates this story pattern. Like Odysseus, she must depart from a sorceress's lair on a journey to a seemingly impossible place ruled by powerful, reportedly hostile deities. Doing so, however, gives her a deeper knowledge about herself and her motivations, reinforcing the positive changes to her character that have occurred since entering the spirit world. Chihiro similarly must return to the original sorceress's house to retrieve loved ones before being allowed to continue home.[13] By alluding to Odysseus's encounter in this way, SA also gains access to the *Odyssey*'s universe of references to other ancient Greek afterlife myths.

One feature that is common to SA and many ancient Greek spirit-world myths is 'chronotopic displacement'. In SA, at the moment the characters stumble into the spirit world and begin to lose their previous identities, they also tumble out of regular time and human space, shifting from one chronotope to another.[14] When Chihiro is employed by the bathhouse, she does not age, and her days and nights are marked by her duties as an employee of the bathhouse. It is not explicit how much time passes while she is there, only that it is long enough for her to make friends, become a valued employee, go on a mission to save her friend Haku, and complete Yubaba's trial to identify her parents from among a group of nondescript pigs. At the end of the film when she and her parents are restored to the real world, there are indications that time has moved at a different rate from what Chihiro and her parents perceived in the spirit world. While the humans have not aged, their car is overgrown and dusty, indicating they may have been in the spirit world for weeks or longer.

Identity and chronotopic displacement pervade the atmosphere of the spirit world. Both SA and the *Nekuia* include a divine mandate for a hero to enter the spirit realm to retrieve something important, the hero's disorientation due to the rapid disappearance of light, and a spirit world whose physical landscape mirrors the real world, operating under an established rule of law. In Homer, Circe orders Odysseus to cross the sea to the edge of the world of the living and get help from Tiresias (*Od.* 10.490–495). Like Chihiro, Odysseus travels through water into an increasingly murky landscape. Upon his arrival, spirits sent by Persephone, the queen of the dead, start to emerge and Odysseus gains access to their stories and hidden information (11.225–227).

Like the goddesses Circe and Persephone, the female deity Yubaba makes decisions about what occurs in her corner of the spirit world. She rules her servants and spirits with an iron hand, making clear that *SA*'s spirit realm is governed by strict laws and a political hierarchy. Yubaba herself is also bound to any contract she signs, and she, like the Greek gods, has limited power. Despite the rules and discouraging signals from the environment and other characters, Chihiro manages to find hidden pathways for getting what she needs by befriending other, less powerful spirits, such as Haku and Kamaji. Chihiro also finds assistance from Yubaba's own son Bou, who defends Chihiro from his mother's cruelty, and from her co-worker Rin, who helps her navigate her bathhouse responsibilities and the internal politics of their co-workers.

SA's supernatural guides and helpers have parallels in Greek afterlife myth, which suggest these elements are also motifs from Greek sources, since no such guides appear in the traditional Japanese Underworld myth of Izanami and Izanagi. Odysseus's divine guides, before he enters the spirit realm, are Hermes and Circe, who assist at different stages; Chihiro's are Haku and Kamaji. Other borrowed features from Greek myth are the mundanity of the spirit world and the portrayal of love as motivation for heroes to journey to the spirit world, breaking the boundary between realms. The food stalls and Yubaba's bathhouse are both commercial enterprises, recognizable from the 'real world', which is why Chihiro's parents felt so comfortable entering them without permission. Mr. Ogino, thinking that he had stumbled into an abandoned amusement park, assumed that he could take the food on display and pay for it later. His treatment of the spirit world's culture as a mirror to the human world's recalls Dionysus's conversation with Herakles in Aristophanes' *Frogs*. In this comedy, the god asks the hero for guidance and, particularly, a list of the Underworld's notable "harbors, bakeries, brothels, rest stops, detours, streams, roads, cities, lodgings, and hostesses" (112–114). Both *SA* and *Frogs* assume that characters in the human and spirit worlds have similar existences.

Indeed, Miyazaki has to prevent the spirit world from becoming too normalized and humanized for the audience when Chihiro's life as Sen becomes routine and the bathhouse characters fill recognizable human roles and designations, such as 'foreman', 'boss', and 'boyfriend'. By inserting small details such as Rin's consumption of a roasted newt, Zeniba's lamppost butler, and the partially sentient grunting and hopping heads of Yubaba's little green men, Miyazaki jolts the audience out of complacency, reminding them that they, along with Chihiro, have been displaced from everyday reality into a fantasy world.

Another way that Miyazaki reflects and displaces notions of reality in *SA* is through the relationship between Chihiro and Haku. When Haku in his dragon form returns injured from a mission and Yubaba leaves him to die, Chihiro does everything within her power to save him, soliciting the help of Kamaji and Rin in the boiler room. She feeds Haku half of the healing medicine from the river god, which leaves him unconscious and vulnerable in boy-form. Because of their bond, Chihiro abandons her original mission to rescue her parents. She chooses instead to save Haku with her special medicine and pursues a seemingly impossible quest deeper into the spirit world to ask Zeniba to lift her curse on Haku. Her love for Haku exceeds all others, and her quest to rescue him from the spirit world's version of death drives her into a story pattern that refigures the Greek myth of Orpheus and Eurydice.

Chihiro and Orpheus

Several characters notice the close relationship between Haku and Chihiro, including Kamaji, who points out to Rin that the bond between the young pair is "love". Zeniba too refers to Haku as Chihiro's boyfriend. *SA* reinforces the theme of their love across the human–spirit world barrier with a re-enactment of a crucial moment from the Greek Orpheus myth. In his final instructions, Haku tells Chihiro that she must walk through the tunnel back into the human world without looking back. By following these instructions, she would save her parents and return to the human world. The mythic poet Orpheus receives similar instructions from chthonic deities when he attempts to rescue his bride Eurydice from the spirit world. The Roman poet Ovid, in one of the most famous retellings of this Greek myth, writes that Orpheus accepts the condition (*legem*) that he not look back (*Metamorphoses* 10.50–52). A second version of this story has Persephone herself, the queen of the dead, issuing this condition (*legem*; *Georgics* 4.497), which Orpheus fails to honour as he, "conquered in spirit, looked back" (*victusque animi respexit*) before Eurydice could cross the threshold into the real world (4.491–493). As a result of his looking back when told not to do so, Eurydice is doomed to stay in the spirit world, separate from Orpheus.

The myth of Orpheus reinforces the importance of following the conditions set by deities in the spirit world. In general, Greek myths assume that the spirit world operates according to a system of laws that its residents and visitors are bound to follow. In the *Homeric Hymn to Demeter*, Persephone is tied to Hades by law because she accepts specific food that he offers to her in the Underworld. To remain in the spirit world, Chihiro must eat food given to her by Haku. This special food anchors her in the supernatural realm so that she does not fade away. Here again, Miyazaki both references and overturns the message of the original Greek myth. Whereas Persephone's consumption of food leads to additional grief because she was forced to return to Hades and separate from her mother Demeter at regular intervals, Chihiro's consumption of food saves her life and allows her to remain in the spirit realm so she can save her parents and ultimately reunite with her mother.[15]

In the case of the Orpheus story, the rulers of the dead set the laws, which Orpheus and the ghost of Eurydice must follow.[16] Similarly, several characters in *SA* talk about the laws and oaths that are required of them. These rules keep the bathhouse running, Yubaba in power, and the spirit world in order. Indeed, Haku relies on these laws to help Chihiro complete the rescue of her parents. Although Japanese myths have the idea of rules governing the spirit world, the level of attention and specific laws that *SA* features all suggest that *SA* is invoking specifically Greek mythic tropes as well as Japanese sources.

Conclusion

Spirited Away appears fresh, familiar, and surprisingly modern to audiences because of its conceptualization of the spirit world along modern, capitalistic lines, but its universal appeal is rooted to a large extent in its incorporation of Greek myths.[17] The proprietress Yubaba and her bathhouse managers are obsessed with making money and are motivated by financial gain. Chihiro's triumph refutes values rooted in acquiring money and power and comes instead from her uniquely human attributes of bravery, intelligence, friendship, and persistence. Miyazaki confirms this, saying that *Spirited Away* is "not a story in which the characters grow up, but a story in which they draw on something already inside them, brought out by the particular circumstances".[18]

Miyazaki shows the audience Chihiro's innate qualities by putting her through the trials of a hero, as conceived from the ancient Greek myths of Odysseus and Orpheus. As an "ordinary girl", however, she accepts different outcomes from those of the Greek heroes. From the ancient Greek mythic perspective, her lack of *nostos* and separation from her beloved are failures. Miyazaki, however, presents these two outcomes in Chihiro's case as intentional and successful. Chihiro exits the spirit world without looking back and willingly re-enters the human world, even though it means she will continue her journey to a new, unseen home, essentially leaving behind two homes – the one she originally left and the one at the bathhouse.

On their return from Zeniba's home, Chihiro and Haku find a space together in the air that is theirs alone, where they finally escape from the displacements that defined their realities for most of the film. Upon their return to the bathhouse, Chihiro successfully completes Yubaba's last trial of identifying which pigs are her parents and faithfully completes Haku's instructions for re-entering the human world without looking back, despite the temptation to see her friend one more time. Likewise, after Chihiro helps him remember his original name, Haku acts with greater self-possession and directly counters Yubaba's will by helping Chihiro return to the human realm. Through their symbiotic connection, these two protagonists reorient themselves into their identities so that they can resist displacements like the ones that led to their initial meetings and continue to operate around them. In the end, Chihiro, like Odysseus, successfully defeats a sorceress's tricks to ensure a return, although not to her original home.

Through Chihiro and Haku, Miyazaki suggests that 'home' resides in the individual and that one's sense of self and relationship with others can overcome the displacements caused by the physical or psychological changes characteristic of the modern world. In

Haku's case, the audience learns that he is a river god whose river was destroyed in the human world by a construction project, so he has no possibility of a return. Chihiro too cannot reverse her family's relocation, so a full return is also impossible for her. Miyazaki thus denies an Odyssean homecoming to both his main characters, yet still gives them a triumphant 'happy ending' that allows them to accept the vicissitudes of fate and resist feelings of displacement through their adaptability. By refiguring the *Odyssey* and the myths of Orpheus in *Spirited Away*, Miyazaki creates a plausible path for the hero in the modern world. By the end of *Spirited Away*, the sulky girl the audience met in the opening scenes has been displaced by a more mature and confident Chihiro, a hero who relocates herself in the human world on her own terms, ready to embrace her future.

Notes

1. See, e.g., Reider 2005, Napier 2006, Knox 2011, Theisen 2011.

2. I use Lorna Hardwick's (2003: 14) definition of 'refiguration' as the adaptation of an older source.

3. Miyazaki (2009: 283), McCarthy (1999: 74), Cavallaro (2006: 48).

4. Miyazaki 1983.

5. Kovacs and Marshall (2016: xxv).

6. These terms are borrowed from Marshall's five-point scheme of how a "modern cultural object" such as a film might relate to classical models: *cosmetic reference, indirect reference, envisioning, revisioning,* and *engagement.* The last two, which are most relevant to this essay, involve direct, active incorporation of classical models (2016: 20–22).

7. In interviews, he has demonstrated his admiration for early French and British cinema where filmmakers, such as Jean Cocteau, often incorporated and adapted Greek myths. For Greek myth in British filmmaking, see Padilla 2016. For the Orpheus myth used by film makers and artists, including Cocteau, see Lee 1961 and Grafton, Most, and Settis (2013: 664–666).

8. Cyrino and Safran (2015: 6).

9. Miyazaki has cited Caesar's *Gallic Wars* and Howard Fast's 1951 novel *Spartacus* as influences in formulating *Nausicaä*'s plot (McCarthy 1999: 74). Western influence on Miyazaki's storytelling started in his college days. As a member of a children's literature research society, he read and analysed famous works of European children's literature (29).

10. While the Japanese Kojiki, an eighth-century CE chronicle of Shinto myths, is an important native source for *SA*, it does not appear to be the film's primary mythic source for its narrative. Several scholars have observed the similarities between some myths of the Kojiki and ancient Greek myths, especially Orphic undertones (Sioris 1987, Kárpáti 1993). For example, the primordial couple Izanami and Izanagi are separated when Izanami dies in childbirth and goes to Yomi, the land of darkness. Izanagi seeks out his wife, but she is not allowed to leave because she has eaten the food of Yomi. Izanagi breaks a taboo by lighting a torch to view his wife and sees that she has decayed beyond recognition. Repulsed, he runs away and places a boulder at the opening to Yomi, thus separating the world of humans and spirits; see Philippi (1968: 56–67).

11. In *SA*, there is also a train, but Kamaji says that it changed its service to run only in one direction. The implication is that there is no return from such a journey, but Chihiro, like Greek katabatic heroes, resolves to do a seemingly impossible quest.

12. Miyazaki (2014: 198).

13. In the *Odyssey*, Odysseus must return to Circe's house to retrieve and bury the body of Elpenor.

14. Bakhtin coined the term 'chronotope' to refer to the space–time continuum in which different characters exist; see Bakhtin and Holquist 1981, Dunn 2002, Bemong et al. 2010. See also Folch's (2017) discussion of how classical references inject the otherworldly into different worlds by offering new chronotopic possibilities.

15. Chihiro demonstrates closeness with her mother when they walk through the tunnel to the spirit world: she clings to her mother while her father walks boldly ahead of them.

16. According to ancient Greek myth, all sentient entities, including gods, were subject to the laws of the cosmos. For example, any deity could be bound by an oath sworn on the waters of the Underworld goddess Styx (Hesiod *Theogony* 782–806); see Clay (1989: 2003).

17. See Napier 2006, Donsomsakulkij 2015.

18. Toyama 2001.

CHAPTER 7

"THE NEAREST TECHNICALLY IMPOSSIBLE THING": CLASSICAL RECEPTIONS IN HELEN OYEYEMI

Benjamin Eldon Stevens

Introduction

Late in Helen Oyeyemi's 2014 novel *Boy, Snow, Bird* (*BSB*), a woman named Snow, speaking to her younger sister, Bird, expresses a resigned acceptance of the strange facts of their lives and strained family history.[1] It is the sort of existential expression that is common in contemporary fiction – but with a twist. Snow refers to a letter in which Bird wrote "about how technically impossible things are always trying so hard to happen to us, and just letting the nearest technically impossible thing happen" (*BSB* 264). In the letter, Bird wrote that "a whole lot of technically impossible things are always trying to happen to us", so many that "you can't pay attention to all of it, so I just pick the nearest technically impossible thing and I let it happen" (237–238). The twist to Snow's expression, then, echoing Bird's, is that their lives are strange indeed, saturated with "technically impossible things". Oyeyemi's language is emphatic: in just two short passages that crucial phrase occurs four times; twice those "impossible things" are described as "always trying" – once "so hard" – to happen; and even these two scenes give the impression of impossibility happening so often that "you can't pay attention to all of it". Living realistically in the world of *BSB* thus involves reconciling oneself to the fantastic. Indeed, Oyeyemi's emphasis on the "technically impossible" is near to how fantasy and the fantastic may be defined as depending on "literal untruth".[2] To examine that connection, in this chapter I focus on how Oyeyemi's novels depict reality as fantastical in part via classical receptions.[3]

A first sense of Oyeyemi's engagement with ancient stories may be suggested by sketches of the five novels to date. In *The Icarus Girl* (2005; *IG*), the titular character is at risk of repeating mythic Icarus's disastrous fall in her own imaginative flights of fancy, airline flights between countries, and flight by supernatural means. The main character of *The Opposite House* (2007; *OH*) similarly recalls a figure from ancient myth, Persephone, who 'falls' into death, snatched by Hades into the Underworld – a 'house' that is 'opposite' to life. Another household's link to deathly powers is emphasized by reference to ancient myth in *White is for Witching* (2009; *WW*): on a descent into a haunted house, the main character compares herself to another Underworld traveller, Eurydice. More ostentatiously aware of literary history, the main character of *Mr. Fox* (2011; *Fox*) is repudiated by his Muse, is married – as the god Apollo wished to be – to a woman named Daphne, and seems to read a masterpiece of ancient mythography. Finally, *BSB* varies the old tale of Snow White via motifs drawn from even older stories, including a supporting character named Alecto – recalling the ancient Fury – and parallels to the Eurydice/Orpheus myth. Thus at least five important characters and plots have meaningful connections to ancient myth. How might this fact of classical reception affect our reading of Oyeyemi's novels? And what light might her fictions shed on the ancient stories?

Oyeyemi's novels suggest that, to represent lived experience meaningfully, literature requires elements that may be considered unrealistic or fantastic. Such elements are emphasized by classical receptions insofar as ancient stories differ from master narratives of the modern world in ways that are similar to how fantasy involves 'displacements' from the real. By departing from ordinary 'realism', Oyeyemi's 'fantastic realism' subverts traditionally more normative modes of storytelling and their ideologies. Oyeyemi thus offers critique of undesirable modern displacements like exploitation of labour, dispossession of heritage and cultural appropriation, diaspora, and alienation from the self.[4] In the face of such lived experience, 'fantasy' becomes a way of representing how the real can be defamiliarizing, estranging, and uncanny – in a word, unreal. By emphasizing displacement, fantasy has the paradoxical potential to represent real life in truly meaningful ways: indeed, from this perspective, literature might be considered 'realistic' insofar as it captures how real life involves fantastic feelings of displacement.[5]

As examples of responding meaningfully to reality-as-fantasy by retelling other stories, Oyeyemi's fictions seek to speak truth to power by being 'strongly mistaken' about the – ideological, political – differences between what is considered true or possible and what is dismissed as "technically impossible" or "literally untrue".[6] Thus in interviews Oyeyemi has emphasized the need for 'argument' in literature: "[r]etelling a story can be a way of arguing with it, or testing its architecture for false walls".[7] One site of such 'false walls' is Western 'classics': perhaps naturally objects of ambivalence or suspicion, classics fascinate and yet may also alienate, causing displacements. Receptions of Greek and Roman classics are thus an important part of how Oyeyemi's fictions 'retell', 'correct', and 'argue with' earlier stories by offering 'strongly mistaken readings' of reality and realism. To return to the language of *BSB*, ancient stories are thus among the "nearest" and most compelling sources for depicting life as involving the "technically impossible".

Paradoxical as that may seem, there is a logic to it that goes beyond Oyeyemi. As this volume's chapters demonstrate, there are many links between ancient stories and the fantastic. Indeed there is something of a natural fit between fantasy and antiquity. As Brett M. Rogers and I have argued, antiquity is similar to the fantastic in requiring us to accept the reality of something that is not – or is no longer – real: reconstructing the past is similar to imagining alternative worlds, requiring interpretive paradigms that differ from lived experience and from contemporary truth-claims about 'the real'.[8] Imagining antiquity thus demands the sorts of epistemological and metaphysical 'displacements' that define fantasy: just as 'the fantastic' seems different from 'the real', so too is 'the ancient' distant from 'the present'. More than merely 'a foreign country', from this perspective the past is a properly *fantastic* place, "technically impossible" to access and yet – therefore – useful for capturing the fantasy that is part of present reality.[9]

Classical reception may thus 'naturally' help generate the sort of readings – argumentative, corrective, critical, subversive, 'strongly mistaken' – that are at work in Oyeyemi's fictions. And yet of course Oyeyemi's retellings are not limited to Greek and Roman stories. This chapter is therefore intended to add to scholarship that has examined how Oyeyemi, a "ravenous" reader, draws on a wide range of sources, above all Western fairy tales and Yoruba myth.[10] Given that complexity, we should wonder about any seemingly 'natural' connection between Greco-Roman classics and the fantastic. Is there anything *specific* to *classical* receptions in Oyeyemi or other authors of fantasy? Or have ancient classics become merely "reliably esoteric, public-domain material for popular cultural ironization"?[11] Probably there is no simple answer even in a single author. It is nevertheless clear that classical reception is an important part of Helen Oyeyemi's fantastic fictions.

To make that argument, I discuss examples from Oyeyemi's novels of fantastic displacements linked to classical receptions. Having touched on *BSB*, in what follows I focus on *IG*, *OH*, and *WW*, examining their 'corrective' retellings of stories about Icarus, Orpheus and Persephone, and Eurydice, respectively.[12] Each novel invites us to reread the ancient stories in light of its own plot, such that Icarus has a *Doppelgänger*, Persephone may take on Orpheus's powers, and Eurydice's Underworld becomes a kind of haunted house. Along the way, some of Oyeyemi's recurrent themes stand out, including doubling or twinning, migration, and 'madness' and mental illness. I conclude by briefly considering *Fox*, whose engagement with antiquity helps strengthen the possibility that Oyeyemi's classical receptions have much to do with Ovid's *Metamorphoses*. This would put Oyeyemi even more squarely in company of other contemporary fabulists working in Ovidian modes.

The Icarus Girl and other Icarian doubles

Oyeyemi's first novel is suggestive of how she links fantastic displacement to classical reception. Near the end (305), the 'Icarus girl', named Jess, dreams that she is

> flying high above all the land, onward and onward, disappearing like a pin into the blue. The rushing wind stung her eyes into slits, and her fluffy hair rippled out in sheets behind her, sometimes whipping in her eyes and lashing across her cheek. She would never fall, because her friend was flying with her and would catch her.

Both the impossible flight and the fact that this is a dream represent displacements from reality. But it is emblematic of Oyeyemi's interest in the "technically impossible" that Jess's dream is not wholly separated from the novel's waking world. Earlier, Jess attempted fantastic motion with the help of her "friend", Tilly (or TillyTilly): the two wished to fly downwards to frighten Jess's babysitter (152–153, italics original):

> TillyTilly's arms enfolded [Jess] from behind and pulled her d o w n and *through* the staircase, the carpet and the actual stair falling away beneath her as if she and

Tilly were going underground in a lift that would never stop descending.... They smashed against the ground so hard that Jess felt broken and winded ... She and TillyTilly had been falling through earth as if it was air! And now they were stuck.

In contrast to Jess's positive dream of flight into a limitless blue sky, this attempt at fantastic motion links realistic fear of falling to the negative feelings of (living) burial and death. The two passages thus contrast a happy dream of flight – a fantastic liberation from gravity and body – with the unhappy feelings of falling and of confinement to the earth and one's earthen form.

The difference between reality and fantasy is developed further in Jess's relationship to Tilly. Tilly is revealed to be a supernatural version of Jess's real twin, Fern, who was stillborn: just after their failed flight, the girls write a poem that reveals Tilly's knowledge of Fern (163). Jess then realizes "with stunning clarity that she was the only person who saw TillyTilly". This realization diminishes Jess – "[s]he suddenly felt very small and a little bit scared" – and makes her wonder: "*Is TillyTilly ... real?*" (164, italics original). Jess thus feels her own existence threatened: instead of fantastic flight she has taken a frightening fall, thanks to a supernatural double who has supplanted her real twin. Reflected as she is in a fantastic being, is Jess herself displaced from the real?

Oyeyemi emphasizes this displacement by having Jess echo another child lost to fantastic flight: mythic Icarus.[13] In an interview, Oyeyemi says:

When I thought of Jess and her mother, I thought of Icarus and Daedalus, in that Daedalus made wings for both himself and his son to enable them to fly away from King Minos' tyranny, and Daedalus managed to fly away safely, but Icarus died. In a similar way, Jess's mum has an imagination that she can rein in and guide in order to write stories, whereas Jess's uncontrollable imagination, Jess's wings, lead her to a force that she can't handle: TillyTilly. It says something about being a child and not being able to guarantee your own safety.[14]

Oyeyemi uses the image of Icarus's failed flight to symbolize the dangers of a child's "uncontrolled imagination" in context of the 'real' – adult – world.[15] Icarus ignores his father's warning in his excitement about flying. His disregard is reflected in Jess's flights, including her expectation that she "would never fall" (305), unrealistic since she has fallen already (153). Like Icarus, Jess has reached that point by ignoring a parent's suggestions, namely her mother's suggestions regarding Yoruba culture. Thus *IG* is filled with the strong feeling that 'flight' must fail, and the would-be flyer fall.

And yet *IG* 'corrects' the ancient story by changing its ending. Near the end, Jess is trapped in "a wilderness" of sorts and has begun "to despair that she'd ever find her way out until *someone* came and bore her away on their back, away, but still not home.... She had stopped flying and had fallen a long time ago, and didn't know the way" (331). Jess has been dispossessed of her body – "as if of a 'home'" – by her fantastic-but-present double, Tilly, and finds herself sharing an unknown place with her literal-but-absent double, Fern. This reinforces the connection between falling and burial or death. But if this is Jess's most Icarian moment, it provides a strong contrast for what follows: unlike Icarus, Jess escapes the downward spiral and turns to endless upwards motion.[16] Having struggled "back into herself", Jess then "woke" and flies "up and up and up and up" (334).

How might this 'correction' encourage rereading the ancient story? The Icarus story features displacements, including flight, technology invented by Daedalus, and even his exile on Crete. Unlike Jess, however, Icarus has no twin and seems to have no obvious double. But certain characters are similar to him in exactly the way that Jess ultimately is not: they are children who die because of imaginative (Daedalan) fantasy. These include the children sacrificed to the Minotaur; the Minotaur himself, Pasiphae's child; and Perdix, Daedalus's nephew. All of these children are in danger due to Daedalus: Icarus because of his father's wings; the children because of the Minotaur made possible by Daedalus and housed in his labyrinth; the Minotaur once the labyrinth is entered; and Perdix at Daedalus's hands. As Oyeyemi puts it in an interview, all are in danger from how the artist's "uncontrollable imagination" represents "being a child and not being able to guarantee your own safety".[17]

The parallels encourage us to wonder whether Icarus, like Oyeyemi's 'Icarus girl', has a double. One possibility is Perdix, a blood relative who first experiences a version of Icarus's flight by being hurled off a cliff by Daedalus and then furthers the story's bird-imagery – and its theme of human–animal hybridity – by being transformed into a partridge by Athena (*Met.* 8.236–259). But in light of *IG*'s focus on monstrous versions of oneself, another possibility is the Minotaur. Not related by blood, the Minotaur was yet made possible by Daedalus, who built the cow suit that let Pasiphae mate with Minos's bull. Similarly, whereas Icarus plays in his father's workshop (195–200), the Minotaur is trapped in another Daedalan invention, the labyrinth (159–168). Icarus is Daedalus's literal child, while the Minotaur is figurative; and whereas Icarus only approximates human–animal hybridity, the Minotaur literalizes it. But both die due to (Daedalan) invention. In context of *IG*, then, the Minotaur seems a strong possibility for Icarus's double or mirror image.

This reading could be raised in reference to the Icarus story alone, but it is clarified in context of Oyeyemi's retelling. And there are further potential parallels between *IG* and the ancient story: for example, Daedalus was exiled for murder and tries to kill Perdix, while Tilly – likewise responsible for flight – contrives physical harm and 'kills' someone's spirit via paranormal lobotomy; the Minotaur's mother, Pasiphae, may be recalled in *IG*'s "tall woman", a mother-figure who embodies unnatural horror; and just as Icarus has a positive double in his inventive blood-relative Perdix, so too would Jess have rather gone on imaginative flights of fancy with Fern. A measure of *IG*'s take on the ancient story is found in how both of those 'real' people, Perdix and Fern, seem to pale next to 'unreal' or unnatural doubles: of greater effect than the real person who could have stood at one's side, in the literal here and now, is the fantastic reflection who moves unnaturally – flying, goring – and thus represents the unreality of reality. If classical reception is reflection, *IG* thus encourages us to wonder what is on the other side of the looking-glass.[18]

Houses of death or *katabasis*: *The Opposite House* and *White is for Witching*

Uncanny doubles and unnatural ways of moving appear in Oyeyemi's other novels as well. In the next two sections, I focus on how *OH* and *WW* depict Underworld journey or *katabasis*.[19] *OH* includes scenes of doubles in a parallel world that draws on the story of Persephone and Hades, with echoes of Orpheus and Eurydice as well.[20] *WW* features a literal twin whose uncanny connection to a haunted house is expressly compared to Eurydice's time in the Underworld. Thus reframing ancient 'houses of death' as fantastic modern labyrinths, these two novels raise the characteristically postmodern question of which version of a story – a person, a life – is the real one, the 'original', and which a simulacrum or 'copy'.[21]

Persephone in *The Opposite House*

OH centres on a woman named Maja who struggles with the conflicting demands of her family, her life, and her aspirations for the future. Maja's family is diverse: her Cuban father is an aggressively rational retired professor of philosophy; her mother, also Cuban, juxtaposes her own philosophical training with Santería; her brother was born in London; and her boyfriend – and father to her unborn child – is a white Ghana-born British citizen. Maja herself is a nexus, a singer whose ability to perform Western jazz standards depends, in her mind, on an episode from her childhood in Cuba in combination with her current life and a mooted return to Christianity.

This complexly multicultural story engages in classical reception by recalling the story of Persephone.[22] Similar to how ancient Persephone splits the year between Underworld and world above, *OH* juxtaposes Maja's 'real-world' experience in London with vignettes from a parallel world, the 'somewherehouse', one of whose residents is named Mama Proserpine. Thus classical reception emphasizes how Maja is caught between places and possible ways of life whose 'reality' is not always clear. Indeed, her first name may suggest 'illusion' as in the Buddhist tradition.[23] Her middle name, Carmen, also has special force: the Latin for 'song', in a Persephone/Underworld story it links her to the poet and singer Orpheus. That link is strengthened via her great-grandmother: also named Carmen, she was "a Santeria priest" (*OH* 37) and therefore similar to Orpheus, combining music with supernatural powers including contact with the dead.

Underworldly fantasy is emphasized by the somewherehouse. Although there is charm – some of its rooms are "so tiny, pale and clean that they are no more than fancies, sugar-cubed afterthoughts" – this "brittle tower of worn brick and cedar wood" evokes fairy-tale towers for keeping captives (1). The surrounding landscape is sinister: "[a]round it is a hush, the wrong quiet of woods when the birds are afraid". The fearful birds could be linked to the ancient folk etymology for the 'birdless place', Avernus, a mythic entrance to the Underworld; in any case, given a singer as main character, the absence of birdsong is a bad sign. If Maja herself is not literally held captive, the somewherehouse yet suggests her Persephonic confinement: a double of Maja's called Yemaya "lives" there (1), "overflow[ing] with *ache*, or power", defined as "energy, damage" (3, italics original). Yemaya "was born that way – powerful, half mad, but quiet about it" (3).[24] She is an *orisha*, a Yoruba spirit, "Yemaya of the ocean" (36), and therefore one of many "deadly friends from stories" (35).[25]

Reflecting those qualities in Maja/Yemaya, the somewherehouse's basement has two doors: one leads to "London and the ragged hum of the city after dark"; the other leads to "the striped flag and cooking-smell cheer of that tattered jester, Lagos – always, this door leads to a place that is floridly day" (1). With classical receptions in mind, these doors may recall the two gates marking the exit from the Underworld in Virgil's *Aeneid* (*Aen.* 6.893–898). Alternatively, the Underworld in question may be not the somewherehouse but London, which is reached "after dark" in contrast to the "flori[d] day" of Lagos as world above. On this mapping, Maja/Yemaya would shuttle between those cities, and between ancestral cultures, like Persephone does between under- and upperworlds. But *OH*'s Persephone-figure, Mama Proserpine, is not the same as Maja or her double Yemaya: instead of being propitiated as queen of the Underworld, Oyeyemi's Mama Proserpine must be stopped.

The complexity of classical receptions in the somewherehouse imagery recurs in the story about Maja's childhood experience mentioned above. "It's the five-year-old Maja," Maja tells us, "that brings jazz into me, blocking my chest so that I have to sing it out" (*OH* 44). She refers here to her family's going-away party from Cuba, at which "a tiny, veiled woman appeared beneath the palm trees at the bottom of the garden of a house" (45). This unknown woman "began to sing to us out of the falling night. We couldn't understand her words . . . but the first notes felled me the way lightning brings down trees without explanation or permission". Simultaneously, in Maja's recollection, a "girl who was under the table with me began to suffer a fit". This girl Maja identifies as an acquaintance named Magalys. Later, however, Magalys remembers the event differently: it is Maja who had the seizure (167–168). Maja is so disturbed by this corrective retelling that she loses her ability to sing. Her original description of the event is ambiguous about who is who, avoiding names: "It was only when the woman had finished singing . . . that *the girl's mother* discovered *her* under the table and carried *her* away" (45, italics added).

Here is another potential recollection of the Persephone story, who was 'carried away', kidnapped, literally from upper- into Underworld, figuratively from innocence into experience. Although young Maja is not physically displaced, death may be evoked in some details of the scene, including the mysterious singer and the way the notes "felled [Maja]". When, then, "the girl's mother . . . carried her away", Oyeyemi seems to retell that ancient story: Hades carrying away Persephone; or Persephone's mother Ceres seeking her; or perhaps even Orpheus seeking Eurydice down below. That last possibility may be the most intriguing, with Maja-as-Orpheus freeing herself. This would resonate with Oyeyemi's interest in 'correcting' older stories. But can even a corrected and empowered Persephone-figure save herself from the Underworld? A similar question is raised by the different sort of underworld experience in Oyeyemi's next novel, *WW*.

White is for Witching and Eurydice's haunted-house tale

WW's most obvious main character is a young woman, Miranda, whose name – recalling Shakespeare's *The Tempest* – resonates with the novel's theme of magic: Miranda is the latest in a line of witches.[26] Miranda has a twin brother, Eliot, as well as a friendship and love-affair with a woman named Ore. The crux of the story, however, is Miranda's relationship with a different sort of being: her family home, 29 Barton Road, a haunted house. With the house as much a main character as Miranda, *WW* develops some of Oyeyemi's recurrent themes by literalizing – making physical – the link between real places and fantastic displacements. In that context, Miranda, true to her name's etymology, 'must be wondered at': as the latest witch, will she become one of the ghosts that haunt her home? Part of the answer comes from how elements of *WW* resonate with Eurydice's relegation to the Underworld.[27] Although Eurydice's story should not be conflated with Persephone's, nonetheless the image of a katabatic or Persephonic Eurydice sheds light on Miranda's journey. To reverse the analysis, what might it mean to read Eurydice's story as a haunted-house tale?

WW signals its interest in Underworlds with an epigraph from poet Gwendolyn Brooks's sonnet "my dreams, my works, must wait till after hell": "I hold my honey and I store my bread / In little jars and cabinets of my will. / I label clearly, and each latch and lid / I bid. Be firm till I return from Hell" (vv. 1–4). Just as Brooks's narrator envisions a journey to Hell, so will Miranda journey down, only hoping to return. Underworldliness is furthered by *WW* being divided into two parts, the first "Curiouser" (11) and the second "And Curiouser" (163), from Alice's exclamation upon 'telescoping' to great size in Lewis Carroll's 1865 *Alice's Adventures in Wonderland*.[28] These two intertexts sharpen Miranda's *katabasis* and its Eurydicean element. Whereas Brooks's narrator "will[s]" her descent into Hell, and whereas Alice's journey is not particularly hellish, Miranda goes down unwillingly in a way that makes her *both* haunted *and* a malevolent force.

There are too many scenes of interaction with the house to describe here. In sum, although the house in itself "is a monster" (244), it is the house and Miranda – as the current woman Silver – *together* who constitute the witch or "goodlady" (251). It is at the very moment of recognizing this that Miranda is identified with Eurydice (273, italics added):

> She looked in the mirror and blood was drying on her chin. When she opened her mouth her teeth lifted, then sliced her bottom lip again. She couldn't see the teeth, only the cuts they made. . . . She swallowed her friend's gift of ten years, or two small watch batteries, as if they were pills. . . . *Miranda went down barefoot, like Eurydice.* She walked with her fingers spread over her face, because no one must see.

In this scene Miranda asks, "What am I?" That displacement from self is framed as physical change or dysmorphism, recalling Miranda's pica as well as Alice's supernatural growth, and evoking lycanthropy or similarly monstrous metamorphosis. Miranda's status as a Eurydice-figure is thus closely linked to (dark) magic.

Miranda would also seem to be like Eurydice in the detail of an injured foot. In one tradition of the ancient story, Eurydice dies from a snakebite (Virgil *Georgics* 4.457–459), leaving her shade with a limp (Ovid *Met.* 10.49). In *WW*, after Miranda disappears, there is question of whether she has left barefoot, and Eliot wonders, "[D]id my sister wound her foot? . . . And if she did cut her foot, is it a clue to something?" (280). Here the similarities may seem to end. Eurydice 'goes down' into the Underworld, but, unlike Miranda, she is not seeking her own death.[29] Nor is Eurydice marked as a monster: although she is liminal – in some versions, a dryad or (oak-)tree-nymph – this would seem to emphasize not uncanny power but desirability. Finally, Eurydice seems to have no twin.

It may be, however, that a focus on literal twinning is misleading. Miranda is identified ultimately not by her twinhood – nor even by selfhood (e.g., she is unrecognizable in a photograph, 187) – but by her connection to the house. We might thus regard Eurydice, too, as being defined not by her most obvious relationship – to Orpheus – but by her involvement with the house of the dead. In one version, Hades and Persephone release only a phantom image of Eurydice, keeping the woman herself (Plato *Symposium* 179d). In a somewhat fainter parallel to Miranda, Eurydice is also a late addition to the story: Miranda follows in the footsteps of her mother and grandmother, while Eurydice plays a role modeled on a figure like Persephone – a woman made to 'go down' into the Underworld against her will – or even Hecate, the chthonic goddess linked to the most 'hellish' part of the Underworld, Tartarus (e.g., *Aen.* 6.35, 564–565).[30] Eurydice could thus be read as like Miranda, an unwilling katabant into a house of ghosts, linked to dark magic.

If Eurydice is changed, what has happened to Orpheus? Having persuaded Persephone and Hades to release her, Orpheus lost her a second time by looking back at her on the ascent. Several characters in *WW* recall Orpheus in trying – and failing – to 'save' Miranda: her twin Eliot, who wonders about her absence; her friend and lover Ore, who sings to her; and a housekeeper named Sade, who recognizes the house's 'monstrosity' but is destroyed by it. These Orpheus-figures would represent twists on the tradition by mirroring Eurydice and by emphasizing themes including race and different cultural traditions of magic. But Orpheus might be changed even further. When Miranda "went down . . . like Eurydice", it was not into the Underworld as such but deeper into the house, from which she gains magical power. Just possibly then the house represents *both* the 'haunted house' of the Underworld *and* an Orpheus-figure that stops at nothing to 'save' its beloved Eurydice. 29 Barton Road continually seeks to bring Eurydices – Miranda and her ancestors – 'up' from the world outside, which the house considers sullied and figuratively 'beneath'.[31] *WW* would thus be 'haunted' by a transformed Orpheus, a sentient house expressing diabolical feeling for multiple Eurydice figures and – also like ancient Orpheus, who spurned love (Ovid *Met.* 10.79–85) – rejecting other women, including Ore and Sade, as unwelcome guests.

Conclusion: *Mr. Fox* and an Ovidian Oyeyemi?

Characters like *IG*'s Jess, *OH*'s Maja, and *WW*'s Miranda are all linked to the fantastic, obligated to let the "nearest technically impossible things" happen. I have tried to show how Oyeyemi achieves this effect – of reality involving displacements intrinsic to fantasy – in part via classical receptions. Thus Jess's flights mark her as an 'Icarus girl', Maja echoes Orpheus as well as (Mama) Proserpine, Miranda is likened to Eurydice, and more. Since, however, this is only one of Oyeyemi's intertextual strategies, I also ask whether there is anything *specific* to her receptions of *classics*.

Ancient classics do seem well-suited to capturing displacements from the present world. Oyeyemi has said that "[i]t feels difficult to find what I need nowadays . . . *I do tend to feel more connected to dead writers*".[32] Her seeming to lump all "dead writers" together, however, emphasizes that ancient Greek and Roman material is not the *only* key to her fictions. But I hope to have shown that a focus on classical receptions unlocks *some* doors into the novels' inner workings. Indeed, insofar as Oyeyemi's stated purpose is to 'correct' earlier stories, ancient material is an important part of how she subverts 'realistic' storytelling so as to criticize normative ideologies. Beyond merely reconciling ourselves to the impossibilities of daily life, we are thus invited to embrace such a 'fantastic realism' as a step towards actualizing the liberating potential intrinsic to speculative fiction.

A final example may be found in a scene partway through *Fox*. The eponymous Fox is at a bar "pretend[ing] to read", when in walk "college men" who "called each other by nicknames that alluded to the classical world" including Castor, Pollux, Patroclus, and Achilles (264). Fox feels excluded from their society: "[t]hey didn't try to get me to call them by their Greek names". The exclusion follows class lines: Fox regards them as "kids who had never been poor and never would be", whereas he is "a farmer's son". And yet this Fox knows enough to recognize their allusions. Indeed, his knowledge sets him apart from the "few guys" in the bar: sitting at a "corner table", Fox "opened my copy of *Metamorphoses*, and pretended to read". The act of reading sets him further apart: "[t]he other guys started giving me the eye then" (263–264). Here literary culture reflects social distinctions.

Such social distinctions are linked to fantastic displacements. *Fox* incorporates metamorphosis as well as metalepsis, in which fictional figures appear in reality: Fox's muse, Mary, becomes real to stop him from writing deaths for his women characters. *Fox* is thus a fantastic retelling of the 'Bluebeard' or 'Robber Bridegroom' folktale.[33] But there is a classical wrinkle: Whose *Metamorphoses* is Fox reading, Ovid's epic poem or Apuleius's novel?[34] Both anticipate *Fox*'s human-animal transformations and embedded narrations.[35] And there is a parallel between the arcs of Oyeyemi's and Apuleius's novels: the protagonist (Fox, Lucius) redeems himself from a dark interest (killing women characters, learning magic) via transformation from animal ('fox', ass) back into human being by acceding to a higher, female power (muse Mary, goddess Isis). But Apuleius too wrote in an Ovidian tradition. The fact that Fox stares at a "line" in his reading (264) *may* indicate poetry. And as noted above, Fox is married to a Daphne, recalling the nymph who escapes Apollo via transformation into a laurel tree (Ovid *Met.* 1.452–567).

Perhaps the strongest reason for suspecting that Fox is reading Ovid, however, lies outside of – and encompasses – the novel. Many of the ancient stories retold by Oyeyemi are to be found in Ovid: Icarus and the Minotaur, Persephone and Hades, Eurydice and Orpheus – all appear in his *Metamorphoses*.[36] Not all of Oyeyemi's classical receptions fit this pattern: for example, *BSB*'s Alecto may recall that Fury in Virgil's *Aeneid*. Yet it is intriguing to consider whether Oyeyemi's classical receptions are retellings of stories told most influentially by Ovid. This would put her work in context of other contemporary Ovidian fabulations like Salman Rushdie's *The Satanic Verses* (1988) and *The Ground Beneath Her Feet* (1999), Kate Atkinson's *Not the End of the World* (2002), David Mitchell's *Cloud Atlas* (2004), and Jane Alison's *Nine Island* (2016).[37] Indeed Oyeyemi's novels would seem to exemplify the sort of (post)modern text Calvino sees anticipated in Ovid: a 'manifold text' that "replaces the oneness of a thinking 'I' with a multiplicity of subjects, voices, and views of the world ... not only to enter into selves like our own but to give speech to that which has no language".[38]

Whether or not this was Ovid's purpose, Calvino's description offers a suggestive way of capturing Oyeyemi's achievement. Her characters – each a "thinking 'I'" – are fantastically displaced from themselves, such that they must embrace – and embody – divergent "views of the world". This sort of displacement in subjectivity is a powerful way of developing critical subversions of the present moment: a way of "giv[ing] speech to that which [traditionally] has no language". I hope to have shown that such displacement assumes a particularly interesting form in the fantastic – and that the fantastic properly includes classical tales retold. By shedding new light on old stories, Helen Oyeyemi's novels consciously 'strongly mistake' the present moment, offering critique of current fantasies and subverting ideologies of the real. As such the novels vividly illustrate the politically and ideologically liberating potential of classical receptions.

Notes

1. A first version of this chapter was presented at *The Once and Future Antiquity* at the University of Puget Sound (March 2015). It is dedicated to my dear friend Tom Anderson, whose recommendation of Oyeyemi's "outstanding" *Mr. Fox* in summer 2014 led me to read all of her work. Special thanks are due to my co-editor Brett M. Rogers.

2. Attebery (2014: 4): "[T]he fundamental premise of fantasy is that the things it tells not only did not happen but *could* not happen." I use 'fantasy' and 'the fantastic' to refer to fictions depending on such 'literal untruth', including 'speculative fiction' and 'science fiction' as well as 'fantasy' as such.

3. Studies have linked Oyeyemi to the Gothic, e.g., Cousins 2012a and Mafe 2012; cf. Warnes 2009, Gaylard 2005, and Cooper 1998 on West African literatures and magical realism. On Oyeyemi otherwise, see Buckley and Ilott 2017, Lau 2016, Gunning 2015, Satkunananthan 2015 and 2011, Tredennick 2015, Ouma 2014 (after Hawley 1995), Stephanou 2014, Cousins 2012b, Stouck 2010, Cooper 2009 and 2008, Cuder-Domínguez 2009, Bastida-Rodriguez 2008, and Bryce 2008. On classics and the fantastic, see Rogers and Stevens (2017a: esp. 7–14), (2015a: 7–8n11), and 2012; Bost-Fiévet and Provini 2014; and Keen (this volume).

4. See Okpewho and Nkiru 2011, Mwangi 2009, Hron 2008, Ashcroft, Griffiths, and Tiffin 2002 [1989], and Brah (1996: esp. 178–210). Cf. Cooper 2009 and 2008 for reference to Oyeyemi.

5. Cf. Doležel 1998, Freedman (2000: 13–23, esp. 16–22). Although Freedman suggests that fantasy *merely* "estranges . . . in an irrationalist, theoretically illegitimate way" (17) – i.e., it does not lead to critical thought – because its subjects are "in principle unknowable" (25), I believe that this confuses such subjects' metaphysics with their epistemology: 'technically impossible' things are yet 'knowable' insofar as they are felt to be part of real life.

6. For 'strongly mistaken' reading or *misprision*, see Bloom (1997: 19–48).

7. Chee 2014; cf. Oyeyemi in Diamond 2014: "I tend to argue with the source story as I write my way into and out of its tropes." For architectural imagery, see further below on *IG*, *OH*, and *WW*, with n. 21.

8. Both fields comprise "texts which are enticingly incomplete . . . self-contained, syntagmatic structures of narrative for which the reader must always supply a missing paradigm"; Rogers and Stevens (2012: 131). Cf. Mendlesohn (2008: xiii).

9. "The past is a foreign country" is attributed to L. P. Hartley's *The Go-Between* (1953); see Rogers and Stevens (2015a: 7n10). Cf. "the future is a foreign country" in Liuzza's chapter in Kears and Paz (2016: 61–78).

10. "Ravenous" reader: Anonymous 2014. On Oyeyemi's other contexts, see above, n. 3.

11. Rogers and Stevens (2012: 131), comparing Paul (2010: 142) on classics and cinema.

12. I mostly pass over Oyeyemi's short stories (2006), a collection entitled *What Is Not Yours Is Not Yours* (2016), and two early plays, *Juniper's Whitening* and *Victimese* (published 2005); see Abram 2017.

13. For Icarus in SF&F literature, see, e.g., Ray Bradbury's "The Golden Apples of the Sun" (1953); Grant Morrison and Frank Quitely's comic *All-Star Superman #1* (January 2006), which recalls Bradbury (Roeg 2005); Brian Greene and Chip Kidd's *Icarus at the Edge of Time* (2008; film 2010); Anna Starobinets's *The Icarus Gland and Other Stories of Metamorphosis* (2013, trans. James Rann 2014); and Zachary Brown's 'Icarus Corps' series (2015–). In film, see, e.g., *Ikarie XB-1* (dir. Polák, 1963); *The Man Who Fell to Earth* (dir. Roeg, 1963), which references Brueghel's painting *Landscape with the Fall of Icarus*; *The Falls* (dir. Greenaway, 1980); and *Sunshine* (dir. Boyle, 2007). In classical sources, see, e.g., Ovid's *Metamorphoses* (*Met.*) 8.152–259 and *Lexicon Iconographicum Mythologiae Classicae* (LIMC), s.v. 'Daidalos et Ikaros', 313–321 (Jacob E. Nyenhuis). For post-classical receptions, see Rudd (1988). Some discussion is to be found under 'Labyrinth' in Grafton, Most, and Settis (2010: 505–506; Hervé Brunon).

14. Taylor 2005.

15. Flight is an ancient image for creative activity: e.g., Ovid says that he will be "borne forever above the high stars" (*super alta perennis / astra ferar*; *Met.* 15.875–876). Cf. Richard Garfinkle's *Celestial Matters* (1996), a story of spaceflight in a Ptolemaic cosmos mixing Aristotelian, classical Chinese, and other ancient metaphysics.

16. Title aside, *IG* makes no explicit reference to the ancient story.

17. Taylor 2005.

18. *IG*'s implicit 'Alice in Wonderland' theme becomes explicit in *WW*; see below.

19. On *katabasis* in literature and the arts, see, e.g., Falconer 2005 and Holtsmark 2001; cf. Edmonds 2004. Relevant SF&F works include literature like Jules Verne's *Journey to the Center of the Earth* (1864) (cf. Stevens 2015), J. R. R. Tolkien's *The Hobbit* (1937) (cf. Stevens 2017) and *The Lord of the Rings* (1954-1955) (cf. Simonis 2014), C. S. Lewis's *The Silver Chair* (1953), Philip Pullman's *His Dark Materials* series (1995–2000) (cf. Syson 2017), and Ursula K. Le Guin's *Lavinia* (2008) (cf. Rea 2010), as well as films like *Cherry 2000* (dir. De Jarnatt, 1987), *Johnny Mnemonic* (dir. Longo, 1995), *The Core* (dir. Arniel, 2003), and *Inception* (dir. Nolan, 2013).

20. Persephone's story (esp. Ovid *Met.* 5.341–571, *Fasti* 4.393–620) recurs in modern writing, e.g., Margaret Atwood's *Two Persephones* (1962), Louise Glück's *Averno* (2006), Gwenaëlle Aubry's *Perséphone 2014* (2014), and many places in the works of A. S. Byatt; on the latter, see also Cox (2011: 135–151) and Slater 2003. See further Hurst 2012, Radford 2007, and Gubar 1979; cf. Grafton, Most, and Settis, s.v. 'Demeter and Persephone' (2010: 254–255; Malcolm Bell). On Orpheus and Eurydice, see below, n. 27.

21. For labyrinth imagery in SF&F, see, e.g., Jorge Luis Borges's "The Garden of Forking Paths" and "The Library of Babel" (both 1941, re-published in 1962 *Labyrinths*), Mark Z. Danielewski's *House of Leaves* (2000), the film *El laberinto del fauno* (dir. del Toro 2006), Catherynne M. Valente's *The Labyrinth* (2004), and David Mitchell's *Slade House* (2014); cf. the Netflix series *The OA* (Marlin and Batmanglij 2016), whose episode "The Garden of Forking Paths" (S1E6) links Borgesian SF&F to Homeric odyssey.

22. Cf. Richard Powers' *The Time of Our Singing* (2003) – whose main characters are members of a multicultural and mixed-race family devoted to music, while the primary singer is compared to Orpheus (165–216) and Aeneas (109–130).

23. See Buswell and Lopez (2013: 535–536), Doniger 1986.

24. This doubling parallels how *IG*'s Tilly doubles Jess, and *OH*'s Mama Proserpine recalls *IG*'s "tall woman", who may then be compared to *WW*'s "goodlady" (discussed below). Also linking *IG* and *OH* is Emily Dickinson: *IG*'s epigraph from her poem #303; *OH*'s title from #547.

25. On 'orisha', see Karade 1994, Awolalu 1979, and, generally, Falola 2016.

26. Nuttall suggests that with *The Tempest* Shakespeare was "inventing science fiction" (2007: 361). See, e.g., H.G. Wells's *The Island of Dr. Moreau* (1896) (cf. Aldiss [1986: 123–124]), Aldous Huxley's *Brave New World* (1931; titled after *Tempest* 5.1.183) (cf. Grushow 1962), the film *Forbidden Planet* (dir. Wilcox 1956) (cf. Amis [1961: 30], Campos 1998, Caroti 2004, and Bucher 2015), and the *Star Trek: The Original Series* episode "Requiem for Methuselah" (Golden 1969 = S3E19) (cf. Morse 2000).

27. SF&F works drawing on the story of Orpheus and Eurydice (esp. Ovid *Met.* 10.1–85 and 11.1–66) include Jean Cocteau's 'Orphic Trilogy' (1930, 1950, 1959), Philip K. Dick's "Orpheus with Clay Feet" (1964), Samuel R. Delany's *The Einstein Intersection* (1967), and Salman Rushdie's *The Ground Beneath Her Feet* (1999) (cf. Falconer 2004). Cf. Grafton, Most, and Settis (2010: 664–666; Elizabeth Sears), Anderson 1982, Robbins 1982, and Bowra 1952b.

28. Originally entitled *Alice's Adventures Underground* (ms. 1864), *Alice* has been a pervasive influence on SF&F, e.g., Roger Zelazny's *Sign of Chaos* (1987), the film *The Matrix* (dir. Wachowski and Wachowski, 1999), and Tad Williams's *Otherland* series (1996–2001); see Mendlesohn (2008: 1–58, esp. 27–28) and cf. (1986: 111–112). Brooks and Carroll link their protagonists' journeys to foodstuffs: Brooks's "jar" may recall the jar of marmalade noticed by Alice during her fall down the rabbit-hole. *WW* also thematizes eating: Miranda suffers from pica, "an appetite for non-food items" (25), as did her mother (186); see Stephanou 2014.

29. Miranda is also implicitly compared (*WW* 248; cf. 209) to the mechanical nightingale of Hans Christian Andersen's "Nattergalen" (1843) that charms Death himself.

30. Ancient Hecate "looms large in ancient magic" with "noctural apparitions, packs of barking hell-hounds, and hosts of ghost-like revenants" and "association with the chthonian realm and the ghosts of the dead" (*Oxford Classical Dictionary* [2012], s.v. 'Hecate'; Albert Henrichs); cf. Johnston 1990 and (1999: 203–249). She appears in Oyeyemi's "'sorry' doesn't sweeten her tea" (2016): described as "someone you see at crossroads" (89) and who "own[s] all thresholds" (90), she is invoked to help punish a violent man, who is then pursued by "three women" (93) who torment him and so recall the Furies of, e.g., Aeschylus's *Eumenides*.

31. The house continues *WW*'s theme of consumption, 'eating' white guests and 'Silver' women while 'spitting out' Black guests and their multicoloured foods. Cf. how "[t]he University Library is a mouth shut tight, each tooth a book" (178).

32. Hoggard 2014, italics added.

33. Oyeyemi has suggested that Bluebeard stories are interesting for showing consequences to rule-breaking (Diamond 2014). Cf. Aarne-Thompson-Uther folktale types 312 ('Bluebeard') and 955 ('Robber Bridegroom'), and Clark 2012.

34. Ovid has been available in English since 1537 (Arthur Golding), Apuleius since 1566 (William Adlington). Fox possibly reads Kafka, whose *Metamorphosis* was released in English in 1937 (A. L. Lloyd), but imprecision does not seem like Oyeyemi.

35. Multiple narrators/narrations have seemed so characteristic of Ovid *Met.* that Italo Calvino describes it as the original 'manifold text' (see below). Apuleius's novel also has many embedded stories, of which 'Cupid and Psyche' has served as "an essential TAPROOT TEXT for fantasy" esp. in the form of 'Beauty and the Beast'; see Clute and Grant (1997: 51, s.v. 'Apuleius'; Clute) and (1997: 241, s.v. 'Cupid and Psyche'; David Langford), and cf. Accardo (2002: 68–87). For 'Cupid and Psyche' in SF via Mary Shelley's *Frankenstein*, see Stevens 2018.

36. I owe this suggestion to Eliana Chavkin.

37. For Ovid's afterlife, see Grafton, Most, and Settis, s.v. 'Ovid' (2010: 667–673; Sarah Annes Brown); Brown 2002 and 2008 (specifically on SF); Ziolkowski 2004; and Kennedy 2002. On Ovid in Rushdie, see Ziogas 2011 and Falconer 2004; in Atkinson, see Sanders (2001: esp. 81–82).

38. Calvino (1988: 117 and 124, respectively).

PART III
DISPLACED IN TIME

CHAPTER 8
DYNAMIC TENSIONS: THE FIGURE(S) OF ATLAS IN *THE ROCKY HORROR PICTURE SHOW*

Stephen B. Moses and Brett M. Rogers

Introduction

It is an oddity of scholarship on *The Rocky Horror Picture Show* – some might even say a 'space oddity' – that critics repeatedly describe the 1975 film (dir. Jim Sharman) in terms that evoke classical antiquity.[1] For James Twitchell, *The Rocky Horror Picture Show* (hereafter *Rocky Horror*) is a "modern saturnalia", evoking the ancient Roman holiday known for its revelry and inversion of social norms.[2] For Mark Siegel, the film offers an "Aristophanic attack against sexually repressive traditional mores and social institutions", recalling that Athenian dramatist's comic lampoons.[3] Amittai Aviram has described Dr Frank-N-Furter (played by Tim Curry) as a "postmodern gay Dionysos", arguing that *Rocky Horror* "can and should be read as a gay rewriting of Euripides [*sic*] *The Bacchae*" and further adding that it "is a pastiche of Great Books and other portions of Western culture, a Bacchic orgy of learned references".[4] John Kilgrove perhaps 'out-classics' them all, referring in one short book chapter to Frank-N-Furter's "Dionysian values" and "Pygmalionesque ecstasy at the sight of his creation", as well as to how Frank's assistant Riff Raff (played by film co-writer Richard O'Brien) "epitomizes the spirit of Saturnalia", desiring to destroy "the loathsome Janus-face of social respectability".[5] The oddity of these repeated invocations of Greco-Roman antiquity becomes even more pronounced when we realize that none of these critics cite or discuss any concrete evidence linking *Rocky Horror* to such Greco-Roman figures and features, and instead project these classicizing images onto the film.

This appropriation of what we might call 'the classical' in order to make sense of *Rocky Horror* is compelling for two reasons. First, these critical responses suggest that there *is* something about *Rocky Horror* that smacks of Greco-Roman antiquity, such that critics feel compelled to invoke ancient classics, despite *Rocky Horror's* decidedly mid-twentieth-century Americana, its backward-looking science fiction (SF), and its forward-looking sexual mores. Second, and more important, we find it perplexing that these scholars neither discuss the few identifiable classical elements in *Rocky Horror* nor use those elements to make a stronger, concrete case about the role of actual Greco-Roman myth for the film. In other words, while we are intrigued that it has been helpful for critics to evoke Dionysos, Aristophanes, Janus, and the Roman Saturnalia to describe the swingin' vibe inside Frank's castle, such descriptions have been *at best* arguments for deep structures of classical thinking based on fairly tenuous evidence, and *at worst* wholly uncritical projections or appropriations of 'the classical' to serve modern and postmodern scholarly agendas. In the process of appropriating 'the classical', we believe that these critics have misunderstood the film's compelling engagement with and displacement of classical antiquity.

One exception appears in Andrew Howe's examination of the loss of innocence in *Rocky Horror*. Howe suggests that "[t]he interplay of innocence and experience, and the subsequent musings upon morality and punishment, serve to situate the film within the Promethean tradition", arguing that "[a]lthough Rocky is equivalent to Frankenstein's monster, Frank as a character represents a postmodern Prometheus".[6] Howe's use of the phrase "postmodern Prometheus" is suggestive here of Aviram's "postmodern gay Dionysos", although it most likely derives from Mary Wollstonecraft Shelley's 1818 novel *Frankenstein; or, the Modern Prometheus*, whose influence on *Rocky Horror* is well known.[7] What exactly makes Frank a "postmodern Prometheus" (as opposed to a 'modern Prometheus') Howe does not say, but the invocation of Prometheus, modern or postmodern, locates *Rocky Horror* within a far more probable genealogical tradition that includes mythic Prometheus and Romantic Victor Frankenstein. The limitation to Howe's identification of this 'equivalence' between Frank and Prometheus, however, is the lack of any concrete evidence in the film for such comparison.[8] The similarity could simply result from the film's more obvious play not with the Promethean tradition but, more narrowly, with the tradition of Frankenstein (see below).

There is, however, a directly identifiable Greco-Roman mythic figure who *does* appear in *Rocky Horror* and yet is overlooked in scholarship on the film: Prometheus's brother, the Titan Atlas. While scholars of *Rocky Horror* have devoted attention to Charles Atlas, who is explicitly referred to just after the creation of Rocky (played by the hunky Peter Hinwood), they have ignored the song's crucial juxtaposition to the image of the mythic Atlas, an image which appears prominently in Frank's bedchamber. The single exception is Sarah Artt, who notes in passing the stained-glass image of Atlas, seeing it as "tied to the camp references to ... Charles Atlas" and part of the film's "semiotic warfare" between images of 'high' art and 'low' culture (including the camp aesthetic), but she takes the point no further.[9]

We argue in this chapter that *Rocky Horror* makes strategic use of ancient, Greco-Roman Atlas to respond to and critique modern norms of hegemonic masculinity embodied and promulgated by Charles Atlas. We trace the history of mythic Atlas and locate his re-emergence in twentieth-century discourses about masculinity as they appear in the popularity of Charles Atlas, comic books, and the *peplum* film genre. We suggest that, in Frank's attempt to replicate these puerile norms in his own universe of queer sexualities, he demonstrates that the pursuit of this masculine ideal instead subjects a person to suffering, imprisoning queer men beneath the weight of an oppressive masculinity – in other words, that trying to make someone into a Charles Atlas results monstrously in making him a classical Atlas. To read *Rocky Horror* in terms of liberatory Dionysos, then, is to miss the point, while reading the film in terms of Prometheus only gets us partway there: this is Atlas's horror show.

Atlas in Greco-Roman antiquity

Mythic Atlas first appears in our earliest ancient Greek sources, most notably in Hesiod's cosmogonic poem, the *Theogony* (*Th.*).[10] In that text, Atlas is the son of Iapetos and Clymene, and brother of Menoitios, Prometheus, and Epimetheus (507–511). This genealogy establishes Atlas as belonging to the generation of Titans, the generation prior to Zeus and the other Olympians. Atlas's family members are noteworthy for coming into conflict with Zeus and for their subsequent sufferings. For example, Iapetos has been condemned to Tartaros (Homer *Iliad* 478–481); his brother Prometheus is famously punished for stealing fire and giving it to humans (*Th.* 521–525); and his brother Menoitios, whom Hesiod tells us is "wanton" or "transgressive" (ὑβριστήν; 514), has been cast into Erebos "for both his acts of recklessness and arrogant manhood" (εἵνεκ' ἀτασθαλίης τε καὶ ἠνορέης ὑπερόπλου; 516). In this same passage, Atlas is also associated with punishment (517–520):

> Atlas holds the wide heaven under strong compulsion
> at the edges of the earth, in front of the clear-voiced Hesperides.
> Standing with it on his head and untiring hands.
> For this fate did all-wise Zeus allot to him.

> Ἄτλας δ' οὐρανὸν εὐρὺν ἔχει κρατερῆς ὑπ' ἀνάγκης
> πείρασιν ἐν γαίης πρόπαρ' Ἑσπερίδων λιγυφώνων
> ἑστηώς, κεφαλῇ τε καὶ ἀκαμάτῃσι χέρεσσι·
> ταύτην γάρ οἱ μοῖραν ἐδάσσατο μητίετα Ζεύς.[11]

As Timothy Gantz observes, no archaic or classical source explicitly tells us the event or action that led to Atlas's punishment, although later sources claim that the punishment was a result of an event known as the Titanomachy, in which the Titans made a failed attempt to overthrow the reign of Zeus.[12] According to the fabulist Hyginus, Atlas was the leader of the Titanomachy (*Fabulae* 150), which fact explains why he suffers a greater punishment than the other Titans. Cause aside, archaic Greek sources emphasize the punishment, as in the passage from Hesiod cited above and elsewhere in Homer (*Odyssey* 1.52–54).[13] Later sources further emphasize Atlas's suffering, as we see in the fifth-century BCE poet Pindar (*Pythian* 4.289–292) and the tragedy *Prometheus Bound* (347–350, 425–430) attributed to the Athenian dramatist Aeschylus.[14] Thus early in the mythic tradition Atlas embodies a dynamic tension between great, masculine power and terrible suffering.

Atlas was also evoked in classical antiquity as a foil to the hypermasculine strength of Herakles. In Herakles's famous labours, the eleventh labour required the hero to retrieve the golden apples of the Hesperides; however, Herakles could not enter their Garden himself. Thus Herakles takes Atlas's place while Atlas goes to retrieve the apples for the hero, as we see on the metopes of the Temple of Olympian Zeus (Fig. 8.1) from the fifth century BCE, as well as in Euripides' *Herakles* (403–407) and the later account in Apollodorus's *Bibliothêkê* (2.5.11).[15] Atlas attempts to renege on his part of the deal and

Fig. 8.1 Athena, Herakles, and Atlas with the Golden Apples of the Hesperides. Marble Relief (fifth century BCE) from the Temple of Olympian Zeus. Archaeological Museum of Olympia. Photo Credit: Erich Lessing/Art Resource, NY.

not take the heavens back, but Herakles tricks him into returning to his state of perpetual punishment. The story emphasizes both the strength and (surprising) cleverness of Herakles, and the pairing of the two figures – especially in terms of masculine strength – resurfaces again later.

There are two notable exceptions to the traditional portrayal of Atlas in classical antiquity. The first story comes from Ovid's epic *Metamorphoses* (8 CE), in which Ovid describes an encounter between the Titan and the hero Perseus (4.631–662). Perseus has travelled to Atlas's home and asks for shelter; Atlas refuses, citing a prophecy that a son of Jupiter will strip Atlas of his glory; here Ovid no doubt means to evoke the common myth (discussed above) of Herakles and Atlas. Perseus then, in a surprising turn of events, inflicts the punishment himself, using the decapitated head of the gorgon Medusa to turn Atlas into a mountain: "Atlas was turned into a mountain as large as he had been: for the his beard and hair turn into forests, his shoulders and hands into mountain ridges; where his head had been before is now a peak on the loftiest mountatin, and his bones become stone" (*quantus erat, mons factus Atlas; nam barba comaeque / in silvas abeunt, iuga sunt umerique manusque,/ quod caput ante fuit, summo est in monte cacumen,/ ossa lapis fiunt;* 657–660).[16] Ovid's version of the Atlas story thus cleverly plays on the learned reader's expectations, making Perseus, rather than Herakles, the son of

Jupiter who brings the prophecy to fruition, adding the detail of Atlas's transformation into stone.

The second notable example comes from the historian Diodorus Siculus, who writes in the mid-first century BCE. Diodorus offers an interpretation of the Atlas myth in the interpretive tradition of Euhemerus, the fourth-century BCE Greek mythographer who argued that myths were based on historical figures but had become distorted or exaggerated over time. In Diodorus's euhemerist account, Atlas is not an immortal Titan who holds the starry heavens and retrieves the apples of the Hesperides, but rather a mortal astronomer with seven beautiful daughters (4.27.2) and a flock of golden sheep (4.27.1). (Diodorus claims here that a confusion of words leads to the myth, as μῆλα, the Greek word for 'sheep', is a homonym for the Greek word for 'apples', also μῆλα.) The Egyptian king Busiris falls in love with Atlas's daughters and hires pirates to kidnap them; Herakles slays both Busiris and the pirates, returning Atlas's daughters to their father (4.27.2–3). In gratitude, Atlas agrees "to teach him astronomy ungrudgingly" (τὴν ἀστρολογίαν ἀφθόνως διδάξαι; 4.27.4), which Herakles subsequently passes on to the Greeks. Diodorus concludes his account with the suggestion that the myth of Atlas stems from Atlas "having worked out matters concerning astronomy and having ingeniously discovered the sphere of the stars . . . as though carrying all the heavens on his shoulders" (περιττότερον γὰρ αὐτὸν τὰ κατὰ τὴν ἀστρολογίαν ἐκπεπονηκότα καὶ τὴν τῶν ἄστρων σφαῖραν φιλοτέχνως εὑρόντα ἔχειν ὑπόληψιν ὡς τὸν κόσμον ὅλον ἐπὶ τῶν ὤμων φοροῦντα; 4.27.5). Diodorus thus rationalizes the older myth of Atlas by depicting the Titan as a pre-historic culture hero of astronomy, a scientist who is only later turned into an object of (not-so-science) fiction.

The accounts of Diodorus Siculus and Ovid aside, the myth of Atlas remains consistent throughout classical antiquity, in both narrative form and visual media. These accounts regularly contain the essential features repeated in the eleventh-century CE Byzantine encyclopedia, the *Suda*: "In myth Atlas is said to hold up the earth and the heavens. And [there is a saying:] 'the iron shoulders of Atlas.' And [there's] a proverb: 'Atlas the heavens,' leaving out 'you took up.' [It is used] when people are thrown into great matters and when they fall upon evil circumstances" (ὁ μυθευόμενος τὴν γῆν καὶ τὸν οὐρανὸν βαστάζειν. καὶ σιδηρέους Ἄτλαντος ὤμους. καὶ παροιμία: Ἄτλας τὸν οὐρανόν. λείπει ὑπεδέξω. ἐπὶ τῶν μεγάλοις πράγμασιν ὑποβαλλομένων καὶ κακοῖς περιπιπτόντων; *Suda* s.v. Ἄτλας). In other words: Atlas is really strong; Atlas supports the dome of the sky; and Atlas suffers whatever weight is placed upon him, be it emotional or physical.

"Yours in perfect manhood": (Charles) Atlas in the twentieth century

I've always felt sorry for Old Man Atlas whenever I spied him crouched in stony loneliness on some pedestal or building, holding this cantankerous world upon his massive shoulders. My invariable reaction has been to wonder who the dickens would want to be an Atlas.

Stewart Robertson

In the early twentieth century, the sorrowful figure of Atlas received new life in an unexpected way. In 1903, a ten-year-old Italian immigrant named Angelo Siciliano arrived with his family in Brooklyn, NY.[17] Siciliano's family moved into an Italian settlement house run by Reverend William E. Davenport, who would take children in the house on weekly trips around New York City. One Saturday, Davenport took the children, including Siciliano, to the Brooklyn Institute of Arts and Sciences (now the Brooklyn Museum), which included a hall of ancient statuary; "the sight of Hercules, Apollo, and the rest of the gods so fascinated [Siciliano]" that the boy stayed in the hall for two hours, returning repeatedly afterwards to view the statues. Siciliano, at the time a "97-pound runt ... skinny and fragile", decided to transform his body in accordance with the aesthetics of those ancient statues. When his friends began comparing him to "a wooden figure upholding the world on top of the Atlas Hotel at Far Rockaway [Beach]", he adopted the name 'Atlas', then 'Charles Atlas'.[18]

Initially working as both a janitor and strongman on Coney Island, Charles Atlas started to be employed as a model for statues in 1916.[19] Subsequently, he was encouraged to enter two contests organized by Bernarr Macfadden, a fitness fanatic and publisher of *Physical Culture* magazine. The first contest, the "Most Beautiful Man", was a photo contest held in 1921, which Charles Atlas won handily, praised as being "like a Greek god".[20] Then, in 1922, Charles Atlas competed in Macfadden's "World's Most Perfectly Developed Man" contest held at Madison Square Gardens, in which he claimed victory over 775 competitors.[21]

Charles Atlas publicized his approach to bodybuilding as a return to classical Greek and Roman traditions, following in the tradition of nineteenth-century bodybuilders such as Eugene Sandow, who had evoked bodybuilding as a return to a Grecian ideal.[22] When he wrote a profile about himself for the November/December 1921 issue of *Physical Culture*, it was entitled "Building the Physique of a 'Greek God'". Starting in 1924, Atlas advertised his 'Secrets of Muscular Power and Beauty' in a brochure whose cover image evoked ancient Atlas, while another image in the same brochure evoked Apollo (now claiming that Atlas's "physique [wa]s more perfect than the Greek Gods"). The following year, Atlas's early business associate Frederick Tilney wrote an article entitled "How to Develop a Perfect Body" for *Artists and Models Magazine* (August 1925), in which Atlas pressed his evocation of the classical further (42):

> One of the first things [Atlas] discovered was the ancients had no modern gymnasia such as we have today. ... He found that the closer these ancient athletes lived to Nature, the more perfect and healthy they were. In [Atlas's] study of how these superb races [i.e., the Greeks and Romans] lived, he found they invariably obeyed certain definite principles and natural laws, which was the secret to their tremendous power. To beautify their bodies, increase their strength, and retain their glorious health, the Greeks, Spartans, and Romans regarded their prime duty. In fact they considered it a disgrace if any one among them lacked physical perfection.

Atlas's presentation of his bodybuilding regimen as a form of recovered classical knowledge – with its focus on living "closer to Nature" and "natural laws", on physical perfection and beautification – went hand-in-hand with his rejection of a fitness culture that was primarily oriented towards modern gymnasia and exercise equipment (such as horizontal bars, trapezes, and weightlifting). Instead of encouraging people to get to the gym, Atlas developed an exercise strategy that "pitted muscle against muscle", eventually marketing this technique as the 'Dynamic Tension Program'. Since his technique did not depend on expensive equipment, it was easy for Atlas to sell the programme by mail order; when the Great Depression hit the United States in the 1930s, the inexpensive programme became more popular still.

Atlas and his second business partner Charles Roman (who had bought Tilney's share of the company) were also savvy about how they defined and reached their target audience: men and young boys feeling insecure about their bodies. Advertisements for the Dynamic Tension Program appeared in magazines featuring Atlas's guarantee that "[i]n just 7 days, I can make you a man!" In the 1940s, Atlas began to produce ads for comic books. These ads typically featured a wimpy individual, named 'Mac', or 'Joe' (or some other stereotypically 'American' name), who is humiliated by a bully in front of his girlfriend. At home, Mac or Joe swears revenge against the bully and sends away for the Dynamic Tension handbook. Within weeks, the wimp doubles in chest size and beats up the bully to the delight of his friends and admirers. As Jonathan Black has observed, "The ads went straight to the male psyche. They preyed upon every man's insecurity – that he wasn't man enough to defend his girl."[23] In this way, Atlas linked the physique of the bodybuilder, based on the classical male nude, with both strength and violence so as to produce and market a particular kind of masculinity that ultimately became *the* template for hegemonic masculinity for at least a generation.[24]

Not only did Charles Atlas's Dynamic Tension ads appear in more than 400 magazines and comic books, but they also had a profound effect on the content in the comic books, and the representation of the Titan Atlas in particular.[25] In 1940, we find Atlas in *Whiz Comics* #2, which introduced the superhero Captain Marvel, an early Superman imitator, but whose powers derived from the magic word "SHAZAM". SHAZAM was an acronym that alluded to several mythical figures and the power Captain Marvel derived from each, including stamina from the Titan Atlas.[26] (For Captain Marvel, strength comes from Hercules.). Not to be outdone, Superman – an important early SF icon himself – also had his fair share of encounters with Atlas, including: *Superman* #28 (May/June 1944), on the cover of which Superman appears standing between Atlas and Herakles in a pose that suggests his superior strength; and *Superman* #121 (June 1948), the cover of which features Atlas in the outfit of a strongman – indirectly evoking Charles Atlas – and which explicitly asks "Is Atlas stronger than Superman?" The answer is, obviously, 'no'.

While the Titan Atlas became a figure identified with strength in the science-fictional and fantastic world of comic books, so too did the physique of Charles Atlas take hold of the popular imagination in film. Famously, the film *Gentlemen Prefer Blondes* (1953) features a sequence in which Jane Russell sings while walking through a gym of scantily clad, muscular men diligently exercising, all strikingly similar in appearance to Charles Atlas.[27] Meanwhile, the rising popularity of superheroes instilled in the public a hunger to see the muscular classical hero in action, giving rise to an entire subgenre of film about ancient superheroes, the 'muscleman epic' or *peplum* film.[28] At heart, muscleman epics were expanded Dynamic Tension ads set in mythical times, which now spoke doubly to the collective male unconscious. Americans became hooked on muscleman epics when the professional bodybuilder Steve Reeves starred in *Hercules* (1958); *Hercules* spawned a slew of further loose retellings of Greco-Roman myths in which, as Jon Solomon puts it, "'might' in its most humanly physical sense [makes] 'right' in its most simplistically narrow sense".[29] Atlas was even the protagonist of his own film in 1961, and his name was used during the period in English translations of titles from Italian films featuring the Hercules-esque hero Maciste. By exposing the public to ancient Atlas's power, Charles Atlas had thus encouraged a generation of boys and men, comic readers and movie goers alike, to worship the Titan's form, strength, and physical violence. These audiences, however, were slow to recall that Atlas had also been a figure of endless suffering.

Body building/building bodies: Frankenstein

Before turning from Charles Atlas and muscle men to *Rocky Horror*, let us return briefly to Andrew Howe's observation that the film belongs to the Promethean tradition. If the figure of Atlas requires us to consider the importance of body building – from Charles Atlas to superheroic muscle men – for the interpretation of *Rocky Horror*, it is also important to take into account another kind of 'body building': the creation of life as depicted in the tradition of stories associated with that 'modern Prometheus', Victor Frankenstein. *Rocky Horror* openly places itself in the tradition that begins with Mary Shelley's *Frankenstein* – the name of Tim Curry's iconic character, Dr Frank-N-Furter, makes this obvious enough.[30] We wish to examine briefly how *Rocky Horror* draws on three aspects of Frankenstein narratives that may influence the film's depiction of Atlas: the tradition's interest in aesthetics; the transformation of those aesthetics throughout Frankenstein's filmic tradition; and the consequences of such transformations for our understanding of masculinity in Frankenstein narratives.[31]

The Frankenstein tradition has displayed, since Mary Shelley's novel, a sustained interest in aesthetics, especially with regards to beauty, ugliness, and monstrosity; that interest is linked with the tradition's reception of the Prometheus myth. In Hesiod's two myths of Prometheus (*Th.* 507–616; *WD* 47–105), Prometheus's theft of fire leads to the creation of an artificial being, the first woman, Pandora; in this account, Hesiod elaborates the care that the gods put into the physical beauty of Pandora, such that she is a καλὸν κακόν or 'beautiful evil' (*Th.* 585) whose exterior beauty stands in stark contrast with her turpitude.

Shelley plays on this tension between (physical) beauty and (ethical) ugliness in *Frankenstein* (hereafter *F*). Victor Frankenstein expends tremendous effort in "collecting and arranging" the various "materials" from which the Creature will be composed, with each part "selected ... as beautiful" (*F* 1.3–4: 33–35).[32] Victor initially aims to construct "an animal as complex and wonderful as a man" (1.3: 33), complete with "hair ... of a lustrous black, and flowing ... [and] teeth of a pearly whiteness" (1.4: 35). Victor then decides to exceed that aim, "to make the being of a gigantic stature ... about eight feet in height, and proportionably large" (1.3: 33). When he finally animates the Creature, however, Victor describes the same assemblage in terms of revulsion and disgust, such as the Creature's "dull yellow eye" and how "[h]is yellow skin scarcely covered the work of muscles and arteries beneath" (1.4: 35). Even the hair and teeth which Victor had formerly selected with such care now "only formed a more horrid contrast with his watery eyes, ... his shriveled complexion and straight black lips" (ibid.). To both Victor and other people that the Creature encounters, the Creature is not the hoped-for apogee of beauty, but rather gives physical form to ugliness and monstrosity, despite his rapidly developing intelligence and his capacity for compassion towards humans.[33]

The novel *Frankenstein*'s concern with aesthetics has subsequently been retained in cinematic receptions, although such receptions have made crucial changes to Shelley's vision of the Creature as physically monstrous but capable of intellectual and ethical beauty.[34] In the first full-length Frankenstein film, *Frankenstein* (1931), director James Whale emphasizes the Creature's monstrous size and physical hideousness, but deprives him of intellect and ethical capacity; Henry (sic) Frankenstein's assistant Fritz steals for the Creature not a normal brain but the brain of a murderer, such that the Creature is predisposed to violence and murder, and ethical ugliness mirrors physical ugliness.[35] Subsequent cinematic adaptations further emphasize such ugliness and monstrosity so as to abandon any aspects of the Creature's intelligence and humanity in favour of a disfigured, lumbering, killing machine. This is perhaps most obvious in the successful 1957 horror film directed by Terence Fisher and produced by Hammer Films Productions, *The Curse of Frankenstein* (hereafter *Curse*). In this film, Victor sets out to create the perfect man, then engages in a series of actions that mark him as a ruthless killer. The Creature, too, is a ruthless killer, and thus takes to an extreme the alignment of physical and ethical monstrosity found in Whale's film. It is noteworthy that *Rocky Horror* was both filmed on the same location (Oakley Court) as *Curse* and used several props belonging to Hammer Films, such that any reading of the Frankenstein tradition in *Rocky Horror* must take into account the influence – or, at least, the lurking spectre – of *Curse*.

These transformations in the aesthetic representation of the Creature must further be understood in terms of the aesthetics of masculinity. From Shelley's novel on, the Frankenstein tradition has carried along with itself a pointed, if not deliberate, queerness, such that critics have often read the story as an allegory for the experience of the male homosexual (the Creature as sexual outcast) or as a barely suppressed homosexual romance (Victor and the Creature as would-be lovers).[36] When Jeffery Weinstock claims that *Rocky Horror* "put[s] a homosexual spin onto the Pygmalion and Frankenstein myths", this surely misses the point that the Frankenstein tradition has already – if not always – been read as a homosocial or homosexual myth.[37] Bette London goes further still, drawing attention to Shelley's "novel's crucially masculine scaffolding", such that *Frankenstein* puts on 'a spectacle of masculinity' that "exposes ... the repression of masculine contradiction at the heart of dominant cultural productions".[38] In other words, from the Frankenstein tradition's very inception, there has been an emphasis on the aesthetics of masculine bodies and the contradictions exposed by masculine bodies, such as the complex interplay between external appearances and interior ethical formation.

In summary, we would suggest that the silver screen's selective reception of Mary Shelley's *Frankenstein* mirrors Charles Atlas's selective reception of mythic Atlas. The Frankensteins of Whale's 1931 film or Fisher's 1957 film work to reduce the Creature to a one-dimensional representation of Shelley's original Creature. In a similar vein, Charles Atlas interpreted mythic Atlas solely in terms of his physical strength and beauty, with no regard for Atlas's suffering, such that Charles Atlas's Titan came to represent a kind of hegemonic masculinity without recognition of the costs Hesiod warns of in *Theogony*. In other words, the persona of Charles Atlas and the cinematic Creature are products constructed out of the exhumed appendages of past traditions, stitched together and resurrected in a new form whose physical exterior attempts to repress the contradictions that lie therein.

Atlas(es) in the *Rocky Horror Picture Show*

Rocky Horror's particular genius, then, is to (dis-)place these two seemingly disparate traditions – on one hand, the 'musculinity' of Charles Atlas in the realm of fitness and comics; on the other hand, the spectacular masculinity of monstrous Frankenstein – into the same, single SF narrative and via the mythic figure of Atlas. The film manipulates its ties to the horror genre to generate the false expectation that a mad scientist – Dr Frank-N-Furter – will create an ugly homicidal monster – his own Frankenstein's Creature – by harnessing the power of electricity. And yet, when Frank reveals his creation to hapless Brad and Janet (played respectively by Barry Bostwick and Susan Sarandon), this creature is not an ugly monster, but a muscular Adonis, "a man / with blond hair and a tan" in a skimpy bikini (Fig. 8.2). Visually, it is not hard to see that Rocky evokes the muscleman of Charles Atlas's ads, but Frank makes the connection explicit by saying that "[Rocky] carries the Charles Atlas seal of approval". Frank further boasts that he too can create Charles Atlas's body, although without the effort or discipline: "Such strenuous living I just don't understand / When in just seven days, I can make you a man." Indeed, Frank seems to critique the Dynamic Tension Program, arguing that the minor science fiction of Charles Atlas may be overcome by the greater science fiction of creating life. There lurks in Frank's boast a hint of megalomania, for, as Liz Locke points out, the creation of man "in just seven days" also evokes Genesis 1:26–27, such that Frank equates himself with the deity who creates mankind.[39] Nevertheless, even if Frank fancies himself a deity who can create the perfect man, he is not able to conceive of a man that exists outside of established norms, instead replicating the same logic of hegemonic masculinity already created by Charles Atlas.

That Frank's creative fantasies have already been constrained is anticipated in two ways. First, when Frank initially enters into the film singing the song "Sweet Transvestite",

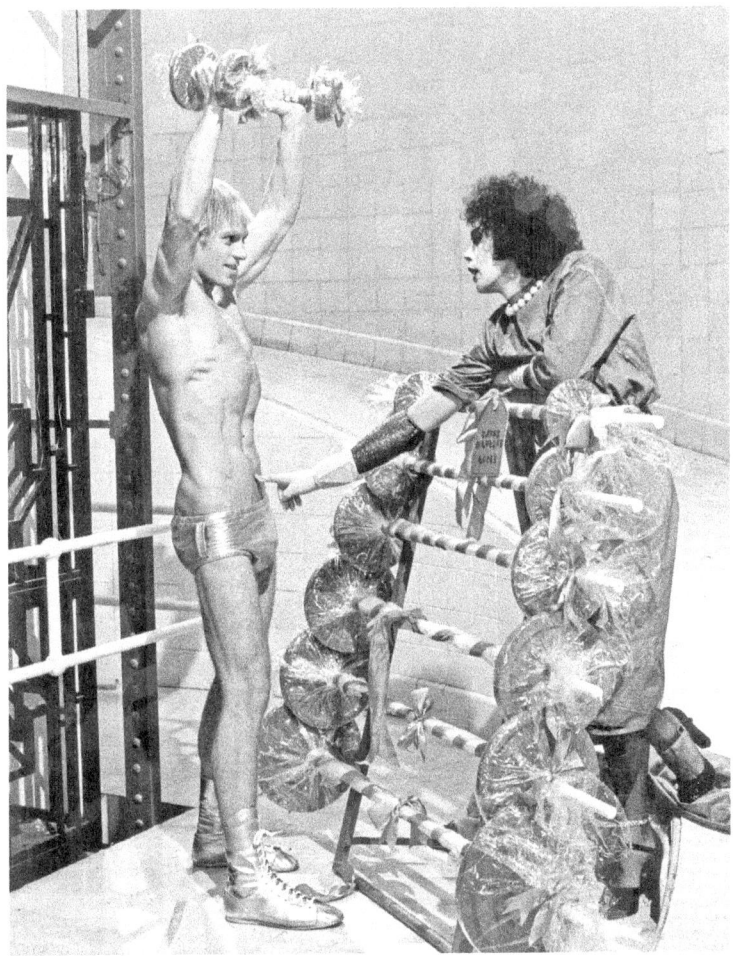

Fig. 8.2 Frank-N-Furter (Tim Curry) and his creation Rocky (Peter Hinwood), who evokes the figure of the muscleman and Charles Atlas. From *The Rocky Horror Picture Show* (dir. Sharman, 1975). 20th Century Fox. Getty Images.

he suggests that he, Brad, and Janet "could take in an old Steve Reeves movie". Reeves evokes the muscleman epic or *peplum* genre, setting up the audience for Frank's repeated references to his great love of muscles; however, in this context, as Daniel O'Brien suggests, the reference to Reeves calls attention to "the latent eroticism associated with displays of bare flesh" in *peplum* films in general.[40] Such musculophilia is also reflected in the décor of Frank's laboratory, which includes some of the other direct evocations of classical antiquity in the film: tall, white, and phallic columns, and, more crucially, gleaming white but cheapish reproductions of two famous male nude statues. One of these statues, the Diskobolos or Discus-Thrower (Fig. 8.3), comes from Greek antiquity itself (*c.* 460–450 BCE), made by the famous sculptor Myron; the other statue is

Fig. 8.3 A copy of the ancient Diskobolos stands above Frank-N-Furter (Tim Curry) in his laboratory. From *The Rocky Horror Picture Show* (dir. Sharman, 1975). 20th Century Fox. Getty Images.

Michelangelo's *David* (*c.* 1501–1504) and consciously draws upon the then-recently-rediscovered aesthetics of Greco-Roman antiquity. (When these statues are eventually damaged, it is good fortune that Frank also has a Medusa Transducer to turn humans into naked statues.[41]) Frank's laboratory thus takes on the appearance of a kind of pagan cult sanctuary dedicated to the worship of an idealized, whitewashed, cheaply reproduced, and recycled classical masculinity. Frank sings that "I'm makin' a man [because] he's good for relieving my tension", evoking Charles Atlas's Dynamic Tension Program, but whereas Frank's tension may be relieved, he effectively displaces that tension onto the shaking, terrified, and suffering body of Rocky himself.

We see this in two key scenes, both of which constitute the other explicit evocations of classical antiquity in the film. First, when Rocky is created, his first words are the lyrics "The sword of Damocles is hanging over my head / And I've got the feeling someone's gonna be cuttin' the thread"; this alludes to the story of Damocles, who, we learn from Cicero's *Tusculan Disputations* (5.21), was a slave of the tyrant Dionysius I of Syracuse. Damocles envied the tyrant's social station; Dionysius offered to teach him what it is like to be a happy tyrant by placing the slave on a throne with a sword "suspended by a single horse-hair, so as to hang over the head of that happy man". Damocles then "entreated the tyrant to give him leave to go, for now he had no desire to be happy". In comparing himself to Damocles, Rocky reveals his unhappiness and terror, intuiting at the very moment of his creation that "my life is a misery", spending much of the subsequent scene attempting to flee Frank's sexual advances. Here Rocky evokes not only the tense terror of Damocles, but also the Creature of Mary Shelley's *Frankenstein*, who describes himself at birth as wandering "half-frightened", a "poor, helpless, miserable wretch" (*F* 2.3: 70).

At the end of Rocky's "Sword of Damocles" song, Frank launches into a reprise of "I Can Make You a Man", which turns into a mock wedding procession leading to Frank's bedchamber. Above the bed we see a stained-glass window emblazoned with the image of the Titan Atlas (Fig. 8.4); here Atlas has the same hyper-masculine musculature and

Fig. 8.4 A stained-glass image of mythic Atlas looms before Rocky (Peter Hinwood), who is chained to Frank-N-Furter's bed. At right Riff Raff (Richard O'Brien) grabs a candelabrum to threaten Rocky with fire. From *The Rocky Horror Picture Show* (dir. Sharman, 1975). 20th Century Fox.

blond hair that characterize Rocky, but appears in a position of servitude, down on one knee, his contorted body straining under the weight of the world. The globe's proportions emphasize the difficulty of Atlas's struggle, showing how his suffering is as great as the beauty of his body. The image of Atlas in his suffering reflects and highlights Rocky's own suffering, re-framing the image of Rocky-as-Charles-Atlas into Rocky-as-Titan-Atlas. Indeed, the next time we see Rocky, once again in Frank's bedchamber and before the image of Atlas, Rocky is bound face down, chained to Frank's bed and tormented with a candelabrum by Frank's assistants, Riff Raff and Magenta (played by Patricia Quinn). In frightening Frank-N-Furter's creation with fire, they evoke yet again the filmic Frankenstein Creature. By juxtaposing Rocky's chained body with the image of the Titan Atlas in his ongoing, dynamic, and tense punishment, the scene visually establishes a connection between Atlas's classical bondage and the bondage of Rocky.

Rocky Horror resists the mythic masculinity promulgated by Charles Atlas, superhero comics, and muscleman films in the mid-twentieth century by exposing a dynamic tension in the reception of the Titan Atlas by Charles Atlas. The film invites viewers to consider Atlas not in the sepia-tone, nigh-monochromatic representation Charles Atlas had produced, but in the vivid polychromatic, stained-glass image of Atlas. Rocky may possess the strength of a Charles Atlas, but that strength comes at a cost known all too well since classical antiquity, the cost of one's own safety and freedom. In this way, the figures of Atlas in *Rocky Horror* warn audiences that although we may possess the scientific or science-fictive knowledge to build a better man, and we may believe in science's fictional ability to lead us to sexual liberation and our deepest fantasies, nevertheless too much suffering awaits. In other words, *Rocky Horror* uses a classical tradition to construct an analogy: just as queer masculinity and sexuality have been oppressed by larger historical forces, so too is the science-fictive figure of Charles Atlas unable to escape the weight and oppression of Atlas's classical past.

Notes

1. This paper began as Moses's thesis at the University of Puget Sound (spring 2014), for which Rogers served as advisor. Subsequently we collaborated to develop and deliver the paper at *The Once and Future Antiquity* conference, also at Puget Sound (March 2015). We thank the audience at that talk, as well as Benjamin Eldon Stevens, for insightful feedback. All mistakes are ours alone.

2. Twitchell (1983: 76).

3. Siegel (1980: 306).

4. Aviram (1992: 183); so too Weinstock (2007: 56–57, 59).

5. Kilgore (1986: 154, 152, 157 and 159, respectively).

6. Howe (2015: 130). This is the only reference to Greco-Roman traditions in that entire volume.

7. On the influence of Shelley's *Frankenstein* and the Frankenstein cinematic tradition on *Rocky Horror*, see below ('Body Building/Building Bodies: Frankenstein'). Much ink has been shed on Shelley's subtitle: see, e.g., Small (1973: 48–67), Baldick (1987: 40–46), Mellor (1988: 71), Dougherty (2006: 108–114), and Weiner, Stevens, and Rogers 2018. Mousley 2016 offers a reading of *Frankenstein* in terms of the closely linked category of the 'posthuman', while Rogers

2018 reads *Frankenstein* and some of its SF descendants in terms of both 'the Postmodern Prometheus' and the posthuman.

8. Here we use the term 'equivalence' in its technical sense for reception studies, as defined by Hardwick (2003), where a figure is "fulfilling an analogous role in source and reception but not necessarily identical in form or content" (9).

9. Artt (2008: 61–62).

10. On Atlas generally, see Helmbold 1906.

11. Text: West (1966: 131). Solmsen (1990: 27), following Guyet, expurgates line 519, noting a repetition of that line at *Th.* 747; Solmsen suggests that 519 may come before 518 ("an ante 518?"); cf. West (1966: 311–312), who nevertheless retains the line. Solmsen also seems to translate the expurgated line differently, amusingly noting that "Atlas stands on his feet, not on his head and hands" (*pedibus stat A[tlas], non capite et manibus*). All translations in this chapter are our own.

12. Gantz (1993: i.40, 46).

13. There is also an unattributed fragment of Aeschylus (fr. 312 Sommerstein = Athenaeus *Deipnosophistae* 11.491a) that refers to Atlas's "great labor upholding the roof of heaven" (μέγιστον ἄθλον οὐρανοστεγῆ; line 2), which is lamented by his seven daughters; see Sommerstein (2008: 300–301).

14. Gantz (1993: i.46) suggests that "possibly the punishment is older than the crime". We must note here that *Prometheus Bound* 425–430 is not without other complications. Both Griffith (1983: 55–56, 161–162) and West (1990: 300) emend the passage significantly, while Podlecki (2005: 106, 175) treats the lines as spurious (following Badham, Dale, and Lloyd-Jones) and deletes them entirely.

15. On visual representations of Herakles and Atlas, see, e.g., Carpenter (1991: 128–129 with plates 209–210), with reference to Pausanias 5.11.5.

16. Text: Tarrant 2004. Cf. Virgil *Aeneid* 4.246–251, who depicts Atlas as a wooded mountain range prior to Ovid. On the Ovidian passage, see Anderson (1997: 481–484), whose description of Perseus's use of this 'secret weapon' as "sadistic" (483) bears some resemblance to Frank-N-Furter's use of the Medusa Transducer (see below).

17. Black 2009.

18. This summary, including quotations, derives from Charles Atlas's own account, reported in Robertson 1939. See also Baines 2014.

19. Charles Atlas posed for several statues, including the statue of George Washington in Washington Square Park, the statue of Alexander Hamilton in front of the US Treasury in Washington, DC, and – perhaps proleptically for *Rocky Horror* – the statue of Sorrow near the Marne River southeast of Paris; see Robertson 1939 and Black 2009.

20. In the article ("The World's Most Handsome Man") published in *Physical Culture* (October 1921) to announce his victory in the photo contest, Atlas is praised in one caption as having "the face, physique, stature and carriage of an Apollo".

21. Black 2009.

22. On Sandow and the classicizing rhetoric of bodybuilding, see Wyke 1997b and Cleveland 2018.

23. Black 2009.

24. For a history of the term 'hegemonic masculinity', see Connell and Messerschmidt 2005. The phrase was not coined until well after Charles Atlas and *Rocky Horror* (in the early 1980s), but we believe it is useful here in describing the particular mode of masculinity promulgated by Charles Atlas, since 'hegemonic masculinity': first, distinguishes one particular mode of masculinity from others and asserts hierarchies of power among masculinities (even as they

may collectively work to assert dominance over femininity); second, is "not ... normal in the statistical sense; only a minority of men might enact it. But it [is] certainly normative" (ibid., 832); and, lastly, does "not mean violence, but [can] be supported by force" (ibid.). In reference to this intensely physical and hyperbolic form of masculinity, scholars in media studies sometimes use Yvonne Tasker's term 'musculinity'; see, e.g., Turner (2009: 140).

25. On 'more than 400 magazines and comic books', see Black 2009.

26. The acronym SHAZAM stands for: S – Solomon (wisdom); H – Hercules (strength); A – Atlas (stamina); Z – Zeus (power); A – Achilles (courage); M – Mercury (speed).

27. Cf. Russo (1981: 78) on this scene: "Probably the most homoerotic sequence in a [Howard] Hawks film ... Russell is surrounded by muscular men in briefs who seem to be oblivious to her charms ('Doesn't *anyone* wanna play?') but are very interested in showing off their bodies to the choreographer Jack Cole."

28. On the muscular male body and the *peplum* film, see most recently O'Brien 2014. Cf. Wyke (1997: esp. 55–70), who also examines antecedents in silent film and homoerotic art.

29. Solomon (1978: 192).

30. Co-writer Richard O'Brien openly admits the debt to Shelley: see, e.g., Michaels and Evans (2002: 40).

31. For readings of *Rocky Horror* in the Frankenstein tradition, see, e.g., Eichler 1987, Hitchcock (2007: 249–53), Locke (2008: 145–146, 149–153), and Matheson (2008: 27).

32. All references to *F* are to the edition of Hunter 2012.

33. Gumpert 2018 argues that critics have misread the Creature as 'ugly' ("as onto-theological failure, a failure of creation due to violation of divine law"; 106), asserting instead that we might read the Creature as an "artistic triumph ... the epiphany of absolute beauty" (106–107) who embodies the transcendent aesthetic of the sublime.

34. On *F*'s reception in cinema, see Hitchcock 2007 and Jancovich 2016.

35. Whale's film is based on Peggy Webling's 1927 play, *Frankenstein: An Adventure in the Macabre*. For a reading of Whale's *Frankenstein* in terms of aesthetics and eugenics/dysgenics, see Smith (2011: 59–81).

36. On queer readings of *F*, see, e.g., Haggerty 2016. James Whale was openly homosexual, and this has affected interpretations of his 1931 film: on Whale's homosexuality and his *Frankenstein*, see Russo (1981: 50–52); the film *Gods and Monsters* (dir. Condon, 1998) offers a fictionalized treatment of Whale's career and sexuality, based on Bram 1995.

37. Weinstock (2007: 55).

38. London (1993: 255 and 260–261, respectively).

39. Locke (2008: 148).

40. O'Brien (2014: 39–40, quotation on 39); cf. Stafford (2012: 232–236) and Wyke 1997b on the *peplum* and Hercules.

41. We cannot help but wonder whether the idea for the Medusa Transducer made its way into *Rocky Horror* via the Ovidian account of Atlas's transformation into stone at the hands of Perseus and the Medusa's head (discussed above). However, given the broad popularity of Medusa in post-classical receptions, such musing is speculative at best. On the tradition of Medusa from Homer to Versace, see, e.g., Garber and Vickers 2003.

CHAPTER 9
DRINKING BLOOD AND TALKING GHOSTS IN DIANA WYNNE JONES'S *THE TIME OF THE GHOST*

Frances Foster

Introduction

Literary conversations between the living and the dead are uncanny events, ones that shift our perceptions of the distinctions between the two states. The idea that the living and the dead occupy separate worlds, but with a divide that can be crossed, is one that extends back to the ancient world. Literary and cultural material from the ancient societies of the Near East, Egypt, Greece, and Rome demonstrates highly complex and developed myths surrounding the dead and how the living related to the dead. In the ancient world, conjuring up the spirits of the dead belongs properly to the domain of necromancy, which Daniel Ogden has defined as "communication with the dead in order to receive prophecy from them".[1] In Greek texts, the technical terms for the act of necromancy and the place where necromantic rites are performed appear quite late: Herodotus uses the word νεκυομαντεῖον to describe a shrine of the dead (*Histories* 5.92); Strabo uses the word νεκυόμαντις (*Geography* 16.2.39) to indicate the 'necromancer' who carries out such rites. The necromancer must first conduct rituals at a specified and appropriate place in order to allow any interaction to take place. The aim of a necromantic rite is primarily to discover information from the dead which is otherwise unavailable to the living, whether a prophecy about the future in the strictest sense of the word or some arcane information that can only be divulged by the dead person.

One of our earliest – though notoriously problematic – accounts of a necromantic ritual (from the Greek world) is that which Odysseus describes in *Odyssey* 11. He performs a ceremony in which he sacrifices two sheep, draining their blood into a pit he has dug and then allowing the shades of the dead to drink the blood so that they may speak to him coherently. Such a ceremony, which enables communication between the living and the dead, forms a central part of the strange rituals performed by the children in Diana Wynne Jones's 1981 *The Time of the Ghost*. When the children observe that there is a ghost among them, they perform rituals to try to communicate with it – indeed, the children are the ghost's living sisters, with whom it, too, is trying to communicate. Jones thus consciously draws on and subverts the Odyssean blood-drinking ritual as a means of communication. In this chapter, I propose to read the rituals and sacrifices in Jones's *The Time of the Ghost* in the context of those Odysseus describes, and examine how Jones reinterprets and refigures Homer's image of communication between the living and the dead via her title's ghost.

The story in *The Time of the Ghost* (henceforth *Ghost*) is set as an extended flashback: the ghost finds herself seven years in the past, seeing her own childhood from the outside. She knows she is one of four sisters – Cart, Sally, Imogen, and Fenella – although she remains uncertain which sister she is for most of the narrative. (Even when she thinks she understands she is Sally, she doubts her identity and decides she is mistaken.) The children identify the presence of a ghost in their midst and try to communicate with it in a séance before attempting to exorcise it with bell, book, and candle. But after the ghost succeeds in writing them a message via their friend Ned, they take more concerted action in their attempts to discover the identity of the ghost and what it wants. At this point, the eldest of the sisters, Cart, races off in search of books to help them make the ghost talk properly (153):

> Then suddenly she was back, red and breathless, hurling fat paperback books on to the table. Thump – *The Odyssey* – thump – *The Iliad* – thump – Virgil's *Aeneid*. 'There!' she said. 'Somewhere in these there's a way to make them speak – it tells you how to make a ghost talk – I know there is! … I *know* it's in one of these somewhere. He made a ghost speak – whoever he was – by letting it drink blood.'

The scene is amusing, not least because when Cart asks Ned and his friend Howard which text contains the episode she described, the boys have no idea – despite learning Latin and having a "classical education", as Cart observes, the boys admit that they have never read any of these texts. The humour continues for the reader who knows that Cart is more accurate than she thinks: in fact, in all three epics, the heroes speak to the shades of the dead at some point. The shade of Patroclus appears as a ghost to Achilles at *Iliad* (*Il.*) 23.65, when he comes to visit the sleeping Achilles without being summoned. Equally, Aeneas is visited twice by uninvited ghosts: first by Creusa's shade at *Aeneid* 2.772; second by the shade of his father Anchises at 5.722. Later, Aeneas journeys down to the Underworld to talk to the dead in their own environment (book 6). But Cart was thinking of Odysseus, who, unlike Achilles and Aeneas, actually calls up the shades of the dead and speaks to them in *Odyssey* 11 by allowing them to drink blood.

Acquiring and preparing the blood

Odysseus's encounter with the dead, or *nekuia*, is a notoriously complex episode. Bruce Louden has suggested that the narrative combines two distinct and separate genres of myth: the *katabasis* (an actual descent to the Underworld) and the 'nekuomantic rite', a cultic ritual involving the consultation of the souls of the dead at a dedicated shrine.[2] In addition, there are two (not quite identical) accounts of the rituals performed within the *Odyssey*: Circe's instructions to Odysseus at the end of *Odyssey* 10 (reported by Odysseus) and Odysseus's own account of what he did at the start of *Odyssey* 11. It is a complex rite. First, Odysseus must journey to the place that Circe has described, located on the far side of the river Ocean, at "a rock and the conflux of two thundering rivers" (πέτρη τε ξύνεσίς τε δύω ποταμῶν ἐριδούπων; *Odyssey* [*Od.*] 10.515).³ Once there, Odysseus draws his sword and uses it to dig a pit into which he pours a libation to the dead, consisting of a honeyed milk drink, followed by wine and then water, over which he sprinkles barley. He then promises that on his return to Ithaca, he will make sacrifices to the dead and separately to the famous (and now deceased) Theban prophet Teiresias. Next, he cuts the throats of the two black animals (a ram and a ewe) he has brought with him, so that "into the pit flowed the dark blood" (ἐς βόθρον, ῥέε δ' αἷμα κελαινεφές; 11.36).⁴ At this point, some of the dead first appear, but immediately Odysseus asks his companions to both burn the dead animals and pray to Hades and Persephone to appease them.

Despite Cart's rather hazy memories of Odysseus's ritual, there are considerable similarities between the necromantic rite performed by the children and that described by Odysseus. Although Cart cannot find a description of the ritual with enough detail to enable the children to carry out the ritual tasks in the correct order, she enthusiastically tells the others, "Everyone go and get some blood. Quick!" (*Ghost* 154). During the search for blood, Cart adds extra details as she thinks of them, remembering, "It was outside in the book. I think they dug a trench for the blood" (158). There is considerable humour as they try to collect the blood since, unlike Odysseus, they do not have an animal at hand for sacrifice. Instead, they raid the school kitchens, draining blood from a tray containing some ox hearts, and then mixing the animal blood with their own by cutting themselves or enforcing nosebleeds. They collect the blood in an enamel bowl rather than a trench so that they have somewhere to store it safely without it draining away. The animal blood from the kitchens turns out to be rather weak and watery, although the children supplement it with undiluted human blood. The resulting mixture parallels Odysseus's libation of water and blood, although it lacks the additional ingredients of honeyed milk, wine, and barley. Despite the unusual mixture of animal blood with human blood – which is not part of ancient offerings to ghosts – there is no suggestion in *Ghost* that we are intended to think of this as some form of human sacrifice for the ghost (as opposed to, e.g., the human sacrifice Achilles performs in his anger over Patroclus's death rather than for a nekuomantic purpose at *Il.* 23.23). Howard brings the pickled corpse of a rabbit from the biology classrooms, claiming it "will do to stand for a sacrifice . . . we ought to have one if we're going to be properly pagan" (*Ghost* 158). Cart omits any direct sacrifices in her rituals to invite the ghost to speak, although true sacrifices take place both before and after this event in the narrative.

The blood and the dead

Before Odysseus sets out, Circe explains to him that he should not let the dead come near the blood until he has heard from Teiresias. She does not suggest that the dead need to drink the blood to talk to him; she implies that simply approaching the blood is enough: "don't let the helpless heads of the dead go nearer to the blood" (μηδὲ ἐᾶν νεκύων ἀμενηνὰ κάρηνα / αἵματος ἆσσον ἴμεν; *Od.* 10.536–537). Odysseus reports that he protected access to the blood with his sword, exactly as Circe has instructed. He repeats her words from 535–537, only changing the tense and person of the verbs in the middle line: "I myself drew my sharp sword from beside my thigh, and sat, but didn't let the helpless heads of the dead go nearer to the blood before I heard from Teiresias" (αὐτὸς δὲ ξίφος ὀξὺ ἐρυσσάμενος παρὰ μηροῦ / ἥμην, οὐδ' εἴων νεκύων ἀμενηνὰ κάρηνα / αἵματος ἆσσον ἴμεν, πρὶν Τειρεσίαο πυθέσθαι; 11.48–50).

Odysseus conducts an initial conversation with the shade of his companion Elpenor, who broke his neck the previous night. Odysseus was unaware of Elpenor's demise until this meeting, and Elpenor is (as yet) unburied. Elpenor does not approach the blood to talk to Odysseus, and Odysseus allows Teiresias to approach the blood, as Circe has instructed. Teiresias speaks to Odysseus, asking that he "withdraw" from the pit "in order that I may drink the blood and speak to you truthfully" (αἵματος ὄφρα πίω καί τοι νημερτέα εἴπω; 11.96). It is thus Teiresias who first introduces the idea of drinking the blood in order to speak. He later clarifies that Odysseus can choose to talk to others of the dead by letting them drink the blood: "Whichever of the dead who have died you let go near the blood will speak to you infallibly" (ὅν τινα μέν κεν ἐᾷς νεκύων κατατεθνηώτων / αἵματος ἆσσον ἴμεν, ὁ δέ τοι νημερτὲς ἐνίψει; 147–148). Odysseus reports that subsequent spirits of the dead, such as his mother, do indeed approach and drink the blood before they speak to him.

Cart recalls enough of this (without the complexities of the original text) to remind the others while they are attempting to collect blood: "What he did in whatever book it was, was to keep other ghosts off with his sword, so that only the one he wanted got a drink" (*Ghost* 156). This leads to the comic horror of the youngest sister, Fenella, stained with blood herself, waving a "mighty" carving knife (in place of a sword) over the bowl of blood "with increasing glee" and intoning, "Unwanted ghosts keep away! ... Lots of lovely gore! ... No foreign ghosts wanted" (156–158). Of course, we know that there are no other ghosts present at this point, making Fenella's efforts unnecessary. It turns out that the children do not need to summon the ghost in the way that Odysseus summons the dead with his initial prayers and sacrifices, but the ghost does need to drink the blood before she can talk to her sisters.

So why does drinking the blood matter, and what does it allow the dead to do, exactly? There has been much scholarly debate surrounding the drinking of blood by the dead in the *Odyssey*, not least because not all the dead who encounter Odysseus seem to need to drink the blood to talk to him. John Heath has observed that "the fully dead do not usually speak like the living", and therefore require some means to enable them to converse with the living.[5] Walter Burkert suggests that, since the dead lack consciousness, they must drink the blood to "recollect themselves and speak" properly rather than like gibbering bats.[6] Alfred Heubeck and Arie Hoekstra refer to Teiresias's words, claiming that the dead who have drunk blood "will recall their previous existence and be able to give information".[7] Daniel Ogden has argued that the blood will "give them the power of recognition and speech", while Christiane Sourvinou-Inwood admits that "the connection between drinking blood and the ability to recognise, speak and think is unstable" within the text.[8] Sarah Iles Johnston points out that the blood is "a striking emblem of the vigorous life they have left behind" to allow them "to become temporarily capable of normal human converse".[9] I shall explore these interpretations in relation to both texts shortly.

The living and the dead

In the *Odyssey*, the dead in Hades are repeatedly called "the souls of the dead … who have died" (ψυχαί … νεκύων κατατεθνηώτων; e.g., 11.37) as a reminder that they have completed their deaths. The perfect participle (κατατεθνηώτων, 'who have died') underscores the idea that they have completed the process of dying and remain dead. They are also called "feeble heads of the dead" (νεκύων ἀμενηνὰ κάρηνα; 11.29) because they are insubstantial and powerless shades. However, the ghost in *The Time of the Ghost* has not quite died yet: she is in fact still (just) alive. Seven years in the future from the flashback that occupies the main part of the narrative, the adult Sally is lying semi-conscious in a hospital bed on a life-support machine and receiving blood transfusions, after being thrown out of a speeding car by her violent boyfriend Julian Addiman. Every moment Sally experiences in the past as a ghost she spends unconscious in the present, in the manner of a thriller, as Farah Mendlesohn notes.[10] She quite literally hovers between life and death since she was critically injured in the accident.

There is an additional reason for Sally's critical condition within the narrative: exactly seven years before the accident, Sally dedicated herself to an ancient goddess, Monigan. This goddess, whom the children thought they had invented but instead had invoked, demands a life from those who dedicated themselves to her after seven years. As a ghost, Sally can hear Monigan inform her, "*I set you aside for seven years … Those seven years are up now*" (*Ghost* 109). Cart calculates that during those seven years there were two leap days: "Count two days for Leap Years and you've got till midnight tonight. Monigan *is* playing fair after all" (126). These two days are the time which Sally experiences as a ghost, hovering between the states of life and death. In this way, she is fundamentally different from the shades in Hades who have finished the process of dying and remain dead, even Odysseus's recently dead (and as-yet unburied) companion Elpenor. Although Sally occupies this peculiar space between life and death, as a ghost in the past she functions in the same way as the shades of the dead.

Drinking the blood

Thus, like Odysseus's feeble dead, as a ghost Sally needs to drink blood in order to talk to the living. But what exactly does it enable her to do? To begin with Burkert's suggestion, "[t]hey are heads without vital force … for indeed they lack consciousness. … They must first drink the blood in order to recollect themselves and speak. Otherwise, they 'flutter as shadows' like gibbering bats in their cave".[11]

The blood does not help Sally recollect herself, nor, even as a ghost, is she totally without consciousness. Her memory is flawed, both as a ghost and as a hospital patient, and "her intelligence as a ghost seemed as limited as a narrow torch beam" (*Ghost* 129), but the blood enhances neither her memory nor her intelligence. The blood does allow people to hear her directly when she speaks to them; otherwise, they only seem to hear her out of the edge of their attention, as when her sister Imogen, intent on her piano practice, replies to the ghost without thinking about whom she might be talking to (141). However, even with the help of the blood, Sally as a ghost cannot talk exactly like the living. She may try to speak in full sentences, but what she and the others hear is a broken echo of what she says (170):

> *Yes*, said the ghost. *Who am I? Don't you know?* This was what she said. But what she heard, and what the others certainly heard, was not so much a voice as a moaning, like the noise of liquid swirling in an enamel bowl, only with words in it. And the words were broken patches of words. It was like a faulty radio circuit. 'Who I – Who I – Oh who I?' she went, like a broken owl.

It appears as if the blood, swirling in the enamel bowl beneath her, provides her with the ability to create sounds, rather than giving her speech as such. Sally is not as helpless as the Homeric dead but resembles the image Burkert recalls from much later in the *Odyssey*, when the dead suitors, on their way to Hades, are compared to squeaking bats (24.6–9). In a similar way, the blood cannot prevent Sally's ghost from making the noise of a different winged animal, recalling the owls hooting when she followed her younger self across the fields at midnight earlier in the story (*Ghost* 104).

Heubeck and Hoekstra's interpretation assumes that the blood allows the dead to remember something about their past: "Teiresias's answer explains the reasons behind both the blood sacrifice and the behaviour of the ψυχαί: spirits which taste the blood will recall, for a little while, their previous existence, and be able to give information."[12] The first half of this reading follows that of Martin Nilsson, who suggests that consciousness and memory return to the dead after they drink the blood.[13] Unfortunately for Sally's ghost, her recollection and memory of events have been poor throughout her experiences as a ghost, and drinking the blood does nothing to change this. As a ghost, she has no memory of the seven years in between the time she observes in the 'past' and the 'present' she experiences in the hospital. Her limited recall of people and events is usually only supported by encountering people and places directly to jog her memory. The blood also does not help her regain a sense of self-awareness or grant her any insight into her own identity, which remains unknown to her, both as a ghost and as a hospital patient. She does give information, or at least try to (*Ghost* 171):

> The ghost spoke. She gave them, as far as she was able, a perfectly clear explanation. . . . But while she spoke, she was listening to a strange broken mutter and moaning pieces of words, and she knew it was what everyone else was hearing. 'Monigan – Monigan – seven years' claim – life help. Help. Help future now – only you – help blood Monigan – seven years help life – dying – seven – help . . .'

There is a gap between what she wants to say (and thinks she is saying) and what she and her living audience actually hear. The blood provides the sound by which the living can hear her, but it appears as a distorted echo of the speech she was trying to make. It does not enable her to communicate coherently the information that she does know. In addition, her poor memory and weak sense of self do not enable her to provide detailed information about the future as Teiresias does. In fact, her first words form a question about her identity, as hopes that the living might be able to identify her. This is an inversion of the more common aim in ancient necromancy, where the living summon the dead in order to ask them for information.[14]

Odysseus Tsagarakis has argued, with reference to the shades of Agamemnon and Ajax in the *Odyssey*, that "the ghosts simply react to the blood and it is only after they taste blood that they can display emotions" on a more complex level.[15] The Homeric shades all gather around the pit as soon as Odysseus drains the blood into it, demonstrating a collective desire to approach the blood, a desire that requires Odysseus to ward them off with his sword. In Jones, although the sound of the blood swirling in the enamel bowl "seemed to draw the ghost" (*Ghost* 166), she does not experience the same urgent desire to drink the blood. The blood, which does not enhance her weak memory, does not grant her any more complex emotions, other than the feelings of panic, fear, and urgency that she has experienced from the outset of finding herself as a ghost. Equally, and even more so after she drinks the blood, her presence inspires fear in the living, as well as fascination (169), just as Odysseus relates how "pale fear gripped me" (ἐμὲ δὲ χλωρὸν δέος ᾕρει; *Od.* 11.43), even though he remains equally intrigued to meet the dead. The same "pale fear" of the crowds of shades is what drives him away at the end of his visit in a repetition of the same words (11.633).

Ogden has proposed that "the blood . . . will give [the shades] the power of recognition and speech". This view is also taken by Robert Garland, who suggests that "the Homeric dead do not immediately recognise their nearest and dearest, but must wait until they have imbibed the sacrificial blood".[16] Sally's ghost correctly identifies everyone she encounters long before drinking blood, and the blood does not grant her any special powers of recognition beyond those she already has; certainly they do not grant her any self-recognition. Of course, Garland's idea does not apply universally to the dead that Odysseus encounters in Hades, as Ajax appears to recognize Odysseus without drinking blood (and still refuses to speak to him). Nor, in turn, does the blood grant the living observers in *Ghost* – Sally's sisters and friends – the power to recognize the ghost's identity, even though Odysseus is able to recognize familiar individuals among the crowds of shades.

As the ghostly Sally prepares to drink, she realizes that, without a body, she cannot drink the blood in a traditional sense, but that drinking is "like having a bath in soda water" (*Ghost* 169). She experiences it as a "fizzing" sensation, the same fizzing she perceives as a ghost when encountering any living creatures. She finds that the blood was "fizzing faintly with the same electric life-feeling that people's bodies had" (169). Sarah Iles Johnston sees blood in the *Odyssey* as an image of life, which therefore allows the dead to talk normally, even though they remain physically insubstantial: "It is only by means of the blood – a striking emblem of the vigorous life they have left behind forever – that they temporarily become capable of normal human converse. Even after they have drunk the blood, the souls of the dead remain physically insubstantial, unable to embrace, much less affect, those who are still alive."[17]

Leaving aside the likes of Elpenor, who speaks without drinking the blood, Johnston's description certainly holds true for Odysseus's mother Antikleia, who approaches him without speaking or visibly reacting until he permits her to drink the blood. When Odysseus later tries to embrace her, he is unable to do so. Antikleia says that the moment of death is when the bones are left behind by the *thumos* (θυμός), a word for which there is no direct English equivalent, but which signifies 'breath' and 'life' itself. Clarke has shown how *thumos* can be the "breath drawn into the lungs", and therefore how its departure becomes the exhalation of the last gasp of a dying person, a gasp taken not just from the lungs but also from the bones.[18] Antikleia explains to Odysseus that after the *thumos* has left the body, the "soul, like a dream, flits and flies away" (ψυχὴ δ' ἠΰτ' ὄνειρος ἀποπταμένη πεπότηται; *Od.* 11.222), so that the soul has no physical substance without breath and life. The blood thus acts as the bodily fluid that partly embodies the soul, taking the place of the *thumos* ('life, breath') temporarily and granting it some physical form.

When the ghost in Jones drinks blood from the bowl she gains some of what Johnston calls "vigorous life", some *thumos*, by temporarily experiencing some of the corporeal senses of the living (*Ghost* 169): "There was a curious roaring in her ears, a blur of green pressing on her eyes, and a sharp rainy smell to her nose. None of it was clear, but she knew what it was. For just a short while, she was hearing, seeing and smelling as people do in bodies." This description concentrates on the senses of sight and smell that the ghost gains by drinking the blood. These senses are more physical and direct than Burkert's sense of consciousness, Heubeck and Hoekstra's recollection of past existence, or Ogden's power of recognition. These physical senses enable her to interact with the living more easily, particularly because they seem to grant her corporeality in another way. While the shades Odysseus summons are visible to him even before they drink blood, the ghost remains invisible to most of the people she encounters until she drinks the blood. The blood thus helps her gain some 'vigorous life' in another sense, as she becomes both visible and audible to the living, albeit not clearly.

This is a significant departure from the nature of the dead in the *Odyssey*, perhaps explicable through a number of circumstances. Odysseus travels to a remote location at the edge of the world – Hades – where the spirits of the dead are imagined to reside, in order to summon up the dead. Perhaps due to the nature of the place, he can see the shades of the dead as soon as they appear, after he has performed the rites to summon them and before they drink the blood. In contrast, Sally's ghost finds herself floating around in the past among the living, and the blood-drinking ritual is not conducted in a place specific to the dead, but simply outside in the back garden. The blood therefore acts as a bridge between the living and the dead. It provides some *thumos* for the ghost and so brings her a little closer to life. This proximity allows the living to see her, since the children have not travelled closer to the dead, as Odysseus did by travelling to the grove of Persephone across the river Ocean. To herself and to others, the ghost appears hanging suspended above the bowl of blood: "'Standing in the bowl!' one was whispering. 'It looks like a girl'. 'Hanging. It's all blurred'" (*Ghost* 169–70).

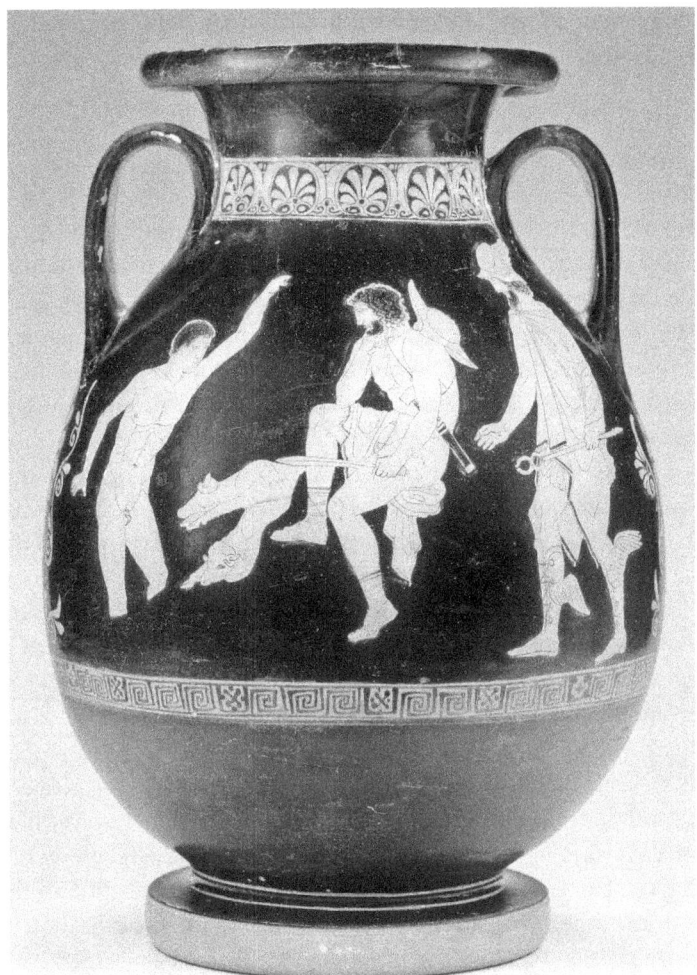

Fig. 9.1 Odysseus speaks to the shade of the recently deceased Elpenor. Attic red-figure *pelike* by the Lykaon Painter, *c.* 440 BCE. Photograph © 2018 Museum of Fine Arts, Boston.

This description makes her resemble Odysseus's dead companion Elpenor, as he is depicted on a fifth-century Attic red-figure *pelike* by the Lykaon Painter (Fig. 9.1). Elpenor appears on the vase as if he is rising out of the earth, but his feet are obscured from view. Odysseus sits opposite him, holding out his sword to protect the blood, which has presumably been drained from the two dead animals lying on the ground next to him. In contrast to the narrative from the *Odyssey*, on the vase Elpenor seems to be rising from the pit of blood itself. By further contrast, in *Ghost*, as Sally's ghost looks down, she sees a "tall vague length of human body, mostly blurred white", but she is alarmed when she observes that "there was a gap between the blurred white and the shining blood in the bowl, where her feet should have been" (*Ghost* 171). Although her appearance is white and blurry (as opposed to Elpenor, who looks clear and substantial), she appears, like Elpenor, to have taken her physical form from the blood itself.

Between life and death

The shades of the dead that Odysseus encounters are all fully dead. Even Elpenor – whom Jan Bremmer thought had "not yet become a full shade" – is dead, since he broke his neck and he describes himself as a shade (*Od.* 11.64–65).[19] However, there are different categories among the dead. Johnston has observed that the "abnormal dead lingered between two worlds and they were a source of potential trouble for the living".[20] Johnston defines these souls as the "restless dead", those who have died violently (such as the "men slain by Ares, killed in battle", ἄνδρες ἀρηΐφατοι; *Od.* 11.41) and who first crowd around the pit when Odysseus drains the blood into it. Elpenor is among these shades, as his death was sudden and violent. Sally's ghost would also belong to this group, since she was thrown out of a speeding car with violent intent. Lars Albinus suggests that the shades of Elpenor and the unburied Patroklos (who died in battle at Hector's hands) are "neither living nor dead in the ritual sense of the word", although they are physically dead. Sally is not fully dead, but while she is unconscious she hovers between the two states of life and death as a ghost, a category that could be defined as 'the restless undead'.[21] Normal rules cease to apply to her, as she is able to act with greater agency than any of the Homeric dead, who lack the ability to act. They can do no more than ask for a proper burial, as Elpenor does. Farah Mendlesohn has suggested that Sally achieves greater agency by changing her attitude towards her past and her memories of it.[22] However, the blood also plays a significant role in granting her an awareness of the past and present.

Regarding the Homeric epics, Bridget Martin has noted that "[o]f all the offerings made to the dead by the living, animal or blood sacrifices seem to be the most honorific".[23] Likewise, in *The Time of the Ghost*, the goddess Monigan is concerned with receiving blood offerings, particularly sacrificial victims. The blood collected by the children is not offered to Monigan, but to the ghost, and is extracted without killing anything. Initially Sally's ghost is disgusted by the idea of drinking the blood, thinking it is "like cannibalism" (*Ghost* 168). When she suddenly hears a voice from the hospital seven years away, saying "we need another bag of blood here" (ibid.), she realizes that in her bodily form she is receiving blood transfusions. She thinks of both sets of blood as gifts or offerings. The blood she receives in the past (as a ghost) and in the future (as a patient) brings together both aspects of her existence. The blood in the bowl and in the bag was donated by the living, without killing sacrificial victims: thus the blood symbolizes life rather than death. Unlike the Homeric dead, Sally (both as a ghost and a hospital patient) occupies a liminal space between life and death, a space that the two blood offerings help her to navigate, particularly as they put her outside the goddess Monigan's power.

Sally's liminality allows her the privilege of communicating with three spheres: the living, the dead, and the divine. As a ghost she can speak with the goddess herself, as well as perceive and talk to the ghosts of the dead among Monigan's barrows. These ghosts are buried kings from long ago who worshipped Monigan. One barrow ghost observes that there is something different about Sally's ghost: "*I hoped you had come to summon me, said the voice. You are both living and dead, as is fitting*" (*Ghost* 212). After drinking the blood, Sally's repeated shifting between the two states and moments – patient in the present and ghost in the past – enables her to understand her identity and the power she holds as an undead ghost, able to control those shifts between states. In this respect she achieves a freedom of power beyond that held by the living and the dead in the *Odyssey*, as she embodies an alternative possibility of existence beyond those in Homer's epic.

This state of being, which grants Sally the power to control the shifting states, enables her to bring her younger sister Imogen from the past into the present by her hospital bed for just a few minutes. The same barrow ghost who noticed Sally's transitional state describes Imogen in similar terms: "*That one. Corn yellow and running, came past me just now, the one bearing within her the power to give life in the realms of death. I took her for the harbinger of my summoning*" (*Ghost* 212–213). The barrow ghost emphasizes how alive Imogen is: she is "*corn yellow and running*", bright and moving among the colourless and static shades, demonstrating Imogen's own transitional state. The shifting liminalities of manipulating the boundaries between life and death allow Sally's ghost – with Imogen's help – to transcend the powerlessness of the "helpless heads of the dead" (νεκύων ἀμενηνὰ κάρηνα) in Homer's Hades.

Stamatia Dova has suggested that "[i]n the *Odyssey* the upper world holds the key to knowledge inaccessible to the dead as much as the underworld contains crucial information for the hero's future back on earth".[24] Odysseus informs Achilles about Neoptolemus's successful role in the sack of Troy, but learns about his future trials from Teiresias and about Antikleia's death by meeting her shade. Sally takes part in such knowledge exchange, but she can only do so through her ability to control her shifting liminality so as to bring Imogen from the past into the present. In so doing, she enables the child Imogen to learn from the adult sisters how to retrieve Sally (and Sally's ghost) from Monigan. Thus Sally can bring together information from the past with that of the present to make a cohesive narrative. It is Sally, as a ghost, who witnesses the child Imogen make an offering to Monigan of her imaginary future musical career. In her ghostly state she can hear what Imogen cannot: Monigan's acceptance of the offering. And it is Sally's ability to cross boundaries that allows her to transmit this information to her adult sisters sitting around her hospital bed. Sally's knowledge exchange is arguably more empowering than Odysseus's: although Odysseus gains knowledge that ought to enable him to navigate his arrival home, he requires considerable divine help to do so successfully. In contrast, Sally's exchange of knowledge enables her to return fully to the world of the living.

Notes

1. Ogden (2001: xix).
2. Louden (2011: 197).

3. All translations from Greek are my own.

4. Odysseus uses the blood from the black sheep he has sacrificed, although elsewhere in the Homeric epics oxen are presented as appropriate sacrificial animals, particularly for large banquets.

5. Heath (2005: 391).

6. Burkert (1985: 196).

7. Heubeck and Hoekstra (1986: 86).

8. Ogden (2001: xxiv), Sourvinou-Inwood (1995: 82).

9. Johnston (1999: 8).

10. Mendlesohn (2005: 55).

11. Burkert (1985: 196).

12. Heubeck and Hoekstra (1986: 86).

13. Nilsson (1992 [1967]: 177).

14. Ogden (2001: xix).

15. Tsagarakis (2000: 108–109).

16. Ogden (2001: xxiv), Garland (2001 [1985]: 2).

17. Johnston (1999: 8).

18. Clarke (1999: 79, 130, and 132).

19. Bremmer (1983: 90).

20. Johnston (1999: 11).

21. Albinus (2000: 50).

22. Mendlesohn (2005: 56).

23. Martin (2014: 3).

24. Dova (2012: 22).

CHAPTER 10
FINDING CASSANDRA IN SCIENCE FICTION: THE SEER OF *AGAMEMNON* AND THE TIME-TRAVELLING PROTECTOR OF *CONTINUUM*

Jennifer C. Ranck

The Cassandra figure from ancient Greek myth has been considered by Karin Beeler as a "mythic prototype" for "women of vision" in postmodern science-fiction (SF) television – women who are portrayed specifically as seers, witches, or psychics, such as River Tam, the 'psychic warrior' in Joss Whedon's television series *Firefly* and film *Serenity*.[1] While this version of the Cassandra figure does appear in SF, focusing on 'women of vision' alone artificially excludes other characters in SF television and film who, although not specifically seers, nevertheless share similarities with Cassandra as a tragic figure. If, then, we shift the focus to how Cassandra is depicted as a character in Greek tragedy, specifically in Aeschylus's *Agamemnon*, we find resonances of her in a different subset of SF characters – namely, police officers or detectives. In this chapter, I consider Kiera Cameron, a time-travelling police officer in Simon Barry's television series *Continuum*.

Bringing the Cassandra of *Agamemnon* into comparative dialogue with Kiera of *Continuum*, I hope to show that Cassandra serves as, in Paula James's terms, a 'cultural companion' to Kiera, with characteristic parallels between the two in their respective stories.[2] Using each as an interpretive lens for the other, I thus, in Dean Kowalski's terminology, establish an "exciting platform" from which to learn about Aeschylus's depiction of Cassandra as well as an "enriched understanding" of Kiera Cameron.[3] Through this link between the two characters and their respective stories, we can examine how these two female characters from different genres, cultures, and times are similarly utilized in dramatic depiction as figures of empowerment and displacement.

Cassandra and Kiera are empowered to be recipients and revealers of truth in their worlds. Cassandra, in Aeschylus's *Agamemnon*, is a seer (Greek *mantis*) of Apollo the god of prophecy. She is empowered with prophetic sight which enables her to see and reveal the evil of the past, present, and future. Kiera is a City Protective Services (CPS) Protector, or police officer, in the year 2077. With the aid of future technology and her own knowledge of the future, she is empowered to reveal information about crimes that are being committed in our present day. This empowerment is a limited one for both Cassandra and Kiera, as we shall see, and will invite discussion of how the limitation of their empowerment contrasts with the empowerment of the modern 'women of vision' Beeler has noted are transformative and active saviours as a result of their powers.[4]

These two characters are part of displaced worlds. *Agamemnon*, performed in front of a fifth-century BCE Athenian audience, utilizes the past mythic world of the Trojan War as its setting; *Continuum* uses a present and future fictional but realistic Vancouver as its setting for a modern twenty-first-century American and Canadian audience. Cassandra and Kiera are also displaced from their own worlds, taken from their homes in Troy and future Vancouver respectively. Both are also utilized as figures of displacement, especially in terms of time and emotion. They see and reveal the unknown past, present, and future. They also suffer and, as a result, are eventually destroyed as collateral damage. Cassandra is a victim who is cursed by Apollo, enslaved as a concubine by Agamemnon, and killed by Clytemnestra. Kiera is imprisoned in the present time, unable to find her way back to the future, and is pursued, arrested, mistrusted, and even killed, literally facing her own death. The displacing combination of empowerment and suffering found in Cassandra has led Pascale-Anne Brault to describe her as a "bearer", or agent, of "time, tragedy, and truth".[5] Kiera, like Cassandra, is an empowered suffering female agent of time, tragedy, and truth.

This comparison of the two characters could invite objections as Cassandra and Kiera are characters from different genres, cultures, and times. First, there is no known direct or intentional reception of the Cassandra figure, or of Greek tragedy in general, in the *Continuum* series. There are, however, some other classical references, direct as well as indirect, found throughout the series. One direct reference is to the name of the mythical figure Theseus, the "warrior who unified Athens", who was also "pushed off a cliff": that name is given to the future revolutionary leader Julian Randol will become ("Family Time", S1E9). One serial murder case Kiera investigates both in the present and in the future, or in her past, is the *Ouroboros* case, the case which resembles the image of "the snake that eats its own tail" ("Second Truths", S2E6).[6] The Freelancers, guardians of the time continuum, tell Kiera that time travel is "Pandora's box" ("Minute by Minute", S3E1). Other more indirect references used with modern definitions include a 'Trojan' virus implemented in the police department network, and the idiomatic term 'Achilles' heel' referring to weaknesses of certain characters. Besides these figures and terms, no explicit connection exists indicating that the series, or its characters, have any specific or intentional basis in Greek tragedy. *Continuum*, according to series creator Simon Barry, is a "marrying" of modern-day elements, a police procedural show with SF time travel whose story blends present-day "social commentary" and "metaphoric storytelling".[7]

A second possible objection: the worlds that the two characters inhabit are quite dissimilar. One significant difference lies in the acknowledgement or apparent lack of divine characters, or more specifically, gods. Besides the Traveler, a mysterious god-like figure from the future who establishes a cult of timeline guardians known as the 'Freelancers', there are no gods in the world of *Continuum*. In *Agamemnon*, the gods are referred to and addressed, but none actually appear directly on stage as they will in the *Eumenides*, the third play of the *Oresteia* trilogy; yet the gods play an important, albeit offstage, role throughout the trilogy. If we employ Joseph Fontenrose's statement that the "Olympian gods are like human rulers" in the *Oresteia*, we can then consider comparisons between the gods in Aeschylus's tragedy and the human characters in Barry's series.[8] For example, the god Apollo plays an important role in the empowering and suffering that Cassandra experiences and, as we will see, the characters Alec Sadler and Matthew Kellog both resemble the Apollo figure in their interactions with Kiera: Alec empowers and causes Kiera to suffer, while Kellog interacts with Kiera similarly to how Cassandra describes her encounter with Apollo. While there is significant discrepancy in the depiction of gods in the two stories, there is an overarching divine order in both, with gods from *Agamemnon* and human characters from *Continuum* resembling each other in terms of function within their respective worlds.

A third possible objection: the Cassandra and Kiera roles are drastically different. Cassandra is neither the protagonist – the lead actor – nor is she a physically active character such as Kiera Cameron. Simon Barry has noted that Kiera is the lead character in the series because she "drives the storytelling" of the show.[9] While Cassandra is not the protagonist of *Agamemnon*, she has a commanding presence on stage: she is silent on stage before her scene, in which she speaks and is spoken to for over 250 lines, and is then on stage as a corpse towards the end.[10] Sommerstein notes that during her scene, Cassandra is in "command of the stage".[11] Cassandra stops the action with her revelation of the evil of the past, present, and future, suspending time and action within the overall story. Both Cassandra and Kiera command the attention of the audience, especially the external audience, with their ability to receive and inform on temporally different visions. Despite some disparities found between these characters, their worlds, and their roles, we still find enough common ground in the functions that Cassandra and Kiera both serve, as well as in other characters and elements in both stories, to make this a worthwhile exploration.

Empowered: "What if she digs deeper?"

Agamemnon's Cassandra and *Continuum*'s Kiera Cameron are empowered as both recipients and revealers of unseen or unknown truth or facts. Cassandra is a seer who has been equipped with the gift of prophetic sight, "set . . . in [that] office" by Apollo (*Agamemnon* [*Ag.*] 1202).[12] She has the ability to see the past, near-present, and future crimes of the house of Atreus in authentic prophetic visions that she receives and reveals to others.[13] She is described as a tracking hound, having a "keen nose . . . like a hound", who will discover whose murder was committed in the past, and she describes herself as "scenting out the evil deeds done long ago" (1093–1094, 1184–1185). She is the only one who sees the children holding their own flesh as her evidence of the past slaughter in the house of Atreus. She also reveals the presence of both the Erinyes, or Furies – the goddesses of vengeance for kindred bloodshed – and Apollo, who drives Orestes to commit matricide to avenge his father Agamemnon's murder; Apollo and the Erinyes are unseen by the audience in the *Agamemnon* but are visible, on-stage characters later in the *Oresteia* trilogy.[14] Cassandra is equipped and authorized to receive and reveal privileged knowledge.

Kiera Cameron, in the SF series *Continuum*, is, like Cassandra, set in her office, by Alec Sadler's future SadTech corporation, as a CPS Protector, with the gift of implanted and external technology that provides enhanced sight and recording capabilities. She is hardwired with a Cellular Memory Review (CMR) device implanted directly into her cerebral cortex, which makes her a "passive recorder" of all that she "sees, hears, and smells", and with special lenses implanted on her eyes ("Fast Times", S1E2). Her CMR and lenses allow her to read human biometrics and to read and utilize satellite and video data. She is also provided with a weapon and multi-tool that also facilitates enhanced vision (ibid.). She can fully restage a crime scene and describe the elements of the crime after it has been committed ("Second Chances", S2E1; "Second Truths", S2E6). Along with this technology, Kiera is provided with intel 'in her head', either visually or audibly through the technological savvy of young Alec, which she then repeats to others. Kiera is also referred to as a good tracker by Jaworski, Kiera's prisoner who is a member of the Liber8 terrorist gang ("Waning Minute", S3E7). Kiera can see victims and perpetrators of a recent murder on her internal CMR screen as images similar to the "dream-shapes" of the murdered children of Thyestes Cassandra sees in her visions (*Ag.* 1217; "The Politics of Time", S1E7). Kiera, like Cassandra, is able to acknowledge and reveal the otherwise unknown presence of key players who resemble other characters in the *Oresteia*, namely the Freelancers, the Fury-like guardians of the time continuum, and the terrorist group Liber8 who start a war to take back the liberty stolen from future citizens reminiscent of the Greeks who start the Trojan War to reclaim Helen (whom they believe was stolen from her husband Menelaus by the Trojan prince Paris). Kiera reveals the presence of the future Liber8 gang in the present time to the Vancouver Police Department (VPD) and, based on her future-*past* experience, she can predict their criminal behaviour and foresee crimes that they commit in the present.

Cassandra and Kiera are both recognized and acknowledged by others in descriptions of their appearance. Cassandra describes herself and is described by the Chorus of elder Argive men with the use of terms that refer to her status as a *mantis*.[15] The Chorus acknowledge that she has the "god's power" in her mind and are aware of her fame as a *mantis* (*Ag.* 1083–1084, 1098–1099). Cassandra is identifiable as a *mantis* in her appearance, decked in prophetic "emblems", which she later describes when she is stripping them off her body (1265).[16] Kiera is identifiable and established in her identity as a CPS Protector, or at the very least as a cop, in the future and present times. As a CPS Protector, she wears a copper-coloured, superhero-like suit, which is bulletproof and offers cloaking technology, along with many other functions that work in tandem with her internal CMR and lenses. In the present time, however, her appearance is noticeably unusual, prompting her to change her suit colour and wear present-time clothing to blend in. Even so, she is known as "the Protector" to both Liber8 and the Freelancers. She is immediately accepted as a cop by Carlos Fonnegra, a present-day VPD detective, based solely on her language and mannerisms during their first encounter ("A Stitch in Time", S1E1).

Kiera and Cassandra are established, or seem to be, in their respective identities by authoritative sources. Mr Escher, Alec Sadler's father, who bequeaths to Alec his technology company Piron, validates Kiera as a Special Agent of the imaginary "Section 6", a cover that Alec and Kiera create to establish a "truth that they [VPD] can accept", as the VPD considers Escher's authorization as legitimate ("Fast Times", S1E2; "Endtimes",

S1E10). Cassandra is also vetted, in a sense, by the god Apollo, the divine source of prophecy, as she is acknowledged as his *mantis*. Apollo, like Alec inheriting Piron, is bequeathed the site of Delphi, home of the oracle and his Pythia, from his mother Phoebe; and he identifies his father Zeus as his source of authentic prophecy (*Eumenides* 1–18, 616–618). Cassandra and Kiera are established by authorized sources in their identities as *mantis* and Protector.

Knowledge and identity: "That is need to know"

Kiera and Cassandra are passive recipients and active revealers of authentic knowledge of crimes that take place in the past, present, and future, whether from another time (Kiera from future Vancouver) or place (Cassandra from war-torn Troy). Their revelation of such knowledge comes in the form of a vision of the past or the future, while they still remain in the present time. In *Agamemnon*, recounting the past is common. The Chorus narrates the past events that led to the Trojan War, including the sacrifice of Iphigenia, and Cassandra, via her prophetic visions, recounts the past crimes of the house of Atreus. Froma Zeitlin states that these visions help the audience to understand the present by "tracing responsibilities" for current present events, and J. C. Kamerbeek notes that they "validate her … knowledge of the future".[17] Cassandra also predicts the impending murder of Agamemnon, as well as her own, and also predicts the future vengeance of Orestes.[18] Cassandra reveals the unknown or unwanted truth of both the past and the future, which also illuminates what is about to happen in the present.[19] Similarly, *Continuum* episodes typically have a flash-forward scene, or, from the time travellers' perspective, a flashback, which recounts events that led to the future and now present war. Kiera and Cassandra are authorized and equipped to manage this temporal displacement all in the present time, seeing and revealing unwanted or unknown truths about crimes in the past, present, or future. Both catch the eye and ear of the external audience as the voice of authentic truth by their appearance as an authorized expositor established by a male Apollo-figure.

The gender of the one chosen to see and disclose the truth in these two stories is female. Cassandra is chosen by Apollo and Agamemnon presumably based on physical appeal. The Chorus assumes that Apollo chose Cassandra because he was attracted to her; Agamemnon describes Cassandra, his chosen war-prize, to his wife and servants as a "flower", possibly suggesting her attractiveness (*Ag.* 955). While Alec does not choose Kiera based on physical attraction, another character, Matthew Kellog, an original member of Liber8 who becomes a tribal warlord in an alternative future, plays the Apollo role: Kellog keeps Kiera in his gaze, engages in a sexual encounter with her, and both deceives and is deceived by her throughout the series.

Both women also seize the attention of the viewer with their silent entrance. Cassandra enters the stage with Agamemnon but is silent for almost 300 lines, approximately the same length as the scene in which she speaks. Oliver Taplin notes that Cassandra, the "woman in unusual costume" is used to capture our attention and that her silence "surrounds her in mystery".[20] Kiera is introduced in the opening scene of the first episode when arresting Edouard Kagame, the leader of Liber8, and similarly does not say a word ("A Stitch in Time", S1E1). Kiera also appears in an unusual futuristic costume – namely, her CPS Protector suit, which is unknown to the audience in the opening scene. Cassandra and Kiera appeal to the audience because, as women, they are portrayed as attractive and mysterious.

Part of their mystery is reflected in their hesitancy to reveal their identity or how that identity was established. Kiera hides her identity as a technologically enhanced police officer from the future by blending in as a present-day detective. Her reason for not disclosing her true identity is that those in the present day would have difficulty accepting the truth, so she creates a more acceptable story. She answers questions using the phrase "need to know" or the term "complicated" to describe herself and her circumstances ("A Test of Time", S1E5). While Cassandra does not deliberately hide her identity as Kiera does, Cassandra, a foreign, Greek-speaking *mantis*, hesitates to reveal the basis of her mantic identity to the Chorus when she tells them, "Before now, I was ashamed to speak of this" (*Ag.* 1203). Cassandra's identity as a seer of Apollo is well-known to the audience since she is identifiable through her dress and mantic garb as such; she hesitates to reveal how she was established as a seer in the first place – namely, her sexual interaction with the god Apollo. Despite the differences in their disclosure, Kiera and Cassandra both hesitate to reveal their full, true identities.

Suffering: "Are you really going to roll the dice with her life?"

The empowered female is also a suffering victim as the empowerment from a divine or superhuman source comes with painful side effects and limitations. One such side effect is the pain from the gift itself. Cassandra suffers from physical pain resulting from the onset of her prophetic visions: she is "agitated and whirled around" by them and "invaded" by their fire, and the chorus describes them as "agonies and the violent onset of possession by a god" (*Ag.* 1215–1216, 1256–1257, 1150–1151). Kiera is similarly physically affected by the vision-enhancing technology implanted in her head. She screams out in pain when her CMR needs to be rebooted or when Alec uploads an encrypted message to her CMR intended for the younger Alec to discover ("Second Chances", S2E1). The gift of specially enhanced sight is accompanied by physical pain.

Forcible physical displacement to a foreign location is another side effect. Cassandra is a former Trojan princess turned foreign slave, chosen especially by or for Agamemnon after Troy was destroyed by Agamemnon and the Greek armies (*Ag.* 954). While taken from Troy by the leader of the Greek armies as a war-prize, she views Apollo instead as the one solely responsible for her current misfortune, calling Apollo her destroyer (1081, 1086), asking to what house he has led her (1087), and later saying "now the prophet-god has exacted his / due from myself as prophet and has led me into captivity for a / deadly fate such as this" (1275–1276).[21] She views the source of her gift as the source of her woe.

Kiera is imprisoned in the present time, having also been forcibly removed from her home and her family, her husband Greg and her son Sam. Unbeknownst to her, Kiera is chosen by Alec to be sent back in time along with Liber8 in an attempt to change his own fate, thus changing the future. When Alec's involvement in Kiera's displacement is eventually made known, Kiera does not hold the present young Alec responsible, as Cassandra does Apollo, nor does Kiera at first seem to show any resentment towards the older Alec. Yet, she later blames younger Alec when he deceives her by going back in time and creating a new, alternative timeline that destroys the one in which Kiera's future-past is set ("Minute by Minute", S3E1). Kiera's imprisonment in the present and then in a new timeline – she is forcibly removed from her own future-past – and Cassandra's status as a captured slave are both viewed as the design of the one who set them up as a voice of truth from another time or place.

Cassandra and Kiera both lament their forcible displacement into a foreign world in which they are isolated and imprisoned. Cassandra mournfully recalls her home, Troy, and her family, and initially mourns the impending death that she will eventually face on her own terms (*Ag.* 1136–1138). Cassandra's status as a victim caught in a net of a wretched fate adds "pathos and pity" to her character; it reinforces her prophecies in that knowing her fate, she faces it head on, and later the Chorus will in turn be forced to face head-on the reality they want to remain unknown and thus do not believe or want to understand.[22] Kiera grieves over the forced removal from her family, especially from her son, Sam. Kiera is confronted with a holographic version of Sam when she is in a simulation of a built-in psychological review program; she tells Sam that she loves him and will let him go, but continually struggles throughout the series with trying to return home to him in particular ("Second Opinion", S2E5).

A limitation that accompanies Cassandra's and Kiera's empowerment is the revelation of their inevitable fate, which they both eventually accept. Cassandra discovers through visions that she will be killed along with Agamemnon by Clytemnestra. She laments her impending death, as well as that of Agamemnon and the Trojans, and despite learning and knowing her fate, is unable to change it and persuade or warn the Chorus of Argive Elders about Agamemnon's lot (*Ag.* 1136–1139, 1305). Cassandra sees her death in a vision, while Kiera, who time-travels from the original timeline in the continuum to an alternative timeline following Alec, sees her own death by literally standing over her own dead body, the body of the Kiera from the alternative timeline created by Alec. The only one who might be able to return her to any future is Alec himself; she cannot do anything herself to facilitate her return. Kiera admits several times that she has to face the possibility that she may never return back to her future and that she may even cease to exist ("Second Truths", S2E6). Yet, Kiera holds on to the hope that she can return home, although she is frequently reminded by the other time-travellers and Alec that the future will most likely not be the future from which she came. Even with a strong possibility that she will not make it back to her own future or timeline and might actually be killed, Kiera walks into the gates of the portal established by Kellog's army that is tethered to a specific point in the future ("Final Hour", S4E6). Cassandra, knowing that she will be killed once inside, approaches the doors of Agamemnon's house, referring to them as the gates of Hades (*Ag.* 1291). Kiera is perceived as dead by others; Alec tells Kiera when she arrives in the future, "I thought you died that day" ("Final Hour", S4E6). Cassandra is revealed as a dead corpse on stage after Clytemnestra murders her. Both Cassandra and Kiera are aware of their own predicaments and struggle with facing their wretched fate that they have no ability to change.

The fate of the discloser of truth has a posthumous effect on those once around her, despite having little effect on the overarching events of the story. While in the present, Kiera cannot stop major events of the past, the history of the future, such as the explosion of a building in 2012 that kills many people and lays the foundation for the future war ("End Times", S1E10). Despite her killing Curtis and Travis of Liber8, both characters appear alive in alternative timelines. Anything she has done in the present is nullified in the alternative timeline and eventual present and future. While Alec and the others think that Kiera died the day she entered the tethered portal, after she is no longer present, Alec tells Kiera that they "steered civilization" because of her "sacrifice" and changed the future ("Final Hour", S4E6). When she arrives in the new future, she is no longer a CPS Protector, nor is Sam her son, but the son of the Kiera of the current timeline. Kiera is an anomaly in the future, removed from everyone she loved or knew except for Alec Sadler, the older version of the younger version she left behind, and was sacrificed in Alec's plan to change the future. While Cassandra's death does not have quite the same effect in terms of 'steering civilization', Cassandra's words, as Pascale-Anne Brault notes, do become more "potent after her death", particularly after Agamemnon has also been killed, in that her words "seem to echo within and transform the Chorus sometime after", evidenced particularly when they "evoke the eventual vengeance of Orestes".[23]

Another limitation of their empowerment is not being believed or trusted but instead hunted to be silenced or repressed. Cassandra is cursed in that no one believes her despite her prophecies being true (*Ag.* 1212). When Cassandra tells the Chorus that they will "look upon Agamemnon's death" (1246), they respond, wanting to silence her, saying, "Hush, o wretched one, put your mouth to sleep" (1247).[24] Their lack of understanding continues when they ask her which *man* will perform the murderous act after she has stated more than once that a *woman*, Clytemnestra, will be the perpetrator (1251). Yet, the Chorus do understand and acknowledge the truth of Cassandra's visions of the past, and they pity her particular fate that she has revealed to them. While they eventually see the truth in her words after Agamemnon is killed, they fall "off the track" when it comes to the imminent death of Agamemnon (1245).

Kiera, like Cassandra, is not always believed or trusted, particularly by police or government officials. She is dismissed in disbelief and scoffed at by both Agent Gardiner and her partner Carlos, who does eventually accept and believe her when Kiera reveals to them that she is from the future ("End Times", S1E10; "Second Truths", S2E6). When talking to Alec via her CMR, she is often mistaken as speaking to herself or others. Once she is accepted as an agent by the VPD, Carlos deems her theories about the Ouroboros serial killer case as crazy, despite her knowledge of the truth having worked on this *past* cold case in the future. Like Cassandra asserting she "knows Greek too well" when the Chorus misunderstand her (*Ag.* 1254), Kiera responds as Carlos storms off, "That's what

I remember" ("Second Truths", S2E6). The typical reaction from others to her unusual knowledge of crimes is disbelief in her ability to have such knowledge or denial that she is an authorized source of truth. Kiera is frequently considered to be working for Liber8, is arrested twice by the VPD, and at one time is declared "public enemy number one" by Inspector Dillon ("Second Time", S2E13). Liber8 pursues her to silence her so that she does not reveal their presence or prevent them from accomplishing their mission; the Freelancers also track her since she is a glitch in the time continuum.

The posthumous effect that both Kiera and Cassandra have in their worlds, as well as their curse of not being believed or understood, provides an alternative to Beeler's view of empowerment and suffering for the Cassandra figure and modern SF and fantasy characters. Beeler views the traditional image of the seer as a "passive victim with little agency", a victim who accepts her fate, while she considers the modern post-feminist woman of vision as a "savio[r]" and transformative "mediator who initiate[s] change in the lives of others" and who may suffer but is not just a "victim who must accept her fate".[25] According to this somewhat strict delineation of the traditional mythic and post-feminist view, Cassandra is a passive victim who has little or no active role in the events of the story, and Kiera is an active saviour who transforms the lives of others and does not have to accept her own fate. As noted, Cassandra, while accepting her death, has a significant effect on the Chorus after her death, and Kiera, while attempting to change others, is more effective after her perceived death than when she is present and, in some ways, ineffective. In their respective stories, one in Greek tragedy and the other in modern SF, the delineation is a bit more blurred: the empowered female agent of time and truth is limited through her suffering and agency. This blurring of empowerment and suffering emphasizes their dual agency of displacement: both Cassandra and Kiera are displacers in time and truth, as well as in emotion and suffering.

Conclusion: "Clarity is a luxury in this business"

Cassandra of *Agamemnon* and Kiera Cameron of *Continuum* find themselves in worlds that, for the external audience, are displaced from reality by the means of time: *Agamemnon* is set in the mythic past of the Trojan War; *Continuum* is based in both a present and future, or future-past, Vancouver setting, as well as in alternative timelines. Both women are also physically displaced themselves in an already temporally displaced world and are utilized in those worlds for further temporal and emotional displacement. Both are empowered with sight and serve as the chosen and authorized vessel to receive knowledge and as the instrument to verbalize and communicate that knowledge. Both act as an expositional informant and intermediary between the worlds of the known and unknown. Both are also afflicted by their special access to truth and are victims of circumstances and misfortune related to the crimes each is seeking out or illuminating, making both agents of calamity. Being displaced in an 'other' world, neither is fully understood, believed, or trusted. They are gifted and cursed by the same source. They attract the attention of the male or divine power players, or major characters, in their respective worlds – and in turn they grab the attention of the external viewer as appealing figures who provide exposition through their special access to divine truth or technological sight, which, in revealing, drives the storytelling. Once they have our attention, we listen to and watch them suffer as collateral damage in the overall story as isolated, foreign, and mistrusted figures whom others try to silence and suppress; we watch and react emotionally to their inability to prevent their own destruction in the end. This ironic suffering and destruction of the empowered and authorized female revealer of truth evokes an emotional response from the viewer and represents the tension of truth itself that we find in Greek tragedy: the tension between "different planes of knowing and revelation", and that truth, being placed on the shoulders of a female, divinely or technologically authorized by a male figure to receive and reveal it, is the "very tension between revelation and concealment".[26] In both Greek tragedy and in modern SF, we learn through the suffering of the female figure who reveals to us the complications of access to, and revelations of, truth.

This empowered, suffering figure exposes similarities between dramatic depictions in Greek tragedy and modern SF, as well as fantasy. In Aeschylus's *Agamemnon*, we see similar characteristics of a modern detective in the seer Cassandra, depicted as a hound that will prophetically sniff out the murder and bloodshed of the past like a modern CPS Protector who is able to sniff out evidence of past crimes through technology and future knowledge. In Simon Barry's *Continuum*, we see characteristics similar to the female seer in the CPS Protector Kiera Cameron, depicted as an empowered, while similarly limited, suffering female agent of time, tragedy, and truth. We see a similar figure in both the Cassandra character of Greek tragedy and the Kiera Cameron character of SF, a figure who is a blend of what have been perceived as separate – the traditional mythical victim and the postmodern feminist action heroine – and whose traits can be found in other SF and fantasy detective-like characters.

Notes

1. Beeler (2008: 1–3). Beeler uses Cassandra and Joan of Arc as models or "icons" for various SF and fantasy "women of vision" characters in postmodern and postfeminist television.

2. James (2009: 239), examining Virgil's Aeneas as 'cultural companion' to Whedon's Buffy (the Vampire Slayer).

3. Kowalski (2011: 71, 80) examines the "literary parallels" between Plato, Aristotle, and Joss Whedon using the figure of Gyges. Rogers 2015 utilizes this methodology.

4. Beeler (2008: 17).

5. Brault (2009: 198). When using the word 'tragedy' alone, I refer to the modern usage of 'tragedy' to mean 'calamity', not to be confused with the genre of ancient Greek tragedy to which Aeschylus's *Agamemnon* belongs.

6. The name of this mythical serpent that seems to be eating its own tail is Greek in origin, while the symbol itself is possibly Egyptian; see Ferber (1999: 190) and Ménez (2003: 9).

7. Golder 2012.

8. Fontenrose (1971: 86).

9. Hogg 2014.

10. See Schein (1982: 11) and Walton (2015: 59). Cassandra enters the stage with Agamemnon at line 784, is directly addressed by Clytemnestra at line 1035, enters the house at line 1331, and is brought back out on stage as a corpse for the rest of *Agamemnon* at line 1371.

11. Sommerstein (2010: 204).

12. Unless otherwise noted, I use Collard 2002 for English translations of the *Oresteia* and Raeburn and Thomas 2011 for Greek text of *Agamemnon*.

13. Brault (2009: 208) argues that Cassandra's function is more to "see and reveal" and less to know the future. Cassandra's visions include: the children of Thyestes weeping as "evidence" of past evil (1095–1097); the bath scene in which Clytemnestra will kill Agamemnon (1101–1104, 1106–1111, 1125–1128); Cassandra's own death (1136–1139, 1146–1149); the presence of the Erinyes at the house (1186–1196); the children of Thyestes holding their own flesh (1214–1222); the retribution and plotting of Clytemnestra and Aegisthus (1223–1240); Cassandra's death at the hands of Clytemnestra (1256–1263); and Orestes, the future avenger of Agamemnon's and Cassandra's deaths by means of matricide (1279–1284).

14. Cassandra calls out to Apollo throughout her scene and describes the presence of the Erinyes at the house (*Ag.* 1186–1196), but they are not active in the trilogy nor seen by others until later in the *Oresteia* trilogy. Mitchell-Boyask (2009: 293) points out that Apollo and the Erinyes are "invisible malefactors" who will later become "visible contestants" in the trilogy.

15. See Mazzoldi 2001 for a complete lexicon of mantic terminology for Cassandra in Greek tragedy; see also Mason 1959, who notes the use of mantic terminology for Cassandra in *Agamemnon*.

16. Walton (2015: 72). Debnar (2010: 129) argues "that the actor's scepter, sacred fillets, and costume" would suggest to the audience that the character is Cassandra.

17. Kamerbeek (1965: 34) argues that validation comes from knowledge of the past, and de Romilly (1968: 72) notes that looking back to the past explains the present. Goldhill (2004: 58) states the past is a "determining factor" in present events.

18. See Grethlein 2013 for his discussion of the Chorus and intertemporality in the *Oresteia*.

19. Kamerbeek (1972: 34), Brault (2009: 201), and Schein (1982: 13) all note that the visions of the past and the future shine light upon the events about to occur in the present.

20. Taplin (1972: 78).

21. See Debnar (2010: 143), who discusses the legal terminology used in 1275–1276.

22. Thalmann (1985: 222) and Knox (1972: 112). The word τάλαινα ('wretched') is used to describe Cassandra and her fate throughout her scene.

23. Brault (2009: 211).

24. This translation is my own.

25. Beeler (2008: 9, 17).

26. Brault (2009: 215).

PART IV
DISPLACING GENRE

CHAPTER 11
CLASSICAL RECEPTION AND THE HALF-ELF CLERIC
C. W. Marshall

Level 1: A wandering monster

Amidst the Caves of Chaos, less than a mile from the Keep on the Borderlands, are the Caves of the Minotaur:

> This labyrinth houses a number of nasty things but worst is a fiendishly clever minotaur who abides herein. Immediately upon entering the place, adventurers will feel slightly dizzy – the effects of a powerful spell which will cause them to lose all sense of direction. . . . When intruders enter the area, the minotaur immediately moves to attack. He knows the area so well that the only way for victims to escape is to go through the secret door . . . or else to run out of the place and climb a large tree.
>
> The cave the minotaur dwells in has skulls and bones arrayed in decorative patterns. The secret door is actually a slab of stone which takes no less than three humans to move.[1]

This description, or a variation on it, has been encountered by tens (and possibly hundreds) of thousands of players of the role-playing game *Dungeons and Dragons* (*D&D*) over the past forty years. *The Keep on the Borderlands* was an adventure included as part of the Basic *D&D* set from 1979–1982, and revisions to it have been made for every generation of the game, most recently as a pre-publication adventure for the fifth edition in 2012.[2] In addition to the decision to decorate his magically cursed cave with bone patterns, *D&D*'s Minotaur is protected by "a great chain mail coat he wears, and [he] carries a **spear+1**" (i.e., a magic spear; see Fig. 11.1).[3] Depending on the adventurers' previous actions, the Minotaur might even be allied with a Bugbear chieftain (a kind of Goblin) in a neighbouring cave.[4] Adventurers might also encounter Fire Beetles or flying, blood-sucking Stirges in the Minotaur's caves.

I was twelve when I first encountered the Caves of Chaos, and since then I have spent a lot of time playing and thinking about table-top role-playing games (what I'll call RPGs, conscious that the term is more often used to describe a type of computer game). To my knowledge, classical reception in RPGs has not been considered previously, but I want to suggest that RPGs do provide a fascinating, if problematic site of reception.[5] To do so will involve some personal reflections that will help isolate some of the aspects of this material that have gone unexplored. Consider the cave just described: the description

Fig. 11.1 The Minotaur from *Keep on the Borderlands*; Gygax (1981: 20). Art by Bill Willingham. © Wizards of the Coast LLC.

was taken from a 'module', a pre-written adventure that would be administered by a referee (called 'the Dungeon Master' or DM), and the text would be presented (either directly or paraphrased) to other players, who would interact with the fantasy world described, battling and killing the Minotaur and his Fire Beetles and taking his treasure for themselves.[6]

This Minotaur is unique in the module, but, unlike his mythic predecessor, he is not unique in the game's fantasy world.[7] He belongs to a race of bull-headed creatures, existing in a world where Goblinoids and Stirges represent the wild evils that adventurers must dispatch. Yet his cave system is labelled a labyrinth, and magical effects make it particularly difficult to navigate.[8] There is ostensibly nothing classical about the Caves of Chaos, and yet players' knowledge of Greek myth provides some clue about the nature of the opponent their characters face. Even though the Minotaur on Crete did not have a magically enhanced spear, the experience created in-game represents a locus around which players partake to some degree in the experience of the hero Theseus, who defeated that ancient monster in the Cretan Labyrinth. On experiencing disorientation in a labyrinthine corridor, it is even possible that some players would recognize the implicit 'script' being presented to them and change their characters' behaviour accordingly.

RPGs constitute a body of material that encourages us to articulate how Greco-Roman sources and classical narrative patterns shape the experience of game-players. In this discussion, my goal is to describe some of the ways that *D&D* and similar games offer players an opportunity to explore classical worlds and themes as part of a collectively generated narrative in fictional worlds, and to consider the methodological implications of studying such games. The discussion considers a range of published source materials that help generate the narrative in play. It is not an exhaustive discussion, but it may prompt further work on classical reception in modern games, as well as highlighting some of the special challenges raised by RPGs.

Level 2: The nature of RPG narrative

Not everyone had a childhood in which they regularly killed Kobolds, so the description above requires clarification. Players in RPGs typically begin by creating characters, fictional avatars for themselves in the game world with extraordinary abilities and great potential for adventure. Often, characters have randomly generated ability scores: through initial rolls of dice, a player might discover that her hero has a high intelligence and a low strength (represented by some numerical value), and this might make one's character more effective in the game world as a wizard rather than as a thief or fighter. Players might choose a species (*D&D* mainstreams the fantasy races from Tolkien's world, offering elves, dwarves, and hobbit-like halflings alongside humans) and a class (a profession in which the hero will develop from novice to expert: warrior, wizard, or whatever). Consequently, one might generate a human rogue, a dwarven paladin (a kind of holy warrior), or (as in my title) a half-elf cleric.[9]

This character then becomes the agent through which the player navigates the world. Guided by the DM, who represents all the non-character elements and individuals in the world, players sitting around a table with paper, pens, books, and polyhedral dice will explore the fictional world, battling opponents (i.e., rolling dice to achieve a randomized result, and describing the consequences of the roll within the fictional world), and 'levelling up' (i.e., gaining new and more powerful abilities as the adventure proceeds).[10] Combat is central: "D & D was designed as an adventure game, pitting good against evil, and was not designed as a sociological simulation."[11] Nevertheless, characters grow, develop, and can even die, and the creation and development of a shared narrative at the table can create an immersive game experience that persists beyond the immediate event.[12]

This shared narrative, and the means by which it is generated, is one of the reasons RPGs have been understudied (and are so fascinating).[13] RPGs developed from tabletop wargames,[14] and so they can be understood as adding at least three elements absent from that earlier pastime:

1. individuation (and personalization) of particular individuals, with the possibility of immersive identification between player and character;

2. the introduction of non-combat elements, including exploration of an unknown world, and social interaction with non-player characters;

3. the possibility of abstraction, away from representation by miniature (plastic or metal) figures to a purely verbal, descriptive representation.

From these differences emerges a variety of features that are shared by many RPGs. Mackey offers the following initial definition: "I define the role-playing game as an *episodic* and *participatory* story-creation *system* that includes a set of quantified *rules* that assist a group of *players* and a *gamemaster* in determining how their fictional *characters'* spontaneous interactions are resolved."[15] This definition applies equally to games played today and to that which emerged more or less spontaneously when Gygax and Arneson invented *D&D*: despite many innovations, the fundamental means by which narrative emerges has remained stable.[16] Mackey isolates the core of an RPG being a story-creation system, involving players and a gamemaster, and he isolates the tension between player and character.

Each element in this definition is (mostly) true.[17] At the same time, the definition fails to identify the true weirdness of the nature of the narrative generated. An RPG game session creates a collective narrative through the efforts of all players at the table: the printed materials (modules, source books, etc.) point to that experience but are not the narrative itself. The analogy of a script to a performance of a play is partially apt, but the ephemerality of the game, and the improvisatory interactions between the players, mean that there is more, as scripted and unscripted elements blend, for an audience that comprises, in the first instance, the players themselves. This creates a unique fictional world at every table.

RPGs are particularly robust as a source for science-fiction and fantasy narratives, but the stories produced are largely inaccessible to researchers. A group of people sitting around a table (or on a shared web-board, etc.), telling a collaborative story about a group of characters working together, the events of which are determined by the roll of dice, produces a product that is qualitatively different from that experienced in most media.[18] As a result, classical material presents itself in equally unique ways. Scholarship can approach the unique narrative space variously. Isolating separate frames of reference is one way. For example, the narrative develops parallel to the game, and the same moment can be described with respect to the several frames: "my quarterstaff knocks the bleeding Kobold to the ground, dislodging its makeshift helmet and revealing the oozing fissure in its skull" is qualitatively different from rolling a twenty-sided die and saying "I got an 18; that's a hit, right?" Both are acceptable contributions to an RPG narrative.[19]

For a scholar considering the literary influences on this narrative, there is an interpretative challenge. The game itself is ephemeral and inward-focused. The presence of an observer would change the result, and transcripts or recordings of the session would lack the immediacy of the ephemeral shared performance event.[20] Because game-play is so challenging to document, in this discussion I focus exclusively on published game books, recognizing that they are an inadequate reflection of the actual play experience. They can point to the ways that game designers (those credited on the covers of the published works) intend or expect narrative to develop in play. Published materials anticipate that moment, they help create it, but they are not the game. Each of the three sections that follow considers a different type of published material (a core reference book, an article in a monthly game magazine, and an optional supplement) to describe its relationship to Greek and Roman sources. Yet there remains a gap between those materials and the immediacy of play itself.

Level 3: Monster Manuals

Where is the classical in all of this? The narratives generated at any given game table might have more or less classical content, depending on the nature of the campaign, the interests and knowledge of players at the table, and the synergies that emerge when creative minds generate narrative together. For an initial approach to the question, we can consider classical monsters in *D&D* Monster Manuals.[21] From the earliest days of RPGs, the Monster Manual has been a repository describing the combat effectiveness and cultural features of the opponents that characters may encounter. The bestiary serves not only as a reference document for DMs, but also as imaginative fuel for players and designers. I examine six bestiaries produced over a span of forty years, using the definitive collection of monsters for each of the seven editions.[22]

While many editions produce many official bestiaries, this single book provides an important reference point for all play, since it is the only collection of monsters that can be presumed to be available at every table. (Note that shorthand reference by the gaming community to different editions is not consistent, and players compare '3.5' to '5e' with disregard for easy diachronic referencing.)

Across these editions, the foundational bestiaries contain up to twenty-five monsters drawn from classical sources. These include eleven that have been present in every

Table 11.1 *D&D* **Monster Manuals consulted in this chapter**

Edition	(Years)	Date	Title
D&D	(1974–1977)	1974	*Monsters and Treasure*
AD&D	(1978–1989)	1977	*Monster Manual*
Cyclopedia	(1977–1999)	1991	*Rules Cyclopedia*
AD&D 2nd ed.	(1989–1999)	1995	*Monstrous Manual*
v. 3.5	(2000–2007)	2003	*Monster Manual v. 3.5*
4e	(2008–2011)	2008	*Monster Manual*
5e	(2014–)	2014	*Monster Manual*

edition, and four more in every edition since 1977.[23] While these volumes contain hundreds of monsters, this classical core remains remarkably consistent (see Table 11.2). All but one of the fifteen classical monsters in the first bestiary appears forty years later in the 5e *Monster Manual*: only 'Titan' is missing. That persistence is surprising, and histories of the reception of each of these monsters could be written. Arguably, many of these persist as legacy creatures: monsters kept out of a sense of tradition, or perhaps obligation to the fantasy mythos. They are familiar monsters, and so help to ground the rest of the book in something that is recognizable to new players.

It is possible to hypothesize why some monsters do not persist. The Triton (a race of aquatic humanoids) and the Hippocampus ("the most prized of the marine steeds") do not survive into the third edition because aquatic adventures are not that common, and space is dedicated to monsters more likely to be encountered.[24] The Phoenix and the Colossus are in a single edition but never find purchase with players, perhaps because there are other gargantuan birds (e.g., roc) and other giants. The absence of 'Erinyes' from 2nd ed. can perhaps be tied to the omission of an entry for 'Devils' (and 'Demons') in that collection, a response to 1980s scaremongering.[25] Subsequent bestiaries may make up for perceived deficiencies: the *Monster Manual 2* for the third edition had the Catoblepas and the Phoenix, for example, and the Cyclops appears in *AD&D*'s *Deities and Demigods*.[26] Accepting the whole list, though, we see that classical monsters are drawn from a variety of sources.

Among the traditional mythic monsters, many are usually associated with a particular hero or mythic cycle: Chimera, Harpy, Hydra, Medusa, Minotaur, Pegasus, Sphinx, and Triton. In these cases, a unique creature has become a race of creatures, living in groups and populating random rooms in dungeons.[27] This process of naturalization into the game world serves a function within the RPG narrative (characters may encounter a nest of Sphinxes, or a pack of Minotaurs; or they may encounter multiple examples over the course of an adventure), and it means that the game designers need to provide combat statistics as well as ecological notes for the creatures.[28]

A second category of classical monsters that persist across these bestiaries is more widely represented mythic species, creatures that exist broadly in mythic representation and can be found in art and literature in a number of narrative contexts implied by myths: Centaur, Cyclops, Dryad, Erinyes, Hippocampus, Nymph and Titan.[29] The nature of gaming materials encourages speculation about the sociology and anatomy of these creatures that seems not to have troubled people in antiquity. For example, the imaginative reconstruction of Centaur anatomy is necessarily speculative and not subjectable to scientific testing. In a pseudo-scientific discussion, Putz argues that parallel internal systems duplicate in human and equine torsos (two sets of lungs, for example); in contrast, an article about *D&D* by Inniss and Adams more plausibly considers the implications of a single involved anatomical system and of a single pair of lungs.[30]

The third category in some ways is the most interesting, because it appears to draw on paradoxography (the ancient genre that described the inexplicable) and the geographic tradition of wondrous creatures at the edge of the world. Two such creatures, the Basilisk and the Catoblepas, are mentioned in Pliny the Elder's *Natural History* ([*NH*] 8.77).

Table 11.2 Classical monsters in principal *D&D* bestiaries, 1974–2014

	D&D 1974	AD&D 1977	Cyclop. 1991	2nd ed. 1995	v. 3.5 2003	4e 2008	5e 2014
Basilisk	X	X	X	X	X	X	X
Catoblepas	–	X	X*	X	–	–	–
Centaur	X	X	X	X	X	–	X
Chimera	X	X	X	X	X	X	X
Colossus	–	–	–	–	–	X	–
Cyclops	X	–	X	X*	–	X	X
Dryad	X	X	X	X	X	X	X
Erinyes	–	X*	–	–	X*	–	X*
Gorgon	X	X	X	X	X	X	X
Griffon	X	X	X	X	X	X	X
Harpy	–	X	X	X	X	X	X
Hippocampus	–	X	–	X	–	–	–
Hippogriff	X	X	X	X	X	X*	X
Hydra	X	X	X	X	X	X	X
Lamia	–	X	–	X	X	X	X
Leucrotta	–	X	–	X	–	–	–
Manticore	X	X	X	X	X	X	X
Medusa	X	X	X	X	X	X	X
Minotaur	X	X	X	X	X	X	X
Nymph	–	X	–	X	X	–	–
Pegasus	X	X	X	X	X	–	X
Phoenix	–	–	X	X	–	–	–
Satyr	–	X	–	X	X	X	X
Sphinx	–	X	X	X	X	X	X
Titan	X	X	–	X	X	X*	–
Triton	–	X	–	X	–	–	–
Unicorn	X	X	X	X	X	X	X
Instances:	15	24	18	25	20	18	19

Note: * Entries so marked appear in the index under other creatures: 'Hippogriff' (under 'Griffon'), 'Erinyes' (under 'Devil'), 'Titan' (under 'Giant'), and 'Catoblepas' (under 'Nekrozon').

Apparently, the Catoblepas is a large cow-like creature whose gaze can kill, and the same power is attributed to the weasel-fearing Basilisk, a kind of fantasy serpent perhaps inspired by the cobra. Aelian (*On Animals* 7.6) suggests that it is the breath of the Catoblepas that is fatal. In *D&D*, fuller details are required. In 2nd ed, "Its most terrifying features are its large bloodshot eyes, from which emanate a deadly ray."[31] The Leucrotta, a hyena-lion-ass hybrid, is described a few chapters earlier in Pliny (*NH* 8.72–73), and is also present in the bestiaries for two editions (see Fig. 11.2).[32]

Some creatures appear to emerge from the surviving memory of lost fifth-century histories of Persia and India, written by Ctesias. The Manticore ('man-eater') is a Persian creature mentioned by Ctesias, but Philostratus gives a fuller description that shapes subsequent medieval appearances: "for they say that the creature has four feet, and that his head resembles that of a man, but that in size it is comparable to a lion; while the tail

Fig. 11.2 The Leucrotta, *AD&D*; Gygax (1977: 60). Art by D. A. Trampier. © Wizards of the Coast LLC.

of this animal puts out hairs a cubit long and sharp as thorns, which it shoots like arrows at those who hunt it" (*Life of Apollonius* 3.45; trans. Conybere). According to the sceptical Pausanias (9.21.4), it is likely describing a tiger. The Unicorn (Greek *monoceros*) is, like the Basilisk, also a heraldic creature, but it too has roots in Greek paradoxography. Again, Ctesias's *Indica* is perhaps the earliest reference, though later references suggest it may represent a confused account of the oryx or perhaps a rhinoceros.[33] The Griffon, a combination of lion and eagle, is found throughout the Bronze Age world in art as well as in literature, where reference to it as the winged guardian of gold may derive from Ctesias.[34] The Hippogriff, apparently the offspring of a mare and a Griffon, with the head and wings of an eagle, and the body of a horse, is mentioned in Virgil (*Eclogues* 8.26–28) but more properly finds company amongst other medieval heraldic creatures. Described in Ariosto's 1516 *Orlando Furioso* (4.18–19), the Hippogriff's classical connection is admittedly slight.

The Lamia is another creature mentioned in ancient sources (e.g., Stesichorus fr. 220 and Horace *Ars poetica* 340) but whose conceptual development remains unclear throughout its history, even in the eponymous poem of John Keats. Early *D&D* editions describe it as a Centaur-like creature with the body and legs of a lion (or some other beast) and the torso, head, and arms of a human woman. In 4e this was completely revised (perhaps inspired by the 1999 film *The Mummy*, dir. Stephen Sommers): "In its true form, a lamia is a swarm of black scarab beetles assembled into a coherent mass around the flesh-stripped bones of a powerful fey creature."[35] 5e has since returned to the lion-centaur form.[36] Beginning in 1981, however, a parallel tradition developed, equating Lamias with Nagas (snake-bodied Hindu deities). The *Fiend Folio* (an additional bestiary compiled mostly from submissions from UK-based players) included 'Lamia Nobles', creatures which "rule over the other lamia and the wild, lonely areas they inhabit".[37] This serpentine tradition has continued alongside the more traditional Lamia in *Pathfinder*, a successful *D&D*-inspired game that emerged in 2008. Curiously, there is stronger classical support for this interpretation of the Lamia: the description at Dio Chrysostom 5.12–13 almost certainly describes the Lamia as a Libyan monster with a serpent's tail.[38]

This points again to conservatism in the RPG system: though new iterations of the game incentivize renewal and innovation, there is a tendency to accept and incorporate disparate narratives into something that is available for use in any game. Denying a pre-existing account (as with the 'Lamia' in 4e) represents a conscious choice, and risks frustrating players who may be willing to accept new system mechanics but not lose the narrative connection they may feel, based on previous exposure, to a given monster in a previous edition.

Classically inspired creatures emerge in the various *D&D* bestiaries drawing from specific heroic legends, general understandings of mythology, and the paradoxographic tradition. Through the succession of subsequent editions, it is possible also to see the mythological becoming environmental, as aspects of a creature are codified within the systems of measurement employed by the game rules and monsters are presented not as one-off opponents, but as something that can be encountered – and battled – repeatedly. This naturalization of mythical creatures points to another aspect of RPG narrative that shapes these results, which is the value of (in-game) innovation. Characters expect to face ever-changing opponents, whose challenge increases as their characters advance.

Level 4: The blood of Medusa

I have suggested that the drive to include classical monsters originated in the 1970s, and that subsequent generations of the game maintained the classical component for the most part, but never expanded it despite the existence of monsters that could have been included. At the same time, a core group of creatures persists through all editions. Among these, the Harpy, the Medusa, and the Minotaur are found in all editions as well as in the Basic game that was sold in the 1980s as an entry into the new hobby (these are the classical creatures in the reduced bestiary found in the Moldvay version of Basic, first published in 1981).[39] It was about this time that I was first exposed to my earliest scholarship on classical myth. I was thirteen, and an article called "The Blood of Medusa" by Michael Parkinson appeared in issue 58 of *Dragon*, a monthly *D&D* magazine. In the short article, Parkinson describes the genealogy of a variety of mythic creatures that can be seen as descendents of Medusa: Pegasus and Chrysaor; Chrysaor's children with Callirhoe, Geryon, and Echidna; Geryoneo, known only from Spenser's *Faerie Queene*; Echidna and Typhon's offspring, Orthus, Cerberus, the Lernaean Hydra, and the monster of Geryoneo; Echidna and Orthus's offspring, the Theban Sphinx and the Nemean Lion; the Chimera, born of the Hydra; and the Blatant Beast, of uncertain parentage.

I had never seen such a beautiful systematization of classical knowledge before; to my teenaged self, this full-page illustrated family tree possessed the elegance of the periodic table, demonstrating connections between monsters I had not imagined (see Figs 11.3 and 11.4). In addition, I now knew the hit points and the magic resistance of each. From my perspective as a Classics professor, I can now perceive the syncretism and other short cuts Parkinson employs. Yet I want to suggest that this systematization is not notably inferior to what might be found in an undergraduate myth textbook. In addition, Parkinson showed his work, quoting both Spenser's *Faerie Queene* and Hesiod's *Theogony* to support his argument. He also adduced a wide range of other mythological facts. For example:

> Bellerophon as a child was called Chrysaor [as well] – but he soon changed his name to 'Bellerus-killer,' a less anonymous appellation. Chrysaor's only important act was to wed the Oceanid Callirhoe and produce two of the foulest offspring ever born: Geryon and Echidna.[40]

He continues: "Edmund Spenser . . . has a wingless Geryon represent Charles V of Spain, and invents for him an identical son, Geryoneo, portraying Philip II of Spain (and the Spanish domination of the Netherlands)".[41]

Seriously, what is this guy thinking? How does this help my game? It didn't at all, but it was important to him that the reader sees he has some literary source to support his

Fig. 11.3 Diagram from "The Blood of Medusa"; Parkinson (1982: 13). Art by David Larson. © Wizards of the Coast LLC.

WHO'S WHO IN MEDUSA'S FAMILY: *Medusa (1), who was beheaded by Perseus, produced Pegasus (2) and Chrysaor (3). Chrysaor wed Callirhoe (4), producing Geryon (5) and Echidna (6). Geryon, according to Spenser, bred Geryoneo (7), whose mother is unknown. The offspring of Echidna and Typhon (8), were several foul monsters: Orthus (9), Cerberus (10), the Lernaean Hydra (11), and the Monster of Geryoneo (12). Echidna and Orthus produced the Theban Sphinx (13) and Nemean Lion (14). The Hydra, whose mate is unknown, bore the Chimaera (15). Finally, the parentage of the Blatant Beast (16) is disputed, being either the offspring of Cerberus and the Chimaera, or of Echidna and Typhon.*

Fig. 11.4 "Who's Who in Medusa's Family"; Parkinson (1982: 12). © Wizards of the Coast LLC.

claims. The "Monster of Geryoneo" is described as such: "This man-eating devil, the creation of Edmund Spenser, represents the Spanish Inquisition."[42] In terms of disseminating knowledge of the classical world, imposing a consistent and critical vision, the article accomplishes a great deal. Typhon is identified as "not the fratricidal Egyptian god of evil, but a like-minded chaotic monster deity, thrown by Zeus into the underworld and trapped there forever".[43] Parkinson attempts, then, not only to expand the types of monsters available to a game, but to make them cohere with each other, to demonstrate that such creatures do not exist independently or solely to be defeated by heroes, but that they have origin stories and a lineage that can be articulated. There are problems with this approach: the systematic integration of all these creatures ignores any diachronic development of myth, washing over the fact that Hesiod and Spenser were separated by more than two millennia. For the thirteen-year-olds reading *Dragon*, of course, that did not matter, because it showed that monsters could have fuller back-stories, existing in the pre-game narrative past, and were more than simply potential occupants of a 20×20 room in a dungeon.

The same issue of *Dragon* also had an article called "Four Myths of Greece", giving stats, narrative, and bibliography for 'Atalanta', 'Daedalus', the 'Sybil of Cumae', and 'Chiron'.[44] The impact on me was less than "The Blood of Medusa", perhaps because none of these creatures were evil: in addition to helping feed my youthful fascination with the monstrous, Parkinson's creatures were things that characters could dispatch without moral anxiety.

Even if I am right about the instincts that motivated the inclusion of classically inspired creatures in the first decade of the hobby, another agenda emerges as time proceeds, which can be seen by again considering the Monster Manuals. An entry for 'Medusa' does not present her as a unique being but as part of a race of petrifying, snake-haired creatures. In *AD&D*, a Medusa is a fierce, mature woman, though the text reassures readers that "[t]he body of a medusa appears quite shapely and human.... However, the face is of horrid visage, and its snakey hair writhes, so that at a close distance (20') this gives the creature away".[45] In 2nd ed., the inspirational art presents her with a sexualized (emaciated, partially clad) body, and minimizes the serpents in the hair. Medusan society is presented in greater detail: they use tools (weapons, in addition to the petrifying stare), and we meet "Maedar [who] are the little-known male version of the medusae".[46] With "medusae" turned into a species, aspects of habitat and society are developed so that they may be more easily integrated into each table's unique fantasy world. In the third edition, Medusas change again, now possessing "scaly, earth-coloured skin" (see Fig. 11.5). They no longer appear human, and the change is largely incompatible with classical sources. Details given in the description are more obviously tied to providing hooks for adventure and plot: "It prizes art objects, fine jewelry, and wealth. Its activities often revolve around obtaining these items. . . . The creature often wears garments that enhance its body while hiding its face behind a hood or veil. . . . A few medusas have formed robbery rings or organized smuggling cabals."[47] The Maedar are also part of the 4e description.

Fig. 11.5 Medusa, v. 3.5; Baker and Williams (2003: 181). Art by Todd Lockwood and David Martin. © Wizards of the Coast LLC.

In 5e, the Medusa has been given a different story: no longer a species, they are men and women, living "forever in seclusion, alienated from the world around them by their monstrous form and caprice", who have struck a deal with an archmage or a devil for beauty, but, "after many years of living like a demigod among mortals, the price for their vanity and hubris is exacted, and they are forever transformed into medusas": "[a] medusa is subject to its own curse. By looking vainly on its reflection, it turns to stone as surely as any living mortal. As a result, a medusa destroys or removes any mirrors or reflective surfaces in its lair".[48] With no necessary consistency from one edition to the next, narrative material can be revised freely. Each new generation of players possesses a story that can be used, adapted, or discarded (as the DM wishes), but there are real ideas there that continue to exist. In this case, the new origin for the monster includes a means of circumventing it (showing the Medusa its own reflection) that explicitly introduces some of the elements present in the Perseus story, where a shield's reflective surface helps the hero.[49]

Three elements combine in all of these creature descriptions: the crunch, the fluff, and the art. The crunch describes its abilities mechanically, with numerical values: its hit points, armour class, and the damage done by its attacks, expressed in multiples of polyhedral dice. The fluff is the rulebook's narrative description, fuel for the imagination that might detail a given creature's life cycle, social habits, or physical appearance. These exist alongside fantasy art. The art is powerful as a source of player inspiration, and one could discuss it helpfully using some of the language that has been developed to describe comics and their juxtaposition of word and image.[50] The Medusa, therefore, possesses a greater (filtered) classical influence now than it has at any time over the past forty years. That it has persisted may be surprising given that in the earliest version of the game (1974), the 'Medusa' illustration, with its languid eyes and torpid serpents, was one of the roughest pieces of fantasy art ever published (see Fig. 11.6).[51]

This discussion of the Medusa leads to another creature that has persisted in every edition of the game: the Gorgon. The Gorgon has nothing to do with Medusa, but is instead a bull (since 1977, with metal scales) with petrifying breath. Comparisons have been made to the *chalcotauroi* ("bronze-bulls"; mentioned at Apollonius *Argonautica* 3.215), and there is considerable overlap with the petrifying Catoblepas, "another significant mythological ungulate".[52] A game designer, J. Wesley Schneider, attempts to explain the origin of the Gorgon in *D&D*, suggesting that they originally were *chalcotauroi*, but changed "in an edit that prioritized accessibility over mythological sanctity". He also suggests, improbably, that the source of the confusion was a 1607 zoological text, *The Historie of Foure Footed Beasts* by Nicholas Topsell. Schneider believes that E. Gary Gygax, one of *D&D*'s main originators, had access to this work and incorporated the creature (equated with the Catoblepas). Schneider also points to the presence of the Lamia in Topsell, which has testicles, the face and breasts of a woman, the body of a goat, and the fore-paws of a lion (see Fig. 11.7). This is close to the presentation of the Lamia in *AD&D* and represents a clear break from the serpentine creature described in antiquity.

There is undoubtedly a bit of hagiography going on, as Gygax is elevated to an implausibly well-read researcher. Nevertheless, Schneider's case is compelling, and is just possible: the

MEDUSA

Fig. 11.6 'Medusa', *OD&D*; Gygax and Arneson (1974: 28). Art by Keenan Powell. © Wizards of the Coast LLC.

work is available on microfilm at the Memorial Library of the University of Wisconsin, Madison, less than two hours' drive from Lake Geneva, Wisconsin, where Gygax lived.

As scholars of classical reception, we can begin to draw a number of lessons from this case study. First, intermediate sources contaminate the hypothesized (or desired) direct line between antiquity and the target text. We must be receptive to the existence of such sources, even if it denies us a classical pedigree. Whether it is seventeenth-century zoology or 1970s stop-action animation, or Hesiod read in translation and filtered through a hobby magazine, cultural literacy at a variety of unexpected (and unpredictable) registers can change what we perceive and how we perceive it. Second, classical references manifest themselves in a complex cluster of aggregated ideas, and it is not possible to isolate a single thread easily. The example of Medusa leads to insights about a variety of

Fig. 11.7 The Lamia in Edward Topsell, *Historie of Foure Footed Beasts* (1607).

other monsters, and the changes when we see the same processes working over a wider range of examples. Third, we must remain sensitive to the nature of the source material at the site of reception. The emergence of RPG narrative as a unique narrative product can be the focus of attention, but it is more natural to refer to something stable (and published), and to do that, we must use (at least, in this preliminary discussion) published game materials, which can only point to the type of narrative that might emerge at the table. Finally, classical material must stand alongside other non-classical sources, jostling for place in the imaginative world created by RPGs.

Level 5: Deities and demigods

One of the easiest ways to see these lessons manifesting in published game materials is in *Deities and Demigods*, a rule book for *AD&D*.[53] The book served as a kind of supplementary Monster Manual, but many of the entries were of gods and heroes from world myth. Various pantheons were arranged alphabetically, and the book could be used to provide specific mythic flavour to a campaign: typical readers might have passing knowledge of the Norse and Egyptian gods, but Finnish and Celtic gods are also presented with the same degree of detail. The book provides ready-made heroes and monsters for the world and could suggest a new range of gods for a player's cleric to worship.

Again, it is hard to describe this book without my personal experience shaping the narrative; this is a problem endemic in any scholarly activity, perhaps, but it feels more confessional and immediate here. Alongside the Greek and Mesopotamian gods and a chapter on the "Arthurian heroes" are also chapters describing H. P. Lovecraft's Cthulhu mythos, the Melnibonéan gods of Michael Moorcock's Elric series, and Fritz Leiber's Nehwon. The presence of these modern literary creations alongside what I understood to be world religions represented another paradigm-shifting change of perspective for adolescent me. Here were Elric and the Greeks together, and I had read bits about both of them. I understood fantasy was perceived to be a fringe-genre of fiction, but here it was being granted a legitimacy by its presence alongside Zeus and Odysseus. Indeed, Aurioch the god of Chaos was more familiar to me than Silvanus – included among the Celtic deities; there is no Roman chapter – because of my familiarity with Moorcock's Elric stories. The Greek chapter was also familiar: indeed, the book claims that "[t]he Greek assembly of gods is probably more familiar to most readers than others of the groups in this work, because they were woven into a literature that has lasted down through the ages".[54] I learned that Prometheus had an alignment of Neutral Good (appropriate for a benefactor of mankind), with additional details that allow him to serve as a patron for player characters (see Fig. 11.8). These can be thoughtful ("Prometheus's clerics also wear an iron ring set with a chip of stone supposedly from the mountain where Prometheus was chained') or silly ("The clerics of Prometheus will take any opportunity to kill a griffon").[55] Having stats for a figure such as Apollo was also fun: readers are told, "In battle, he casts a purple haze around any single being (usually himself) that will act as a +5 *ring of protection*," and this fostered a great deal of the solo-play ("reading"), even if I never knew of a player who actually encountered Apollo in a game.[56]

What is more, the book also contained a chapter of completely made-up gods for the non-human monsters. It was there I learned that Maglubiyet was the god of goblins and hobgoblins, and Garl Glittergold the god of gnomes.[57] The continuity between myth, fantasy fiction, and free invention was explicit and served as a great leveller, reducing – in some cases erasing – the distinctions between high and low art (even if this is not the way I phrased it at the time). *Deities and Demigods* encouraged players to imagine Maglubiyet taking over Asgard and other such paradigm-shifting possible stories. In light of this, the formulation by Rogers and Stevens is particularly helpful:

> it is important for Classicists in particular to acknowledge that … 'the classics' have been transformed into something like 'reliably esoteric, public-domain material for popular cultural ironization.' In this way 'the classics' are being made into vivid signifiers *neither* of the ancient past, *nor* even of professional knowledge of antiquity, *but* of a present moment: an advanced postmodern moment marked by recomposition of past cultural products that is omnivorous and, from the scholarly perspective, generally uncritical.[58]

Fig. 11.8 Prometheus in *Deities and Demigods*; Ward and Kuntz (1980: 74). Art by Jim Roslof. © Wizards of the Coast LLC.

Game materials encourage this recompositional practice in every session and provide the tools to do so largely separated from primary sources. That is not to say these materials are without value. They point to a body of knowledge and present it in a way that removes many implicit cultural hierarchies.

The book served as a leveller in other ways, too. Each pantheon was presented with identical complexity, which means that a less well-attested mythos (from my perspective as a young reader in Western Canada at least) was treated with equal seriousness and detail as the Egyptians and the Greeks. That is a result of the constraints of the format, and even if it required greater free invention for (e.g.) the Finnish mythos, to my eyes the book proposed a multicultural equivalence. *Deities and Demigods* also obscured the chronological relationships between cultures. For a historian, that is potentially quite limiting; however, in terms of the possibilities for narrative generation and the universalizing effects of literature, this approach was liberating.[59] It is also the case that it was only in this year that this particular set of virtues could be found, for in the 1981 reprinting of *Deities and Demigods*, the Cthulhu and Melnibonéan chapters had been removed for copyright reasons.[60]

The presence of classically inspired creatures, narrative patterns, and other vectors of reception exist widely in these published materials that facilitate gameplay and narrative development at the table, and this list is not exhaustive. A 1987 adventure module for high-level adventurers involves players rescuing the Greek gods from the Immortals of Entropy.[61] Some game designers might make whole rulebooks dedicated to helping recreate a particular era or tone for an adventure campaign (as with *The Trojan War*, a guide to setting a campaign at the end of the Greek Bronze Age).[62] There are economic forces at work here as well, as smaller publishers jostle for position in the marketplace, and such accessories are one approach. Another is to write an 'independent' RPG, such as *Agon*, a small, self-contained game that employs a mechanism that aims to recreate a particular feel of hoplite combat, or *Hellas*, which takes classical material and imposes it on a game that offers a sweeping space opera.[63] The possibility of using tabletop rules to replicate the experience of ancient warfare or maritime trade in antiquity is another vector along which classical reception in tabletop RPGs might be investigated.

The study of RPGs provides an opportunity to explore the dissemination of classical ideas in a medium that has not received wide academic study but which impacts its readership in a unique way, often first at a time when the possibilities of narrative are new and yet to be aggressively explored. It is a rich and complex area that affords many opportunities for research in classical reception. I take a set of platonic solids in my hand – shapes that represent the elements and the universe, but which I think of as d4, d6, d8, d12, and d20 – and I roll to hit or to see if my half-elf cleric makes his saving throw against confusion.[64] If I roll higher than a certain number, he can successfully raise his mace against a Minotaur and a Bugbear chieftain in *The Keep on the Borderlands*. In doing so, I contribute to the dissemination of classical myth and classical values in the modern world.

Notes

1. Gygax (1981: 20). My thanks to the editors for the invitation to participate in *Once and Future Antiquities* and for the patient support they provided in encouraging me to pursue this topic, and to Craig Hardiman for his helpful insights. This chapter is unofficial Fan Content permitted under the Fan Content Policy. Not approved/endorsed by Wizards. Portions of the materials used are property of Wizards of the Coast. ©Wizards of the Coast LLC.

2. Gygax 2012. Schick (1991: 135) speculated that there were more copies printed of this adventure than any other role-playing-game scenario.

3. Gygax (1981: 20; bold in original).

4. Gygax (1978: 12).

5. I use the term 'classical reception' broadly, to embrace the appropriation and use of ideas and imagery from the Greco-Roman world, both direct and indirect, in a more recent cultural product. Some tentative applications have been made applying classical philosophy to RPGs and the narratives they produce, as when Merli 2012 asks "Does *Dungeons and Dragons* refute Aristotle?" (Spoiler: the answer is no.) See also the use of Aristotle in Littman 2012 and Nicholas 2014, Robichaud (2014: 65–67) on Plato's *Phaedo*, and Hummel 2014 on *The Republic*. None of these are reception studies.

6. For 'modules', see Cover (2010: 134–138); ibid. (54–71, 79–84) for her description of *The Temple of Elemental Evil*, another influential adventure; Silcox and Cogburn (2012: 122–124) for *The Tomb of Horrors*.

7. In 1999, a sequel module was written (Rateliff 1999), which tied the adventure to the larger fictional world of 'Greyhawk', a published campaign setting for *D&D* since the 1970s.

8. For players exploring the caves, the DM might not show them the map, but would instead describe it, with one player attempting to reproduce the unfamiliar terrain on graph paper. The disorienting effects of the 'powerful spell' would only then become evident, as the hand-drawn map no longer corresponds to the players' experiences. This emphasis on mapping was central to the game in the early 1980s (Iosue 2015), but has become less central, in part because the theme of exploration has been reduced, and the back-and-forth between DM and the mapper provided less engagement for other players. *Keep on the Borderlands* as an introductory module makes the function explicit, encouraging the use of graph paper with the DM providing approximate descriptions but not correcting errors; see Gygax (1981: 5–6). Röhl and Herbrik 2008 consider the function of maps in the creation of an imaginary world. For some groups, miniature figures placed on a tabletop mat (gridded with squares or hexes to mark position) also sidestep this issue.

9. The speciation of elves in *D&D* has yielded a wide diversity of genetically unique groups, which can energize fans; see Rocha and Rocha 2012. A half-elf is the product of an elf–human union. The cleric is a kind of warrior-priest, originally inspired by the vampire hunter played by Peter Cushing in 1970s Hammer films; see Old Geezer 2006 and Peterson (2012: 172–179).

10. Nachos are also important. Call me a purist.

11. Fine (1983: 18).

12. The description in these two paragraphs is meant only as a representative description for non-players, and it does not describe the actual range of possible dynamics provided by tabletop RPGs. Further, not all games are face-to-face, and online chat-boards and other technologies allow players geographically dispersed to share in the process of narrative generation.

13. Others include the perceived association with young male (geek) culture and the overall bias against academic study of popular culture. There is also a holdover from scaremongering in the 1980s, with exaggerated misperceptions about what was then a new medium for play: see Martin and Fine 1991, Lancaster 1994, Ewalt (2013: 153–166), and Laycock (2015: 76–136).

14. Rule-based systems for fighting imaginary wars go back to H. G. Wells (1913), though the concept of pretend soldiers goes back much further.

15. Mackey (2001: 4–5; italics in original).

16. There are many accounts of *D&D*'s origins: see, e.g., Wolfendale and Franklin (2012: 207–209), Ewalt (2013: 91–113 and 132–152), and Mizer (2014: 1300–1305).

17. Exceptions exist, such as games without a gamemaster or where players represent things other than individual characters, but these exceptions are self-consciously deviating from the presumptive formula as described here.

18. For the use of dice, see Fine (1983: 90–102), Peterson (2012: 312–320), Bateman (2012: 229–231), Rose (2012: 274–277), and White (2014: 89–91).

19. Borgstrom 2007 explores the nature of RPG narrative space. Fine (1983: 177–204) introduces the language of 'frames', and Mackey (2001: 7) distinguishes cultural, formal, social, and aesthetic frames. My formulation here is closer to the emergent narrative described by Hendricks (2006: 51); see also Cover (2010: 94).

20. See Fine (1983: 243–252) and MacCallum-Stewart 2014.

21. See Peterson (2012: 152–157).

22. Gygax and Arneson 1974 (henceforth *OD&D*, marking the Original game); Gygax 1977; Allston 1991; Beach 1995; Baker and Williams 2003; Mearls, Schubert, and Wyatt 2008; and Perkins 2014. This selection means that I consider 1995's *Monstrous Manual* rather than the *Compendium* that came out in 1989, and the v. 3.5 *Monster Manual* and not the 3.0. I believe these choices will not affect the overall conclusions. I have also included the *Rules Cyclopedia* (Allston 1991), which represents a summative statement for the Basic Rules, a parallel edition that was kept in print alongside *Advanced D&D* (*AD&D*) and was expanded to include "Expert" and other levels. Year range in the table indicates the time that this edition was the primary version of the game supported by the company. Some decisions are subjective: the *AD&D Monster Manual* was released before the *Player's Handbook*, and served as a kind of teaser for the game's release. Midway through its life cycle the third edition was revised, and it was this version that led to the spin-off game *Pathfinder* (published by Paizo, a classically inspired company name from the Greek verb 'to play'), which continues to be played. In 2012 and 2013, 5e was in a period of public playtest, but was not commercially available.

23. I have excluded: some monsters that have connection with the classical world but not specific ancient roots (such as Werewolves, Living Statues, and Ghosts); medieval creatures (such as the Wyvern and Cockatrice; see Peterson [2012, 153 n115]); the Kraken, despite *Clash of the Titans* and its retro-projection on the mythic past; the Sylph (2nd ed.), which comes from Paracelsus in the fifteenth century; and things with classical names referring to non-classical monsters, such as v. 3.5's 'Archon' and 4e's 'Eidolon'. Peterson (2012: 135–136) makes a case for classical and Near Eastern Dragons, but the connection is not direct.

24. Hippocampus: Beach (1995: 189).

25. On 1980s scaremongering, see n. 13 above. This was partially circumvented by the inclusion of, e.g., Baatezu, "the primary inhabitants of the Nine Hells"; see Beach (1995: 11). This suggests game authors did not expect censuring adults to look beyond the alphabetic entries. The absence of 'Erinyes' in that edition may represent a missed opportunity, since their classical heritage separates them from the popular Christian frame that was generating panic.

26. 'Catoblepas' and 'Phoenix': Bonny et al. (2002: 41 and 168–169). Ward and Kuntz (1980: 67–68) present two versions of the Cyclops for *AD&D*, the 'Greater' (Hesiodic; cf. *Theogony* 139–146) and the 'Lesser' (Homeric; cf. *Odyssey* 9.357–358 and 399–402).

27. One exception is the Harpies, a flock, which remain un-individuated in their connection to the blind hero Phineus. Curiously, Sirens have not been introduced as a *D&D* monster. Their connection to Odysseus and the potential threat that they pose to wandering adventurers is significant, and yet they exist in none of these seven core bestiaries. My hypothesis is that they were confused with Harpies: this blurring is found in antiquity, as on the name vase for the Siren Painter, a red-figure stamnos in the British Museum (London E440, Beazley *ARV* 177). While Homer, *Odyssey* 12.39–52 and 165–191 presents them as women, later sources do present them as human/avian hybrids (Apollodorus *Epitome* 7.19; Hyginus *Fabulae* 125.13). The omission of 'Sirens' from the *Monster Manual* might also point to an issue of persistence: while new classically themed monsters are introduced after the publication of *AD&D* in 1977, the list remains surprisingly stable. This may suggest that the drive to include classical creatures resided primarily with the earliest players. Once *D&D* found a footing, the pressures were directed to expanding the bestiary in ever-new directions.

28. Knowledge of monsters was sometimes unofficially supplemented with journal articles with no reference to classical associations (e.g., Gerard 1986 on the Minotaur).

29. Titans are absent from 5e, but 'Titan' is introduced as a game term describing "divine creations of deities" (Crawford, Perkins, and Wyatt [2014: 11]), describing hypermassive creatures such as the Kraken (a giant sea monster), the Bullette, and the Empyrian (the last of which conforms to expectations of a classical Titan; see Perkins [2014: 130]).

30. Putz (2006: 10); Inniss and Adams (1985: 36).

31. Beach (1995: 39); see also Peterson (2012: 154).

32. Gygax (1978: 61): "This monster is very sly and can imitate the voice of a man or a woman. They will do this to trick prey to approach within attack distance."

33. Aelian *On Animals* 3.41, 4.52, 16.20; Aristotle *Historia animalium* 2.1 (499b18), *De partibus animalium* 3.2 (663a18); Strabo 15.1.56; Pliny *NH* 8.31.

34. Herodotus 3.116, 4.13; ps.-Aeschylus *Prometheus Bound* 803–804; Pausanias 1.24.6; etc. See also Peterson (2012: 153–154n114).

35. Mearls, Schubert, and Wyatt (2008: 174).

36. Perkins (2014: 201).

37. Turnbull (1981: 59; Philip Masters).

38. Scobie (1977: 7–10) makes the connection explicit.

39. Moldvay (1981: B36 and B39).

40. Parkinson (1982: 12).

41. Ibid., 12.

42. Ibid., 15.

43. Ibid., 14.

44. Moore and Kerr 1982. I was disappointed later to learn that the author Roger Moore was not the actor who played James Bond, something I continued to believe until widespread access to the internet. This Moore was a prolific writer and future editor of *Dragon*.

45. Gygax (1978: 66).

46. Beach (1995: 248): "The typical maedar is a monogamist who mates for life … A widowed maedar will pursue his mate's killer for years."

47. Baker and Williams (2003: 180).

48. Perkins (2014: 214).

49. The petrifaction of Medusa herself originates (I believe) in the film *Clash of the Titans* (1981, dir. Desmond Davis). Interestingly, the film presents her as a serpent-bodied Lamia, creating a new kind of mythological hybridity.

50. For comics as a site of classical reception, see Kovacs and Marshall 2011 and 2016.

51. Hughes 2012: 'Keenan Powell's amateur, almost outsider-art pictures set the tone, for me, for the OD&D aesthetic. The whole book gives the feeling of being illustrated by gamers who draw pictures, not by artists who play games.'

52. Schneider 2014.

53. Ward and Kuntz 1980.

54. Ibid., 63.

55. Ibid., 74. Presumably, the aquiline elements of the Griffon remind the clerics of the torture suffered from Zeus's eagle by Prometheus, though this must be inferred.

56. 'Ring of protection': ibid., 65; compare *Iliad* 5. Walter 2015 describes the joy of reading manuals for RPGs even if the game is not played. This is increasingly a way the hobby is enjoyed. Peterson 2012 describes a more hostile reaction from some players to this supplement (602), and to a similar volume for the previous edition (566–567). These players objected to the specific decisions made describing (beloved) fictional characters in game terms, especially when their heroes were not as powerful as the players felt they should be.

57. Ward and Kuntz (1980: 109).

58. Rogers and Stevens (2012: 131; italics in original).

59. For historiographical problems associated with video games, see Gardner 2007 and 2008, and Bembeneck 2013. For the representation of historical buildings in virtual worlds (with ideas easily transferable to classical examples), see Dow 2013.

60. See Ward and Kuntz (1980: 86–104).

61. Blake 1987.

62. Rosenberg 2004.

63. *Agon*: Harper 2006. *Hellas*: Fiegel and Grayson 2008.

64. Plato selects as the basic corpuscles (*sômata*, 'bodies') four of the five solids: the tetrahedron for fire, the octahedron for air, the icosahedron for water, and the cube for earth. The remaining regular solid, the dodecahedron, is "used for the universe as a whole" (*Timaeus* 55c4–6), since it approaches most nearly the shape of a sphere; see Peterson (2012: 313).

CHAPTER 12
THE GODS PROBLEM IN GENE WOLFE'S
SOLDIER OF THE MIST
Vincent Tomasso

One of the most prominent ways in which modern popular culture relates to ancient Greece is through the latter's mythic narratives about the gods.[1] Novels, films, television programmes, and video games set in ancient Greece tend to feature deities like Zeus, Athena, or Apollo as characters – or at the very least name-drop them. Such depictions of the Greek gods are closely associated – to an extent even equated – with modern popular culture's understanding of what ancient Greece was, and so modern artists' shifting ways of depicting the gods' presence (or lack thereof) is an important key to understanding the moving target that is the modern reception of antiquity. In this chapter I seek to illuminate a facet of this relationship through the stance taken by Gene Wolfe in his 1986 novel *Soldier of the Mist* (*Mist*). I argue that by positioning his text as a piece of lost history (a marker of the historical fiction genre) and simultaneously depicting the gods as physically present entities (a marker of the fantasy genre), Wolfe uses *Mist* to complicate the mythologizing and rationalizing modes of conceptualizing the gods that have existed since ancient Greece itself. Furthermore, Wolfe's way of representing the divine leads to a radical destabilizing of the modern audience's understanding of the nature of ancient Greece.

Mist is the first novel in Wolfe's series about the adventures of Latro, a Latin mercenary for the Persian king Xerxes in the fifth century BCE. In the course of the battle of Plataea in 479 BCE, Latro receives a head wound. This injury makes him an anterograde amnesiac, resulting in his inability to remember anything in the recent past for more than 24 hours or so. As a half-measure, he writes down some of his thoughts and experiences in a scroll that he carries with him. This scroll was neglected by subsequent generations until it was discovered in the basement of the British Museum and translated by an editor (*Mist* xi).[2] This frame is typical of the modern historical-fantasy genre, as examples like Umberto Eco's 1980 novel *The Name of the Rose* demonstrate.[3] This historical frame is embellished further by the incidents in which Latro meets and interacts with real historical characters. Early in the novel, for example, a group of Theban citizens sends one of their own to help Latro on his sacred journey to the sanctuary of Demeter in Eleusis. This man, an important secondary character throughout the novel, is the late-sixth-century to mid-fifth-century BCE poet Pindaros (often Anglicized as 'Pindar'). Closer to the end of *Mist*, Latro meets two historical characters who feature prominently in Herodotus's fifth-century BCE *Histories*, the Spartan regent Pausanias and the Athenian general Xanthippus.[4] Through such elements, Wolfe generates the atmosphere and generic expectations of historical fiction for his audience.

But this superficially straightforward exercise in genre is complicated from the outset. Latro's wound also gives him an amazing (and sometimes terrifying) ability: to see and interact with gods and other supernatural entities. In the course of the novel Latro encounters Hades, Aphrodite, Demeter, Aesculapius, Heracles, and several other divine beings. Nor are these meetings limited to dreams, though this does happen very occasionally. For instance, Latro happens upon Hades walking along a seashore, accompanied by the ghost of a recently deceased acquaintance of Latro's (*Mist* 66–67). Latro receives tips from Heracles when the former is locked in a wrestling match with the Spartan Basias (147–148). Such "non rational phenomena" are characteristic of the modern fantasy genre.[5]

Wolfe's representation of the divine in a narrative that is primarily historical taps into an issue whose roots reach back to classical antiquity itself. Narratives in what I will call 'the mythologizing mode' depict the Olympians as real entities who regularly intercede in the mortal world and who effect such fantastical events as teleportation and metamorphosis.[6] On the other side of the spectrum are narratives that make use of what I will call 'the rationalizing mode'. Rationalizing interpretations "recast myth as misunderstood accounts of actual events" because of "the desire to preserve the place of myths as powerful cultural property, and ... the recognition that these stories violate empirically perceived norms of reality".[7] It is important to note that *both* modes acknowledge the existence of the gods, so the difference between them is not simply a matter of (mythological) belief and (rational) non-belief, but an issue of how the gods are represented and their role in human history.

It will be instructive to look at a specific episode from the Trojan War, insofar as that event in particular triggered both modes of interpretation in antiquity. An excellent example of the mythologizing mode is the eighth-century-ish BCE *Iliad* by Homer, an epic poem in which the gods come down to Earth to support their favourite heroes, engage in petty squabbles, eat and drink at feasts, and have sex. On the other hand, Dictys of Crete's fourth-century CE Latin prose text *Journal of the Trojan War* best represents the rationalizing mode.[8] In Dictys's allegedly eyewitness narrative the gods never appear, even when audiences knowledgeable of Homer's mythologizing interpretation of the Trojan War might expect it.[9] For example, in *Iliad* book 3, Aphrodite, the goddess of love, snatches the Trojan prince Paris from the battlefield to save him from an ignominious death at the hands of the Greek leader Menelaus, who has been cuckolded by his opponent (380–382). Dictys, by contrast, reports this same episode in prosaic terms: a "throng of barbarians [Trojans]" (*globus barbarorum*; 2.40) rushes Paris away from battle.[10]

The ancient bifurcation of the mythologizing and rationalizing modes of representing the gods has been adopted by modern genres, specifically by fantasy in the first case and by historical fiction in the second.[11] Fantasy, which William Bainbridge describes as narratives with "events caused by supernatural agents", parallels the ancient mythologizing mode in that it portrays the Greek gods as physically present, important actors in the narrative.[12] Thus for some the fantasy genre is inappropriate to understanding the ancient world, since, in David Sandner's words, it "displaces" the audience from reality (or history).[13] This mode has been and continues to be especially popular in films, comics, and literature. Let us consider examples with which Wolfe and his audience for *Mist* in 1986 might have been familiar. Several scenes are set in the gods' home on Mount Olympus in Don Chaffey's 1963 film *Jason and the Argonauts* and Desmond Davis's 1981 film *Clash of the Titans*. In the first issue of the comics series *Wonder Woman* (1942), the gods Ares and Aphrodite quarrel over the role of war and love in the world. The time spent by Hephaestus in the care of the goddesses Thetis and Eurynome after his parents cast him from Mount Olympus is the subject of Leon Garfield and Edward Blishen's *The God Beneath the Sea* (1970). We should also consider that popular compendia of mythological tales, such as Edith Hamilton's *Mythology* (1942) and Bernard Evslin's *Heroes, Gods, and Monsters of the Greek Myths* (1966), are essentially re-tellings of Greek myths in a modern fantasy mode.[14]

On the other end of the spectrum, the rationalizing mode is paralleled in historical fiction. Whereas fantasy displaces audiences from 'reality', from accepted constructs of 'history', historical fiction generates narratives that are plausible according to rationalist approaches to history.[15] As Tomas Hägg defines the genre, "it is – or gives the impression of being – true, *as far as the historical framework is concerned*".[16] For Veronica Schanoes, historical fiction is "a genre grounded in realism and historically accurate events".[17] In the twentieth century and beyond, the historical fiction genre has become immensely popular for its ability to portray the Greek gods in ways that have been and continue to be more coincident with the rationalistic orientation of many contemporary audiences. Perhaps the rise in the employment of historical fiction in conjunction with subjects set in classical antiquity may be associated with, as Jonathan Burgess argues, the archaeological discoveries of Heinrich Schliemann at Mycenae and Troy in the late nineteenth century, which "seemed to uncover the reality under myth".[18] This contributed to the popularity of novels about Bronze-Age Greece, such as Mary Renault's *The King Must Die* (1958), the first entry in a trilogy about the adventures of the hero Theseus. Renault rationalizes the most 'outlandish' mythic stories in her fictional universe. For instance, Theseus claims to be a son of Poseidon, but the god himself never appears. There is no Minotaur; Theseus and his fellow Athenians are sent to Crete as ritual victims in a bull-leaping game, such as those depicted on Minoan frescoes.

Although *Mist* is not, even loosely speaking, science fiction (SF), it is useful in this case to consider how that genre's conventions overlap with historical fiction's, both because the two genres use the rationalizing mode and because Wolfe has been connected so often with the SF genre. In SF, which has "the natural world operating according to rational, mechanical principles", the Greek gods are not really gods.[19] Instead, they are beings enhanced by technology beyond human understanding. Examples of this trope before *Mist* was published abound, from 1932's "The Lemurian Documents" by John Lewis Burrt, to the 1967 *Star Trek* episode "Who Mourns for Adonais?"[20] This mode continues to be popular into the early twenty-first century, as Dan Simmons's novels *Ilium* (2003) and *Olympos* (2005) show; in that duology, meta-humans have enhanced themselves with technology to seem like the Greek gods to mortals.[21] Thus, although SF and historical fiction are, epistemologically speaking, entirely separate genres, they are related in this case through the rationalizing lens that they tend to use on subjects from classical antiquity.

Before the publication of *Mist* in 1986, Wolfe's literary output had mostly consisted of what many considered to be SF, like *The Fifth Head of Cerberus* (1972) and the *Urth of the New Sun* tetralogy (1980–1987), because of their inclusion of 'straight-ahead' elements of the genre like futuristic settings, space travel, and so on. As Joan Gordon points out, however, Wolfe's work "refuses to fall clearly within a specific genre. Though he writes within the science-fiction network, Wolfe prefers to identify his writing as speculative fiction".[22] Peter Wright argues that even though *Urth of the New Sun* has the trappings of SF, it is full of mystical elements.[23] This is what Wolfe himself has called "science fantasy", a mixture of SF and fantasy that blurs the typical boundaries of the genres.[24] Famed SF author Ursula Le Guin's remarks on the back of the dust jacket of the 1986 US edition of *Mist* confirm this blend of generic elements: "Every time Gene Wolfe writes a new book, we need a whole new definition of 'science fiction.'" I would argue that this redefinition of genre is characteristic of Wolfe's work in general, and in the case of the *Soldier* novels, he melds fantasy, not with SF, but with the related genre of historical fiction.

I am now going to examine the particular aspects of *Mist* that allow it to intervene in this bifurcated debate over how to represent antiquity through the gods. *Mist* deconstructs the differences in representing the Greek gods in the fantasy and historical fiction genres by combining elements characteristic of *both* genres. Wolfe's aim in doing this is to combine the mythological (fantasy) and rational (historical fiction) modes to create a more authentic representation of the Greek past that acknowledges the demands of both modern historical fiction and fantasy.

The full title, *Soldier of the Mist*, already signals that Wolfe's novel will be a mixture of genres. Latro refers to his amnesiac condition as a "mist" again and again (e.g., "there is a mist before my eyes that the sun cannot drive away"; 4), which parallels the mist that clouds mortal vision in the ancient Greek and Roman epic genre.[25] Consider book 5 of the *Iliad*, in which the goddess Athena tells the Greek warrior Diomedes how she will enable him to see mortals and immortals on the battlefield clearly: "And from your eyes I snatched the mist that was on them before, so that you may be able to distinguish god and mortal easily" (ἀχλὺν δ' αὖ τοι ἀπ' ὀφθαλμῶν ἕλον ἣ πρὶν ἐπῆεν, / ὄφρ' εὖ γιγνώσκῃς ἠμὲν θεὸν ἠδὲ καὶ ἄνδρα; 127–128).[26] Just as Athena removes the mist that prevents Diomedes from seeing the corporeal presences of the Olympians on the Trojan plain, before the events of *Mist* Demeter shrouded Latro with a mist that wipes his short-term memory clean every day but that also allows him to perceive and engage with the divine world. This mist symbolizes how Wolfe's novel mixes the mythological and the rationalizing modes as well as generic structures of fantasy and historical fiction.

From the outset, Wolfe partakes of a typical convention of historical fiction in setting *Mist* in the aftermath of a battle, in particular between Greeks and Persians at Plataea in 479 BCE. The historicity of the battle of Plataea, for which we have considerable evidence, is reinforced by Wolfe's invocation of the ancient historian Herodotus, whose *Histories* is a treatise on the Persian War that took place in the fifth century BCE. On the opening page, Wolfe dedicates *Mist* to Herodotus "with the greatest respect and affection", and on the following page, he quotes the *Histories*' description of an episode in the battle of Plataea: "First there was a struggle at the barricade of the shields; then, the barricade down, a bitter and protracted fight, hand to hand, at the temple of Demeter" (= *Histories* 9.62).[27] From this, readers are to imagine that *Mist* picks up right where Herodotus left off (or at least fill in details that the ancient historian could not be bothered with), and thus this citation of Herodotus is a critical component of establishing its place in the historical fiction genre.

The *Histories* is often considered the first work of historical thinking in the western world. Indeed, in his very first sentence Herodotus describes his work with the Greek term ἱστορίη, *historiē* ('inquiry'), from which the English word 'history' ultimately derives. And yet, Herodotus has also been accused of lies, both in antiquity and in the modern world.[28] This is due in no small part to the fact that in his writing humans encounter the gods. At the end of *Mist*'s preface, the translator cites such an incident in Herodotus's account, the Athenian messenger Pheidippides' meeting with the god Pan after the battle of Marathon in 490 BCE (*Histories* 6.106). A closer analysis of this episode actually reveals Herodotus's scepticism about events that he has not witnessed himself. The historian reports Pheidippides' story via indirect statement – that is, he does not independently credit that the runner actually met Pan.[29] This does not mean that Herodotus was an atheist; rather, he was careful to emphasize that he was reporting things that he did not personally witness.[30] In other words, Herodotus acknowledges the supernatural because it was part of what the Greek people believed affected their history, regardless of his personal view on the gods' ontology.[31] For Wolfe, too, the ancient Greek gods are a vital part of the 'authenticity' of his novel, for they are inextricable from the matrices of ancient Greek culture and history. That is, "[m]odern skeptics should note that Latro reports Greece as it was reported by the Greeks themselves" (*Mist* xiii).

The contrast between Wolfe's use of Herodotus and Neil Gaiman's in his 2001 fantasy novel *American Gods* illustrates the divide that typifies the differences between the fantasy and historical fiction genres. In Gaiman's chapter 7, the protagonist Shadow is driving through Wisconsin when he decides to give a ride to a hitchhiking college student named Sam. After dismissing Sam's question about Herodotus being "the father of lies" ("He wrote what he'd been told"), Shadow tells the same story that appears in *Mist*'s preface, Pheidippides' encounter with Pan.[32] But whereas for the editor of *Mist* this story is an access point into the ancient Greek thought-system, a story that is true for *them*, Gaiman's Shadow asserts it as fact.[33] Odin, Anubis, Anansi, and all the other divine beings that populate the novel's landscape actually exist in the narrative world of *American Gods*.[34] "'So there are stories with gods in them. What are you trying to say? That these guys had hallucinations?' 'No,' said Shadow. 'That's not it.'"[35]

Another aspect of *Mist* that illustrates the difficulty of representing and comprehending the Greek gods is Wolfe's use of unfamiliar names. As Peter Wright has noted, Wolfe "deconstructs the reader's familiarity with the Greek world".[36] This parallels David Sandner's notion of fantasy as 'displacement' in that it indicates spatial and temporal displacement.[37] *Mist* is cognitively estranged from popular culture representations of the gods, with which Wolfe's ideal audience members are likely to be familiar. From the perspective of the internal mechanics of the novel, it is completely understandable that Latro himself is also in the position of not being familiar with the Greek gods, given that he is a Latin mercenary and thus a foreigner to Greece and its customs. This is demonstrated by his very mangled memory of worshipping at "the house of some small god" (*Mist* 6) – presumably one of the Roman household gods known as the Lares.[38] The external audience shares Latro's cognitive estrangement as well. As in the *Urth of the New Sun* tetralogy, characters employ various titles like "strategist" (= Greek στρατηγός, 'general') without any explicit definition within the narrative (though there is a glossary at the end of the novel).[39]

Another way that Wolfe achieves this is by having his characters employ names for Greek deities unfamiliar from their modern popular culture representations. Apollo is "the Swift God", Zeus is "the Descender", Persephone is "the Maiden", and so on.[40] At some points, characters tell mythic narratives involving these gods, but often these are lesser-known tales. For instance, a Theban priest narrates to Latro and his companions how "the Lady of Thought" (Athena) saved the heart of "the God in the Tree" (Dionysus) when he was torn apart by the machinations of the jealous "Teleia" (Hera; *Mist* 18–21). This story was not a mainstream narrative even in the ancient world, though it does appear prominently in Orphism, a mystery religion.[41] More importantly for my purposes, it is not often portrayed in, and is therefore unfamiliar to, modern popular culture.[42] Adding to the reader's bewilderment, the priest's story is itself fragmentary. Since Latro's interactions with his travelling companions interrupt the story, the reader misses a crucial portion of the priest's discussion of Dionysus. The priest begins with Zeus seducing Semele in disguise and Hera's plot to have Semele incite Zeus to kill her inadvertently, but the reader's comprehension breaks off with Hera's advice to Semele, "'Make him promise to reveal –'" with an intrusion from Latro's friends (20). But the story goes on, and the reader eventually does re-enter the narrative after their conversation ("' – gave to the child god the form of a kid.'") This is a microcosmic representation of *Mist*'s and Wolfe's view of the representation of the Greek gods more generally: fragmentary and foreign.[43]

Nor do the gods have an existence independent of Latro's perception. The audience never witnesses, nor is even told about, the typical set-pieces of ancient epic, such as councils of the gods, which would ratify their independent existence on Mount Olympus.[44] *Mist*'s gods only interact with Latro individually on earth, a situation that is reflected in Apollo's words to him in his temple in Thebes: "Only the solitary may see the gods" (9).[45] Indeed, Latro typically interacts with the supernatural by himself because he alone can see them; only if he touches deities or supernatural figures are other mortals able to observe them. For instance, when he and his friends are prisoners of Spartan helots, Latro touches "the King of Nysa" (Silenus), so that the helots are able to see him. Many of the human characters believe that they have truly met a divine being in this encounter. Pindaros later remarks of the meeting with the King of Nysa, "It's just that I've never actually seen an immortal before" (24). This attitude speaks both to Wolfe's commitment to showing the theistic attitude of a large number of people in antiquity and to the inability of most characters to grasp what they have experienced. Aside from Latro's description of the effect of the King of Nysa's pipe-playing (causing the helots to dance) and his wine ("There is no describing how it tasted – as earth, rain, and sun must taste to the vine, I think. Or perhaps as the vine to them"; 25), there is no objective way for the reader to know that the characters have definitely interacted with a god.

In fact, other characters cast doubt on Latro's assertions that he encounters gods. A Spartan healer, for instance, describes Latro's interactions with divine beings as "occasional hallucinations" (*Mist* 174). In the city of Thebes, Latro thinks he sees and then embraces "the Swift God" (Asopus, a river deity), but it turns out to be a statue in a fountain (8). In his record of the event in his scroll, Latro acknowledges that he was talking to a statue of Asopus, and later the Spartan regent Pausanias echoes that sentiment: "You'd tried to embrace a statue of the River God" (211). When Latro first points out the King of Nysa, one of his Spartan helot captors remarks, "No, that is only the shadow of the vines" (24). Later Latro himself asks a helot how he can be certain that they had encountered a god, to which the helot replies, "We danced. I too – I couldn't stand still. It was a god, and you saw him when none of the rest of us could" (30). It is important to note that the human characters never question the *existence* of the gods, even though some of them doubt Latro's experiences. At one point even Latro interrogates his own memory of encounters with the supernatural: "So many strange things – events I cannot credit – are described here" (42) and later he muses, "If I had ever known them [the divine beings Europa and Kore], they were lost in the mist, lost forever as though they had never been" (191). Even though the audience reads the encounters between Latro and supernatural entities, we wonder along with the Latin mercenary whether these meetings are hallucinations stemming from Latro's head injury (historical fiction) or happen in reality (fantasy). Wolfe thematizes this issue through the first-person account of Latro's scroll; *Mist* is the result of one man's imperfect recollection of the past.

In addition to these markers within the narrative that cast doubt on the ontology of the gods, *Mist*'s prefatory letter presents the reader with the most problems. The 'translator' informs us that, although Latro speaks Greek fluently, he writes in a form of Old Latin, misunderstands a number of Greek proper nouns, and abbreviates his writing. Like a scholar commenting on ancient text, he informs the reader that he has filled out these gaps.[46] The translator uses the facetious initials "G.W.", which, of course, are the initials of the external author himself, "Gene Wolfe". Yet an informed reader knows that "G.W." is a persona, as the real Wolfe was an industrial engineer, not an academic Classicist. Through such extradiegetic dimensions Wolfe is encouraging his audience to be sceptical about Latro's divine encounters.

Soldier of the Mist thus challenges the frequent modern separation between 'fiction' and 'fact', between myth and history, between non-rational and rational, between fantasy and historical fiction. Wolfe has done this to flesh out his conception of the ancient Greek world, which in his vision cannot be understood completely through history alone or through myth alone. While most twentieth- and early-twenty-first-century popular culture texts suggest that it is only possible for modern audiences to know the ancients truly through a rationalizing lens, through 'straightforward' history, *Soldier of the Mist* asserts that it is only through "the uncomfortable experience of disjunction, an ill-fitting conception of the presence of the impossible of fantasy", through the window on culture offered by the ancient Greek gods, that we can partially grasp what ancient Greece was.[47] Latro's severely imperfect perception of his experience also defamiliarizes ancient Greece, compelling us to reconsider what we think we know about antiquity. For Wolfe, the gods were real to ancient Greek culture, but for a modern audience they are inaccessible and in the end unknowable. He represents this situation by deploying elements of the genres of fantasy and historical fiction that contradict – or at least are at cross-purposes with – one another. The ancient Greeks filtered their experiences of the divine through the lenses of the mythological and the rationalizing modes in diverse texts. *Soldier of the Mist* makes use of both of these lenses and thus is positioned at the interstices of fantasy and historical fiction, embodying Hawes' observation about the mythologizing and rationalizing modes in antiquity as "an ongoing rivalry between poetry and *historia* over the correct way of telling stories about the past".[48]

Notes

1. I would like to thank this volume's editors, Brett M. Rogers and Benjamin Eldon Stevens, for their support, encouragement, and helpful comments. Without the conference that they convened at the University of Puget Sound in March 2015, I would not have had the impetus to put these ideas together in the first place. The audience at the conference also had many helpful suggestions and ideas.

2. References to *Mist* are to Wolfe 1986.

3. Schanoes discusses several examples of historical fantasies in which scholars are central characters who "disrupt . . . the usual divisions between what is practical and what is theoretical/academic" (2012: 244).

4. Latro is thus "[t]he typical man . . . whose life is shaped by world-historical figures and other influences", a characteristic of historical fiction, according to Fleishman (1971: 11).

5. Tymn, Zahorski, and Boyer (1979: 3).

6. Bost-Fiévet and Provini (2014: 23) list elements of Greek and Latin literature that would now be considered part of what they call "littératures de l'imaginare" (or fantastika), several of which fall under the 'science fiction' and others under the 'fantasy' genre: "the desire to imagine beyond knowledge and human possibilities really did exist in antiquity" ("le désir d'imaginer au-delà des connaissances et des possibilités humaines existe bien dans l'Antiquité"; my translation). I put 'fantasy' in quotation marks because such events were perceived as supernatural in antiquity, whereas modern SF and historical fiction writers might describe them as the results of science and/or technology. Rogers and Stevens also see in the ancient Roman Ovid's epic poem *Metamorphoses* reflections of what SF can do (2015a: 5–6) and point to Roberts's list of elements in SF that can be found in the ancient Greek novel (14).

7. Hawes (2014: 2–3). The two modes that I identify as 'mythologizing' and 'rationalizing' have been recognized and named differently. Hawes (2014: 10), for instance, speaks of 'poetic' and 'historical' modes in antiquity, while Roberts uses the labels 'religious (supernatural)' and 'technical (materialist)' (2005: 21). Rogers and Stevens speak of 'theological' and 'magical' versus

'materialist' (2015a: 16), building on Suvin's 'Ovidian' and 'Lucretian' dichotomy (1979: xv). In my chapter on the SF television series *Battlestar Galactica* I use the terms 'mythical hermeneutic' and 'cognitive hermeneutic'; see Tomasso (2015a: 249).

8. For a discussion of the issue of the probable Latin translation of the earlier Greek version, see Merkle (1996: 577).

9. "[T]he Homeric poems were the touchstone of authenticity by which all subsequent Greek culture defined itself" (ní Mheallaigh [2014: 236]), because for ancient Greeks the *Iliad* and the *Odyssey* enshrined communal values (on which see, e.g., Nagy 1999 and Zeitlin 2001). Thus it is quite likely that any given ancient audience member would interpret Dictys's depictions against the culturally dominant background of the Homeric poems.

10. Latin text: Eisenhut 1994. All English translations of Greek and Latin in this chapter are my own.

11. I do not argue that we can trace modern literary genres back directly to ancient models; in this chapter I speak in terms of 'analogues' and 'parallels' instead.

12. Bainbridge (1986: 118). Cf. James and Mendelsohn (2015: 1): "fantasy is about the construction of the impossible whereas science fiction may be about the unlikely, but is grounded in the scientifically possible".

13. Sandner (2004: 9). He also tellingly uses words like "bewilder", "overwhelm", "lack", and "disruption" to describe the relationship between fantasy and its audience.

14. James and Mendelsohn (2015: 3) argue that "writers within the modern genre of fantasy have been inspired by them and have frequently reused and referenced them" (i.e., "earlier fictions about the fantastical", including the *Odyssey* specifically). Just as we may see in Lucian's second-century CE text *True History* the first example of literary science fiction (see the discussion in Georgidou and Larmour [1998: 45–48] and the bibliography in Keen [2015a: 107n9]), so too might Homer's *Odyssey*, with its theological dimension, be understood as an early example of (what would become) the fantasy genre.

15. The genre of historical fiction thus has an interesting parallel with ancient "rationalistic interpretations [which] are not so much historically accurate as historiographically plausible" (Hawes [2014: 10]).

16. Hägg (1999: 145); emphasis mine.

17. Schanoes (2012: 236).

18. Burgess (2009: 169). Cf. Hawes (2014: 1): "myths may capture the imagination, but they are more valuable when historical proof can be offered".

19. Bainbridge (1986: 118).

20. See Kovacs 2015 and Tomasso (2015a: 251–252) and (2015b: 151) on "Who Mourns for Adonais?"

21. For further thoughts on Simmons's duology, see Grobéty's 2015.

22. Gordon (1986: 3). Cf. Cape, Jr. (2015: 330): "Wolfe often poses his stories at the intersection of genres") and Sleight (2012: 249): "Gene Wolfe is an author primarily known for science fiction rather than fantasy").

23. Wright (2003: 86–103). Cf. Gordon's claim (1986: 8) that "Wolfe's stories don't 'feel' like science fiction precisely because they de-emphasize the empirical reality so many science-fiction writers stress to give their concocted worlds credibility" and Sleight's claim that *Urth of the New Sun* "occupies an unusual place between science fiction and fantasy" (2012: 249).

24. Wright (2003: 88). Cf. Clute and Nicholls's summation of Wolfe: "a spongelike ability to assimilate generic models and devices" (1993: 134).

25. The motif appears most prominently in Homer (see Kirk [1990: 69] with further bibliography) and in Virgil (see Lovatt [2013: 90]).

26. Allen 1931.

27. Given the nearly identical phrasing, Wolfe probably used Ernle Bradford's English translation of the *Histories* (1993: 241).

28. For an analysis of this phenomenon, see Evans 1968.

29. "At that time this Pheidippides, having been sent by the generals, when <u>he claimed</u> that Pan had appeared to him ... upon his arrival said the following to the archons ..." (Τότε δὲ πεμφθεὶς ὑπὸ τῶν στρατηγῶν ὁ Φιλιππίδης οὗτος, ὅτε πέρ οἱ <u>ἔφη</u> καὶ τὸν Πᾶνα φανῆναι ... ἀπικόμενος δὲ ἐπὶ τοὺς ἄρχοντας ἔλεγε ...). Greek text: Legrand 1963.

30. Herodotus at several points in the *Histories* asserts his own belief in the role of the divine in historical events; see Munn (2006: 297–298).

31. Ibid., 296: "classical Greek historical thought was not only sensitive to the claims of widely held religious belief, but was even designed, with selective discretion, to provide historical affirmation of them".

32. Gaiman (2001: 132).

33. Cf. Schanoes's analysis of the 1999 novel *A Secret History: The Book of Ash*, which she argues thematizes the question of whether "the function of historical narrative ... [is] to reproduce a lost historical viewpoint so as to illuminate how 'these people' understood their world, or ... to explicate how we, looking back, understand what took place" (2012: 238).

34. As Gaiman remarks in a prefatory disclaimer about the fictional nature of his novel, "Only the gods are real" (2001: no pagination).

35. In the first chapter, Gaiman also uses Herodotus for what Swanstrom describes as a "classic moment of misdirection" (2012: 6), a device employed to distract Shadow from the fact that he is being manipulated by Odin.

36. Wright (2003: 187).

37. Sandner (2004: 9). This is parallel to Suvin's description of SF as "cognitive estrangement" (1979: 7–8).

38. On the Lares, see Beard, North, and Price (1998: 185).

39. For an analysis of Wolfe's use of de-familiarizing vocabulary in the *Urth of the New Sun* novels, see Andre-Driusi 2008.

40. It is crucial to note that these titles are *not* estranging from the point of view of the ancient Greeks themselves, since they are derived from epithets found in their literature. Persephone, for example, is called *Kore* ('the Maiden') at Pausanias 1.14.1, Apollodorus *Bibliotheca* 1.33.1, and Diodorus of Sicily 5.2.3. In this way, Wolfe attempts to give modern readers some sense of what the relationship between ancient Greek culture and its gods was 'really' like.

41. See Burkert (1985: 127, 296–298).

42. See Tomasso (2015b: 148).

43. This is also a major theme within modern receptions of classical antiquity; cf. Porter's "fragments and fragmentary wholes" (2007: 474).

44. Cf. Keen's review of the *Mist* 'threequel' *The Soldier of Sidon*, in which he notes the fact that there are "no great epic narratives, no wars of gods and men" in the Latro series (2007b).

45. In Simmons's novels, by contrast, readers are treated to scenes of the posthuman 'gods' on Mars' Olympos Mons, but the point of this is precisely to confront (and deconstruct) the generic expectations of epic.

46. Cf. Schanoes's analysis of fantasy novels in which "the dynamic between history and fantasy is embodied in the troubled relationship between researcher and topic" (2012: 237).

47. Sandner (2004: 9).

48. Hawes (2014: 10).

CHAPTER 13
THE DIVINE EMPEROR IN VIRGIL'S *AENEID* AND THE *WARHAMMER 40K* UNIVERSE

Alex McAuley

> From that noble line will arise a Trojan Caesar, who will bound his rule with the oceans and his fame with the stars . . . he too will be summoned with prayers, and then the bitter centuries, with wars put aside, will become gentle.
>
> Virgil *Aeneid* 1.286–291

On its face, Virgil's *Aeneid* is worlds apart from the universe of Games Workshop's *Warhammer 40k* series.[1] In the quotation above, the *Aeneid* (*Aen.*) prophesies the future of Rome's first emperor Augustus in the closing decades of the first century BCE.[2] In contrast, the standard preface to the *Warhammer 40K* codices and novels describes the grim status quo of a dystopian, science-fiction (SF) vision of 41st-millennium humanity: "For more than a hundred centuries the Emperor has sat immobile on the Golden Throne of Earth. He is the master of mankind by the will of the gods, and master of a million worlds by the might of his inexhaustible armies." The various historical and literary influences on *Warhammer 40K* (henceforth *40K*) have been the subject of long discussion and debate among enthusiasts of the tabletop game and the elaborate literary universe it has inspired.[3] Sources range from Norse berserkers (World Eaters) and World War I regiments (the Death Korps) to Frank Herbert's *Dune* and J. R. R. Tolkien's *Lord of the Rings*. The universe that emerges combines displaced threads of SF, ancient and contemporary history, and literature woven together to create a dark, though not entirely unfamiliar, view of the far future.

Rome figures prominently in the 41st-millennium as described by Games Workshop and its publishing subsidiary, the Black Library. There is something unmistakably Roman in the Imperium of Man in the *40K* universe: it is a highly militarized empire, stretching across vast territory and maintaining its dominion with complex administration and unstoppable military might. This Imperium – with its governors, sectors, legions, and cohorts, not to mention dozens of "High Gothic" (pidgin Latin) terms – makes it obvious that the human side of *40K* is consciously modeled on the High Roman Empire.[4] As we shall see below, the educational background of the creative minds behind *40K* makes this displacement of Rome into the far future central to its design. But Rome is not the only empire that seems to have influenced *40K*: we can also find echoes of the Soviet Union (commissars, regiments of the Imperial Guard), the Spanish Empire (the Holy Inquisition), the Third Reich, and some aspects of the ideology of the British Empire, among others. To those interested in ancient history, however, the far future of *40K* poses two unique problems from two different methodological perspectives. First, in a comparative sense, how does the Imperium of Man relate to the Roman Empire in both structure and ideology? And second, from a historical perspective, how can we explain the prominence of Rome in the far future of *40K*, and how does the collaborative and serialized nature of the *40K* universe, shaped by dozens of authors across different media over several decades, subsequently re-work these ancient echoes?

There is one lens through which we might glimpse some of the answers to these methodological questions. At the heart of both Rome's imperial past and *40K*'s bleak future lies a figure who embodies the empire and society of each universe: the divine emperor. I argue that the place of the God-Emperor in the cosmology of *40K* is remarkably and consciously similar to that of Augustus in the cosmology of Rome. This chapter will investigate this echo of the Augustan age in the distant future of *40K* by first examining Augustus's depiction in Virgil's *Aeneid*, and then turning to the parallels that can be drawn with the God-Emperor of the *40K* Universe as described by the *Horus Heresy* prequel series along with other novels set in the 41st millennium. From there I shift to a historical perspective in order to explain how these parallels were drawn. Tracing the biography and education of the most prominent authors in the *40K* canon, I argue that they were aware of the Roman precedent and used it to shape the character of the God-Emperor of Mankind. Next I review my own correspondence with several authors of *40K* novels who describe their own creative process, in order to determine how this reception of Augustus evolves in a collaborative and serialized universe, in which echoes are transmitted from one author to another and modified by each. Because we are not dealing with a monolithic or single-authored SF universe, the dynamics of reception become still more complicated. However, in better understanding how many hands sculpt and reshape ancient precedent, we may consider *40K* an illustrative case study for examining other collaborative SF universes, not least among them *Star Wars*, *Star Trek*, and *Dune*.

Before examining all of this, however, a few critical distinctions must be made. There are essentially two components to *40K*: the tabletop strategy game in which players build, paint, and command their armies in battles against other players according to a complex turn-based rulebook; and the increasingly expansive literary universe that has been developed through novels, short stories, and audio dramas to provide the backstory to the tabletop game. In what follows, I focus primarily on the latter, the narrative universe of *40K*. Rulebooks, codices, and other materials related to the rules of the game will be treated as literary material and examined for how they provide further information on the universe's backstory.

The Divine Emperor of Virgil

This man, this is he whom you often hear promised to you: Augustus Caesar.

Virgil's *Aeneid*, composed between 29 and 19 BCE, is ostensibly set in the mythical past (*c.* 1150 BCE) and relates the journey of Aeneas, a Trojan prince, who, after the sack of

Troy, travels across the Mediterranean on his destined path to found Rome.[5] Once he reaches Italy, the second half of the epic becomes a tale of civil war among the kings and warriors of Latium, from which Aeneas emerges victorious after defeating the daunting Turnus.[6] But Virgil's contemporary present, the reign of the first emperor Augustus, lurks in the poem's backdrop as the future towards which Rome is inescapably marching.[7] The seeds of the distinct brand of one-man rule that would become a reality during the reign of Augustus are sprinkled by Virgil throughout the poem. The poem displaces its contemporary present throughout Rome's mythical past: allusions to the arrival of the man who will answer Rome's prayers and usher in centuries of golden prosperity suffuse the work and remind the reader that the narrative present is merely prequel to Rome's glorious future.[8] The work as a whole thus revolves around a figure who, paradoxically, is only indirectly present: the first emperor himself.

For centuries the *Aeneid* formed the backbone of Latin curricula throughout Europe, and such a wide readership has inspired numerous divergent responses. Scholars of this "classic of all Europe", as T. S. Eliot branded it, have traditionally fallen into one of two camps: those who consider the poem to be a pessimistic narrative of the individual trapped in the inevitability of history; and those who read it as an optimistic panegyric to the city of Rome and Virgil's indirect patron, Augustus.[9] For the purposes of this chapter, I align myself with the latter camp, in the sense that the poem's optimism means that the cosmological order established by Augustus is implicitly a good thing, although a more pessimistic reading in which Augustus simply sets the pattern for future tyranny could resonate equally well with the dark view of the far future put forward in *40K*. Out of the *Aeneid* as a whole there are two principal motifs that recur prominently in the *40K* narrative: the shadows of the civil war that preceded the Emperor's victory, and his subsequent place in the cosmology of Rome. These two motifs provide the basis of the God-Emperor's place in the distant future of *40K*.

In the closing lines of *Aeneid* book 8 (678–719), Virgil offers an account of the future history of Rome (as forged by the god Vulcan on the shield of Aeneas) that culminates with the ferocious Battle of Actium, the pinnacle of a long line of conflicts fought by heroic Romans since the city's foundation. Historically speaking, the battle itself, in 31 BCE, was the final and decisive clash pitting Augustus (then named Octavian) and his allies against the forces of Mark Antony and Cleopatra. Augustus's victory at Actium made him the sole surviving power in Rome and resulted in his unchallenged supremacy in the city. In the memory of the victors, Augustus's opponent in the conflict is a vile traitor. According to the *Aeneid*, Actium outstrips all the other clashes of the civil war(s) in grandeur and import.

On the shield, Augustus cuts a divine figure whose victory seems inevitable: as he leads the Senate and people of Rome into battle alongside the household gods and principal deities of the Roman pantheon (679–680), Augustus stands at the stern of his ship with flames shooting forth as the star of his divine (adoptive) father Julius Caesar rises above his head (680–681). Arrayed against him are the uncivilized hordes of Mark Antony including forces drawn from the barbarous East, while Cleopatra trails in his wake with her army and the gods of Egypt in tow (685–700). Once the battle is engaged, it becomes a cosmic conflict between the forces of order and chaos, another Titanomachy or Gigantomachy in which, as Philip Hardie puts it, "the balance of power in heaven itself" hangs in the balance.[10] The noble Olympian deities of the Romans clash with the alien Egyptian gods – the latter of whom are described as monstrous, bestial, and bent on chaos (695–704). Led by Augustus, the Roman deities emerge victorious and, with the shot of Apollo's arrow, the battle is decided. The Arabs, Egyptians, Indians, and Sabaeans (so Virgil tells us) are driven into flight along with the clacking queen Cleopatra towards the personified Nile River, who invites all of the conquered into his watery embrace (704–714).

With the victory of Augustus, order has triumphed over chaos, civilization over barbarism, and Rome emerges victorious over the traitor Mark Antony and his eastern legions. On the cosmic plane, the Olympian gods of the Romans have defeated their foreign counterparts and, as the primacy of Rome in the mortal realm is established, so too is the reign of the Olympians restored in the divine realm.[11] All of this, of course, is thanks to the clash of the young Emperor with his traitorous arch-rival. Although Virgil narrates the battle directly with only a few lines in book 8, the conflict pervades the rest of the epic. The Shield of Aeneas, with its numerous scenes of Roman triumph in civil conflicts, immediately prefaces both the midnight attack against the Trojan camp by Turnus and his allies that follows in book 9 and the epic clashes that follow once Aeneas returns with his allies. The disruption of the Italian civil war is paralleled by various disruptions in nature itself, again emphasizing that this clash is about more than just politics or territory. The storm of book 1 is narrated using military language as an attack against the Trojans by the angry Juno, and its power is only equalled by the fleet of Cleopatra and Antony churning up the sea with their oars to the point that it seems the Cyclades will be ripped up by their roots. In the end, Augustus is the only figure able to calm both storms and restore order to the cosmos.[12]

This triumph of order lies at the core of the figure of Augustus in the poem. Over the course of the epic, a city is lost and a city is gained, as the sack of Troy is balanced by the Trojan refugees' future foundation of Rome. Augustus's victory at Actium becomes his ascent to godhood: the roads of Rome fill with joy at his return; crowds in temples clap their hands in delight above the animals they have sacrificed to his cause (*Aen.* 8.717–819). Augustus himself sits (*sedens*) at the threshold of the temple of Apollo, receiving the tribute of all the conquered peoples of the world (720–728). The universal empire has thus been established, with the universal emperor at its head.

Augustus, in his guise as the future divine ruler of Rome, reappears elsewhere in the epic, again providing regular reminders of the glorious future for which Rome is destined. During Aeneas's journey to the Underworld in book 6, his father Anchises bids him to look and see the glorious future that lies in store for Rome (791–805). Immediately after Romulus comes Augustus, again hailed as the second founder of Rome (791–797):

This man, this is he whom you have often heard promised to you: Augustus Caesar, born of the divine, the man who will usher in golden centuries to Latium where Saturn once ruled, he will bring forth his empire, over the Garamants and the

Indians, and his reign will extend beyond the paths of the years and stars, where Atlas bears the sky, and turns the axis of the burning stars on his shoulder.[13]

This imagery recurs in the *40K* universe: a golden age, a massive imperial dominion stretching beyond the stars, bringing order and control to all conquered peoples – these characteristics apply equally to both Augustus and the God-Emperor of the distant future. The passage from *Aeneid* book 6 reiterates the divine place of the emperor in society that Virgil introduces in book 1 (285–291), where Jupiter tells Juno of the destined reign of Augustus. The man will be born from Trojan stock, his power and fame will be bounded only by the sky and the ocean, and he, like the Olympian gods, will be summoned with prayers and vows. His reign will soften hard centuries, and peace – the *pax Augusta* – will extend throughout the universe.

There is one subtle point to be made before turning our attention to the God-Emperor of the distant future: Augustus's divine rule as the guarantor of order in society comes with some measure of personal sacrifice.[14] He sets aside his own ambitions and desires in the selfless service of the Roman people and the cosmos itself. All of this comes after his defeat of a one-time ally and confidant-turned-traitor to the forces of barbarism, Mark Antony. And therein, perhaps, lies the role played by the character Horus in the *40K* universe.

Making the God-Emperor of mankind: The *Horus Heresy*

As Actium was to Augustus, so too is the *Horus Heresy* to the God-Emperor of *40K*. At the height of his personal power, the Emperor delegates military control of the expanding Imperium to his most favoured son, the primarch Horus. At first Horus is a loyal servant, but then the corrupting influence of Chaos creeps in and leads him to revolt against the Emperor: the *Horus Heresy*. The *Heresy* is told by a series of (to date) 46 novels, 17 novellas, and various anthologies and audio dramas penned by a team of Black Library authors. In terms of mass-market appeal and sheer selling power, they have created one of the most successful *40K* sub-brands in the gaming universe's history, with many novels appearing on the *New York Times* bestselling lists.[15] This series of novels, along with many of its predecessors, has created an entirely separate strand of *40K* fans who have never played the tabletop game but are nonetheless familiar with its universe.[16] These contributions join a product line introduced by Games Workshop featuring new models, units, and scenarios for the tabletop game.[17] The events of the *Heresy* take place roughly 10,000 years before the 'main' *40K* canon set in the 41st millennium, and describe the *apotheosis* (ascent to divinity) of the Emperor of Mankind as a result of the betrayal of Horus.

Horus cuts a figure akin to the *Aeneid*'s Mark Antony: rather than remaining a loyal servant of truth, justice, and civilization, he is seduced by the wealth and power offered by barbarous powers, in this case the gods of Chaos. The character's name Horus reinforces his connection to Egypt, evoking Cleopatra and her bestial deities as well as a sense of

'Oriental excess'. According to Dan Abnett's novel *Horus Rising* (2006), the first in the series, Chaos is able to clench Horus in its talons by leading him to believe that the Emperor is about to declare himself a god and mandate his worship by the Imperium's citizens. Horus, unable to brook such hubris, gathers his allies and his nascent treachery expands. The *Horus Heresy* conflict thus arises out of the question of the Emperor's divinity.

The betrayal of Horus divides the Imperium along two lines: those who support the civilized light of the Emperor of Mankind, and those who ally themselves with the destructive gods of Chaos and their denizens.[18] The Primarchs, superhuman demigods created by the emperor as his successors and ideal warriors at the head of vast legions, align themselves with both sides as the conflict broadens. After a near-apocalyptic war that tears the galaxy apart, Horus besieges Terra itself, and a massive battle ensues. The Emperor resists and boards Horus's flagship, and in the ensuing duel he emerges victorious though gravely wounded. The Emperor then restores some measure of peace to a reunified Imperium and ascends the Golden Throne.

The cosmic stakes of this conflict are essentially the same as those for Actium in the *Aeneid*: chaos clashes with order, barbarism with civilization, and disturbance with tranquility, while the fate of the cosmos hangs in the balance. As the *40K Rulebook* describes, "if the Emperor fails, then the daemons of Chaos will flood into the galaxy. Every living human will become a gateway for the destruction of mankind . . . there will be no physical matter. No space. No time. Only Chaos".[19] As with Actium in *Aeneid* book 8 and the war in Italy of books 7–12, the *Horus Heresy* conflict is essentially a civil war, splitting the Imperium in two and setting it against itself. Both conflicts likewise come to a dramatic end with a massive battle involving superhuman forces. In *Aeneid*'s Actium, Romans and their Olympian deities clash with the hordes of the East and their Egyptian deities in a cosmic battle between west and east; in *40K*'s Battle of Terra, the loyal forces of the Emperor, bolstered by his psychic ability, contend with Horus's legions and their daemons of Chaos in a similar orientalizing clash.[20] There is also a mortal and cosmic plane to the *Horus Heresy* that may provide another parallel to Actium in the *Aeneid*: all of *40K*'s space marines and their primarchs are essentially immortal – they can be killed in battle but cannot die of natural causes – and their involvement in the conflict makes it seem like the clash of gods. That each primarch has his own distinct character, weapons, and abilities further makes them seem like futuristic Olympians.

In the aftermath of each conflict comes the establishment of some measure of peace and order within the cosmos, enabled by the Emperor's victory. The prophecy regarding Augustus in *Aeneid* book 6 comes to fruition after Actium, ushering in the golden centuries of peace and prosperity promised to Aeneas by the shade of Anchises. According to the subsequent tradition of the *40K* universe, the Emperor's victory over Horus ensures the continued existence of the Imperium and saves its denizens from Chaos. While far from a Golden Age in the Augustan sense, the aftermath of the Heresy is at least not as terrible as it could have been. With his ascent to the golden throne, the Emperor channels his psychic power into the creation of the Astronomican, an immensely powerful warp beacon that enables safe navigation throughout the Empire and calms the storms of Chaos – again calling to mind the tranquility forged by Augustus.[21]

Perhaps most importantly, this cosmic clash and the victory that ensues in both the *Aeneid* and *40K* become a path to divinity for each emperor. Augustus is described by Virgil as the son of a god, and his accomplishments make him into a superhuman figure who is the object of prayers and supplication as the guarantor of stability. Although the Emperor of *40K* initially refuses to be worshipped as a deity (just like Augustus) and forbids religion or superstition on his conquered worlds, eventually his subjects come to view his abilities and accomplishments as proof of his divinity. Numerous characters in the *Heresy* series begin as sceptics but are gradually drawn to believing in the Emperor's divinity. Among them is Captain Garro, who in the *Flight of the Eisenstein* is described by another believer as "gradually turning to the same path that he had already walked, a path that led to Terra and the only truly divine being in the cosmos, the God-Emperor himself".[22] And this, of course, in both the *Aeneid* and *40K* is the inevitable future for which all were fated: as Euphrati Keeler, an historian who becomes an ardent worshipper of the Emperor, says, "we are all of purpose".[23] Shattered by the fight against Horus, the Emperor ascends the Golden Throne of Terra, an arcane device built to keep his withered husk alive forever, and with this he becomes the immutable God-Emperor of humankind.[24]

Fast forward: The God-Emperor long after the *Horus Heresy*

Turning our gaze ten millennia forward, in the later series that form the core of the *40K* universe we glimpse a God-Emperor whose place in the ideology and governance of the Imperium is remarkably similar to that of Augustus and the Julio-Claudians in the Early Empire. On a structural level, the notion, which figures so prominently in Virgil, that the city of Rome embodies the entire Roman world is echoed in *40K* with a slight twist: Terra, the centre of the Imperium, is described as a planet-wide city. Terra is the font of the Imperium's sprawling bureaucracy, all of which is built around the Imperial Palace and the Golden Throne. From there, the Imperium is administered in the God-Emperor's name. The eternal city at the figurative centre of the Empire becomes the eternal planet at the figurative centre of the galaxy. The God-Emperor himself exists as something of a passive figurehead in whose name all business, laws, and decrees are enacted by subordinates. To again quote the *Rulebook*: "the Imperium is ruled in the Emperor's name by the incalculably vast Adeptus Terra, the ancient priesthood of earth ... the Emperor has become a god and saviour to sprawling mankind".[25] God and saviour, yes, but as with many of the Julio-Claudians and their successors, the emperor does not often directly intervene in minute affairs – perhaps leading us to think of the reigns of Commodus, Nero, or Claudius.

Yet the figure of the God-Emperor pervades Imperium, and other *40K* series afford us some insight into his place in Imperial society when glimpsed from the bottom up. Dan Abnett's *Eisenhorn* series narrates the inner workings of the Inquisition in the Helican Sector, the institution tasked with finding and eliminating traces of Chaos. The piety of characters such as Godwyn Fischig and Inquisitor Eisenhorn himself is noteworthy;

even here in a distant province the imperial cult is ubiquitous.[26] Cathedrals and temples dominate city skylines; even small and remote settlements have a temple to the God-Emperor with regular services. He is a figure of organized public worship and the object of prayers and supplications, like Augustus in the *Aeneid*. Faith among the imperial elite can sometimes seem like a cursory nod to social propriety, calling to mind some aspects of Roman imperial cult, and in both societies worship of the divine emperor is requisite for access to the imperial bureaucracy.

Vast armies continue to fight in the God-Emperor's name on far-flung planets in order to preserve the relative integrity of the Imperium and the stability that it guarantees to its citizens. Among these soldiers of the Imperial Guard, devotion to the God-Emperor is widespread and institutionalized.[27] The Tanith First and Only regiment under Colonel-Commissar Ibram Gaunt is nearly always accompanied by one of the Emperor's priests, Ayatani Zweil, whose services in the makeshift regimental chapel are obligatory for the guardsmen. Gaunt, along with fellow commissars Hark and Ludd, exhorts the troops by recourse to the majesty of the God-Emperor and to the duty of each guardsman to act in the service of his divine will. Questions of the individual's standing with, and his sense of personal duty to, the God-Emperor pervade the inner monologues of many officers and guide both actions and tactical decisions. Though these soldiers will never even glimpse the God-Emperor, it is thanks to their efforts that his dominion, like Augustus's, stretches to the firmaments of the heavens. Service to the emperor and service to the Imperium, as in the ideology of Augustan Rome, are one and the same in the grim, far-off future of the 41st millennium.

Future imperfect: Spinning the web of *40K*

There are dozens of other examples of the God-Emperor's structural and ideological prominence in the Black Library's *40K* series, but there remains a rather more pressing question: where did all of this Roman inspiration come from? In such a sprawling collaborative universe shaped by so many creative hands, can we posit an original source for this Virgilian inspiration, and then track its development as the universe was elaborated? A biographical examination of the early origins of Games Workshop and the Black Library may hold some answers. At the heart of Games Workshop's creative staff we find a small group of writers and designers who are highly educated and would likely have been exposed to the ancient world and, more importantly, Latin literature. It would seem likely, then, that the minds that shaped the overall structure of the *40K* universe would be the initial source of its Virgilian and Roman inspiration.

As noted earlier, Virgil's *Aeneid* has enjoyed centuries of popularity in European primary and secondary school curricula, and this trend holds for the United Kingdom in the 1960s and 1970s. The prominence of Latin in general and the *Aeneid* in particular for schoolchildren across the United Kingdom during the formative decades for Games Workshop's creative staff makes it highly likely that they would have at least been exposed to the poem – and Roman history more broadly – at an early age; those who pursued an A-level in Latin would have studied it in greater depth. There was, at the time, a general cultural awareness of Virgil's poetry simply because of its popularity in formative education.[28]

The early history of Games Workshop was shaped by a small group of creative staff who were intimately familiar with the Roman world. The precursor to *40K*, the tabletop fantasy game *Warhammer*, was created in the early 1980s by Rick Priestly, Bryan Ansell, and Richard Halliwell. Although Halliwell has had a fairly unconventional career path and is somewhat difficult to track down, the biographical details of Priestly and Ansell allow us to identify them as likely sources of the fictional future's Roman characteristics. Ansell and Priestly both hail from Nottingham, and Ansell was educated at the Nottingham Boys High School, in which Latin would have figured in his secondary curriculum.[29] Priestly, for his part, began working as the Creative Director for the newly founded Games Workshop in 1982, after graduating from Lancaster University with a BA in Archaeology in 1981. In an interview from 2013, he speaks of the high level of education among *Warhammer*'s founders and the impact of their study on the universe they shaped: "the GW writers in those days were a pretty literate and well educated bunch – and this at a time when only about 5% of the population were university educated. I mean – we had three archaeology degrees between us! Phil Gallagher could speak Russian and Persian for goodness sake!"[30]

40K was developed five years later by the same creative team as the futuristic SF complement to the fantasy universe of the original *Warhammer*. In the same year, Games Workshop asked Scott Rohan, a Scottish author, to pen the first spin-off books filling in the *40K* backstory, which would subsequently be developed into the Black Library publishing house.[31] Rohan was educated at the Edinburgh Academy in the 1950s and 1960s – where he would likely have been exposed to Latin literature – and then studied English and Law at Oxford in the 1970s.[32] The classical influences in each environment would have been abundant. Marc Gascoigne, one of the lead creative writers of Games Workshop in the early 1980s and later editor of the Black Library press, likewise had an impressive education, first at the Chatham House Grammar School in Kent, then leading to a BA at Nene College in Northampton.[33]

From there *40K* took on a life of its own as Games Workshop grew exponentially. The addition of new units and models was matched by an ever-expanding literary universe meant to provide the backstory to new campaigns and additions, and with this enlargement came new creative influences. But even among the dozen or so subsequent Black Library 'regulars' who came to produce most of the universe's book series, we find the same prevalent exposure to the classical tradition. Dan Abnett, the most prolific and best-selling of the Black Library's authors, graduated from St Edmund's college in Oxford in 1987. Ben Counter, author of the *Grey Knights* series and a contributor to the *Horus Heresy*, graduated with a degree in Ancient History before first publishing in 2000. Biographical details of other Black Library authors are difficult to come by, but even with these few examples the trend is clear: *40K* novels continue to be written by authors who are familiar with ancient history and Latin literature, and who continue to carry the torch first lit by Priestly and his colleagues in the 1980s.[34]

Nevertheless, the mechanics of the literary production of the *40K* universe have changed somewhat in recent years, as the narrative has gone from backstory, to a game played by a small but passionate community, to mass-market paperbacks with a much broader audience that is not necessarily interested in gaming or painting. With serialization comes an entirely different set of concerns: serialized novels, like comic books, are the work of many creative minds overseen by an editorial board, and they are not meant to be completely self-contained narratives but rather employ many devices to ensure the continued interest of readers: allusion, cross-reference, suspense, and cliffhangers.[35] To better understand the mechanics of how a collaborative series like the *Horus Heresy* or its fellow *40K* franchises are transformed from initial concepts to serially published novels written by multiple authors, I contacted two authors who have written extensively for both: Graham McNeill and Dan Abnett.[36]

According to McNeill, when the Black Library was in its infancy and a new book was planned, "lots of us sat in a big room at GW and thrashed out the plots we needed to hit, and by a certain osmosis of interest, the projects kind of naturally found the right fit in terms of author".[37] Once the general idea and a few main events had been decided on, it was up to the author to find the plot. The synopsis of the plot was then sent off to the editors, who modified certain elements in dialogue with the author and requested some revisions to the story. Then the author gradually produced the final work.[38] Here we can see how the seed of Virgilian and Roman influence germinated among Games Workshop's initial creative team and then passed through several generations of authors.

The author of a book in the series then shaped his work according to a combination of his personal influences and those which were already established in the canon. Dan Abnett, when asked about his specific sources of inspiration, relates that "first and foremost [is] the Games Workshop lore, of course", to which he added elements drawn from TV, movies, newspapers, more focused research, and the like. He admits to having a "huge interest" in ancient history, "and so do the guys at Black Library", leading him to have modeled *Prospero Burns* on Norse myth and the warrior lodges of the Legions on the cult of Mithras in the Roman army.[39] Graham McNeill echoes this awareness of antiquity, stating that the classical past influenced everything from names, battles, plots, and set pieces: "too many to mention . . . but loads of them borrowed from the *Odyssey*, the *Iliad*, and the *Aeneid*". As noted above, the classical world is only one influence among many, and care must be taken not to overstate the case. McNeill states that, for the *Horus Heresy* series, "the inspiration came very much from Milton's *Paradise Lost*", though the well-discussed influence of the *Aeneid* on Milton suggests that many, though by no means all, roads lead to Rome eventually.[40]

The universe of *Warhammer 40K* is complex. Comments by Abnett and McNeill, along with the biographies of Games Workshop's founders, reveal that the Roman past in general and the *Aeneid* in particular shaped the distant future of the 41st millennium, but only as one influence among many. In the evolution of this particular aspect of classical reception, we see how an idea or parallel between the historical or literary past and the fictional far future can arise out of a small group of creative minds and then be passed on, re-worked, and embroidered by subsequent authorial hands collaborating to weave a universe marked by both great variety and essential unity. Perhaps the same mechanism is at work in *Star Wars*, *Star Trek*, and many other serially published collaborative narrative universes, be it in comics, video games, or television series. An initial mythos of a series is conceived by an author or screenwriter, who is consciously modelling something on what to them is a familiar classical precedent; then this element is reshaped by subsequent creative minds with different backgrounds.

To bring us back to the topic at hand, Dan Abnett's comments on the God-Emperor provide a fitting conclusion – and could equally describe Augustus and his successors in the Roman world. When asked how he thought the God-Emperor of the *Horus Heresy* series relates to the God-Emperor of the later *Warhammer 40K* canon, Abnett wrote:

> They are two sides of the same character really, but there is a key difference. In the *Horus Heresy* he is alive and active. Albeit god-like in power, he is still an active, demonstrably 'provable' individual. He is an actor in the story. By *40K*, though he technically still exists, he is a distant myth, a concept, a deified thing, remote and disconnected but still with a deep and prevailing influence presence. He moves from being a living proxy of a god, like a Pharaoh or a Roman Emperor, to a symbolic, conceptual deity.[41]

Notes

1. I would like to thank the editors for their patience and feedback, as well as my friend and colleague C. W. Marshall (UBC) for recommending this chapter in the first place. An early version of this paper was presented at the Science Fiction Foundation Conference at the University of Liverpool on June 29, 2013, and I also thank the organizers and attendees for their feedback and insight. The feedback of the anonymous readers was eminently helpful as well.

2. The original Latin for the first quotation is: *Nascetur pulchra Troianus origine Caesar, / imperium oceano, famam qui terminet astris,—/ Iulius, a magno demissum nomen Iulo. / Hunc tu olim caelo, spoliis Orientis onustum, / accipies secura; vocabitur hic quoque votis. / Aspera tum positis mitescent saecula bellis.* All translations from the *Aeneid* are my own; the text is Greenough 1900.

3. E.g., the community forums of Relic News, (http://forums.relicnews.com/showthread.php?254954-WH40K-influences), as well as sections of Reddit and Kotaku.

4. While Low Gothic is the *lingua franca* of the Imperium, High Gothic seems to be simplified Latin and is used as the language of Imperial administration, literature, and communication.

5. Section epigraph: *Hic vir, hic est, tibi quem promitti saepius audis, Augustus Caesar; Aen.* 6.791–792.

6. For a concise overview of the *Aeneid*, its literary context, and its reception, see Conte (1999: 249–291).

7. Galinsky (1996: especially chs. 3 and 5) provides a useful description of Augustan culture and the Augustan ideological programme; cf. Galinsky 2012.

8. Augustus is mentioned directly only three times in the *Aeneid*: Jupiter's prophecy at 1.257–296; the shade Anchises' description of Rome's future at 6.791–805; and on the shield of Aeneas at

8.671–728. For thorough discussion of each of Augustus's appearances in the text, see Grebe 2004.

9. Martindale (1997: 3) gives the quotation from Eliot, as well as a general discussion of the scholarly and popular tradition of the work. In the optimistic camp, for instance, see Hardie (1986: 1–15); for the pessimistic, Dyson 2001.

10. Hardie (1986: 98). The Titanomachy and Gigantomachy are mythical battles in which the Olympian gods defeated the Titans and the Giants, respectively, in the process securing their supremacy in the cosmos. For a full discussion of Actium as an analogue to the Gigantomachy, see ibid. (98–110).

11. See Hardie (1986: 98–107) and Braund 1997 on the cosmological resonance of this battle and the *Aeneid* as a whole.

12. Hardie (1986: 107–110).

13. *Hic vir, hic est, tibi quem promitti saepius audis, / Augustus Caesar, Divi genus, aurea condet / saecula qui rursus Latio regnata per arva / Saturno quondam, super et Garamantas et Indos / proferet imperium: iacet extra sidera tellus, / extra anni solisque vias, ubi caelifer Atlas / axem umero torquet stellis ardentibus aptum.*

14. The notion of the sacrificial victor pervades the *Aeneid*; see Dyson 2001.

15. For instance, *A Thousand Sons* (Graham McNeill) reached 22 on the list in February 2010; *Nemesis* (James Swallow) 26 in August 2010; *The First Heretic* (Aaron Dembski-Bowden) 28 in November 2010; and *Prospero Burns* (Dan Abnett) 16 in January 2011.

16. Cf. Marshall's discussion (this volume) of the "joy" to be had in reading role-playing game manuals without actually playing the game.

17. The *Horus Heresy*'s literary component seems to have outstripped the tabletop game itself, while previous novel series were intended as only a complement to newly released models or product lines. Despite the vast number of books and novellas published in the series, the only addition to the tabletop game is the "Betrayal at Calth" set and associated paints.

18. The first three novels in the series – by Abnett (2006), McNeill (2006), and Counter (2006) – establish the general arc of the fall of Horus and the emergence of the heresy in various other legions. After Swallow (2007), the series breaks away from its linear narrative to focus on a specific legion or group.

19. *Rulebook* (Troke, Vetock, and Ward 2012: 4). This Chaos might be compared to the storm with which the *Aeneid* begins.

20. Although the Battle of Terra has not yet been narrated directly by the *Horus Heresy* series, there are dozens of scattered descriptions of and allusions to it in the Space Marine, Chaos Marine, and Imperial codices, as well as the four volumes of the *Index Astartes* published by Games Workshop in 2002–2003.

21. The Astronomican was originally described in the 1987 edition of *Rogue Trader*, the first *40K* rulebook; see, e.g., Priestly (1992: 140). The *Rulebook* is currently in its eighth edition, released in 2017.

22. Swallow (2007: 121).

23. Ibid., 234.

24. The Golden Throne and the Emperor's entombment therein are described, e.g., in Merrett (2007: 322–328, 350) and the sixth edition *Rulebook* produced by Troke, Vetock, and Ward (2012: 170).

25. *Rulebook* (Troke et al. 2012: 141). On the place of the Emperor, see also *Rulebook* (Troke et al. 2012: 136–139, 158–163, and 187–188).

26. Abnett 2004a contains the original three novels published in 2001–2002.

27. Abnett's *Gaunt's Ghosts* series, as contained in the collected volumes published in 2003, 2004, and 2010.

28. On the 'Classic' Virgil and his place in primary and secondary education, see Haskell 2010 and Richard 2010.

29. These biographical details have been reconstructed from Priestly's and Ansell's *LinkedIn* profiles. There is a fascinating post from March 2013 in the *Realm of Chaos* blog that provides a detailed discussion of Halliwell's tumultuous career. That Latin still figures prominently in the curriculum of the Nottingham Boys School (as outlined on their website) leads me to conclude that it would have been equally, if not more entrenched, when Priestly was attending.

30. Jafnakol 2013.

31. This history of Games Workshop and Black Library has been reconstructed from ibid., as well as Mark Rohan's biographical page on his personal website. An *IGN* article on the history of Games Workshop, as well as the corporation's own informational pages on its website, also prove quite helpful.

32. Latin is a prominently featured subject in the upper year education of the Academy's pupils, and this was likely the case decades ago.

33. Taken from Gascoigne's *LinkedIn* profile and Rohan's personal website.

34. On the broader question of why historians, particularly ancient historians, seem well-prepared and well-disposed to write SF, see the introduction to Rogers and Stevens 2015.

35. See the case studies of classical receptions in the serialized medium of comics in Kovacs and Marshall 2011 and 2016.

36. I owe an immense debt to Dan Abnett and Graham McNeill for their kindness and generosity in responding to my various queries.

37. Author's e-mail correspondence with Graham McNeill, 19 January 2016.

38. Author's e-mail correspondence with Dan Abnett, 21 January 2016.

39. Author's e-mail correspondence with Dan Abnett, 5 October 2015.

40. All of the above are taken from my e-mail correspondence with Graham McNeill, dated 6 November 2015.

41. Author's e-mail correspondence with Dan Abnett, 5 October 2015.

PART V
EPILOGUE: FINDING A PLACE IN DISPLACEMENT

CHAPTER 14
JUST YOUR AVERAGE TUESDAY-MORNING MINOTAUR
Catherynne M. Valente

I have spent the better part of my life in a torrid love triangle with classics and speculative fiction. They are the great passions of my heart – I could never choose between them. For me, they are forever intertwined, one feeding the other, and it's been that way for as long as I can remember being a thinking, reading, storytelling person, which all mean the same thing, really. For as long as I've been alive.

When I was a child, you could not separate me from *D'Aulaires' Book of Greek Myths*. In my memory, the book is huge, half as big as myself, the colour of the sun, with everything in the world inside it. I used to read it under my desk in my classroom, thinking I was very clever and hidden. Every kid knows that a desk is a magic shield and no teacher has the power to see what's happening underneath it. I read it over and over again. I can still picture each whacked-out 1970s illustration perfectly. I read everything else I could get my hands on, too, and for me, there was no difference between Zeus and Dionysus and Athena and the Childlike Empress and Bilbo Baggins and the Watchdog. They were all equally real, equally powerful, equally deserving of worship, equally in control of my entire tiny world, moving the seasons, demanding sacrifices, promising a universe greater and more full of magic than the one I knew.

Like many kids', my parents were divorced. Like somewhat fewer children, this held an almost religious significance for me. You see, during the winter, I lived with my father in Seattle, where it was dark and cold and the main crop was a big, round, red fruit. During the summer, I lived with my mother in the San Joaquin Valley in California, where everything is hot and golden and growing. When this visitation arrangement was reached, I recognized it instantly. I was eight years old and I was Persephone. What a relief! It wasn't that my parents hated each other and abandoned me – I was a seasonal goddess who had probably picked a crocus like a year ago without even noticing it. Everything made sense. The universe had order.

I think, in some sense, all small children are classicists. They have none of the adult sciences to explain the inexplicable world, so they throw story after story at what they observe until one makes sense to them in a personal way. Pre-teens become medievalists, clinging to the God of their parents while making great strides in their personal development, hoping that the bricks they lay down now become cathedrals after college. The Reformation comes with teenage years, rejecting that God and defining personal sacraments to replace them. University brings the Industrial Revolution, both creative and destructive, learning to make and do and consume and waste with equal enthusiasm.

Life after graduation heralds the disillusionment of modernism, the bitter realizations that old forms no longer hold, and adult, working life is a journey through the long, meandering postmodern wilds, where every trick and tool is necessary to tell the simplest story about living from one end of the day to the other. We are the history of literature embodied – we play out this process over and over.

Back then, when I was eight and I was Persephone, I dwelt in a classical universe where the sun being a ball of helium and hydrogen and being a man in a golden chariot seemed equally plausible. For me, there was no difference between myth and real life, between what I read and what I lived. The two agreed. They were an equation that meant me.

Years later, when I was fifteen and had almost entirely stopped believing I was Persephone, my mother, a political science professor and academic jaguar of the first degree, brought up the idea that, as I hated high school, I might graduate early and go straight on to college. All I heard was the word "college", because, in my mind, college meant "you can take Latin". That's what you do in college, a lifetime of *Dead Poets Society* and other movies about earnest young men in places with more bricks and ivy than sense had taught me. College means Latin classes. I am a product of public schools from kindergarten to graduate school – taking Latin had never been a possibility. I didn't like the idea of leaving what friends I had and the promise of playing Juliet the next year, but Latin was more important than all those things.

And in my first admission counsellor meeting for my new school with *far* more bricks and ivy than sense, I was told "We don't offer Latin."

I said: "I don't understand. What do you mean you don't offer Latin?"

"It's a dead language. We don't offer it. We have Japanese. Why? Are you Catholic?"

I was as full of white-hot indignity as only a sixteen-year-old girl can be. Some girls get told they can't have a new car. I'd been told I couldn't have Latin. To me, it was a tragedy. But in the end, I'm glad I was thwarted. I only wanted Latin because I hadn't met Greek yet.

In my last year before transfer, a woman named Kathryn Holwein, a retired professor, decided she wanted to teach a somewhat unusual course. The university told her she could, if she could get enough students for it. It would be a year long, and it would study only the *Iliad* and the *Odyssey*. Nothing else. She'd been a poetry professor, and wanted to teach it the way she had taught Eliot or Byron, as poetry first. She was an amazing teacher and I fell in love with her. She was a profound influence on me as a writer, and I didn't even think of myself as a writer yet. Kathryn asked me once why I was writing all these sonnets about Helen of Troy and Persephone and the Oracle at Delphi. Because I love them, I answered. And she said – yes, I can see you do. But this has nothing to do with you, with your life, with your experience. Writing sonnets like Elizabeth Barrett Browning isn't you, and if it isn't you, what's the point? And I started to put it together. To stop drawing a difference between what you write poetry about (heroes and magic and war) and what you know (divorce and poverty and abandonment). There was no difference.

At the end of the year, a lot of odds and ends came together to make something extraordinary. I thought that we should all get together one night and take turns reading from the *Iliad*. It was my favourite and it was better read aloud, obviously, as it was intended to be. In the midst of discussing what parts to read and what food to bring, Kathryn Holwein thought she could do us one better. We could do the whole thing. In one night. We got together with the Sacramento Poetry Center and the Sacramento Homeric Salon (which was a real thing that really existed in 1999 in Central California), and rented a farmhouse and the field around it for a June evening. We set up a little stage and microphone. A local Greek restaurant came out and roasted two whole lambs over fires for us. In the end, about a hundred people brought drums and couches and baklava and stuffed grape leaves and about a cistern worth of coffee. We divided the book up into numbered sections and everyone drew four or five lots to read.

And Kathryn brought her friend, a classicist, and he read the first fifteen lines of each book in Greek. In perfect dactylic hexameter. And right there, on wet grass under the June stars, my life changed. I heard Greek and I had to have it. I had to know it inside and out. It was the strangest and most alien and most beautiful thing I'd ever heard, and I was going to chase it down and make it love me. As the sun came up, I read out Hecuba's grief over the body of her son and cried and knew I'd never be the same.

A year later, the group performed the *Odyssey* in the same fashion. The major difference was that I read the first fifteen lines of the book in Greek. Incidentally, these readings have continued on for sixteen years, in locations from New York to Los Angeles to Crete, showing no signs of stopping.

I spoke Hecuba's words that night – and I didn't write for three years. All I did was Greek and Latin until subject-verb-object charts were coming out my nose. I sat outside my Latin classes reading Seneca for fun and Colleen McCullough for guilty pleasure. My classmates called me 'the Last Roman'. (Not a joke.) I forgot any verb existed that wasn't λύω in its endless conjugations. The map of λύω became the map of my world. I couldn't even read billboards anymore. My head was so full of Greek that I swapped V's for N's (v/ν) and W's for O's (w/ω) and N's for E's (n/η) until In-N-Out just became totally unpronounceable.

This was my state of mind just after I graduated. I came home from Edinburgh University where I'd done my last year, a stranger in the very strange land of Rhode Island. Six months after seeing Delphi for the first time, I took a job as an Oracle – a fortune teller in a little room at the top of a stone tower in the Old Armory, a room which also served as storage space for the Newport Shakespeare Festival. I was twenty-two, delivering my oracles from Lear's throne. And between supplicants, I would pull out my laptop and write what became my first novel, *The Labyrinth*.

I did not have a great deal of luck in finding a publisher for it. Too weird, on every level. One evening, my then-boyfriend asked if I'd considered submitting it to a science-fiction or fantasy publisher. I said: why would I? I don't write science fiction or fantasy.

Well, he said, I mean, you've got a sentient maze in there, and talking animals, and carnivorous doors, and a minotaur. It's not exactly what you'd call realism, is it?

I know it's hard to believe, but until that moment, I had not considered that I was not writing literary realism. It's not that I was stupid, or that I looked down on SFF in any conceivable way, or that I didn't know that as a young American writer I wasn't supposed to be writing about the deep pain of suburbia. But I was a classicist. Mazes, talking animals, magic, curses, witches, prophecies, minotaurs? In ancient Greece, that's not fantasy. That's Tuesday. Euripides is realism, right? Of course he is and he isn't. What he believed about the world is not what we believe, which, to some people, makes all the difference. But not to me. To me there was no difference. Of course I wrote about minotaurs. Literature involves minotaurs. It's a universal law. Sure, sometimes they look like Holden Caulfield or Sarah Woodruff, but they're still minotaurs, waiting in the dark of the story to take their tribute.

Once I accepted that because my minotaurs look like minotaurs, I was writing fantasy, it only took a few months before I had a contract with a publisher. When *The Labyrinth* came out, much was made of my prose style, how unusual and different it was, whether this was a good or a bad thing. But my prose, especially those first few books, was unhinged and unique not because at twenty-five I was some crazy genius, but because I had three languages banging around my head. I still confused V's and N's. Greek and Latin kept imposing their syntax on English and it made for some truly Neptunian sentences. And my stories, from the first to the next, from my labyrinth to the Braurion in *Palimpsest* to the fact that the protagonist of *Radiance* is named Anchises, have always grown from old soil. They've circled around those underworlds where Persephone and the minotaur walked, around Dionysus's antics and Artemis's cruelties. I am still living in that book the colour of the sun, half as big as myself.

There have been twenty-nine other books in the ten years since that first one. Some are for children, most are for grown-ups. Some are fairy tales, some are histories, some are laments, some are dreams, most are all of these. But I can't think of one that doesn't dig its heels into the classical world and refuse to be moved. I took half a chapter out of one of my middle grade books to teach kids what *katabasis* means and why they should care – and that was *after* the reviews said I used too many big words.

I would never have been a speculative fiction writer if I had not been a classicist. For me, there is no difference. Those dead languages gave me my living voice, and those stories taught me how to be a human being – and how to write about the alien, the impossibly possible, the logic of ritual, the numinous. We're raised by our parents as children, but it's what we read that raises us as writers. Whatever age you start writing, you have to go through that process of growing up all over again. The writer part of you is still a baby, frustrated and prone to tantrums and saying no to everything and thinking you're the first one in the world to tell a story in second person, then imitating other writers in the safety of pre-adolescence, rebelling as a teenager and running around in deconstructed leather jackets, then reconciling and surviving on your own. And I'll tell you, all through that process, Homer was my babysitter. He taught me how to do exposition, the power of epithets, and how to care about the smallest thing, even if it's just a helmet sitting on the ground. Euripides taught me how to get my lament on and how to look at traditional stories from every angle, clever old fanfic writer that he was. Aristophanes taught me that there is always, always a time and a place for fart jokes, and Sappho taught me everything else.

But perhaps, as a writer of fantasy, a genre that often looks toward the past for inspiration and authority, most important were my snickering, gossipy besties Suetonius and Catullus. Because I read them, and I knew that human beings had never changed, not even a little, in the whole history of civilization. We are as petty and jealous and brilliant and crude and romantic and dumb and hopeful and depressed and horrible as we've ever been. There is no difference. The past is not magic. It is not ennobling. It has no authority – though it does have power. Just because you wear togas doesn't mean your ex-girlfriend isn't the worst. Just because your house has columns doesn't mean you weren't super into fart jokes. If I ever had an ounce of awe left for a historical figure, Catullus would always be there, snorting in derision. When I began writing historical fiction, Catullus was my personal patron saint. When writing any larger-than-life person who really lived and walked the earth, I ask myself: What would Catullus say? And the answer is usually that Catullus would say he was a cocksucker.

There is nothing I loved I could not find in the ancient world. From the rap battles of the *Frogs* to Hephaestus's terrifyingly awesome robot horse guardians, from Euripides' alt-continuity fanfic to Lucian's unreliable narrator to Daedelus the mad geek scientist, nothing is postmodern that is not premodern. Some might find that depressing, but I have always found it extraordinarily freeing. You cannot live without your bones, and our bones are flutes upon which old, old songs play forever. Part of the mission statement of my life is perpetrating acts of classical penetration – singing those old songs with a techno beat. I have been accused, with a straight face and a frown, of tricking people into reading classical poetry since the day my first book came out.

The fact is, the person I am does not exist without that night in California when the dactyls were dancing and the hexameters were hexing. The writer I am vanishes without classics. She would have nowhere to stand. Hell, *Radiance* is best described as a decopunk noir Venusian space opera alt-Hollywood mystery with space whales and it is easily the most Greco-Roman thing I've ever written. In fact, I've made my publishers very happy by providing my own translations of my epigraphs from Homer, Ovid, and Hesiod, so that no one has to pay the estates of Mr Fagles or Mr Hughes.

I have always harboured a little tugboat of regret and vague shame that I didn't finish my graduate work. I can only plead that I was abducted by aliens. Whether by that I mean science fiction or New York publishers, I can't really say. I am at best a non-practising classicist. But for the whole of my life, classics has been my fuel and my destination, my heart and my hearth. I am always in the labyrinth, and sometimes I am the minotaur and sometimes I am Theseus, but down there in Daedelus's digs is where I make my works and days. Whatever it looks like I'm talking about, in the end, I am always talking about Persephone, about minotaurs, about the rock at Aulis where Iphigenia got swapped out for a deer at the last possible moment. Out of these, I make fantasy and science fiction. Because there is no difference.

WORKS CITED

Abnett, Dan. 2003. *Gaunt's Ghosts: The Founding*. Nottingham: Black Library Publishing.

Abnett, Dan. 2004. *Gaunt's Ghosts: The Saint*. Nottingham: Black Library Publishing.

Abnett, Dan. 2004a. *Eisenhorn: The Omnibus*. Nottingham: Black Library Publishing.

Abnett, Dan. 2006. *Horus Rising*. Nottingham: Black Library Publishing.

Abnett, Dan. 2010. *Gaunt's Ghosts: The Lost*. Nottingham: Black Library Publishing.

Abram, Nicola. 2017. "Sensory Signification in *Juniper's Whitening* and *Victimese*". In *'Telling it Slant': Critical Approaches to Helen Oyeyemi*. Chloe Buckley and Sarah Ilott, eds. Brighton, Portland, OR, and Toronto: Sussex Academic Press. 93–112.

Accardo, Pasquale. 2002. *The Metamorphosis of Apuleius: Cupid and Psyche, Beauty and the Beast, King Kong*. Teaneck, NJ: Fairleigh Dickinson University Press.

Adams, Douglas. 1985. *The Hitch-Hiker's Guide to the Galaxy: The Original Radio Scripts*. London and Sydney: Pan Books.

Albinus, Lars. 2000. *The House of Hades: Studies in Ancient Greek Eschatology*. Aarhus: Aarhus University Press.

Aldiss, Brian, with David Wingrove. 1986. *Trillion Year Spree: The History of Science Fiction*. London: Victor Gollancz.

Allen, T. W. 1931. *Homeri Opera*. Oxford: Clarendon Press.

Allston, Aaron. 1991. *Dungeons and Dragons Rules Cyclopedia*. Renton, WA: Wizards of the Coast.

Amis, Kingsley. 1961. *New Maps of Hell*. London: Victor Gollancz.

Anderson, William S. 1982. "The Orpheus of Virgil and Ovid: *flebile nescio quid*". In *Orpheus: The Metamorphoses of a Myth*. J. Warden, ed. Toronto: University of Toronto Press. 25–50.

Anderson, William S., ed. 1997. *Ovid's Metamorphoses Books 1–5*. Norman, OK: University of Oklahoma Press.

Andersson, Pia. 2012. "Alternative Archaeology: Many Pasts in Our Present". *Numen* 59: 125–137.

Andre-Driusi, Michael. 2008. *Lexicon Urthus: A Dictionary for the Urth Cycle*. Albany, CA: Sirius Fiction.

Anonymous. 1965. "Doctor Who and the Trojan War". *Radio Times*. 14 October 1965. London: British Broadcasting Corporation. 6.

Anonymous. 2014. "Helen Oyeyemi: By the Book". *New York Times Book Review*. 16 March 2014. http://www.nytimes.com/2014/03/16/books/review/helen-oyeyemi-by-the-book.html?_r=0.

Arentzen, Wout. 2001. "An Early Examination of the 'Mask of Agamemnon'". *L'Antiquité Classique* 70: 189–192.

Armstrong, Richard. 2005. *A Compulsion for Antiquity: Freud and the Ancient Word*. Ithaca, NY: Cornell University Press.

Artforum. 2017. "Classicist Receives Death Threats from Alt-Right over Art historical Essay". *Artforum*. 15 June 2017. https://www.artforum.com/news/classicist-receives-death-threats-from-alt-right-over-art-historical-essay-68963.

Artt, Sarah. 2008. "Reflections on the Self-reflexive Musical: *The Rocky Horror Picture Show* and the Classic Hollywood Musical". In *Reading Rocky Horror: The Rocky Horror Picture Show and Popular Culture*. Jeffrey A. Weinstock, ed. New York, NY: Palgrave Macmillan. 51–68.

Ashcroft, Bill, Gareth Griffiths, and Helen Tiffin. 2002 [1989]. *The Empire Writes Back: Theory and Practice in Post-colonial Literatures*. London and New York, NY: Routledge.

Attebery, Brian. 2014. *Stories about Stories: Fantasy and the Remaking of Myth*. Oxford: Oxford University Press.

Aviram, Amittai F. 1992. "Postmodern Gay Dionysus: Dr. Frank N. Furter". *Journal of Popular Culture* 26.3: 183–192.

Awolalu, J. Omosade. 1979. *Yoruba Beliefs and Sacrificial Rites*. London: Longman.

Bainbridge, William Sims. 1986. *The Dimensions of Science Fiction*. Cambridge, MA: Harvard University Press.

Baines, David. 2014. *Charles Atlas: The Man, The Myth, and the Muscles*. Birch Tree Publishing.

Baker, Rich and Skip Williams. 2003. *Monster Manual: Core Rulebook III v. 3.5*. Renton, WA: Wizards of the Coast.

Bakhtin, M. M., and Michael Holquist. 1981. *The Dialogic Imagination: Four Essays*. Austin, TX: University of Texas Press.

Baldick, Chris. 1987. *In Frankenstein's Shadow: Myth, Monstrosity, and Nineteenth Century Writing*. Oxford: Clarendon Press.

Bastida-Rodriguez, Patricia. 2008. "Evil Friends: Childhood Friendship and Diasporic Identities in Meera Syal's *Anita and Me* and Helen Oyeyemi's *The Icarus Girl*". *Philologia: Naučno-Stručni Časopis za Jezik, Književnost i Kulturu/Scientific-Professional Journal for Language, Literature and Cultural Studies* 6: 163–171.

Bateman, Chris. 2012. "The Rules of Imagination". In *Dungeons and Dragons and Philosophy: Raiding the Temple of Wisdom*. Jon Cogburn and Mark Silcox, eds. Chicago, IL: Open Court. 225–238.

BBC. 2014. "Myth Makers – Reviews". http://www.bbc.co.uk/doctorwho/classic/cd/mythmakers/review.shtml. Accessed 21 April 2018.

Beach, Tim. 1995. *Monstrous Manual*. Lake Geneva, WI: TSR.

Beard, Mary, John North, and Simon Price, eds. 1998. *Religions of Rome*. Vol. 1. Cambridge: Cambridge University Press.

Beeler, Karin. 2008. *Seers, Witches and Psychics on Screen: An Analysis of Women Visionary Characters in Recent Television and Film*. Jefferson, NC: McFarland & Company.

Bembeneck, Emily Joy. 2013. "Phantasms of Rome: Video Games and Cultural Identity". In *Playing the Past: Digital Games and the Simulation of History*. Matthew Wilhelm Kapell and Andrew B. R. Elliott, eds. London: Bloomsbury. 77–90.

Bemong, Nele, Pieter Borghart, Michel De Dobbeleer, Kristoffel Demoen, Koen De Temmerman, and Bart Keuen, eds. 2010. *Bakhtin's Theory of the Literary Chronotope: Reflections, Applications, Perspectives*. Gent: Academia Press.

Bergstein, Mary. 2003. "Gradiva Medica: Freud's Model Female Analyst as Lizard-Slayer". *American Imago* 60.3: 285–301.

Binder, Eando. 1939. "I, Robot". *Amazing Stories* January 1939: 8–18.

Binford, Lewis. 1989. *Debating Archaeology*. San Diego, CA: Academic Press.

Black, Jonathan. 2009. "Charles Atlas: Muscle Man". *Smithsonian Magazine*. August 2009. http://www.smithsonianmag.com/history/charles-atlas-muscle-man-34626921/?no-ist. Accessed 7 April 2018.

Blake, Robert J. 1987. *The Wrath of Olympus*. Lake Geneva, WI: TSR.

Bloom, Harold. 1997. *The Anxiety of Influence*. Oxford: Oxford University Press.

Blum, Alex A. (a.). 1950. *Classics Illustrated No.77: Homer's* Iliad. New York, NY: Gilberton Co., and Leicester: Thorpe & Porter.

Blum, Cinzia Sartini. 2008. *Rewriting the Journey in Contemporary Italian Literature: Figures of Subjectivity in Progress*. Toronto: University of Toronto Press.

Boeckh, August. 1968 [1877]. *On Interpretation and Criticism*. John Paul Pritchard, ed. and trans. Norman, OK: University of Oklahoma Press.

Bond, Sarah. 2017. "Why We Need to Start Seeing the Classical World in Color". *Hyperallergic*. June 7, 2017. https://hyperallergic.com/383776/why-we-need-to-start-seeing-the-classical-world-in-color.

Works Cited

Bonny, Ed, Jeff Grubb, Rich Redman, Skip Williams, and Steve Winter. 2002. *Monster Manual II.* Renton, WA: Wizards of the Coast.

Booth, Paul. 2015. *Game Play: Paratextuality in Contemporary Board Games.* London: Bloomsbury.

Borgstrom, Rebecca. 2007. "Structure and Meaning in Role-Playing Game Design". In *Second Person: Role-Playing and Story in Games and Playable Media.* Pat Harrington and Noah Wardrip-Fruin, eds. Cambridge, MA: MIT Press. 57–66.

Bost-Fiévet, Mélanie, and Sandra Provini, eds. 2014. *L'Antiquité dans l'imaginaire contemporain: fantasy, science-fiction, fantastique.* Paris: Classiques Garnier.

Bost-Fiévet, Mélanie and Sandra Provini. 2014a. "Introduction Générale". In *L'Antiquité dans l'imaginaire contemporain: fantasy, science-fiction, fantastique.* Mélanie Bost-Fiévet and Sandra Provini, eds. Paris: Classiques Garnier. 15–34.

Bourke, Liz. 2011. "SFF and the Classical Past". *Tor.com.* 30 March 2011. http://www.tor.com/features/series/sff-and-the-classical-past.

Bowra, C. M. 1952a. *Heroic Poetry.* London: MacMillan.

Bowra, C. M. 1952b. "Orpheus and Eurydice". *Classical Quarterly* 2.3/4: 113–126.

Bradford, Ernle. 1993. *Thermopylae. The Battle for the West.* New York, NY: Da Capo Press.

Brah, Atvah. 1996. *Cartographies of Diaspora: Contesting Identities.* London: Routledge.

Bram, Christopher. 1995. *Father of Frankenstein.* New York, NY: Dutton [Penguin].

Brault, Pascale-Anne. 2009. "Playing the Cassandra: Prophecies of the Feminine in the Polis and Beyond". In *Bound by the City: Greek Tragedy, Sexual Difference, and the Formation of the Polis.* Denise Eileen McCoskey and Emily Zakin, eds. Albany, NY: State University of New York Press. 197–220.

Braund, Susanna M. 1997. "Virgil and the Cosmos: Religious and Philosophical Ideas". In *The Cambridge Companion to Virgil.* Charles Martindale, ed. Cambridge: Cambridge University Press. 204–221.

Bremmer, Jan. 1983. *The Early Greek Concept of the Soul.* Princeton, NJ: Princeton University Press.

Brown, Sarah Annes. 2002. *The Metamorphosis of Ovid: from Chaucer to Ted Hughes.* London and New York, NY: Bloomsbury.

Brown, Sarah Annes. 2008. "'Plato's Stepchildren': SF and the Classics". In *A Companion to Classical Reception.* Lorna Hardwick and Christopher Stray, eds. Malden, MA: Wiley-Blackwell. 415–427.

Brown, Shelby. 1993. "Feminist Research in Archaeology: What Does It Mean? Why Is It Taking So Long?" In *Feminist Theory and the Classics.* Nancy Sorkin Rabinowitz and Amy Richlin, eds. New York, NY: Routledge. 238–263.

Bruner, Kurt and Jim Ware. 2007. *Shedding Light on His Dark Materials: Exploring Hidden Spiritual Themes in Philip Pullman's Popular Series.* Colorado Springs, CO: Tyndale House Publishers.

Bryce, Jane. 2008. "'Half and Half Children': Third-Generation Women Writers and the New Nigerian Novel". *Research in African Literatures* 39.2: 49–67.

Bucher, Gregory S. 2015. "A Complex Oedipus: The Tragedy of Edward Morbius". In *Classical Traditions in Science Fiction.* Brett M. Rogers and Benjamin Eldon Stevens, eds. Oxford: Oxford University Press. 123–144.

Buckley, Chloe, and Sarah Ilott, eds., 2017. *'Telling it Slant': Critical Approaches to Helen Oyeyemi.* Brighton, Portland, OR, and Toronto: Sussex Academic Press.

Budelmann, Felix, and Haubold, Johannes. 2008. "Reception and Tradition". In *A Companion to Classical Reception.* Lorna Hardwick and Christopher Stray, eds. Oxford: Blackwell. 13–25.

Bull, Donald and Alice Frick. 1962. "SCIENCE FICTION: Report by Donald Bull to HSD, Television". *The Genesis of Doctor Who: Creating a Science Fiction Hero.* BBC Archives, 2014. http://www.bbc.co.uk/archive/doctorwho. Accessed 21 April 2018.

Burgess, Jonathan S. 2009. "Achilles' Heel: The Historicism of the Film *Troy*". In *Reading Homer. Film and Text.* Kostas Myrsiades, ed. Madison, NJ: Fairleigh Dickinson Press. 163–185.

Burkert, Walter. 1985. *Greek Religion*. Peter Bing, trans. Cambridge, MA: Harvard University Press.

Buswell, Robert E., and Donald S. Lopez, Jr., eds. 2013. *The Princeton Dictionary of Buddhism*. Princeton, NJ: Princeton University Press.

Butler, Robert. 2007. "The Art of Darkness. An Interview with Philip Pullman". *Intelligent Life*. 3 December 2007. http://www.moreintelligentlife.com/node/697.

Butler, Shane, ed. 2016. *Deep Classics: Rethinking Classical Reception*. London: Bloomsbury.

Butler, Shane. 2016a. "Introduction. On the Origins of 'Deep Classics'". In *Deep Classics: Rethinking Classical Reception*. Shane Butler, ed. London: Bloomsbury. 1–19.

Cacoyannis, Michael, dir. 1971 [film]. *The Trojan Women*. Josef Shaftel Productions.

Calder, William M. III. 1980. "Wilamowitz on Schliemann". *Philologus* 124.1: 146–151.

Calder, William M., III. 1981. "Research Opportunities in the Modern History of Classical Scholarship". *Classical World* 74.5: 241–251.

Calvino, Italo. 1988. *Six Memos for The Next Millennium*. New York, NY: Vintage International.

Campos, Miguel A. G. 1998. "Shakespeare in Outer Space: *Forbidden Planet* as Adaptation of *The Tempest*". *Sederi* 9: 285–291.

Cape, Jr., Robert W. 2015. "Suggestions for Further Reading and Viewing". In *Classical Traditions in Science Fiction*. Brett M. Rogers and Benjamin Eldon Stevens, eds. Oxford: Oxford University Press. 327–338.

Caroti, Simone. 2004. "Science Fiction, Forbidden Planet, and Shakespeare's the *Tempest*". *CLCWeb: Comparative Literature and Culture* 6.1. Special thematic issue *Shakespeare on Film in Asia and Hollywood*. Charles S. Ross, ed. http://clcwebjournal.lib.purdue.edu/clcweb04-1/caroti04.html/.

Carpenter, Thomas H. 1991. *Art and Myth in Ancient Greece*. London: Thames & Hudson.

Cary, Earnest and Herbert B. Foster, trans. 1925. *Dio Cassius: Roman History, Volume VIII: Books 61–70*. Cambridge, MA: Harvard University Press.

Cavallaro, Dani. 2006. *The Animé Art of Hayao Miyazaki*. Jefferson, NC: McFarland & Co.

Chabon, Michael. 2005. "Dust & Daemons". In *Navigating the Golden Compass: Religion, Science and Daemonology in Philip Pullman's His Dark Materials*. Glenn Yeffeth, ed. Dallas, TX: Benbella Books. 1–14.

Chadwick, John. 1959. *The Decipherment of Linear B*. Cambridge: Cambridge University Press.

Chadwick, Whitney. 1970. "Masson's *Gradiva*: The Metamorphosis of a Surrealist Myth". *The Art Bulletin* 52.4: 415–422.

Chapman, George. 1609. *Euthymiae Raptus: or The Teares of Peace with interlocutions*. London: Humphrey Lownes.

Chee, A. 2014. "An Interview With Helen Oyeyemi: 'Nothing Happens Without My Teapots'". *Buzzfeed*. 10 March 2014. http://www.buzzfeed.com/alexanderchee/an-interviews-with-helen-oyeyemi-nothing-happens-without-my#1ptev6l.

Clark, Nick. 2012. "Bluebeard's Muse". [Review of *Mr. Fox*, by Helen Oyeyemi.] *The Cascadia Subduction Zone* 2.1 (January 2012). http://thecsz.com/past-issues/csz-v2-n1-2012.pdf.

Clarke, Lindsay. 2004. *The War at Troy*. London: HarperCollins.

Clarke, Michael. 1999. *Flesh and Spirit in the Songs of Homer: A Study of Words and Myths*. Oxford: Clarendon Press.

Clay, Jenny Strauss. 1989. *The Politics of Olympus: Form and Meaning in the Major Homeric Hymns*. Princeton, NJ: Princeton University Press.

Clay, Jenny Strauss. 2003. *Hesiod's Cosmos*. Cambridge: Cambridge University Press.

Cleveland, Kyle. 2018. "Eugene Sandow's 'Grecian Ideal' and the Birth of Modern Body-Building". *Philomathes: A Journal of Undergraduate Research in Classics* 2.1: 31–43.

Clute, John and Peter Nicholls, eds. 1993. *The Encyclopedia of Science Fiction*. New York, NY: St Martin's Press.

Clute, John, and John Grant, eds. 1997. *The Encyclopedia of Fantasy*. New York, NY: St Martin's Press.

Works Cited

Cogburn, Jon, and Mark Silcox, eds. 2012. *Dungeons and Dragons and Philosophy: Raiding the Temple of Wisdom*. Chicago, IL: Open Court.

Cohn, Matt. 2015. "Was God an Astronaut? Ridley Scott's Prometheus on the Classics, the Past, and the Alien". *Eidolon*. 9 July 2015. https://eidolon.pub/was-god-an-astronaut-4d6dc500f889.

Collard, Christopher, trans. 2002. *Aeschylus: Oresteia*. Oxford: Oxford University Press.

Collins, Walter P., ed. 2010. *Emerging African Voices. A Study of Contemporary African Literature*. New York, NY: Cambria Press.

Condon, Bill, dir. 1998 [film]. *Gods and Monsters*. Lions Gate Films.

Conkey, Margaret W. and Joan M. Gero. 1991. "Tensions, Pluralities, and Engendering Archaeology: An Introduction to Women and Prehistory". In *Engendering Archaeology: Women and Prehistory*. Joan M. Gero and Margaret W. Conkey, eds. Oxford: Basil Blackwell. 3–30.

Connell, R. W. and J. W. Messerschmidt. 2005. "Hegemonic Masculinity: Rethinking the Concept". *Gender and Society* 19.6: 829–859.

Conrad, Joseph. 2008. *Heart of Darkness and Other Tales*. Cedric Watts, ed. Oxford: Oxford University Press.

Conte, Gian Biagio. 1999. *Latin Literature: A History*. Joseph B. Solodow, trans. Baltimore, MD: The Johns Hopkins University Press.

Cook, Chris. 2002. *Index Astartes*. 4 vols. Nottingham: Black Library Publishing.

Cooper, Brenda. 1998. *Magical Realism in West African Fiction: Seeing with a Third Eye*. London: Routledge.

Cooper, Brenda. 2008. "Diaspora, Gender, and Identity: Twinning in Three Diasporic Novels". *English Academy Review* 25.1: 51–65.

Cooper, Brenda. 2009. "The Middle Passage of the Gods and the new Diaspora: Helen Oyeyemi's *The Opposite House*". *Research in African Literatures* 40.4: 108–122.

Counter, Ben. 2006. *Galaxy in Flames*. Nottingham: Black Library Publishing.

Cousins, Helen. 2012a. "Helen Oyeyemi and the Yoruba Gothic: *White Is for Witching*". *The Journal of Commonwealth Literature* 47.1: 47–58.

Cousins, Helen. 2012b. "Unplaced/Invaded: Multiculturalism in Helen Oyeyemi's *The Opposite House*". *Postcolonial Text* 7.2: 1–16.

Cover, Jennifer Grouling. 2010. *The Creation of Narrative in Tabletop Role-Playing Games*. Jefferson, NC: McFarland.

Cox, Fiona. 2011. *Sibylline Sisters: Virgil's Presence in Contemporary Women's Writing*. Oxford: Oxford University Press.

Crawford, Jeremy, Christopher Perkins, and James Wyatt. 2014. *Dungeon Master's Guide*. Renton, WA: Wizards of the Coast.

Csicsery-Ronay, Jr., Istvan. 2003. "Marxist Theory and Science Fiction". In *The Cambridge Companion to Science Fiction*. Edward James and Farah Mendlesohn, eds. Cambridge: Cambridge University Press. 113–124.

Csicsery-Ronay, Jr., Istvan. 2011. *The Seven Beauties of Science Fiction*. Hanover, NH: Weslyan University Press.

Cuder-Domínguez, Pilar. 2009. "Double Consciousness in the Work of Helen Oyeyemi and Diana Evans". *Women: A Cultural Review* 20.3: 277–286.

Culler, Jonathan. 1997. *Literary Theory: A Very Short Introduction*. Oxford: Oxford University Press.

Cyrino, Monica S., and Meredith E. Safran, eds. 2015. *Classical Myth on Screen*. New York, NY: Palgrave Macmillan.

D'Angour, Armand. 2001. "Men in Wings: Fantasies of Flight in Ancient Greece (Part 1)". *Omnibus* 42: 24–26.

Däniken, Erich von. 1968. *Erinnerungen an die Zukunft*. Econ-Verlag: Dusseldorf.

Davis, S. 1964. "Cretan Hieroglyphs: The End of a Quest?" *Greece & Rome* 11.2: 106–127.

de Romilly, Jacqueline. 1968. *Time in Greek Tragedy*. Ithaca, NY: Cornell University Press.

Debnar, Paula. 2010. "The Sexual Status of Aeschylus' Cassandra". *Classical Philology* 105.2: 129–145.

Delcourt, Marie and Robert L. Rankin. 1965. "The Last Giants". *History of Religions* 4.2: 209–242.

Denniston, John Dewar and Denys Page, eds. 1957. *Aeschylus: Agamemnon*. Oxford: Clarendon Press.

Dethloff, Craig. 2011. "Coming up to Code: Ancient Divinities Revisited". In *Classics and Comics*. George Kovacs and C. W. Marshall, eds. Oxford: Oxford University Press. 103–114.

Diamond, J. 2014. "Flavorwire Interview: 'Boy, Snow, Bird' Author Helen Oyeyemi on Fairy Tales and Feminists with Flawless Prose". *Flavorwire.com*. 7 March 2014. http://flavorwire.com/443678/flavorwire-interview-boy-snow-bird-author-helen-oyeyemi-on-fairy-tales-and-feminists-with-flawless-prose.

Doležel, Lubomír. 1998. *Heterocosmica: Fiction and Possible Worlds*. Baltimore, MD: The Johns Hopkins University Press.

Doniger, Wendy. 1986. *Dreams, Illusions, and Other Realities*. Chicago, IL: University of Chicago Press.

Donsomsakulkij, Weeraya. 2015. "Spirited Away: Negotiation between Capitalism and Reminiscent Environmental Ethics". *Resilience: A Journal of the Environmental Humanities* 2.3: 147–151.

Dougherty, Carol. 2006. *Prometheus*. London: Routledge.

Dova, Stamatia. 2012. *Greek Heroes in and out of Hades*. Plymouth, MA: Lexington Books.

Dow, Douglas N. 2013. "Historical Veneers: Anachronism, Simulation, and Art History in *Assassin's Creed II*". In *Playing the Past: Digital Games and the Simulation of History*. Matthew Wilhelm Kapell and Andrew B. R. Elliott, eds. London: Bloomsbury. 215–231.

Downing, Eric. 2006. *After Images: Photography, Archaeology, and Psychoanalysis and the Tradition of Bildung*. Detroit, MI: Wayne State University Press.

Dryden, John. 1679. *Troilus and Cressida, or, Truth Found too Late a Tragedy, as It Is Acted at the Dukes Theatre: To Which Is Prefix'd, a Preface Containing the Grounds of Criticism in Tragedy*. London: Printed for Jacob Tonson at the Judges-Head.

Duhoux, Yves. 2000. "How Not to Decipher the Phaistos Disc: A Review Article". *American Journal of Archaeology* 104.3: 597–600.

Dunn, Francis. 2002. "Rethinking Time: From Bakhtin to Antiphon". In *Bakhtin and the Classics*. Robert Bracht Branham, ed. Evanston, IL: Northwestern University Press. 187–219.

Dyson, Julia T. 2001. *King of the Wood: The Sacrificial Victor in Virgil's Aeneid*. Norman, OK: University of Oklahoma Press.

Easton, D. F. 1981. "Schliemann's Discovery of Priam's Treasure: Two Enigmas". *Antiquity* 55: 179–183.

Easton, D. F. 1984a. "Schliemann's Mendacity: A False Trail?" *Antiquity* 58: 197–204.

Easton, D. F. 1984b. "Was Schliemann a Liar?" In *Heinrich Schliemann: Grundlagen und Ergebnisse moderner Archäologie 100 Jahre nach Schliemanns Tod*. Joachim Hermann, ed. Berlin: Akademie Verlag. 191–198.

Easton, D. F. 1994. "Priam's Gold: The Full Story". *Anatolian Studies* 44: 221–244.

Easton, D. F. 1998. "Heinrich Schliemann: Hero or Fraud?" *Classical World* 91.5: 335–343.

Eccleshare, Julia. 1996. "Northern Lights and Christmas Miracles". *Books for Keeps* 100: 15.

Edmonds, Radcliffe G., III. 2004. *Myths of the Underworld Journey: Plato, Aristophanes, and the "Orphic" Gold Tablets*. Cambridge: Cambridge University Press.

Eichler, Rolf. 1987. "In the Romantic Tradition: *Frankenstein* and *The Rocky Horror Picture Show*". In *Beyond the Suburbs of the Mind: Exploring English Romanticism*. Michael Gassenmeier and Norbert H. Platz, eds. Essen: Verlag Die Blaue Eule. 95–114.

Eisenhut, Werner. 1994. *Dictys Cretensis*. Stutgardiae et Lipsiae: Teubner.

Ephron, Henry D. 1962. "Hygieia Tharso and Iaon: The Phaistos Disk". *Harvard Studies in Classical Philology* 66: 1–91.

Evans, J. A. S. 1968. "Father of History or Father of Lies; The Reputation of Herodotus". *The Classical Journal* 64.1: 11–17.

Ewalt, David M. 2013. *Of Dice and Men: The Story of Dungeons and Dragons and the People Who Play It*. New York, NY: Scribner.

Fagles, Robert, trans. 1990. *Homer: The Iliad*. New York, NY and London: Penguin.

Fagles, Robert, trans. 1996. *Homer. The Odyssey*. New York, NY: Viking.

Falconer, Rachel. 2004. "Shape-changing in Hell: Metamorphosis and Katabasis in Rushdie's *The Ground Beneath Her Feet*". *E-rea* 2.2. http://erea.revues.org/449. Accessed 9 March 2016.

Falconer, Rachel. 2005. *Hell in Contemporary Literature: Western Descent Narratives since 1945*. Edinburgh: Edinburgh University Press.

Falola, Toyin. 2016. *Encyclopedia of the Yoruba*. Bloomington, IN: Indiana University Press.

Fehling, Detlev. 1977. *Amor und Psyche: Die Schöpfung des Apuleius und ihre Einwirkung auf das Märchen, eine Kritik der romantischen Märchentheorie*. Wiesbaden: Franz Steiner.

Ferber, Michael. 1999. *A Dictionary of Literary Symbols*. Cambridge: Cambridge University Press.

Fiegel, Michael L. and Jerry D. Grayson. 2008. *Hellas: Worlds of Sun and Stone*. Seattle, WA: Khepera.

Fine, Gary Alan. 1983. *Shared Fantasy: Role-Playing Games as Social Worlds*. Chicago, IL: Chicago University Press.

Fisher, Terence, dir. 1957 [film]. *The Curse of Frankenstein*. Hammer Film Productions.

Fitch, John G., ed. and trans. 2002. *Seneca VIII: Tragedies I*. Cambridge, MA: Harvard University Press.

Fleishman, Avrom. 1971. *The English Historical Novel. Walter Scott to Virginia Woolf*. Baltimore, MD: The Johns Hopkins Press.

Folch, Marcus. 2017. "A Time for Fantasy: Retelling Apuleius in C. S. Lewis's *Till We Have Faces*". In *Classical Traditions in Modern Fantasy*. Brett M. Rogers and Benjamin Eldon Stevens, eds. Oxford: Oxford University Press. 160–186.

Fontenrose, Joseph. 1971. "Gods and Men in the Oresteia". *Transactions and Proceedings of the American Philological Association* 102: 71–109.

Fox, Matthew. 2015. "Winckelmann's Legacy: Decorum, Textuality, and National Stereotype in the Eighteenth-Century Reception of Homosexuality". In *Ancient Rome and the Construction of Modern Homosexual Identities*. Jennifer Ingleheart, ed. Oxford: Oxford University Press. 74–92.

Frazer Jr., R. M. 1966. *The Trojan War: The Chronicles of Dictys of Crete and Dares the Phrygian*. Bloomington, IN: Indiana University Press.

Fredericks, Sigmund C. 1975. "Science Fiction and the World of Greek Myths". *Helios* n.s. 2: 1–22.

Fredericks, Sigmund C. 1976. "Lucian's *True History* as SF". *Science Fiction Studies* 3.1.8: 49–60.

Fredericks, Sigmund C. 1977. "Revivals of Ancient Mythologies in Current Science Fiction and Fantasy". In *Many Futures, Many Worlds: Theme and Form in Science Fiction*. Thomas D. Clareson, ed. Kent, OH: Kent State University Press. 50–65.

Fredericks, Sigmund C. 1978. "Lucian's *True History* as SF". *Science Fiction Studies, Second Series: Selected Articles on Science Fiction 1976–1977*. R.D. Mullen and Darko Suvin, eds. Boston, MA: Gregg Press. 1–12.

Fredericks, Sigmund C. 1980. "Greek Mythology in Modern Science Fiction: Vision and Cognition". In *Classical Mythology in Twentieth Century Thought: Proceedings of the Comparative Literature Symposium, Texas Tech University*. Wendell M. Aycock and T. M. Klein, eds. Lubbock, TX: Texas Tech Press. 98–106.

Freedman, Carl. 2000. *Critical Theory and Science Fiction*. Middletown, CT: Wesleyan University Press.

Freud, Sigmund. 1953–1974. *The Standard Edition of the Complete Psychological Works of Sigmund Freud*, 24 vols. J. Strachey, ed. and trans. London: Hogarth Press.

Frost, Laurie. 2008. *The Definitive Guide to Philip Pullman's His Dark Materials*. London: Scholastic.

Gaiman, Neil. 2001. *American Gods*. New York, NY: W. Morrow.

Galinsky, Karl. 1996. *Augustan Culture: An Interpretive Introduction*. Princeton, NJ: Princeton University Press.

Galinsky, Karl. 2012. *Augustus*. Cambridge: Cambridge University Press.

Gantz, Timothy. 1993. *Early Greek Myth: A Guide to Literary and Artistic Sources*. Two volumes. Baltimore, MD: The Johns Hopkins University Press.

Garber, Marjorie and Nancy J. Vickers, eds. 2003. *The Medusa Reader*. New York, NY: Routledge.

Gardner, Andrew. 2007. "The Past as Playground: The Ancient World in Video Game Representation". In *Archaeology and the Media*. Timothy Clack and Marcus Brittain, eds. Walnut Creek, CA: Left Coast Press. 255–272.

Gardner, Andrew. 2008. "Playing with the Past: A Review of Three 'Archaeological' PC Games". *European Journal of Archaeology* 10: 74–77.

Gardner Coates, Victoria C. 2012. "Pompeii on the Couch: The Modern Fantasy of 'Gradiva'". In *The Last Days of Pompeii: Decadence, Apocalypse, Resurrection*. Victoria C. Gardner Coates, Kenneth Lapatin, and Jon L. Seydl, eds. Los Angeles, CA: Getty Publications. 70–77.

Garland, Robert. 1985. *The Greek Way of Death*. Cornell, NY: Cornell University Press.

Gaylard, Gerrard. 2005. *After Colonialism: African Postmodernism and Magical Realism*. Johannesburg: Wits University Press.

Gemmell, David. 2005. *Troy: Lord of the Silver Bow*. Ealing: Bantam Press.

Georgiadou, Aristoula and David H. J. Larmour. 1998. *Lucian's Science Fiction Novel* True Histories. Leiden: Brill.

Gerard, Anthony. 1986. "The Ecology of the Minotaur". *Dragon* 116: 32–35.

Gessert, Genevieve S. 2017. "The Mirror Crack'd: Fractured Classicisms in the Pre-Raphaelites and Victorian Illustration". In *Classical Traditions in Modern Fantasy*. Brett M. Rogers and Benjamin Eldon Stevens, eds. Oxford: Oxford University Press. 63–91.

Giesecke, Annette L. 2003. "Homer's Eutopolis: Epic Journeys and the Search for an Ideal Society". *Utopian Studies* 14.2: 23–40.

Gilbert, James. 2006. "Auteur with a Capital *A*". In *Stanley Kubrick's 2001: A Space Odyssey. New Essays*. Robert Kolker, ed. Oxford: Oxford University Press. 29–41.

Gloyn, Liz. 2015a. "Classics and Sci Fi – Some Initial Thoughts". *Classically Inclined*. https://lizgloyn. wordpress.com/2015/03/10/classics-and-sci-fi-some-initial-thoughts. Accessed 29 April 2018.

Gloyn, Liz. 2015b. "In a Galaxy Far, Far Away: On Classical Reception and Science Fiction". *Strange Horizons*. 27 April 2015. http://strangehorizons.com/non-fiction/articles/in-a-galaxy-far-far-away-on-classical-reception-and-science-fiction.

Golder, Dave. 2012. "Continuum: Creator Simon Barry Interview". *gamesradar.com*. 27 September 2012. http://www.gamesradar.com/continuum-creator-simon-barry-interview. Accessed 22 October 2015.

Goldhill, Simon. 2004. *Aeschylus: The Oresteia, A Student Guide*. Second edition. Cambridge: Cambridge University Press.

Goldhill, Simon. 2010. "Cultural Theory and Aesthetics: Why Kant Is Not a Good Place to Start with Reception Studies". In *Theorising Performance: Greek Drama, Cultural History and Critical Practice*. Edith Hall and Stephe Harrop, eds. London: Duckworth. 56–70.

Gordon, Joan. 1986. *Gene Wolfe*. Mercer Island, WA: Starmont House.

Grady, Hugh and Terrence Hawkes. 2007. "Presenting Presentism". In *Presentist Shakespeares*. Hugh Grady and Terence Hawkes, eds. Abingdon: Routledge. 1–5.

Grafton, Anthony, Glenn W. Most, and Salvatore Settis, eds. 2010. *The Classical Tradition*. Cambridge, MA: Harvard University Press.

Grebe, Sabine. 2004. "Augustus' Divine Authority and Virgil's 'Aeneid'". *Vergilius* 50: 35–62.

Greene, Thomas. 1982. *The Light in Troy: Imitation and Discovery in Renaissance Poetry*. New Haven, CT: Yale University Press.

Greenhalgh, Claire. 2015. "Classical Receptions Theory and Ancient World Television Drama". Unpublished.

Works Cited

Greenough, J. B., trans. 1900. *Bucolics, Aeneid, and Georgics of Vergil.* Boston, MA: Ginn & Co.

Grethlein, Jonas. 2013. "Choral Intemporality in the Oresteia". In *Choral Mediations in Greek Tragedy.* Renaud Gagné and Marianne Govers Hopman, eds. Cambridge: Cambridge University Press.

Griffith, Mark. 1983. *Aeschylus: Prometheus Bound.* Cambridge: Cambridge University Press.

Grobéty, Gaël. 2015. "Revised Iliadic Epiphanies in Dan Simmons' *Ilium*". In *Classical Traditions in Science Fiction.* Brett M. Rogers and Benjamin Eldon Stevens, eds. Oxford: Oxford University Press. 263–279.

Grünschloß, Andreas. 2007. "'Ancient Astronaut' Narrations". *Fabula* 48.3: 1–24.

Grushow, Ira. 1962. "*Brave New World* and *The Tempest*". *College English* 24.1: 42–45.

Gubar, Susan. 1979. "Mother, Maiden and the Marriage of Death: Woman Writers and an Ancient Myth". *Women's Studies* 6: 301–315.

Gumpert, Matthew. 2018. "The Sublime Monster: *Frankenstein*, or the Modern Pandora". In *Frankenstein and Its Classics: The Modern Prometheus from Antiquity to Science Fiction.* Jesse Weiner, Benjamin Eldon Stevens, and Brett M. Rogers, eds. London: Bloomsbury Academic. 102–120.

Gunning, Dave. 2015. "Dissociation, Spirit Possession, and the Languages of Trauma in Some Recent African-British Novels". *Research in African Literatures* 46.4: 119–132.

Gurd, Sean. 2004. "On Text-Critical Melancholy". *Representations* 88.1: 88–101.

Gygax, G. 1978 [1977]. *Monster Manual.* Lake Geneva, WI: TSR Hobbies.

Gygax, G. 1981. *Dungeon Module B2: Keep on the Borderlands.* Lake Geneva, WI: TSR Hobbies.

Gygax, G. 2012 [unpublished]. *Dungeon Module B2: The Caves of Chaos.* Robert J. Schwalb and Bruce R. Cordell, rev. Renton, WA: Wizards of the Coast.

Gygax, G., and Dave Arneson. 1974. *Monsters and Treasure.* Lake Geneva, WI: Tactical Studies Rules.

Hägg, T. 1999. "*Callirhoe* and *Parthenope*: The Beginnings of the Historical Novel". In *The Greek Novel.* Simon Swain, ed. Oxford: Oxford University Press. 137–162.

Haggerty, George E. 2016. "What Is Queer about *Frankenstein*?" In *The Cambridge Companion to Frankenstein.* Andrew Smith, ed. Cambridge: Cambridge University Press. 116–127.

Hall, Edith. 2010. *Greek Tragedy: Suffering Under the Sun.* Oxford: Oxford University Press.

Hallett, Judith P. and Thomas Van Nortwick, eds. 1997. *Compromising Traditions: The Personal Voice in Classical Scholarship.* London: Routledge.

Hanfmann, G. M. A. 1980. "The Continuity of Classical Art: Culture, Myth, and Faith". In *Age of Spirituality.* K. Weitzmann, ed. New York, NY: Metropolitan Museum of Art. 75–99.

Hardie, Philip. 1986. *Cosmos and Imperium.* Oxford: Clarendon Press.

Hardwick, Lorna. 2003. *Reception Studies.* Oxford: Oxford University Press.

Hardwick, Lorna, and Christopher Stray, eds. 2008. *A Companion to Classical Reception.* Malden, MA: Wiley-Blackwell.

Harper, John. 2006. *Agon.* Seattle, WA: one.seven design.

Hartman, Geoffrey H. 2008. "Psychoanalysis as a Cultural Ideal: 'Form Feeling' in Freud's Essay on *Gradiva*". *American Imago* 65.4: 505–522.

Haskell, Yasmin. 2010. "Practicing What They Preach? Vergil and the Jesuits". In *A Companion to Vergil's* Aeneid *and Its Tradition.* Joseph Farrell and Michael C. J. Putnam, eds. Oxford: Blackwell. 203–216.

Hatlen, Burton. 2005. "Pullman's *His Dark Materials*, a Challenge to the Fantasies of J. R. R. Tolkien and C. S. Lewis, with an Epilogue on Pullman's Neo-Romantic Reading of *Paradise Lost*". In *His Dark Materials Illuminated: Critical Essays on Philip Pullman's Trilogy.* Millicent Lenz and Carole Scott, eds. Detroit, MI: Wayne State University Press. 75–94.

Hauser, Friedrich. 1903. "Disiecta membra neuattischer Reliefs". *Jahreshefte des österreichischen archäologischen Institutes in Wien* 6.

Hawes, Greta. 2014. *Rationalizing Myth in Antiquity.* Oxford: Oxford University Press.

Hawkes, Terrence. 2002. *Shakespeare in the Present*. London: Routledge.

Hawley, John. 1995. "Ben Okri's Spirit-Child: Abiku Migration and Postmodernity". *Research in African Literatures* 26.2: 38–48.

Hayes, Marisa C., ed. 2015. *Fan Phenomena: The Rocky Horror Picture Show*. Bristol and Chicago, IL: Intellect Books.

Heath, John. 2005. "Blood for the Dead: Homeric Ghosts Speak Up". *Hermes* 133.4: 389–400.

Helmbold, Julius. 1906. *Der Atlasmythus und verwandtes*. Mülhausen: Buchdruckerei Wenz & Peters.

Hendricks, Sean Q. 2006. "Incorporative Discourse Strategies in Tabletop Fantasy Role-Playing Gaming". In *Gaming as Culture: Essays on Reality, Identity and Experience in Fantasy Games*. J. Patrick Williams, Sean Q. Hendricks, and W. Keith Winkler, eds. Jefferson, NC: McFarland. 39–56.

Heubeck, Alfred, and Arie Hoekstra. 1989. *A Commentary on Homer's Odyssey: Volume II: Books IX–XVI*. Oxford: Clarendon Press.

Higgins, Charlotte. 2009. "*Battlestar Galactica* revealed as the new Virgil's *Aeneid*". *The Guardian*. 24 February 2009. http://www.theguardian.com/culture/charlottehigginsblog/2009/feb/24/classics-classics.

Hiscock, Peter. 2012. "Cinema, Supernatural Archaeology, and the Hidden Human Past". *Numen* 59: 156–177.

Hitchcock, Susan T. 2007. *Frankenstein: A Cultural History*. New York, NY: W. W. Norton & Company.

Hite, Christian. 2011. "Bas-Relief: Footnotes on Statue-Love and Other Queer Couplings in Freud's Reading of *Gradiva*". *Postmodern Culture* 21.3.

Hodkinson, Owen, and Helen Lovatt. 2018. "Introduction". In *Classical Reception and Children's Literature: Greece, Rome and Childhood Transformation*. Owen Hodkinson and Helen Lovatt, eds. London: I. B. Tauris. 1–37.

Hogg, Trevor. 2014. "Perspectives: Simon Barry and Rachel Nichols talk about Continuum". *flickeringmyth.com*. 14 May 2014. http://www.flickeringmyth.com/2014/05/perspectives-simon-barry-rachel-nichols-talk-continuum.html. Accessed 22 October 2015.

Hoggard, L. 2014. "Helen Oyeyemi: 'I'm Interested in the Way Women Disappoint One Another'". *The Observer*. 1 March 2014. http://www.theguardian.com/books/2014/mar/02/helen-oyeyemi-women-disappoint-one-another.

Holderness, Graham. 2007. "'The Undiscovered Country': Philip Pullman and the 'Land of the Dead'". *Literature and Theology* 21.3: 276–292.

Holtsmark, Erling B. 2001. "The *Katabasis* Theme in Modern Cinema". In *Classical Myth & Culture in the Cinema*. Martin M. Winkler, ed. Oxford: Oxford University Press. 23–50.

Howe, Andrew. 2015. "Mercy Killing: Rocky Horror, the Loss of Innocence and the Death of Nostalgia". In *Fan Phenomena: The Rocky Horror Picture Show*. M. C. Hayes, ed. Bristol and Chicago, IL: Intellect Books and the University of Chicago Press. 124–131.

Hron, Madeleine. 2008. "Oran a-au nwa: The Figure of the Child in Third Generation Nigerian Novels". *Research in African Literatures* 39.2: 27–48.

Hughes, Paul. 2012. "art by gygax and arneson". *Blog of Holding*. 25 June 2012. http://blogofholding.com/?p=4871. Accessed 4 March 2018.

Hummel, Matt. 2014. "Menzoberranzan: A Perfect Unjust State". In *Dungeons & Dragons and Philosophy: Read and Gain Advantage on All Wisdom Checks*. Christopher Robichaud, ed. Hoboken, NJ: John Wiley and Sons. 121–131.

Hunter, J. Paul, ed. 2012. *Mary Shelley: Frankenstein; or, The Modern Prometheus*. Second edition. New York, NY: W. W. Norton.

Hurst, Isobel. 2012. "'Love and Blackmail': Demeter and Persephone". *Classical Receptions Journal* 4.2: 176–189.

Inniss, Stephen and Kelly Adams. 1985 (November). "The Centaur Papers". *Dragon* 103: 35–46.

Works Cited

Iosue. 2015. "The Caller and the Mapper". *Enworld.org* post 59. 4 September 2015. http://www.enworld.org/forum/showthread.php?356094-The-Caller-and-the-Mapper/page3&p=6693913&viewfull=1#nspost6693913. Accessed 4 March 2018.

Jackson, John, trans. 1937. *Tacitus: Annals Books 13–16*. Cambridge, MA: Harvard University Press.

Jackson, Rosemary. 2003. *Fantasy*. New York, NY: Routledge.

Jacobs, Alan. 2000. "The Devil's Party: Philip Pullman's Bestselling Fantasy Series Retells the Story of Creation – with Satan as the Hero". *The Weekly Standard* 6: 6. 23 October 2000. http://www.weeklystandard.com/Utilities/printer_preview.asp?idArticle=11746&R=138EFF2.

Jafnakol, Orlygg. 2013. "Rick Priestley Interview: From the Realms of Chaos to the Gates of Antares". *Realm of Chaos 80's Blog*. http://realmofchaos80s.blogspot.ca/2013/01/rick-priestley-interview-from-realms-of.html. Accessed 26 January 2016.

James, Edward, and Farah Mendlesohn, eds. 2003. *The Cambridge Companion to Science Fiction*. Cambridge: Cambridge University Press.

James, Edward and Farah Mendlesohn. 2015. "Introduction". In *The Cambridge Companion to Fantasy Literature*. Edward James and Farah Mendlesohn, eds. Cambridge: Cambridge University Press. 1–4.

James, Paula. 2009. "Crossing Classical Thresholds: Gods, Monsters and Hell Dimensions in the Whedon Universe". In *Classics for All: Reworking Antiquity in Mass Culture*. Dunstan Lowe and Kim Shahabudin, eds. Newcastle upon Tyne: Cambridge Scholars Publishing. 237–260.

Jancovich, Mark. 2016. "*Frankenstein* and Film". In *The Cambridge Companion to Frankenstein*. Andrew Smith, ed. Cambridge: Cambridge University Press. 190–204.

Jauss, Hans Robert. 1970. "Literary History as a Challenge to Literary Theory". Elizabeth Benzinger, trans. *New Literary History* 2.1: 7–37.

Jenkins, Thomas E. 2015. *Antiquity Now: The Classical World in the Contemporary American Imagination*. Cambridge: Cambridge University Press.

Jensen, Wilhelm and Sigmund Freud. 2003. *Gradiva and Delusion and Dream in Wilhelm Jensen's Gradiva*. Helen M. Downey, trans. Los Angeles, CA: Green Integer.

Johnson, W. R. 1976. *Darkness Visible: A Study of Vergil's Aeneid*. Chicago, IL: University of Chicago Press.

Johnston, Sarah Iles. 1990. *Hekate Soteira: A Study of Hekate's Roles in the Chaldean Oracles and Related Literature*. Atlanta, GA: Scholars Press.

Johnston, Sarah Iles. 1999. *Restless Dead: Encounters between the Living and the Dead in Ancient Greece*. Berkeley, CA: University of California Press.

Jones, Diana Wynne. 2001 [1981]. *The Time of the Ghost*. London: Collins.

Jong, Irene J. F. de. 2005. "Convention versus Realism in the Homeric Epics". *Mnemosyne* 58.1: 1–22.

Kallendorf, Craig. 2007. *The Other Virgil*. Oxford: Oxford University Press.

Kamerbeek, J. C. 1965. "Prophecy and Tragedy". *Mnemosyne* Fourth Series 18.1: 29–40.

Kapell, Matthew Wilhelm and Andrew B. R. Elliott, eds. 2013. *Playing the Past: Digital Games and the Simulation of History*. London: Bloomsbury.

Karade, Baba Ifa. 1994. *The Handbook of Yoruba Religious Concepts*. York Beach, NY: Weiser Books.

Kárpáti, János. 1993. "Amaterasu and Demeter: About a Japanese–Greek Mythological Analogy". *International Journal of Musicology* 2: 9–21.

Kears, Carl, and James Paz, eds. 2016. *Medieval Science Fiction*. London: King's College London.

Keen, Tony. 2006a. "The 'T' Stands for Tiberius: Models and Methodologies of Classical Reception in Science Fiction". *Memorabilia Antonina*. 10 April 2006. http://tonykeen.blogspot.co.uk/2006/04/t-stands-for-tiberius-models-and.html.

Keen, Tony. 2006b. "Is *2001* an *Odyssey* or an *Argonautica*?" Concussion: British National Science Fiction Convention. Glasgow. 16 April 2006. Unpublished.

Keen, Tony. 2007a. "'T for Tiberius': The Original *Star Trek*". *Memorabilia Antonina*. 23 April 2007. http://tonykeen.blogspot.co.uk/2007/04/april–23rd-is-apparently-international.html.

Keen, Tony. 2007b. "*Soldier of Sidon* by Gene Wolfe". *Strange Horizons*. 2 November 2007. http://www.strangehorizons.com/reviews/2007/11/soldier_of_sido.shtml.

Keen, Tony. 2009. "Reception Theory: Some Preliminary Thoughts". *Memorabilia Antonina*. 4 January 2009. http://tonykeen.blogspot.co.uk/2009/01/reception-theory-some-preliminary.html.

Keen, Tony. 2010. "It's about Tempus: Greece and Rome in 'Classic' *Doctor Who*". In *Space and Time: Essays on Visions of History in Science Fiction and Fantasy Television*. D. C. Wright Jr. and A. W. Austin, eds. Jefferson, NC: McFarland. 100–115.

Keen, Tony, 2011. "Reinventing the Past in the Future". *Iris Online*. http://irisonline.org.uk/index.php/features/59-reinventing-the-past-in-the-future. Accessed 29 April 2018.

Keen, Tony. 2012a. "I, Sidious: Historical Dictators and Senator Palpatine's Rise to Power". In *Star Wars and History*. Nancy R. Reagin and Janice Liedl, eds. Hoboken, NJ: Wiley. 125–149.

Keen, Tony. 2012b. "Science Fiction". *Tools for Classical Reception Studies*. https://crsnseminar.wordpress.com/science-fiction-2. Accessed 29 April 2018.

Keen, Tony. 2014a. "The Fantastika and the Greek and Roman Worlds". *Foundation* 118: 5–8.

Keen, Tony. 2014b. "Does Catullus Sing Smokey? A Meditation on the Fannish Academic and the Return of the Personal Voice". *Memorabilia Antonina*. 8 October 2014. http://tonykeen.blogspot.co.uk/2014/10/does-catullus-sing-smokey-meditation-on.html.

Keen, Tony. 2015a. "Mr. Lucian in Suburbia: Links between the *True History* and *The First Men in the Moon*". In *Classical Traditions in Science Fiction*. Brett M. Rogers and Benjamin Eldon Stevens, eds. Oxford: Oxford University Press. 105–122.

Keen, Tony. 2015b. "The Fantastika and the Greek and Roman Worlds". *Academia.edu*. https://www.academia.edu/11753150/The_Fantastika_and_the_Greek_and_Roman_Worlds. Accessed 29 April 2018.

Keen, Tony. 2015c. "The Odyssey". In *The Slings and Arrows: Graphic Novel Guide*. http://theslingsandarrows.com/the-odyssey. Accessed 21 April 2018.

Keen, Tony. 2016a. "Are Fan Fiction and Mythology Really the Same?" *Transformative Works and Cultures* 21. 15 March 2016. http://journal.transformativeworks.org/index.php/twc/article/view/689.

Keen, Tony. 2016b. "Thinking about Theories and Methods". *The Open University: Personal Blogs*. 27 October 2016. https://learn1.open.ac.uk/mod/oublog/viewpost.php?post=185363.

Keen, Tony. 2017. "Prometheus, Pygmalion, and Helen: Science Fiction and Mythology". In *A Handbook to the Reception of Classical Mythology*. Vanda Zajko and Helena Hoyle, eds. New York, NY: Wiley-Blackwell. 311–322.

Keen, Tony, 2018. "Homer Beyond the Stars: *2001* as a Reception of the *Odyssey*?" Classical Association Annual Conference, University of Leicester. 7 April 2018. Unpublished.

Kennedy, Duncan F. 2002. "Recent Receptions of Ovid". In *The Cambridge Companion to Ovid*. Philip Hardie, ed. Cambridge: Cambridge University Press. 320–335.

Kenney, E. J. 1990. *Apuleius: Cupid & Psyche*. Cambridge: Cambridge University Press.

Kenward, Claire. 2016. "The Reception of Greek Drama in Early Modern England". In *A Handbook to the Reception of Greek Drama*. Betine van Zyl Smit, ed. Chichester: Wiley-Blackwell. 173–198.

Kenward, Claire. 2017. "Sights to Make an Alexander? Reading Homer on the Early Modern Stage". *Classical Receptions Journal* 9.1: 79–102.

Kilgore, John. 1986. "Sexuality and Identity in *The Rocky Horror Picture Show*". In *Eros in the Mind's Eye: Sexuality and the Fantastic in Art and Film*. Contributions to the Study of Science Fiction and Fantasy No. 21. Donald Palumbo, ed. New York, NY and Westport, CT: Greenwood Press. 151–160.

Kincaid, Paul. 2008. *What It Is We Do When We Read Science Fiction*. Harold Wood: Beccon.

King, Noel. 1998. "Hermeneutics, Reception Aesthetics, and Film Interpretation". In *The Oxford Guide to Film Studies*. John Hill and Pamela Church Gibson, eds. Oxford: Oxford University Press. 212–223.

Works Cited

Kirk, G. S. 1990. *The Iliad: A Commentary*. Volume II: Books 5–8. Cambridge: Cambridge University Press.

Kleu, Michael. 2015. "Tagungsbericht: Antikenrezeption in der Science-Fiction-Literatur". *Academia.edu*. https://www.academia.edu/21687053/Tagungsbericht_Antikenrezeption_in_der_Science-Fiction-Literatur. Accessed 29 April 2018.

Knight, Damon. 1996 [1956]. *In Search of Wonder: Essays on Modern Science Fiction*. Third edition. Chicago, IL: Advent.

Knight, Diana. 2004. "From Painting to Sculpture: Balzac, Pygmalion and the Secret of Relief in Sarrasine and The Unknown Masterpiece". *Paragraph* 27.1: 79–95.

Knox, Bernard M. W. 1972. "Aeschylus and the Third Actor". *American Journal of Philology* 93.1: 104–124.

Knox, Julian. 2011. "Hoffmann, Geothe, and Miyazaki's 'Spirited Away'". *The Wordsworth Circle* 42.3: 198–200.

Kober, Alice E. 1948. "The Minoan Scripts: Fact and Theory". *American Journal of Archaeology* 52.1: 82–103.

Kölzer, Christian. 2008. *Fairy Tales Are More Than True: das mythische und neomythische Weltdeutungspotenzial der Fantasy am Beispiel von J. R. R. Tolkiens* The Lord of the Rings *und Philip Pullman's* His Dark Materials. *Studien zur anglistischen Literatur- und Sprachwissenschaft*, No. 32. Trier: Wissenschaftlicher Verlag Trier.

Kovacs, George. 2011. "Comics and Classics: Establishing a Critical Frame". In *Classics and Comics*. George Kovacs and C.W. Marshall, eds. Oxford: Oxford University Press. 3–26.

Kovacs, George. 2015. "Moral and Mortal in *Star Trek: The Original Series*". In *Classical Traditions in Science Fiction*. Brett M. Rogers and Benjamin Eldon Stevens, eds. Oxford: Oxford University Press. 199–216.

Kovacs, George, and C. W. Marshall, eds. 2011. *Classics and Comics*. Oxford: Oxford University Press.

Kovacs, George, and C. W. Marshall, eds. 2016. *Son of Classics and Comics*. Oxford: Oxford University Press.

Kowalski, Dean A. 2011. "Plato, Aristotle, and Joss on Being Horrible". In *The Philosophy of Joss Whedon*. Dean A. Kowalski and S. Evan Kreider, eds. Lexington, KY: The University Press of Kentucky. 71–87.

Kubrick, Stanley, dir. 1968 [film]. *2001: A Space Odyssey*. Metro-Goldwyn-Mayer.

Lafferty, R. A. 1968. *Space Chantey*. New York, NY: Ace.

Laimé, Arnaud. 2014. "De la marge à la trame: le personnage du scholiaste dans *Ilium* et *Olympos* de Dan Simmons". In *L'Antiquité dans l'imaginaire contemporain: Fantasy, Fantastique, Science-Fiction*. Mélanie Bost-Fiévet and Sandra Provini, eds. Paris: Classiques Garnier. 117–134.

Lancaster, Kurt. 1994. "Do Role-Playing Games Promote Crime, Satanism and Suicide among Players as Critics Claim?" *Journal of Popular Culture* 28.2: 67–79.

Larson, Glen A., prod. 1978 [TV show]. *Battlestar Galactica*. Glen A. Larson Productions.

Latacz, Joachim. 1998. *Homer, His Art and His World*. Ann Arbor, MI: University of Michigan Press.

Lau, Kimberly J. 2016. "Snow White and the Trickster: Race and Genre in Helen Oyeyemi's *Boy, Snow, Bird*". *Western Folklore* 75.3/4: 371–396.

Laycock, Joseph P. 2015. *Dangerous Games: What the Moral Panic Says about Play, Religion, and Imagined Worlds*. Berkeley, CA: University of California Press.

Lee, M. Owen. 1961. "Orpheus and Eurydice: Some Modern Versions". *Classical Journal* 56.7: 307–313.

Leeston-Smith, Michael, dir. 1965 [TV show]. *Doctor Who*: "The Myth Makers". BBC.

Legrand, Phillipe Ernest. 1963. *Hérodote. Histoires*. Vol 6. Paris: Les Belles Lettres.

Lenz, Millicent. 2001. "Philip Pullman". In *Alternative Worlds in Fantasy Fiction*. Peter Hunt and Millicent Lenz, eds. London: Continuum. 122–169.

Lenz, Millicent and Scott, Carole eds. 2005. *His Dark Materials Illuminated: Critical Essays on Philip Pullman's Trilogy*. Detroit, MI: Wayne State University Press.

Littman, G. 2012. "Aristotle's Dungeon". In *Dungeons and Dragons and Philosophy: Raiding the Temple of Wisdom*. Jon Cogburn and Mark Silcox, eds. Chicago, IL: Open Court. 3–15.

Liveley, Genevieve. 2011. "Delusion and Dream in Théophile Gautier's *Aria Marcella: Souvenir de Pompéi*". In *Pompeii in the Public Imagination from Its Rediscovery to Today*. Shelley Hales and Joanna Paul, eds. Oxford: Oxford University Press. 105–117.

Locke, Liz. 2008. "'Don't Dream It, Be It': Cultural Performance and Communitas at *The Rocky Horror Picture Show*". In *Reading Rocky Horror:* The Rocky Horror Picture Show *and Popular Culture*. Jeffrey A. Weinstock, ed. New York, NY: Palgrave Macmillan. 141–156.

London, Bette. 1993. "Mary Shelley, Frankenstein, and the Spectacle of Masculinity". *Proceedings of the Modern Language Association* 108.2: 253–267.

Lothane, Zvi. 2010. "The Lessons of a Classic Revisited: Freud on Jensen's *Gradiva*". *The Psychoanalytic Review* 97.5: 789–817.

Louden, Bruce. 2011. Homer's Odyssey *and the Near East*. Cambridge: Cambridge University Press.

Lovatt, Helen. 2013. *The Epic Gaze: Vision, Gender and Narrative in Ancient Epic*. Cambridge: Cambridge University Press.

Lowe, D. Forthcoming. "The Lightning Scar: Classical Antiquity in Harry Potter".

Lowe, Nick. 2012 "Popular Culture". In *The Oxford Classical Dictionary*. Simon Hornblower, Anthony Spawforth, and Esther Eidinow, eds. Oxford: Oxford University Press. 1185.

MacCallum-Stewart, Esther. 2014. "'Kill Her, Kill Her! Oh God, I'm Sorry!': Spectating *Dungeons and Dragons*". In *Dungeons & Dragons and Philosophy: Read and Gain Advantage on All Wisdom Checks*. Christopher Robichaud, ed. Hoboken, NJ: John Wiley and Sons. 175–188.

Mackay, Alan. 1965. "On the Type-Fount of the Phaistos Disc". *Statistical Methods in Linguistics* 4: 15–25.

Mackay, Daniel. 2001. *The Fantasy Role-Playing Game: A New Performing Art*. Jefferson, NC: McFarland.

Mafe, Diana Adesola. 2012. "Ghost Girls in the 'Eerie Bush': Helen Oyeyemi's *The Icarus Girl* as Postcolonial Female Gothic Fiction". *Research in African Literatures* 43.3: 21–35.

Maltby, Richard. 2003 [1995]. *Hollywood Cinema: An Introduction*. Second edition. Oxford: Blackwell Publishing.

Mann, Anthony, dir. 1964 [film]. *The Fall of the Roman Empire*. Samuel Bronston Productions.

Marchand, Suzanne L. 1996. *Down from Olympus: Archaeology and Philhellenism in Germany, 1750–1970*. Princeton, NJ: Princeton University Press.

Marshall, C. W. 2016. "Odysseus and *The Infinite Horizon*". In *Son of Classics and Comics*. George Kovacs and C. W. Marshall, eds. Oxford: Oxford University Press. 3–31.

Martin, Bridget. 2014. "Blood, Honour and Status in *Odyssey* 11". *Classical Quarterly* 64.1: 1–12.

Martin, Daniel, and Gary Alan Fine. 1991. "Satanic Cults, Satanic Play: Is 'Dungeons and Dragons' a Breeding Ground for the Devil?" In *The Satanism Scare*. James T. Richardson, Joel Best, and David G. Bromley, eds. Hawthorne, NY: Aldine de Gruyter. 107–123.

Martindale, Charles A. 1993. *Redeeming the Text: Latin Poetry and the Hermeneutics of Reception*. Cambridge: Cambridge University Press.

Martindale, Charles. 1997. "Introduction: 'The Classic of all Europe'". In *The Cambridge Companion to Virgil*. Charles Martindale, ed. Cambridge: Cambridge University Press. 1–18.

Martindale, Charles. 2007. "Reception". In *A Companion to the Classical Tradition*. Craig W. Kallendorf, ed. Malden, MA: Wiley-Blackwell. 297–311.

Martindale, Charles. 2013. "Reception–A New Humanism?" *Classical Receptions Journal* 5.2: 169–183.

Martindale, Charles and Lorna Hardwick. 2012. "Reception". In *The Oxford Classical Dictionary*. Simon Hornblower, Anthony Spawforth, and Esther Eidinow, eds. Oxford: Oxford University Press. 1256–1257.

Works Cited

Martindale, Charles and Richard Thomas, eds. 2006. *Classics and the Uses of Reception*. Oxford: Blackwell.

Mason, P. G. 1959. "Kassandra". *Journal of Hellenic Studies* 79: 80–93.

Matheson, Sue. 2008. "'Drinking Those Moments When': The Use (and Abuse) of Late-Night Double Feature Science Fiction and Hollywood Icons in *The Rocky Horror Picture Show*". In *Reading Rocky Horror: The Rocky Horror Picture Show and Popular Culture*. Jeffrey A. Weinstock, ed. New York, NY: Palgrave Macmillan. 17–34.

Mathews, Richard. 1997. *Fantasy: The Liberation of Pure Imagination*. New York, NY: Twayne Publishers.

Matthews, Susan. 2005. "Rouzing the Faculties to Act: Pullman's Blake for Children". In *His Dark Materials Illuminated: Critical Essays on Philip Pullman's Trilogy*. Millicent Lenz and Carole Scott, eds. Detroit, MI: Wayne State University Press. 125–134.

Maurer, Kathrin. 2009. "Archaeology as Spectacle: Heinrich Schliemann's Media of Excavation". *German Studies Review* 32.2: 303–317.

Mayer, Andreas. 2012. "Gradiva's Gait: Tracing the Figure of a Walking Woman". *Critical Inquiry* 38.3: 554–578.

Mazzoldi, Sabina. 2001. *Cassandra, la vergine e l'indovina: Identità di un personaggio da Omero all'ellenismo*. Roma: Istituti Editoriale e Poligrafici Internazionali.

McCarthy, Helen. 1999. *Hayao Miyazaki Master of Japanese Animation: Films, Themes, Artistry*. Berkeley, CA: Stone Bridge Press.

McCloud, Scott. 2003 [1993]. *Understanding Comics: The Invisible Art*. Northampton, MA: Kitchen Sink.

McDevitt, Jack. 1994. *The Engines of God*. New York, NY: Ace.

McDevitt, Jack. 2007. *Odyssey*. New York, NY: Ace.

McDougall, Sophia. 2005. *Romanitas*. London: Orion Books.

McManus, Barbara. 1997. *Classics and Feminism*. New York, NY: Twayne.

McNeill, Graham. 2006. *False Gods*. Nottingham: Black Library Publishing.

Mearls, Mike, Stephen Schubert, and James Wyatt. 2008. *Monster Manual*. Renton, WA: Wizards of the Coast.

Mellor, Anne K. 1988. *Mary Shelley: Her Life, Her Fiction, Her Monsters*. New York, NY: Methuen.

Mendlesohn, Farah. 2005. *Diana Wynne Jones: Children's Literature and the Fantastic Tradition*. London: Routledge.

Mendlesohn, Farah. 2008. *Rhetorics of Fantasy*. Middletown, CT: Wesleyan University Press.

Ménez, André. 2003. *The Subtle Beast: Snakes, from Myth to Medicine*. New York, NY: Taylor and Francis.

Merkle, Stefan. 1996. "The Truth and Nothing but the Truth: Dictys and Dares". In *The Novel in the Ancient World*. Gareth Schmeling, ed. Leiden: Brill. 563–580.

Merli, D. 2012. "Does Dungeons and Dragons Refute Aristotle?" In *Dungeons and Dragons and Philosophy: Raiding the Temple of Wisdom*. Jon Cogburn and Mark Silcox, eds. Chicago, IL: Open Court. 17–27.

Merrett, Alan. 2007. *The Horus Heresy: Collected Visions. Iconic Images of the Imperium, Betrayal and War*. Games Workshop.

ní Mheallaigh, Karen. 2014. *Reading Fiction with Lucian. Fakes, Freaks and Hyperreality*. Cambridge: Cambridge University Press.

Michaels, Scott and David Evans. 2002. *Rocky Horror: From Concept to Cult*. London: Sanctuary.

Michelakis, Pantelis. 2012. "Film". In *The Oxford Classical Dictionary*. Simon Hornblower, Anthony Spawforth, and Esther Eidinow, eds. Oxford: Oxford University Press. 575–576.

Mitchell-Boyask, Robin. 2009. "The Marriage of Cassandra and the "Oresteia": Text, Image, Performance". *Transactions of the American Philological Association* 136.2: 269–297.

Miyazaki, Hayao. 1983. *Nausicaä of the Valley of the Wind, Volume I*. David Lewis and Toren Smith, trans. Tokyo: Tokuma Shoten Co.

Miyazaki, Hayao. 2009 [1996]. "On *Nausicaä*". In *Starting Point: 1979–1996*. Beth Cary and Frederik L. Schodt, eds. San Francisco, CA: Viz Media. 283–284.

Miyazaki, Hayao. 2014 [2008]. "Chihiro, from a Mysterious Town – The Goal of This Film". In *Turning Point: 1997–2008*. Beth Cary and Frederik L. Schodt, eds. San Francisco, CA: Viz Media. 197–199.

Mizer, Nicholas J. 2014. "The Paladin Ethic and the Spirit of Dungeoneering". *The Journal of Popular Culture* 47: 1296–1313.

Moldvay, Tom, ed. 1981. *Basic Rulebook*. Lake Geneva, WI: TSR Hobbies.

Moore, Roger, and Katherine Kerr. 1982 (February). "Four Myths of Greece". *Dragon* 58: 18–21.

Moore, Ronald D. (developer). 2003–2009. *Battlestar Galactica*. Eick Productions and R&D TV.

Morley, Neville. 2000. "Trajan's Engines". *Greece and Rome* n.s. 47: 197–210.

Morley, Neville. 2014. "Wir Rezeptionsgelehrten". *Sphinx: Exploring Antiquity and Modernity*. November 21, 2014. https://thesphinxblog.com/2014/11/21/wir-rezeptionsgelehrten.

Morse, Ruth. 2000. "Monsters, Magicians, Movies: *The Tempest* and the Final Frontier". *Shakespeare Survey* 53: 164–174.

Mousley, Andy. 2016. "The Posthuman". In *The Cambridge Companion to Frankenstein*. Andrew Smith, ed. Cambridge: Cambridge University Press. 158–172.

Munn, Mark H. 2006. *The Mother of the Gods, Athens, and the Tyranny of Asia. A Study of Sovereignty in Ancient Religion*. Berkeley, CA: University of California Press.

Mustich, James. 2007. "Philip Pullman: The Storyteller's Art. A Conversation with James Mustich". *Barnes & Noble Review*. 3 December 2007. http://www.barnesandnoble.com/bn-review/interview.asp?PID=20784&btob=I.

Mwangi, Even Maina. 2009. *Africa Writes Back to Self: Metafiction, Gender, Sexuality*. Albany, NY: State University of New York Press.

Nagy, Gregory. 1999 [1979]. *The Best of the Achaeans*. Second edition. Baltimore, MD: The Johns Hopkins University Press.

Napier, Susan Jolliffe. 2006. "Matter out of Place: Carnival, Containment, and Cultural Recovery in Miyazaki's 'Spirited Away'". *Journal of Japanese Studies* 32.2: 287–310.

Nicholas, Jeffrey L. 2014. "'Others Play at Dice': Friendship and Dungeons and Dragons". In *Dungeons & Dragons and Philosophy: Read and Gain Advantage on All Wisdom Checks*. Christopher Robichaud, ed. Hoboken, NJ: John Wiley and Sons. 202–216.

Nilsson, Martin. 1992. *Geschichte der griechischen Religion*. Munich: CH Beck.

Nisbet, Gideon 2011. "Prolegomena to a Steampunk Catullus: Classics and SF". *Academia.edu*. https://www.academia.edu/543120/Prolegomena_to_a_Steampunk_Catullus_Classics_and_SF. Accessed 29 April 2018.

Nisbet, Hugh Barr, ed. 1985. *German Aesthetic and Literary Criticism: Winckelmann, Lessing, Hamann, Herder, Schiller, Goethe*. Cambridge: Cambridge University Press.

Nokes, Richard Scott. 2006. "Caprica Six and Baltar". *Unlocked Wordhoard*. February 27, 2006. http://unlocked-wordhoard.blogspot.com/2006/02/caprica-six-and-baltar.html.

Nuttall, Anthony D. 2007. *Shakespeare the Thinker*. New Haven, CT: Yale University Press.

O'Brien, Daniel. 2014. *Classical Masculinity and the Spectacular Body on Film*. Hampshire, UK and New York, NY: Palgrave Macmillan.

Ogden, Daniel. 2001. *Greek and Roman Necromancy*. Princeton, NJ: Princeton University Press.

Okpewho, Isidore and Nzegwu Nkiru, eds. 2011. *The New African Diaspora*. Bloomington, IN: Indiana University Press.

Old Geezer. 2006. "Re: [Historical] Where did the Cleric/Mage split come from?" *Forum. rpg.net* post 27. 3 May 2006. https://forum.rpg.net/showthread.php?264684-Necro-Historical-Where-did-the-Cleric-Mage-split-come-from&p=5787205#post5787205. Accessed 4 March 2016.

Orrells, Daniel. 2010. "Derrida's Impression of Gradiva: *Mal d'archive* and Antiquity". In *Derrida and Antiquity*. Miriam Leonard, ed. Oxford: Oxford University Press. 159–184.

Works Cited

Orrells, Daniel. 2011a. "Rocks, Ghosts, and Footprints: Freudian Archaeology". In *Pompeii in the Public Imagination from Its Rediscovery to Today*. Shelley Hales and Joanna Paul, eds. Oxford: Oxford University Press. 185–198.

Orrells, Daniel. 2011b. "Burying and Excavating Winckelmann's *History of Art*". *Classical Receptions Journal* 3.2: 166–188.

Orrells, Daniel. 2014. "Introduction: Inventive Inscriptions – The Organization of Epigraphic Knowledge in the Nineteenth Century". *Journal of the History of Collections* 26.3: 329–336.

Ouma, Christopher. 2014. "Reading the Diasporic *Abiku* in Helen Oyeyemi's *The Icarus Girl*". *Research in African Literatures* 45.3: 188–205.

Oyeyemi, Helen. 2006. "i live with him, i see his face, i go no more away". *New Statesman*. 18 December 2006. https://www.newstatesman.com/node/198002.

Pache, Corinne O. 1990. "'So Say We All': Reimagining Empire and the *Aeneid*". *The Classical Outlook* 87: 132–136.

Padilla, Mark William. 2016. *Classical Myth in Four Films of Hitchcock*. Lanham, MD: Lexington Books.

Papadimitropoulos, Loukas. 2008. "Heracles as Tragic Hero". *Classical World* 101.2: 131–138.

Parkinson, Michael. 1982 (February). "The Blood of Medusa". *Dragon* 58: 11–16.

Parsons, Wendy and Catriona Nicholson. 1999. "Talking to Philip Pullman: An Interview". *The Lion and the Unicorn* 23: 116–134.

Paul, Joanna. 2007. "Working with Film: Theories and Methodologies". In *A Companion to Classical Receptions*. Lorna Hardwick and Christopher Stray, eds. Oxford: Blackwell Publishing. 303–314.

Paul, Joanna. 2010. *Film and the Classical Epic Tradition*. Oxford: Oxford University Press.

Paz, James, and Kears, Carl, eds. 2016. *Medieval Science Fiction*. Martlesham: Boydell and Brewer.

Perkins, Christopher. 2014. *Monster Manual*. Renton, WA: Wizards of the Coast.

Petersen, Wolfgang, dir. 2004 [film]. *Troy*. Helena Productions and Plan B Entertainment.

Peterson, John. 2012. *Playing at the World: A History of Simulating Wars, People, and Fantastic Adventures, from Chess to Role-Playing Games*. San Diego, CA: Unreason Press.

Philippi, Donald L. 1968. *Kojiki*. Tokyo: University of Tokyo Press.

Pinch, Trevor J. and Wiebe E. Bijker. 2012. "The Social Construction of Facts and Artifacts: Or How the Sociology of Science and the Sociology of Technology Might Benefit Each Other". In *The Social Construction of Technological Systems: New Directions in the Sociology and History of Technology*. Wiebe E. Bijker, Thomas P. Hughes, and Trevor J. Pinch, eds. Cambridge, MA: MIT Press. 11–44.

Podlecki, Anthony J., ed. with intro. 2005. *Aeschylus: Prometheus Bound*. Liverpool: Aris & Phillips.

Poe, Edgar Allan. 1919 [1845]. "To Helen". In *The Oxford book of English verse, 1250–1900*. Arthur Quiller-Couch, ed. Oxford: Clarendon. 694.

Pomerance, L. 1976. *The Phaistos Disk: An Interpretation of Astronomical Symbols*. Goteborg: Paul Astroms.

Porter, James I. 2002. "Homer: The Very Idea". *Arion* 10.2: 57–86.

Porter, James I. 2006. "What is 'Classical' about Classical Antiquity?" In *Classical Pasts: The Classical Traditions of Greece and Rome*. James I. Porter, ed. Princeton, NJ: Princeton University Press. 1–68.

Porter, James I. 2007. "Reception Studies: Future Prospects". In *A Companion to Classical Reception Studies*. Lorna Hardwick and Christopher Stray, eds. Malden, MA: Blackwell. 469–481.

Potter, Amanda. 2009. "Hell Hath No Fury like a Dissatisfied Viewer: Audience Responses to the Presentation of the Furies in *Xena: Warrior Princess* and *Charmed*". In *Classics for All: Reworking Antiquity in Mass Culture*. Dunstan Lowe and Kim Shahabudin, eds. Newcastle upon Tyne: Cambridge Scholars Press. 217–236.

Potter, Tiffany and C. W. Marshall, eds. 2008. *Cylons in America: Critical Studies in Battlestar Galactica*. London: Bloomsbury.

Potts, Alex. 2000. *Flesh and the Ideal: Winckelmann and the Origins of Art History*. New Haven, CT: Yale University Press.

Pretzler, Maria. 2010. "From One Connoisseur to Another: Pausanias as Winckelmann's Guide to Analysing Greek Art". *Classical Receptions Journal* 2.2: 197–218.

Priestly, Rick. 1992 [1987]. *Warhammer 40,000: Rogue Trader*. Eastwood: Games Workshop.

Provini, Sandra and Mélanie Bost-Fiévet. 2014. "L'antiquité gréco-latine dans l'imaginaire contemporain: introduction générale". In *L'Antiquité dans l'imaginaire contemporain. Fantasy, science-fiction, fantastique*. Mélanie Bost-Fiévet and Sandra Provini, eds. Paris: Classiques Garnier. 15–34.

Pullman, Philip. 1996. *The Golden Compass* [British title: *Northern Lights*]. New York, NY: Knopf.

Pullman, Philip. 1997. *The Subtle Knife*. New York, NY: Knopf.

Pullman, Philip. 2000. *The Amber Spyglass*. New York, NY: Knopf.

Putz, H. C. Reinhard V. 2006. "Anatomy of the Centaur". *Annals of Improbable Research* 12.5: 6–13. http://www.improbable.com/airchives/paperair/volume12/v12i5/centaur-12-5.pdf. Accessed 4 March 2018.

Quinn, A. 2014. "The Professionally Haunted Life of Helen Oyeyemi". *NPR.org*. March 7, 2014. http://www.npr.org/2014/03/07/282065410/the-professionally-haunted-life-of-helen-oyeyemi.

Quinn, Sarah. 2016. "Sci-Fi's Obsession with Ancient Greece and Rome". *Omni*. https://omni.media/sci-fi-s-obsession-with-ancient-greece-and-rome. Accessed 26 November 2016.

Radford, Andrew D. 2007. *The Lost Girls: Demeter-Persephone and the Literary Imagination, 1850–1930*. Amsterdam: Rodopi.

Raeburn, David and Oliver Thomas. 2011. *The Agamemnon of Aeschylus: A Commentary for Students*. Oxford: Oxford University Press.

Rand, Nicholas, and Maria Torok. 1997. *Questions for Freud: The Secret History of Psychoanalysis*. Cambridge, MA: Harvard University Press.

Rateliff, John D. 1999. *Return to the Keep on the Borderlands*. Lake Geneva, WI: TSR.

Rathje, William. 1978. "The Ancient Astronaut Myth". *Archaeology* 31.1: 4–7.

Realm of Chaos Blog. http://realmofchaos80s.blogspot.com. Accessed 16 January 2016.

Reed, J. D. 2007. *Virgil's Gaze: Nation and Poetry in the* Aeneid. Princeton, NJ: Princeton University Press.

REF 2014. 2015. "Research Excellence Framework 2014: Overview Report by Main Panel D and Sub-panels 27 to 36". REF. http://www.ref.ac.uk/2014/media/ref/content/expanel/member/Main%20Panel%20D%20overview%20report.pdf. Accessed 29 April 2018.

Reider, Noriko T. 2005. "'Spirited Away': Film of the Fantastic and Evolving Japanese Folk Symbols". *Film Criticism* 29.3: 4–27.

Rice, Philip and Patricia Waugh, eds. 2001 [1989/1992]. *Modern Literary Theory: A Reader*. 4th edn. London: Arnold.

Richard, Carl J. 2009. *The Golden Age of the Classics in America*. Cambridge, MA: Harvard University Press.

Richard, Carl J. 2010. "Vergil and the Early American Republic". In *A Companion to Vergil's* Aeneid *and Its Tradition*. Joseph Farrell and Michael C. J. Putnam, eds. Oxford: Blackwell. 355–356.

Richardson, Edmund. 2013. *Classical Victorians: Scholars, Scoundrels and Generals in Pursuit of Antiquity*. Cambridge: Cambridge University Press.

Richardson, James T., Joel Best, and David G. Bromley, eds. 1991. *The Satanism Scare*. Hawthorne, NY: Aldine de Gruyter.

Richter, Jonas. 2012. "Traces of the Gods: Ancient Astronauts as a Vision of Our Future". *Numen* 59.2–3: 222–248.

Robbins, Emmet. 1982. "Famous Orpheus". In *Orpheus: The Metamorphoses of a Myth*. J. Warden, ed. Toronto: University of Toronto Press. 3–23.

Roberts, Adam. 2005. *The History of Science Fiction*. Basingstoke: Palgrave Macmillan.

Roberts, Adam. 2006. *Science Fiction*. London: Routledge.

Works Cited

Robertson, Stewart. 1939. "Muscles by Mail". *The Family Circle* 14.3. January 20, 1939. Reprinted on *The Official Website of Charles Atlas*. http://www.charlesatlas.com/articletoc.html. Accessed 15 August 2016.

Robichaud, Christopher, ed. 2014. *Dungeons & Dragons and Philosophy: Read and Gain Advantage on All Wisdom Checks*. Hoboken, NJ: John Wiley and Sons.

Robinson, Kim Stanley. 1993. *Red Mars*. New York, NY: Spectra.

Robinson, Kim Stanley. 1994. *Green Mars*. New York, NY: Spectra.

Robinson, Kim Stanley. 1996. *Blue Mars*. New York, NY: Spectra.

Rocha, J. and M. Rocha. 2012. "Elf Stereotypes". In *Dungeons and Dragons and Philosophy: Raiding the Temple of Wisdom*. Jon Cogburn and Mark Silcox, eds. Chicago, IL: Open Court. 91–105.

Roeg, Joe. 2005. "On Allusion: *All-Star Superman* and 'The Golden Apples of the Sun'". *Double Articulation*. http://doublearticulation.blogspot.com/2005/12/on-allusion-all-star-superman-and.html. Accessed 24 June 2017.

Rogers, Brett M. 2015. "Hybrids and Homecomings in the *Odyssey* and *Alien Resurrection*". In *Classical Traditions in Science Fiction*. Brett M. Rogers and Benjamin Eldon Stevens, eds. Oxford: Oxford University Press. 217–242.

Rogers, Brett M. 2017. "Orestes and the Half-Blood Prince: Ghosts of Aeschylus in the *Harry Potter* Series". In *Classical Traditions in Modern Fantasy*. Brett M. Rogers and Benjamin Eldon Stevens, eds. Oxford: Oxford University Press. 209–232.

Rogers, Brett M. 2018. "The Postmodern Prometheus and Posthuman Reproductions in Science Fiction". In *Frankenstein and Its Classics: The Modern Prometheus from Antiquity to Science Fiction*. Jesse Weiner, Benjamin Eldon Stevens, and Brett M. Rogers, eds. London: Bloomsbury Academic. 206–227.

Rogers, Brett M. and Benjamin Eldon Stevens. 2012. "Classical Receptions in Science Fiction". *Classical Receptions Journal* 4: 127–147.

Rogers, Brett M. and Benjamin Eldon Stevens, eds. 2015. *Classical Traditions in Science Fiction*. Oxford: Oxford University Press.

Rogers, Brett M. and Benjamin Eldon Stevens. 2015a. "Introduction: The Past is an Undiscovered Country". In *Classical Traditions in Science Fiction*. Brett M. Rogers and Benjamin Eldon Stevens, eds. Oxford: Oxford University Press. 1–24.

Rogers, Brett M. and Benjamin Eldon Stevens, eds. 2017. *Classical Traditions in Modern Fantasy*. Oxford: Oxford University Press.

Rogers, Brett M. and Benjamin Eldon Stevens. 2017a. "Introduction: Fantasies of Antiquity". In *Classical Traditions in Modern Fantasy*. Brett M. Rogers and Benjamin Eldon Stevens, eds. Oxford: Oxford University Press. 1–22.

Röhl, Tobias and Regine Herbrik. 2008. "Mapping the Imaginary – Maps in Fantasy Role-Playing Games". *Forum Qualitative Sozialforschung / Forum: Qualitative Social Research* 9.3: Art. 25. http://nbn-resolving.de/urn:nbn:de:0114-fqs0803255. Accessed 4 March 2018.

Rose, Jason. 2012. "The Gunpowder Crisis". In *Dungeons and Dragons and Philosophy: Raiding the Temple of Wisdom*. Jon Cogburn and Mark Silcox, eds. Chicago, IL: Open Court. 265–278.

Rosenberg, Aaron. 2004. *The Trojan War: Roleplaying in the Age of Homeric Adventure*. Renton, WA: Green Ronin.

Ross, David O. 1975. *Backgrounds to Augustan Poetry*. Cambridge: Cambridge University Press.

Rudd, Niall. 1988. "Daedalus and Icarus (i) From Rome to the End of the Middle Ages" and "Daedalus and Icarus (ii) From the Renaissance to the Present Day". In *Ovid Renewed: Ovidian influences on literature and art from the Middle Ages to the twentieth century*. Charles Martindale, ed. Cambridge: Cambridge University Press. 21–54.

Russo, Vito. 1981. *The Celluloid Closet: Homosexuality in the Movies*. New York, NY: Harper & Row Publishers.

Salzman-Mitchell, Patricia. 2008. "A Whole out of Pieces: Pygmalion's Statue in Ovid's *Metamorphoses*". *Arethusa* 41.2: 291–311.

Sanders, Julie. 2001. *Novel Shakespeares: Twentieth-century Women Novelists and Appropriation.* Manchester: Manchester University Press.

Sandner, David. 2004. *Fantastic Literature. A Critical Reader.* Westport, CT: Praeger.

Satkunananthan, Anita Harris. 2011. "Textual Transgressions and Consuming the Self in the Fiction of Helen Oyeyemi and Chimamanda Ngozi Adichie". *Hecate* 37.2: 41–69.

Satkunananthan, Anita Harris. 2015. "The Baby's Not for Burning: The Abject in Sarah Kane's *Blasted* and Helen Oyeyemi's *Juniper's Whitening*". *3L: Southeast Asian Journal of English Language Studies* 21.2: 17–29.

Sayer, Derek. 2014. "Five Reasons Why the REF is Not Fit for Purpose". *The Guardian.* 15 December 2014. https://www.theguardian.com/higher-education-network/2014/dec/15/research-excellence-framework-five-reasons-not-fit-for-purpose.

Saylor, Steven. N.d. "The Ancient World in Science Fiction, Fantasy & Alternate History". *Steven Saylor.com.* http://www.stevensaylor.com/StevensBookshopSci-Fi.html. Accessed 29 April 2018.

Schanoes, Veronica. 2012. "Historical Fantasy". In *The Cambridge Companion to Fantasy Literature.* Edward James and Farah Mendlesohn, eds. Cambridge: Cambridge University Press. 236–247.

Schein, Seth L. 1982. "The Cassandra Scene in Aeschylus' 'Agamemnon'". *Greece & Rome* 29.1: 11–16.

Schick, Lawrence. 1991. *Heroic Worlds: A History and Guide to Role-Playing Games.* Buffalo, NY: Prometheus Books.

Schindler, Wolfgang. 1992. "An Archaeologist on the Schliemann Controversy". *Illinois Classical Studies* 17.1: 135–151.

Schneider, J. Wesley. 2014. "So, I Have a Question about Pathfinder's Bestiary . . ." *F. Wesley Schneider* [blog]. http://wesschneider.tumblr.com/post/92511929906/so-i-have-a-question-about-pathfinders-bestiary. Accessed 4 March 2018.

Schwartz, Benjamin. 1959a. "The Phaistos Disk". *Journal of Near Eastern Studies* 18.2: 105–112.

Schwartz, Benjamin. 1959b. "The Phaistos Disk II". *Journal of Near Eastern Studies* 18.3: 222–226.

Schwartz, Benjamin. 1959c. "Notes and Afterthoughts on the Phaistos Disk Solution". *Journal of Near Eastern Studies* 18.3: 227–228.

Scobie, Alex. 1977. "Some Folktales in Graeco-Roman and Far Eastern Sources". *Philologus* 121: 1–23.

Scott, Carole. 2005. "Pullman's Enigmatic Ontology: Revamping Old Traditions in *His Dark Materials*". In *His Dark Materials Illuminated: Critical Essays on Philip Pullman's Trilogy.* Millicent Lenz and Carole Scott, eds. Detroit, MI: Wayne State University Press. 95–105.

Sharman, Jim, dir. 1975 [film]. *The Rocky Horror Picture Show.* Michael White Productions, 20th Century Fox.

Shone, Russell. 1999. "Alien Landscapes in Lucian". Classical Association Annual Conference, University of Liverpool. 9 April 1999. Unpublished.

Siegel, Mark. 1980. "*The Rocky Horror Picture Show*: More Than a Lip Service". *Science Fiction Studies* 7.3: 305–312.

Silcox, Mark and Jon Cogburn. 2012. "The Laboratory of the Dungeon". In *Dungeons and Dragons and Philosophy: Raiding the Temple of Wisdom.* Jon Cogburn and Mark Silcox, eds. Chicago, IL: Open Court. 121–132.

Silk, Michael, Ingo Gildenhard, and Rosemary Barrow. 2014. *The Classical Tradition: Art, Literature, Thought.* Hobokonen, NJ, and Chichester: Wiley Blackwell.

Silverberg, Robert. 1969. *The Man in the Maze.* London: Sidgwick & Jackson.

Silverberg, Robert. 2003. *Roma Eterna.* New York, NY: Eos Books.

Simmons, Dan. 2003. *Ilium.* New York, NY: HarperCollins.

Simmons, Dan. 2005. *Olympos.* New York, NY: HarperCollins.

Simonis, Annette. 2014. "Voyages mythiques et passages aux Enfers dans la littérature fantastique contemporaine: *Le Seigneur des Anneaux* et *À la croisée des mondes*". In *L'Antiquité dans l'imaginaire contemporain: Fantasy, science-fiction, fantastique*. Mélanie Bost-Fiévet and Sandra Provini, eds. Paris: Classiques Garnier. 241–252.

Simpson, Paul. 2007. *The Rough Guide to Philip Pullman's His Dark Materials*. London: Rough Guides.

Sioris, George. 1987. *Mythology of Greece and Japan: Archetypal Similarities*. New Delhi: Sterling Publishers.

Slater, N. 2003. "Looking for Proserpina: A. S. Byatt's Notes on the *Aeneid*". *Literary Imagination* 5.2: 194–208.

Sleight, Graham. 2012. "Fantasies of History and Religion". In *The Cambridge Companion to Fantasy Literature*. Edward James and Farah Mendlesohn, eds. Cambridge: Cambridge University Press. 248–256.

Small, Christopher. 1973. *Mary Shelley's* Frankenstein: *Tracing the Myth*. Pittsburgh, PA: University of Pittsburgh Press.

Smith, Angela M. 2011. *Hideous Progeny: Disability, Eugenics, and Classic Horror Cinema*. New York, NY: Columbia University Press.

Smith, Karen Patricia. 2005. "Tradition, Transformation, and the Bold Emergence: Fantastic Legacy and Pullman's *His Dark Materials*". In *His Dark Materials Illuminated: Critical Essays on Philip Pullman's Trilogy*. Millicent Lenz and Carole Scott, eds. Detroit, MI: Wayne State University Press. 135–152.

Solhaug, Sigrid I. 2008. "The Fantastic Identity: De/constructing the Feminine Hero in Philip Pullman's *The Golden Compass*". *Nordlit* 23: 317–335.

Solmsen, Friedrich, ed. 1990. *Hesiodi Opera*. Third edition. Oxford: Clarendon Press.

Solomon, Jon. 1978. *The Ancient World in the Cinema*. South Brunswick and New York, NY: A. S. Barnes and Company.

Sommerstein, Alan H., ed. and trans. 2008. *Aeschylus: Fragments*. Cambridge, MA: Harvard University Press.

Sommerstein, Alan H. 2010. *Aeschylean Tragedy*. Second edition. London: Duckworth Publishers.

Sourvinou-Inwood, Christiane. 1995. *'Reading' Greek Death to the End of the Classical Period*. Oxford: Clarendon Press.

Squires, Claire. 2006. *Philip Pullman, Master Storyteller – A Guide to the Worlds of His Dark Materials*. New York, NY: Continuum.

Stafford, Emma. 2012. *Herakles*. New York, NY: Routledge.

Stahl, Hans-Peter. *Virgil's* Aeneid: *Augustan Epic and Political Context*. London: Duckworth.

Stanford, W. B. 1961. *The Odyssey of Homer*. London: Macmillan.

Stephanou, Aspasia. 2014. "Helen Oyeyemi's *White is for Witching* and the Discourse of Consumption". *Callaloo* 37.5: 1245–1259.

Stevens, Benjamin Eldon. 2016. "Virgilian Underworlds in A. S. Byatt's *The Children's Book*". *Classical Receptions Journal* 8.4: 529–553.

Stevens, Benjamin Eldon. 2017. "Ancient Underworlds in J. R. R. Tolkien's *The Hobbit*". In *Classical Traditions in Modern Fantasy*. Brett M. Rogers and Benjamin Eldon Stevens, eds. Oxford: Oxford University Press. 121–144.

Stevens, Benjamin Eldon. 2018. "Cupid and Psyche in *Frankenstein*: Mary Shelley's Apuleian Science Fiction?" In *Frankenstein and Its Classics: The Modern Prometheus from Antiquity to Science Fiction*. Jesse Weiner, Benjamin Eldon Stevens, and Brett M. Rogers, eds. London and New York: Bloomsbury Academic. 123–144.

Stouck, Jordan. 2010. "Abjecting Hybridity in Helen Oyeyemi's *The Icarus Girl*". *ARIEL* 41.2: 89–109.

Subramanian, Aishwarya. 2015. "Helen Oyeyemi Symposium, Teesside University, 18 February 2015". *Science Fiction Film & Television* 44.1: 113–114.

Suvin, Darko. 1979. *Metamorphoses of Science Fiction: On the Poetics and History of a Literary Genre*. New Haven, CT: Yale University Press.

Suvin, Darko. 2014. "Estrangement and Cognition". *Strange Horizons*. 24 November 2014. http://strangehorizons.com/non-fiction/articles/estrangement-and-cognition.

Suvin, Darko. 2016. *Metamorphoses of Science Fiction: On the Poetics and History of a Genre*. New edition. Oxford: Peter Lang.

Swallow, James. 2007. *The Flight of the Eisenstein*. Nottingham: Black Library Publishing.

Swanson, Roy A. 1976. "The True, the False, and the Truly False: Lucian's Philosophical Science Fiction". *Science Fiction Studies* 3.3: 228–239.

Swanstrom, Elizabeth. 2012. "Mr. Wednesday's Game of Chance". In *Neil Gaiman and Philosophy: Gods Gone Wild*. Tracy L. Bealer, Rachel Luria, and Wayne Yuen, eds. New York, NY: Open Court. 3–20.

Symes, Carol. 2106. "Ancient Drama in the Medieval World". In *A Handbook to the Reception of Greek Drama*. Betine van Zyl Smit, ed. Chichester: Wiley-Blackwell. 97–132.

Syson, Antonia. 2017. "Filthy Harpies and Fictive Knowledge in Philip Pullman's *His Dark Materials* Trilogy". In *Classical Traditions in Modern Fantasy*. Brett M. Rogers and Benjamin Eldon Stevens, eds. Oxford: Oxford University Press. 233–249.

Taplin, Oliver. 1972. "Aeschylean Silences and Silences in Aeschylus". *Harvard Studies in Classical Philology* 76: 57–97.

Tarrant, R. J., ed. 2004. *P. Ovidi Nasonis Metamorphoses*. Oxford: Clarendon Press.

Taylor, Isabel. 2005. "Helen Oyeyemi's *The Icarus Girl*. Review and Author Interview". *Albion Magazine*. 7 September 2005. http://www.zyworld.com/albionmagazineonline/books5_fiction.htm.

Thalmann, W. G. 1985. "Speech and Silence in the 'Oresteia' 2". *Phoenix* 39.3: 221–237.

Theisen, Nicholas. 2011. "Declassicizing the Classical in Japanese Comics: Osamu Tezuka's *Apollo's Song*". In *Classics and Comics*. George Kovacs and C.W. Marshall, eds. Oxford: Oxford University Press.

Thomas, Julian. 2000. *Interpretive Archaeology: A Reader*. Leicester: Leicester University Press.

Thomas, Rosalind. 1989. *Oral Tradition and Written Record in Classical Athens*. Cambridge: Cambridge University Press.

Thomas, Roy. 1979. "An Ounce of Troy". In *Thor Annual #8: Thunder Over Troy*. Roy Thomas (w.), John Buscema (a.), and Tony DeZuñiga (i.). New York, NY: Marvel Comics Group. 47.

Thomas, Roy (w.), John Buscema (a.), and Tony DeZuñiga (i.). 1979. *Thor Annual #8: Thunder Over Troy*. New York, NY: Marvel Comics Group.

Tilney, F. W. 1925. "How to Develop a Perfect Body. Charles Atlas's Secrets of Success". *Artists and Models* August 1925: 41–48.

Timm, Torsten. 2004. "Der Diskos von Phaistos – Anmerkungen zur Deutung und Textstruktur". *Indogermanische Forschungen* 109: 204–231.

Tomasso, Vincent. 2015a. "Classical Antiquity and Western Identity in *Battlestar Galactica*". In *Classical Traditions in Science Fiction*. Brett M. Rogers and Benjamin Eldon Stevens, eds. Oxford: Oxford University Press. 243–259.

Tomasso, Vincent. 2015b. "The Twilight of Olympus: Deicide and the End of the Greek Gods". In *Classical Myth on Screen*. Monica Cyrino and Meredith E. Safran, eds. New York, NY: Palgrave Macmillan. 147–157.

Toyama, Ryoko, trans. 2001. "An Interview: Miyazaki on Sen to Chihiro no Kamikakushi". *Animage*. May 2001. http://www.nausicaa.net/miyazaki/interviews/sen.html. Team Ghiblink. Accessed 23 April 2018 via *Nausicaa.Net*.

Traill, David A. 1983. "Schliemann's Discovery of Priam's Treasure". *Antiquity* 57: 181–186.

Traill, David A. 1984. "Schliemann's Discovery of Priam's Treasure: A Re-examination of the Evidence". *Journal of Hellenic Studies* 104: 96–115.

Traill, David A. 1986. "Schliemann's Mendacity: A Question of Methodology". *Anatolian Studies* 36: 91–98.

Traill, David A. 1988. "Hisarlik, 31 May 1873 and the Discovery of Priam's Treasure". *Boreas* 11: 227–234.

Works Cited

Traill, David A. 1993. *Excavating Schliemann*. Atlanta: Scholars Press.

Tredennick, Bianca. 2015. "'I Think I Am a Monster': Helen Oyeyemi's *White Is for Witching* and the Postmodern Gothic". In *Monsters and Monstrosity from the Fin de Siècle to the Millennium: New Essays*. Sharla Hutchison and Rebecca A. Brown, eds. Jefferson, NC: McFarland & Company. 12–28.

Tringham, Ruth E. 1991. "Households with Faces: The Challenge of Gender in Prehistoric Architectural Remains". In *Engendering Archaeology: Women and Prehistory*. Joan M. Gero and Margaret W. Conkey, eds. Oxford: Basil Blackwell. 93–131.

Troke, Adam, Jeremy Vetock, and Matt Ward. 2012. *Warhammer 40,000 Rulebook*: Sixth edition. Nottingham: Black Library Publishing.

Tsagarakis, Odysseus. 2000. *Studies in* Odyssey *11*. Stuttgart: Franz Steiner Verlag.

Tucker, Nicholas. 2007. *Darkness Visible: Inside the World of Philip Pullman*. Second edition. Thriplow: Wizard.

Turnbull, Don, ed. 1981. *TSR Fiend Folio: Tome of Creatures Malevolent and Benign*. Lake Geneva, WI: TSR Hobbies.

Turner, Susanne. 2009. "'Only Spartan Women Give Birth to Real Men': Zack Snyder's *300* and the Male Nude". In *Classics for All: Reworking Antiquity in Mass Culture*. Dunstan Lowe and Kim Shahabudin, eds. Newcastle upon Tyne: Cambridge Scholars Publishing. 128–149.

Twitchell, James B. 1983. "*Frankenstein* and the Anatomy of Horror". *The Georgia Review* 37.1: 41–84.

Tymn, Marshall B., Kenneth J. Zahorski, and Robert H. Boyer. 1979. *Fantasy Literature: A Core Collection and Reference Guide*. New York, NY: R. R. Bowker Co.

Valdez, Damian. 2014. *German Philhellenism: The Pathos of the Historical Imagination from Winckelmann to Goethe*. New York, NY: Palgrave Macmillan.

Venuti, Lawrence. 2008 [1995]. *The Translator's Invisibility: A History of Translation*. London: Routledge.

Walcot, Derek. 1990. *Omeros*. New York, NY: Farrar, Straus & Giroux.

Walter, Damien. 2015. "The Joy of Reading Role-playing Games". *The Guardian*. 19 June 2015. https://www.theguardian.com/books/booksblog/2015/jun/19/the-joy-of-reading-role-playing-games. Accessed 4 March 2018.

Walton, Michael J. 2015. *The Greek Sense of Theatre: Tragedy and Comedy Reviewed*. Third edition. New York, NY: Routledge.

Ward, James M. and Robert J. Kuntz. 1980. *Deities and Demigods*. Lake Geneva, WI: TSR Games.

Warnes, Christopher. 2009. *Magical Realism and the Postcolonial Novel: Between Faith and Irreverence*. Basingstoke: Palgrave Macmillan.

Weinbaum, Stanley G. 1934. "A Martian Odyssey". *Wonder Stories* July 1934: 174–190.

Weinbaum, Stanley G. 1949. *A Martian Odyssey and Others*. Reading, PA: Fantasy Press.

Weiner, Jesse. 2015. "Lucretius, Lucan, and Mary Shelley's *Frankenstein*". In *Classical Traditions in Science Fiction*. Brett M. Rogers and Benjamin Eldon Stevens, eds. Oxford: Oxford University Press. 46–74.

Weiner, Jesse, Benjamin Eldon Stevens, and Brett M. Rogers, eds. 2018. *Frankenstein and Its Classics: The Modern Prometheus from Antiquity to Science Fiction*. London: Bloomsbury Academic.

Weinstock, Jeffrey Andrew. 2007. *Rocky Horror Picture Show*. Cultographies. London and New York, NY: Wallflower Press.

Weinstock, Jeffrey A., ed. 2008. *Reading Rocky Horror:* The Rocky Horror Picture Show *and Popular Culture*. New York, NY: Palgrave Macmillan.

Wells, H. G. 1913. *Little Wars: A Game for Boys from Twelve Years of Age to One Hundred and Fifty and for that More Intelligent Sort of Girls Who Like Boys' Games And Books*. London: F. Palmer.

Wendland, Albert. 1985. *Science, Myth, and the Fictional Creation of Alien Worlds*. Ann Arbor, MI: UMI Research Press.

Wenskus, Otta. 2011. *Umwege in die Vergangheit: Star Trek und die griechisch-römische Antike*. Innsbruck, Vienna, and Bozen: Studien Verlag.

Wenskus, Otta. 2017. "'Soft' Science Fiction and Technical Fantasy: The Ancient World in *Star Trek*, *Babylon 5*, *Battlestar Galactica*, and *Dr Who*". In *A Companion to Ancient Greece and Rome on Screen*. Arthur J. Pomeroy, ed. Malden, MA: Wiley-Blackwell. 449–466.

West, David, trans. 2003 [1990]. *Virgil: The Aeneid*. Revised edition. London: Penguin.

West, M. L., ed. 1966. *Hesiod: Theogony*. Oxford: Clarendon Press.

West, M. L., ed. 1978. *Hesiod: Works & Days*. Oxford: Oxford University Press.

Whale, James, dir. 1931. [film] *Frankenstein*. Universal Pictures.

Wheat, Leonard F. 2000. *Kubrick's 2001: A Triple Allegory*. Lanham, MD, and London: The Scarecrow Press.

White, William J. 2014. "Player-Character is What you Are in the Dark: The Phenomenology of Immersion in *Dungeons and Dragons*". In *Dungeons & Dragons and Philosophy: Read and Gain Advantage on All Wisdom Checks*. Christopher Robichaud, ed. Hoboken, NJ: John Wiley and Sons. 82–92.

Whittaker, Helène. 2005. "Social and Symbolic Aspects of Minoan Writing". *European Journal of Archaeology* 8.2: 157–181.

Williams, J. Patrick, Sean Q. Hendricks, and W. Keith Winkler, eds. 2006. *Gaming as Culture: Essays on Reality, Identity and Experience in Fantasy Games*. Jefferson, NC: McFarland.

Willis, Ika. 2007. "'She Who Steps Along': Gradiva, Telecommunications, History". *Helios* 34.2: 223–242.

Willis, Ika. 2017. *Reception*. London and New York, NY: Routledge.

Winckelmann, Johann Joachim. 1985 [1755]. "Thoughts on the Imitation of the Painting and Sculpture of the Greeks". Hugh Barr Nisbet, trans. *German Aesthetic and Literary Criticism: Winckelmann, Lessing, Hamann, Herder, Schiller, Goethe*. Hugh Barr Nisbet, ed. Cambridge: Cambridge University Press. 32–54.

Winkler, Martin M. 2001. "*Star Wars* and the Roman Empire". In *Classical Myth and Culture in the Cinema*. Martin M. Winkler, ed. Oxford: Oxford University Press. 272–290.

Winterson, Jeanette. 2005. *Weight: The Myth of Atlas and Hercules*. Edinburgh: Canongate Books.

Wohlleben, Joachim. 1990. "Homer in German Classicism: Goethe, Friedrich Schlegel, Hölderlin and Schelling". *Illinois Classical Studies* 15.1: 197–211.

Wolfe, Gene. 1986. *Soldier of the Mist*. New York, NY: Tor.

Wolfe, Gene. 1989. *Soldier of Arete*. New York, NY: Tor.

Wolfe, Gene. 2010. *Soldier of Sidon*. New York, NY: Tor.

Wolfendale, Pete and Tim Franklin. 2012. "Why *Dungeons and Dragons* Is Art". In *Dungeons and Dragons and Philosophy: Raiding the Temple of Wisdom*. Jon Cogburn and Mark Silcox, eds. Chicago, IL: Open Court. 207–224.

Wordsworth, William. 1974. *The Prose Works of William Wordsworth*. W. J. B. Owen and Jane Worthington Smyser, eds. Oxford: Oxford University Press.

Wright, Peter. 2003. *Attending Daedalus: Gene Wolfe, Artifice and the Reader*. Liverpool: Liverpool University Press.

Wright, Rita P, ed. 1996. *Gender and Archaeology*. Philadelphia, PA: University of Pennsylvania Press.

Wrigley, Amanda and Stephen Harrison, eds. 2013. *Louis MacNeice: The Classical Radio Plays*. Oxford: Oxford University Press.

Wyke, Maria. 1997a. *Projecting the Past: Ancient Rome, Cinema and History*. London: Routledge.

Wyke, Maria. 1997b. "Herculean Muscle! The Classicizing Rhetoric of Bodybuilding". *Arion* Third Series 4.3: 51–79.

Wylie, Alison. 1991. "Gender Theory and the Archaeological Record: Why Is There No Archaeology of Gender?" In *Engendering Archaeology: Women and Prehistory*. Joan M. Gero and Margaret W. Conkey, eds. Oxford: Basil Blackwell. 31–54.

Works Cited

Wylie, Alison. 1997. "The Engendering of Archaeology: Refiguring Feminist Science Studies". *Osiris* 12: 80–99.

Zeitlin, Froma I. 1996. *Playing the Other: Gender and Society in Classical Greek Literature*. Chicago, IL: University of Chicago Press.

Zeitlin, Froma I. 2001. "Visions and Revisions of Homer". In *Being Greek Under Rome*. Simon Goldhill, ed. Cambridge: Cambridge University Press. 194–265.

Ziogas, Ioannis. 2011. "Ovid in Rushdie, Rushdie in Ovid: A Nexus of Artistic Webs". *Arion* 19.1: 23–50.

Ziolkowski, Theodore. 2004. *Ovid and the Moderns*. Ithaca, NY: Cornell University Press.

INDEX

Index

Index